2020:

AMERICA
ON THE
BRINK

A NOVEL
WILLIAM J. LAWRENCE

"A good read! In part, a thriller about how an academic might influence an election. In part, a story of one way the 2020 election could have played out. But at its core, a tale that enlightens us about the importance of voter participation."

—James Knickman, retired professor at NYU's Wagner School of Public Service

"You can take a very enjoyable ride with Dr. Pryce through the Trump era and learn a great deal to boot about us and our country. You will smile, be depressed, and understand how we can make America ours again."

—Richard Scheffler, Distinguished Professor of health economics and public policy in the Graduate School, UC Berkeley

"With a brilliant mind and deeply moral soul, William Lawrence is the best possible author for this provoking novel. It is his first foray into fiction but I hope not his last. The book's topic could not be more timely and the value of the lessons contained in it will last forever."

—Elisabeth Martin, FAIA, Principal, MDA designgroup architects & planners

"What Dr. Lawrence has delivered is a sorely needed narrative addressed to the average American about the economic and political reality that set the stage for a Trump victory, and the ensuing existential threats to the survival of the United States as a beacon of democracy and social advancement."

—Donald Matteson, former Wall Street hedge fund analyst, trader, and manager

"2020: America on the Brink is a densely written historical fiction encased in amazingly witty and professionally informed dialogue by characters who know lots about government policy and tantalizing views of our American political drift. All this is in service of an objective to get concerned but clueless Americans to realize the strength of their vote, just as Stacey Abrams has done in the state of Georgia. A must-read for political junkies, policy wonks, and people who secretly wish they were."

—Craig Schelter, former head of the City of Philadelphia's city planning commission and economic development corporation

EDITORS@EMERALD-BOOKS.COM

EMERALD BOOKS
959 NE Wiest Way,
Bend OR, 97701

Printed in the USA
Illustrations by Rob Zammarchi
www.zammarchi.com

SUMMARY:

The work of democracy is hard; but with a pandemic and a tyrant in the presidency it was nearly impossible.

But retired economics professor Benson Pryce has a plan. Using top-secret espionage techniques, Professor Pryce and his team aim to save our democracy by restoring trust. To achieve his mission, he must dodge federal agents and a deadly virus. Desperate to save the country he loves, Pryce will risk it all.

BISAC CATEGORIZATION:
FIC037000   FICTION / Political
FIC031060   FICTION / Thrillers / Political

Identifier for the paperback edition:
ISBN: 978-1-954779-00-6

EMERALD BOOKS

CONTENTS

ACKNOWLEDGEMENTS   1

INTRODUCTION   4

CHAPTER 1: 2019   8

CHAPTER 2: JANUARY 2020   22

CHAPTER 3: FEBRUARY 2020   37

CHAPTER 4: FEBRUARY 2020   59

CHAPTER 5: MARCH 2020   79

CHAPTER 6: MARCH 2020   93

CHAPTER 7: MARCH 2020   108

CHAPTER 8: APRIL 2020   119

CHAPTER 9: MAY 2020   142

CHAPTER 10: MAY 2020   169

CHAPTER 11: JULY 2020   183

CHAPTER 12 : JULY 2020   205

CHAPTER 13: JULY 2020   218

CHAPTER 14: AUGUST 2020   240

CHAPTER 15: SEPTEMBER 2020   268

CHAPTER 16: SEPTEMBER 2020   288

CHAPTER 17: OCTOBER 2020   307

CHAPTER 18: SEPTEMBER 2020   340

CHAPTER 19: OCTOBER 2020   363

CHAPTER 20: OCTOBER 2020   387

CHAPTER 21: OCTOBER 2020   426

AFTERWORD   440

APPENDIX   469

ABOUT THE AUTHOR   481

Acknowledgements

THE MAJOR THEME OF THIS BOOK has been in my mind for more than twenty years. However, I could not decide how I wanted to present it. Happenstance knocked in the shape of a roundtable discussion I saw with a small group of fiction writers. They were each lamenting how difficult it was, in this upside-down, topsy-turvy world, to create entertaining stories when much of what is actually happening out there was stranger than any fiction they could imagine. Reality has become more farfetched than fiction. It was at that moment that I decided that rather than struggle with that problem, I wanted to embrace it.

2020: America on the Brink is a novel concerned with how urgent it is that Americans dramatically increase our abysmal voting participation. A vast body of informational resources were publicly available every day for me to call upon. I interpreted the Trump administration as the perfect case study on how an informed voter can make all the difference in the world as to what kind of nation we will live in.

The Trump administration with all its drama, disorder, ambiguity, and deception provided daily fodder for the message I wanted to give my readers. I have used only information gleaned from print and broadcast news sources to carry the reader through 2020 as we moved steadily toward Election Day, to highlight the importance of an informed electorate. I was guided by the following publications: *The New York Times*, *The Washington Post*, *Huffington Post*, *The Hill*, *Wall Street Journal*, *Axios*, *BuzzFeed*, Fox News, *Slate*, and others. CNN, MSNBC, PBS, and Fox are the broadcast information sources I have followed for as long as I can remember. I am also addicted to NPR and BBC and absorb as much of their insightful broadcasts as possible. As a novelist, I have admittedly taken literary license on the timing of events to facilitate the flow of my story.

As with any writing experience, I have many people to thank. Ted Curtin, Jack Gallagher, and Mike Kazan read and commented helpfully on earlier drafts. Countless friends, family, students, and business contacts have unwittingly contributed through general discussions that provided insight into a range of impressions on the events that have found their way into this book. Bette Soloway has masterfully slogged her way through a multitude of sidetracks I cannot resist taking. She expertly reduced or eliminated them to a text that is a more readable experience. Paul Kutasovic, an economist and former colleague of mine, offered invaluable insights that were most appreciated. Most of all, I thank my wife, Sybil, who has taught writing for many years and never ceased to marvel at how I can still take two or more pages to say something that could best be said in one paragraph. I am forever thankful to her for keeping this novel significantly shorter and more to the point than if she had not dedicated many hours to each draft.

I want to acknowledge and highly praise the daily newsletter by Dr. Heather Cox Richardson, "Letters from an American." Heather has a unique ability to take events, no matter how convoluted they might be, and boil them down to roughly a thousand succinct words that have efficiently informed and enlightened her readers every day. She will find many of her thoughts and contributions over the years expressed herein. Thank you, Heather, you have many followers who count on your scholarship and insight.

I also want to thank my patient publisher, Isaac Peterson and editor, Jessica Hammerman at Emerald Books, who put the final stamp on this novel as it was sent off to be printed. Special thanks go to Rob Zammarchi, whose creative talents as an illustrator perfectly captured the characters I sought.

All errors found herein are mine and mine alone. This book is my first attempt at fiction, which I have learned is far more difficult to write than professional papers on econometrics, statistical inference, theoretical, or empirical economics. I deeply admire every writer for the fortitude and endurance needed every day to keep plowing ahead, and not succumbing to those demons inside telling us to just hit the delete button and go for a walk.

★ ★ ★

INTRODUCTION

2020: AMERICA ON THE BRINK MIGHT BE SEEN as a doomsday novel. It is not. It is a wakeup call and a civics lesson, focused on how America has fallen far below its potential. Our constitutionally defined checks and balances were designed to maintain an equilibrium of power among our three branches of government. They were not perfectly conceived, but they did form a functioning democracy that was the envy of the post-WWII civilized world. That same Constitution gave most Americans the right to pursue their dreams with built-in freedoms that respected the rights of others. However, through decades of mismanagement, our economic, social, and political systems have enabled an effective minority to seize power over the very capitalistic and democratic institutions that were originally established to serve everyone, not just the few.

The universal prosperity all income classes had enjoyed during the immediate post-WWII period came to a dramatic end as we entered the 1970s, when an increasing income and wealth gap steadily eroded the purchasing power of middle-class workers. American working families and voters consequently developed a serious mistrust that their government and many business entities they had always relied on no longer served them or their needs. This novel strives to establish the critical role of the informed and active voter as the best weapon available to preserve our representative democracy and our economic prosperity. It employs the evolution of the 2020 election as a case study to prove its point.

4

America has become more polarized than at any time in recent history. Our historic two-party system has become defined by political parties each comprised of fundamentally divergent groups in which the participants are highly charged and less willing to tolerate the opinions of others, even those within their own party. Democrats are struggling with a rising number of progressives who push decidedly to the extreme left. Republicans have, especially under the presidency of Donald J. Trump, succumbed to the radical right, and are equally intolerant, to the point that the world now views Republicans as the party of Trump.

America has long embraced representative democracy and capitalism as flawed systems, but symbolic of how we individually prefer to function as a free society. We have, however, learned with increasing urgency that each of these cherished systems is highly vulnerable to a takeover by those who, through money and power, are able to neutralize the constitutional and traditional checks and balances we thought were eternal.

This condition has been festering for several decades. Trump chose the perfect time to run for president. Whatever his faults and limitations, we must recognize his brilliance and his ability to continually enhance his brand, unfortunately doing so at any cost. He has manipulated our legal system and the media, to enshrine that brand with checkered success throughout his career.

A game-changing event occurred when Trump entered the public world of politics and the presidency. As hard as he tried, Trump could no longer control the narrative needed to support his narrow vision of the world. This has given us the perfect case study to better understand why, in a democracy, the voter must be both engaged and informed if that democracy is to survive.

This novel's protagonist, Dr. Benson Pryce, is a retired professor of economics. He is a veteran and a patriot who has dedicated his professional life to meeting the challenges like those we are now facing. Born into poverty, Dr. Pryce has become independently wealthy, committed to righting what he and a recognized majority of Americans feel is wrong with the polarized path his country has taken. Pryce is an endlessly curious person, competent and passionate about all he cares about. Pryce also values the simpler things in life that can only be achieved when our nation and our communities are politically, economically, and socially stable—a condition that he strongly feels has been compromised. Pryce has chosen to dedicate a significant portion of his wealth and energy to the creation of a concentrated attack on inequality and social injustice by targeting those who are using their economic and political power to subvert our nation and its core values. These same people seek to compromise our Constitution and our representative democracy for their own personal financial and political gain. Power over country is their mantra.

The year 2020 opened with a worldwide pandemic. America was hit especially hard, and that soon led to the collapse of our economy. COVID-19 set states and individuals against each other as some strived to protect themselves with health-preserving practices that became politicized. The uncertainty of the impending election combined with this drama and a morally absentee president made 2020 unfold as a fraught time and a year we could not wait to put in the history books.

That great twentieth-century philosopher, Pogo, once lamented: "We have met the enemy, and he is us." Pogo's creator, Walt Kelly, was trying to tell us that we need to take a serious look inward if we are to live happily in a world of our own making.

Historically, the citizens in America have been able to make choices, but we have not kept our eyes on the ball. As Pogo tried to tell us, in a democracy, it is our responsibility as citizen voters to be informed about the candidates and the issues if we want our freedoms preserved. Our hesitancy to vote and our carelessness at staying informed has cost us the freedoms we cherish, no matter where on the political spectrum we stand.

One major reason we have become so polarized is that we are listening to distinct bodies of questionable information. As the late Senator Moynihan said, "You are entitled to your opinion. But you are not entitled to your own facts." Unfortunately, we have not been diligent, which has allowed divergent and often unsupportable commentary and opinion, not facts, to rule. Technology and social media are major contributors that have made it extremely difficult for average Americans to separate truth from a myriad of misleading statements and deliberate lies specifically designed to confuse the voter. If we are to come together as a nation, we are going to have to begin by accepting only verifiable facts as the foundation of any debate.

Benson Pryce and his team confront these crises by focusing on the uncertainty as we moved toward an election of tremendous importance. *2020: America on the Brink* should be read as a civics course that uses actual events to illustrate that the American citizen voter is our best line of defense against tyranny. The citizen voter must become more of an active and a properly informed participant in our democracy—if it is to survive.

2020: America on the Brink can help us understand who we are as a nation and what we have become. Most importantly, it is a story of what we can achieve if and only if we open our hearts and minds to seek that more perfect union—one that respects our differences under the banner of justice and equal opportunity for all.

★ ★ ★

Chapter 1

2019

"**Thank you, everyone, this is our last class.** Please do not miss the final exam. I will not be around this summer, and I won't be able to schedule a makeup exam. Your final is scheduled for 10 a.m. on Thursday, May 23, in our regular classroom. No excuses."

I have always lamented the end of a semester. This time, I knew that it probably would be the last class I would ever teach. I had first entered a classroom at Hofstra University in the summer of 1970. That was my first year at NYU Graduate School in the Department of Economics. A colleague who was about to graduate, gave me the opportunity to give a lecture to his class. My lecture was on monetary theory and, at that instant, I finally knew, at the age of thirty, exactly what I was going to do for the rest of my working life.

Forty years after a wonderful career as a professor of economics at Pace University, consulting for the City of New York, and several entrepreneurial efforts, I was asked to join the faculty of a university outside of the city. I was hired to help their business school get academic accreditation that I soon realized they did not deserve. The administra tion and some of the faculty had a vastly different perception of education than I did—one that I felt did not serve our students or the faculty dedicated to education and traditional academic standards. I realized that I could no longer participate. I finally decided to retire. I was not leaving teaching but knew that it had left me.

Fortunately, I had made some wise financial decisions, making it possible for me to earn more retired than employed. I have always loved being an educator, but only when I was in an academic environment conducive to learning. Saying goodbye to friends and colleagues, especially the students, was the only difficult part of my choice. Most of them knew about my decision to leave. As I was driving back to Brooklyn, where I lived at the time, my mind suddenly switched to that marvelous book, *Passages*, written by Gail Sheehy and published in 1977. I knew that this was most certainly a passage for me. I had other fish to grill.

⁂

IT WAS NOW JUNE 2019 and the three years since the presidential election that had been rough for anyone who cherishes our nation's core values. I called an old friend who was working in Washington. I needed to talk about some ideas that were floating around in my head. I was concerned that America was becoming a highly polarized nation, alien to those of us who respect our Constitution and our admired (but flawed) democracy. Most of all, our longstanding model of capitalism, also flawed, was still the envy of the post-WWII world, though it was not functioning as hoped. The fifty-year movement toward the extreme right had culminated with the election of Trump, an excessively vain businessman who had no public sector experience and was largely ignorant of the responsibilities of the presidency.

★ ★ ★

I DECIDED THAT I NEEDED TO TALK to someone I trusted. Andrew Lawson was my oldest and dearest friend and a professional colleague. We both have PhDs in economics from NYU and enjoyed rewarding but different careers. Andrew worked in a well-known economics research think tank in DC and independently as a consultant. I chose the academic world. As graduate students, we began to compile and maintain a rather extensive database on a host of social, political, and economic information and events. We used our databases over the years for research and consulting, with a long-term goal of producing a newsletter geared toward increasing voter participation. America has one of the worst voting participation rates per eligible voter in the industrialized world.

I called him and learned that he was consulting in the city, so we decided to meet downtown in the Battery, formerly known as Battery Park. It was originally built as a fort in the late seventeenth century and fortified with a battery of artilleries, installed to protect the growing settlement on the island of Manhattan. The Battery is now a major tourist attraction and historical site. Andrew and I chose a bench overlooking the majestic entrance of New York Harbor. We spread out the coffee and bagels I had brought for us. We caught up on our lives until Andrew looked up at me and said, "Something is wrong. Are you not healthy?"

"I'm fine. I wanted to talk about something I know bothers you as much as me, and that is the circumstances leading to Trump."

He nodded. I continued. "I'm sure that we agree that the 2020 election is going to be a game changer for America. You and I have wanted to get more people to the polls for years, and I think now is the time to get it done. There are a lot of well-funded groups all along the political spectrum that are going to do their best to influence the outcome. I'm not interested in just throwing our hats into that ring without a plan. We both want to make a difference, and that means that we have to do everything in our power to get people to the polls. We also want to prevent another four years of Trump, who we recognize as an existential threat to our democracy. We have agreed for years that the best means of change in America must come from the voter."

Andrew studied me carefully and could tell that I was serious. "Benson, it's been our goal to get more people to register and vote intelligently for years. We also know that many voters do not know their own best interests, and candidates often don't present themselves as who they really are. I've been giving this question a lot of thought. A few years ago, I did a modified cost-benefit analysis on our options. I concluded that we had the time to commit, since you were thinking of retiring. I would also need to either retire or take a leave. We have the funds, since both of us made a killing betting on high-tech companies. We know a lot about the economics and politics of what's happening, and we're connected to the social issues, all of which will play a major role in the next election. Like you, I think we need to get involved. I am ready to take it on."

I was really happy to see that we were thinking alike. We had no idea at the time that 2020 was going to turn out to be a year to remember. Our next task was to define a strategy that would build on the work that was already done. We wanted nothing more than to get involved and to make a difference. Andrew continued. "We need to distribute the information in our data banks to eligible voters who are not voting. We need highly trained technicians to program the access we need. We also know that the public will be subject to misleading messages and outright lies, similar to the 2016 election. This means that to be successful, we have to tap into the platforms and distribution channels used by domestic and foreign entities that thrived on distorting the election process. To accomplish this, we have to gain access to several computers, essentially imputing a virus that tags our posts directly to theirs. This is hacking, and in most states and countries a crime punishable by fines and jail time. We will be hacking the hackers. Becoming hackers is not exactly an honored profession."

"I know," I said and gave him a serious look. "I've given this a lot of thought. The voters we want are on the fringe and do not get their information from establishment sources. The only way to reach these people who are inundated with misleading propaganda is to hack into the distributors and sources familiar to them."

"Benson," he said, "you know that hacking is a felony. To go forward, we must do so knowing the dangers we will face."

I took a sip of coffee, finished the last bite of my bagel, and turned to Andrew. "I know this. That is why I wanted to speak to you. Neither of us wants to go to jail, but we're not interested in doing what a bunch of other pro- and anti-Trump groups will be doing. There is nothing to gain by blending in with them. We need to go beyond normal political activity if we are going to make a difference. And we will need help. We are not doing this for money—we are doing it specifically to get documented facts to voters who, if 2016 is our guide, receive a ton of questionable and biased information."

"But can we do this? And in time for the election cycle?" asked Andrew, ever the pragmatist.

We knew what we had to do. We also knew it was not going to be easy and a lot of sacrifices were ahead for us. We had to have total confidence in our hired help. We knew that we would be crossing a line, and that our personal and professional lives could be in danger.

Andrew and I stopped talking to gaze out at the harbor. The Staten Island Ferry had just left its pier to the one borough not connected by subway. It was one of those clear days where the water and the sky were almost the same color. There was a light breeze, and we could hear children playing on the grass behind us. Two lovers were holding onto each other as they also appreciated the timeless beauty of the sea and the city.

Taking a moment like this has always been important to me, especially when making major decisions. These moments ground me on what is important. The serenity of this view, the sounds of the children, and the lovers convinced me that we really did not have a choice. We had a responsibility to them and to our country.

I looked at Andrew and knew that he thought the same. We smiled at each other, got up, put our garbage in the bin, and shook hands.

"We have a lot of work to do, let us stay in close touch," he said to me as we parted.

I RETURNED TO BROOKLYN and made myself an espresso. Sipping coffee on my stoop, I enjoyed watching the kids playing street games. I also reflected on being unemployed for the first time since I was nine years old. I had sold my Brooklyn home and was looking for an apartment in Greenwich Village. Selling this home was part of the retirement plan. I was apparently downsizing in all directions.

I had sent a note to the chair of the economics department at NYU and asked for an appointment as a visiting scholar. I needed only office space and access to the university libraries and computers. I wanted to start after the New Year. I had decided to spend a month or so sailing out of Greenport on Long Island. I bought plane tickets to London for the fall and planned to spend about three months touring Europe. I had also booked a berth on the *Queen Mary II* out of Southampton in November. I would cross the Atlantic heading southwest to the Caribbean for several weeks of stopovers before pulling into New York harbor around the first of January 2020. That was when I had planned to gear up for the project that Andrew and I were discussing. I had never in my life taken so much time off. It was just what I needed.

I called Andrew to ask if he would let me use his sailboat for about a month starting mid-June. "Of course. Where are you going?"

"Wherever the wind takes me. I just need some time with nature."

"I wish I had the time to go with you. You know where the key is. I wanted to let you know that if we decide to go ahead with this project, we will have to set up offshore, and I will have to disappear. Given the risks, I do not want anyone to be able to track me down."

I agreed. "I would suggest you meet with Anna and let her know your plan. Do not let her know anything about our project. I would hate to make her vulnerable, should she be contacted in any way."

"She is my daughter," he said, "and we tend to share everything." He paused. "I do think you are right, though. I will come up with something."

We both have been there for Anna since her parents' divorce. She suddenly grew up, graduated from college, and found a job as a social worker, and she loves what she's doing. She thinks of me as a second dad. At a young age, she learned the art of playing Andrew and me off each other to get what she wanted. We invariably gave in.

I had no idea how Andrew would handle the situation. I left it up to him to find the best strategy.

I hired movers to put everything I didn't sell with the house into storage. I then began provisioning *Satori*, Andrew's thirty-five-foot sloop. With family and friends, I had sailed that boat for many years. For this trip, I had hoped to sail up to Salem and Marblehead in Massachusetts. One aspect of sailing is that you are totally dependent on the whims of nature; she always determines your course. If the winds are favorable, you can go where you want. If not and you still want to sail, you go where Mother Nature says.

ON THE SCHEDULED MORNING, I drove out to Greenport where *Satori* was docked. I spent a day filling water and fuel tanks and packing the non-perishables. I fully checked the running gear and electronics. In two days, I cast off with the early morning tide. I love to sail stress-free, without an agenda or planned route. Fortunately, the prevailing southwest winds were with me, so I headed out toward Block Island, one of my favorite stopovers.

Block Island was named after Adriaen Block, whose original ship the *Tyger* burned down to the waterline in 1613 while moored off the southern tip of what is now called Manhattan. With the help of the Lenape Indians, Block and his crew, who were reported to have been the first white men to winter on the island, built *Onrust*, so he could continue his journey. The *Onrust* took off the following spring, sailing up the East River. He worked his way through the treacherous strip that connects the East River with Long Island Sound. He named that strip Hell's Gate. That name was listed on his surveys and survives today on all maritime charts. Block and his crew worked their way along Long Island Sound, surveying the Connecticut and Long Island coastlines for the New Netherland Company. Their journey ended on an island about thirty miles off the eastern tip of Long Island. The *Onrust* was only ten feet bigger than the boat I was on—not suitable for crossing the North Atlantic. Block settled on the island he later named after himself. He and his crew remained on Block Island until an English ship entered Old Harbor and took him and his crew on board for the return trip to England.

It took *Satori* and me about six hours to reach Great Salt Pond on the west coast of Block about thirty nautical miles from Greenport. I stayed there on a mooring for several days, enjoying the beaches, birds, and other sailboats, like *Satori*, straining on their moorings. I was also waiting for good weather. I finally took off for Buzzard's Bay, the Cape Cod Canal, and points north. I made it to Salem and Marblehead, where some of the best sailboats of the nineteenth and twentieth centuries were designed. I stayed for about a week, and then made my way back to Greenport enjoying every moment. The entire cruise took a little over a month.

I returned to Manhattan in early August and began to look for an apartment. I found one on Thirteenth Street in the Village, in the same building where I used to live as a graduate student. It was a sublet and perfect for me until I figured out my long-term plans. My short-term plan was already set. I was scheduled to fly to London in August, rent a car, and tour England for a few days, before getting on the Eurostar direct to Paris's Gare du Nord. This trip of 306 miles by train took less than two and a half hours. I have wanted to take that tunnel, sometimes called the Chunnel, ever since it was finished in 1994.

I had almost three months before I had to be in Southampton to board the *Queen Mary II*. I refused to plan, getting up every morning and heading off to any of Europe's enchanting preserved cities. Despite being able to afford first-class hotels, I traveled as I always have. I prefer B&Bs, now Airbnb. I like to eat in local pubs and hang out at a corner café and watch locals go about their day. I always keep a handwritten log on a steno pad. I bought about ten of them for the trip. I rented an inconspicuous and comfortable stick shift diesel car. I wanted nothing flashy—to blend in wherever I go. The car rental and fuel were expensive, but I liked going wherever and whenever I want. I am not a person who can adjust to the schedule of a tour bus. My travel plans always provide surprises along the way.

I ended up visiting twenty-one countries and countless cities and villages. I packed light, so getting up and taking off each day was not a chore. I will have many memories that I can easily call upon when I can no longer make such trips. I got back to the UK to meet up with the *QMII*. I met with some friends and chose to hang out until it was time to board. I had not been on the North Atlantic in more than sixty years, while in the Navy. I really looked forward to having the horizon all around me and the frigid North Atlantic seas giving way to our powerful engines as we worked our way west. I knew that I was aboard one of the finest of ocean cruise ships ever built.

Our departure was a miniature exhibition of royal splendor. A full-dress British marching band, fireworks, horns blasting, our railings, and the docks were lined five deep with *bon voyage* wishes and clinking champagne glasses as the splendor of Southampton drifted off our stern. The pungent smells of a busy port and tugboats steaming unattached alongside in case of emergency complemented the cooling of the late afternoon English winter day. Our ship picked up speed as we neared the end of the channel at the head of the harbor. One lone vessel cruised comfortably off our starboard quarter, awaiting the signal from the bridge that the pilot would soon be disembarking. The setting sun guided our ship toward open water and points west.

I stayed on deck, remembering my time as a naïve teenage sailor on the USS *Skywatcher*, a Navy radar picket ship that would spend thirty days at sea about 400 miles off the East Coast guarding against possible enemy missile attack. Upon being relieved of duty we would go back to our home port in Rhode Island for ten days after which we went back to sea. I spent three years on that ship learning everything I could about the sea and the nuances of living on a ship. Most of my shipmates were bored to death knowing it would be more than a month before they could grab a beer and see that waitress they had been dating. I was the black sheep. Whether it was learning celestial navigation, weather observations, or how our ancient 2500hp triple expansion steam engine managed to push 14,000 tons of steel through the ever-demanding north Atlantic, I loved being at sea where nature was our constant companion.

The elegance of the *QMII* cannot be overstated. Everything is white-glove royalty. Far too much food, too many deserts, fantastic entertainment, and that ever-present horizon that bends into the dark sky and frequently sends a shooting star our way. I wanted peace and quiet; I wanted to read and watch movies. I wanted to enjoy the marvelous stage performers and take brisk walks around the deck's measured mile. The queen of the North Atlantic provided it all.

Dinner conversations surprised me. Almost every American aboard was a staunch Trump advocate. Admittedly, those who could afford a cruise of this nature did not represent a cross-section of American voters, but they were American, and they vote. I found it more comfortable to listen and not reveal my own political leanings. Most of my dinner companions were openly conservative—whatever that now means. They protect their money and their station. It is unfair to try to put any demographic into a box because they could certainly do the same to me. It appeared that most of my shipmates were single-issue voters: the money they were making, *Roe v. Wade*, taxes, guns, their definition of freedom, or fiscal restraint. Like most of us, they lived in a bubble that echoed their values. Among them, there was a complete absence of European gentility I found prevalent in almost all of our non-American travelers—probably because that social trait is not needed to be successful in America. We are cut from a different cloth.

I did not confront any of the meanness and vitriol found in the press, talk radio, or TV frequently occurring in the States. Each of the American passengers I met was very pleasant. None seemed mean-spirited or unkind, but they did seek a comfort zone that tended to restrict the type of information that entered their bubble. Hard data was not as important as the accepted belief among their peers that matched and defined what mattered. They vocally excused the crude or inappropriate behavior of someone in power, as long as it did not affect their bottom line or station.

My perspective could not have been further from theirs. Almost all of the European friends I met were truly flabbergasted that any nation, much less America, could ever raise a person like Trump to the presidency. They were also sure that he was the least-qualified person to ever sit in the White House. They were perfectly happy that he had separated our country from the activities of most of our trading and diplomatic partners rather than engage—something that I learned long ago rarely produces a meaningful solution. I chose to listen and observe. The takeaway for me, however, resulted in a major shock to my perspective. Those of us who devote a lot of our energy to try to do the right thing often become convinced of the wisdom behind our own truth. To see a completely different truth in someone who is diametrically opposed to most of what you believe in is not easy to absorb. Economists like me try to understand a decision in terms of what we decided *not* to do. Watch a ballgame on TV, or go to the ballpark? Buy an American car, or the European model? Send your kids to college, or not? Be devoutly religious, or declare yourself an atheist? Have a quiet meal at home or dine out? We make such decisions every day and can only hope that we make the right ones. Often, we do not, and usually that is okay. Other times, we make decisions that can be damaging and possibly life-threatening. Whom we vote for fits into that category.

Is the decision to commit to rightwing politics a rational one for a social being? Is it based on your true beliefs, or is it motivated by the neighborhood you chose to live in, your parents, your friends, or your boss? Did you choose where you live, or your place of employment because of your political values? Maybe it was an economic one, perhaps ethnically comfortable, or maybe it was that four-bedroom house with the white-picket fence on a cul-de-sac that you have long coveted. Did you make personal choices because of your education, life experiences, or because of the person you love? Many reasons underlie each decision we make. Unfortunately, we do not get to choose our parents, and most of us learn to live with that. Some follow in their footsteps, others fight to do the opposite. Whenever possible, we are constantly making decisions, and we can only hope that we make the right ones. It is a learning curve of life that we are always on.

Democracy encourages us to use our experiences to do the right thing for us. Who among us is qualified to sit in judgement of decisions others make, even if they differ from what we would have done? Most of my American shipmates voted for a man who to me is nothing short of a tyrant. Does that make them wrong and me right? Most certainly not. If we arrange our lives by negatively judging other people's actions, we will never resolve any controversies. We all walk around with our own moral compasses in our pockets. Unless we are blind or driven to irrational behavior, our moral compass is ours and ours alone. Our compass is rarely the same as another's, which is why societies create laws and codes of behavior so that we all have a basic benchmark from which to live and interact and do so from a basis of truth and verifiable facts.

I have learned by living among people who do not think like me. I had to shut down my mind and listen to others. I learned that they are as convinced of their facts as I am of mine. I learned that to negate them would create a communication vacuum. They will negate me, and I them. Two negatives will pull apart. A positive force is necessary to bring negative forces together.

Where does the positive force come from? What if the desire is to enlighten? The first step to move opposing forces together is to have facts, supportable truths, and to know and understand the opponent's facts and determine if they are supported. Life is complicated. A second step involves having compassion for others, we all think and behave the way we do for a reason.

On the cruise, I split my time between connecting to nature and trying to connect with a herd of decent people who looked at the world very differently from me. I saw that each one of us was convinced that our wisdom was superior and theirs was not. I saw that each of us is equally convinced of that one fact from which all other disputes are launched. Is the goal to change minds and convince others that your facts are right? That will at least open the door to conversation. We can also choose to dig into positions that stop dialogue. The former path is more complicated than the latter, but it will take you further toward enlightenment.

The crossing went smoothly. The North Atlantic and I reconnected with a bond much warmer than its frigid winter waters. As we entered New York Harbor and passed under the Verrazano Bridge, I was happy to see the Lady of Freedom off our port bow and the inviting skyline of the City of New York. I had taken the time I needed to recharge. I saw and learned much during my travels. We berthed in Brooklyn to a vastly different world than the one I left behind, four months ago. The path of impeachment of the president had just unfolded. Returning from my absence and confronting the chaos surrounding our nation quickly brought me back to earth. I found Andrew's words rattling through my brain. We had a lot of work to do. I was glad to be back home.

★ ★ ★

CHAPTER 2

JANUARY 2020

IT WAS 4:30 ON A CHILLY JANUARY AFTERNOON. I walked down to NYU and stopped by to check out my new office in Tisch Hall overlooking Washington Square Park. I have cherished this park ever since I first moved to New York. It is a delightful public space where visitors are forever new and changing while its enchanting character manages to remain the same. There was a note on my desk that I'd be sharing the office with another visiting professor I had yet to meet.

Gazing out at Washington Square Park, I thought about how fortunate I was to have lived my privileged life. Education was never a priority in my dysfunctional family. My childhood circumstances kept my long-held goal of going to college out of reach. I was twenty-eight when I first entered college. Once accepted by the university of my choice, I thundered through my undergraduate courses, soaking up every ounce of academic knowledge available. Two years later, in 1968, I was awarded a bachelor's degree in economics with a minor in philosophy. Five years after that, I walked out of NYU with a master's and PhD in economics in my head and a postdoc at Princeton in my pocket.

I was thirty-five years old at the time and had launched myself into an entirely new career that would excite me every day for the next forty-five years. I always consider my education among my most gratifying and important accomplishments.

I had some time to kill, so I decided to take a walk through the familiar streets of Greenwich Village. It was early in the evening and the winter sun had already drifted behind the skyline. Leaving my office, the elevator and lobby were empty of their usual throng of students. I turned left on West Fourth Street and decided to walk through the park; entering from the southeast corner, I headed for the fountain at its center. The basin surrounding the fountain has not been filled with water for decades. It once floated boats for children and boasted many species of waterfowl. Now these have been replaced by a flock of minstrels, magicians, political activists, and skateboarders who defy gravity as they speed in and out of the entertainers.

Despite the hour and cold, the paths in the park were filled with people strolling, playing music, singing, or just hanging out. I watched each performer, giving some change to those whose need for money outstripped their talent. I then wandered over to the chess tables to watch the action. Casual players beware there is a stiff price to be paid for losing at these tables, although money is never visible. All the boards were full and surrounded by players standing by for a chance to beat one of the unrated, yet incredibly competent regulars.

I watched the games from a safe distance before heading up Fifth Avenue toward my new home on Thirteenth Street. As I walked out of the park, I noticed several surveillance cameras on poles and trees. I had never seen them before. Trying to remain discreet as I strolled, I counted seventeen cameras. Washington Square Park has historically been the site of protests and marches, but that was in the past. The park was now filled with students escaping classes, mothers strolling with their babies, and street performers. *Why were there cameras and who installed them?*

More importantly, who was monitoring them?

Taxis, busses, private cars, and horse-drawn buggies filled the avenue. Joggers breathed smoke into the evening air as they competed with the more casual night strollers for a path forward. We were all weaving in and out, managing to avoid bumping into each other. Tired, homebound, late-night workers like me were somewhat less alert.

I counted the different languages I heard within a single block, rarely hearing less than three, more often as many as five or six. I was beginning to really feel at home here again and wondered why I had ever left. Many find the city to be too crowded, too loud, too busy. I do not—I cherish the anonymity it provides, not to mention its diversity and ever-present chemistry. Every corner one turns offers a new and changing world to savor. My return to NYU ushered in a happy time in my life, despite the hard times we as a nation have endured in recent decades: 9/11, the 2008 crash, and most recently, the election of Trump, which had taken me and the world as much by surprise as, I suspect, it had shocked Trump himself.

I began to realize how much I had missed all that the Big Apple had done for me for the many years I lived there in the seventies. Cooperative and dense apartment life such as in the building where I was living might be one of the reasons all this works as well as it does. Economists think of apartment buildings as cluster living, an environmentally friendly choice. Cluster living puts a lot of people on significantly less land than most suburban homes. City dwellers typically use about 50% less energy and resources per capita than do our nation's suburban residents. Urban dwellers create a much smaller carbon footprint on our struggling planet.

I suddenly decided to turn left and check out the block that used to be called Shoe Alley. Eighth Street between Fifth and Sixth Avenues was for years chock-a-block with the widest assortment of shoe stores imaginable. During the Victorian period, Eighth Street was labeled the Ladies' Mile. It was redefined as Bohemia's Main Street at the turn of the twentieth century, before eventually becoming a Mecca for shoes. Whatever style or price range you sought; this was where you would find it. Alas, as with most of the city's changing landscape, restaurants, internet cafés, banks, and nail salons have pretty much taken over most of the old retail spaces.

As a graduate student, I would take this walk almost every night after my classes, which usually ended around 10:30. Graduate school was giving me all the tools to understand the world and how it functioned, but these streets gave me purpose. Complex economic theories that delve into virtually every aspect of life—each of which is backed by econometric, statistical, and mathematical tools—filled every moment of my academic life. I needed these tools to understand the issues that drove me toward a PhD in the first place. But it was my walks through my neighborhood that complemented all that I'd learned from my professors. The economist is a social scientist. What separates us from other social scientists is the power of theories to help solve extremely complex problems. In addition to my coursework, I needed to stay in touch with those who were living the problems—the retail workers, shoppers, and street artists. Coming back to these same streets as a seasoned professional grounded me even more. The only difference from fifty years ago was that everything was much more complex, and that people were more vulnerable than they were in the seventies. I became more committed to using my skills as a positive force on behalf of those struggling to survive the digital age. The diversity and energy of Eighth Street was the same, but time had brought major economic change to the composition of the shops that filled the dynamic corner of this perpetually bustling urban neighborhood.

I was getting cold, but not tired, so I continued walking. Do people just wake up one day and decide to open a bakery, a bar, a clothing store? How do they decide where to locate it? Are they aware of the effort it takes to run a business? How do they know that among the millions of people in this city, enough of them will come into their store to ensure its survival? I turned down Bleecker Street, past Sixth Avenue, and took a right onto MacDougal Street to Dante's Italian restaurant where I was to meet Ari, a longtime friend who had the perfect contacts and knowledge to help Andrew and me launch our project.

Dante's was known for its homestyle Italian cooking at prices favorable to students. The taste was exceeded only by the large portions. I walked down the familiar stairs and immediately felt at home. I took my favorite table in the far corner. Gazing out at the street with my glass of Amarone, an Italian red I could not have afforded as a student, I recalled the many reasons I had spent so much time after my classes walking the streets of the city.

I watched a man I barely recognized as he entered the restaurant. He kind of looked like Ari but I had not seen him in years. It was him, and I knew that as soon as I looked into his eyes. I would never have known him if I didn't. He has developed the art of disguise to a science.

We first met at a protest in Washington Square in 1968, when I was still an undergraduate living on Long Island. He had taken a year off from his work in Israel and moved to the Village. We were both in our late twenties, still young enough to be idealistic but older than most of the other protesters. I had done a tour of military service right out of high school, and Ari was a well-trained Israeli operative. Neither of us was directly connected to the antiwar effort, but we both believed in the cause and wanted to get America out of that unforgivable war.

Ari went to school in Haifa, Israel. Like every Israeli citizen, he served in the army and ended up in intelligence. The army sent him to college where he studied foreign affairs and computer science. The army recognized his skills and continued to train him in intelligence, and by the end of his degree, he was promoted to the higher echelon of the Mossad, Israel's Institute for Intelligence and Special Operations. He was eventually assigned to covert operations, which worked independently from the government and reported only to the prime minister. Ari was sent to the UK and then to the United States where he worked for twenty years at the embassy until retiring about five years before me. He decided to stay in the States and set up a small, highly selective cybersecurity firm. You could not hire him unless he personally knew you. In fact, you would not even know he existed; he learned how to be almost invisible to anyone he did not want to know. You did not ask him many questions, you simply told him about the problem you were having, and he would find out what he needed, and somehow the job got done perfectly and discreetly.

My call to Ari was Code Green, meaning there was no emergency. That did not alter the surveillance he would have completed before our meeting. In fact, he always chose the place and time to meet. He walked directly to me and took a chair facing the entrance.

We greeted each other warmly. He was well. His business was thriving, and he looked relaxed. He was happy to see that I'd moved back to the city, surprised that I had retired and told me that the years had been kind to me.

We ordered dinner and talked about how different the world of 2020 was from that of the sixties. One never asks about his life—he tells you what he wants you to know. All I got was that he was comfortable and working much less, but still had his crew on payroll, but mostly on standby.

I mentioned that I'd just gotten a sublet in the same building I used to live in. I told him about my teaching and research over the past four decades. I mentioned my frequent trips to meet colleagues from graduate school. I did not recall if he knew Andrew. I let him know that Andrew and I had decided that Trump had become a worse threat than we could ever have imagined and that we wanted to do something to prevent him from being reelected. We knew that we wanted to update our voter participation database and get it out to fringe voters who are generally not connected to establishment news.

"I don't remember you telling me about that database," he said.

"At the time, it was an academic exercise to support why we need to vote and be involved with our communities if we wish to preserve our democracy. The data are all pretty much up to date. What we need is a distribution mechanism to reach out to potential voters who tend not to be on traditional mailing lists."

Ari was pleased to hear that Andrew and I had both become very wealthy, thanks to Andrew's insight into the then-burgeoning tech companies of the nineties. I told Ari that I had received an inheritance from a family I'd lived with as a teenager. I turned most of it over to Andrew, who invested it. In any case, we sold most of our securities and separately placed everything in conservative growth stocks and bonds. I put a lot offshore as a precaution. We are both now multimillionaires and living comfortably on the returns of our portfolios. I had to establish this wealth to convince him that we could do what I was about to ask of him.

"Ari, we're concerned about where the country is going. I came back to New York to work on the database project. The data will be central to our plans, but we will need to work on the down-low because of the methods we want to implement. The only way to get to our intended audience is to hack our way into several sites and organizations who feed misinformation to these groups. We need skilled programmers knowledgeable in cybersecurity. We need to hire a couple of extremely high-level, big data, computer, and intelligence-savvy people to set us up."

"You know that hacking is illegal," he reminded me.

"We do and have accepted the risk. We want to find the most qualified people we can to help us set the project up and to design the distribution systems we need. Can you help us find those people? I think we will need two."

"Of course. Does it matter where they're from? Where will they be working?"

"We have yet to decide, but it will be in Europe. I thought about Iceland. Andrew is checking various places out. We think we will need the staff to be onsite for about a year, but after that they can work from anywhere. We can pay them well, and we must be absolutely sure we can trust them. We want to distribute information in a format that the average voter can digest and appreciate as important to them and their families."

"I don't understand. What's so secretive about that?"

"Reasonable question," I acknowledged. "The data we are working with are publicly available, but not to the average citizen. They are used for research and planning. The problem is distribution. We want to hack into the underground and foreign sources that have been meddling with our elections. We want to reach the fringe elements who do not, for a host of reasons, get establishment news. Not all but many of these families in the Rust Belt do not have internet services and ready access to professional journalism. Those who do tend to share information with those who are living off the grid. We will reach out to those who are online and hope that their normal community networks will see our posts. They do, however, vote, and because of the selected information they get, they do not often vote in their own best interests. Rush Limbaugh is a prime example. His daily feeding trough of BS influences a lot of people who rarely listen to anyone else. There are a lot of talk shows, websites, and podcasts we want to tap into. We want to get to those using Facebook, Twitter, and other social media to disseminate their false messages. To the extent that those who are spreading false information to this demographic, we will infiltrate their sites as they do to others, we will be hacking the hackers. We also, to the extent possible, want to tap into Trump's feed so that we can directly counter his lies to the eighty million people who follow him. Every time any of these people hit the send button, they will also be sending out a message from us."

"Whoa, now I know why you need to be on the down-low. I need some time to make calls to see if I can get the people you need. The skills are out there for you, but I need to see who can take that much time out. Where did you go on your trip?"

"Europe for about three months then came back to the UK where I hopped on board the *Queen Mary II* to sail back via the Caribbean."

"Nice trip. Did you go to Iceland?"

"No, why do you ask?"

"Because if you are planning to set up shop in Iceland and had recently gone there, you will increase the chances of getting caught. They watch passports..." He paused and looked at me knowingly.

"Understood," I said quickly. This is why I trust this man so much. He somehow manages to think of everything.

We talked about our memories, our food preferences, and our lives. I then asked, "How is your dinner?"

"Great, and this is really a wonderful wine. Did you choose it?"

"Angelo made some suggestions, and I chose from his list. Would you like some coffee? I'm going to have an espresso and a sfogliatella, my all-time favorite Italian pastry."

"I would love one—I have not had one since the last time we ate here, which I think was around 1970."

"It was." I placed the order and asked for the check. We talked for a while, finishing off our dessert, which we both enjoyed. Ari rarely stays in one place for too long. I was surprised he was still at our table. I knew he would be going soon, and out the back door. We nodded at each other. He let me know that he would contact me within a week. Ari is a master at disappearing whenever he knows it is time. I ordered a brandy and decided to relax for a while. Whenever we meet, I never leave with him. We go separate ways as though the meeting never happened.

I knew that he would come through for me. I was surprised that he did not ask more about what Andrew and I were doing. He did not even try to say that it could not be done. He supported our effort. That was more of an endorsement than I expected.

I finished my brandy, paid Angelo, and walked out into the West Village once again. I headed toward Sheridan Square on Seventh Avenue and Christopher Street. That section has a few tiny jazz bars that hum till the early morning. Most feature musicians just drop by to jam. These guys are a tight-knit group. It was a totally improvisational experience to behold, and therein lies the true beauty of jazz.

A favorite haunt for the musicians, especially those who thrive on jazz, is Bradley's on University Place. Bradley's stopped serving paying customers around two or three in the morning, and that's when musicians drop by for an early morning bite after their gigs. The Village remains a legendary neighborhood in the city due largely, I suspect, to the efforts of Bradley and his wife Wendy Cunningham.

It was getting late, so I had to leave. I stopped at the supermarket for some breakfast supplies and then headed home. It was about one in the morning, and Mr. Bonaparte was on duty. Born in Barbados, his melodious, East Indian island chain accent makes his native English sound like a symphony of blended harmonics. This beautiful man was a true pleasure to know. A handsome gentleman, always polite and professional, he never ceased to make our building a comfort for all of us. He would always greet me by name. He would help elderly neighbors with packages and give a particularly warm reception to the resident children who adored him. Mr. Bonaparte would tip the brim of his cap as a sign of respect to everyone going through our doors, in or out.

He and I had a deep respect for each other that went as far back as my graduate studies. After I had finished my studies and moved out of the city, I always found time to stop by and say hello whenever I was in town. He had taken a great personal interest in my studies. I would let him know what classes I was taking and how they were going. He always laughed when I would say that he was getting an honorary PhD. I would have loved to have had him graduate with me.

Last fall, when I decided to move back to the city, I stopped by to say hello. I told him I was looking for an apartment. He told me that a one-bedroom sublet would soon be available in the building. The owner had retired and was taking time off to travel. I filled out an application and met with the board. Armed with a reference from Mr. Bonaparte and my previous ownership of a unit in the building, my apartment search, never an easy task in this town, was happily over.

"Still keeping your late hours, Dr. Pryce?" He always called me doctor, knowing how hard I worked for that title.

"You know me well, Mr. Bonaparte. I just came from my office and dinner with a friend and, as usual, I needed to check out our hood before calling it a day. Tell me is Ramon still working here?"

"Yes, he is. He did move his family out to Queens. They wanted to have their own home."

"I'm glad to hear it. I have always like him and his family—good people."

"You're right. By the way, I received this message today from Ms. Anna. She's been trying to get in touch with you. She did not know where you were, and assumed I would."

"She is right, I forgot to tell her that I sold my Brooklyn home and left the country for several months. I had also disconnected my phone."

"Here's her number. Call her tonight."

"I will."

"Dr. Pryce, do you think things have changed in the Village since you last lived here?"

"Yes and no. I do miss the older cafés, but the overall character of the Village remains pretty much the same, and for that I am grateful." Like Ramon and his wife, Mr. Bonaparte is an immigrant who got citizenship several years ago. He loves his native country but is happy to be living in America. He dropped his professional face and stared directly at me. I could tell that there was a lot on his mind. He leaned forward over the counter and pushed his cap up to give me a clear view of his face.

"What has changed, Dr. Pryce, is something I can best describe as a pall over the streets and alleys, and even the people. I cannot put my finger on it, but it is there, and I do feel it."

I knew exactly what it was. I told him how upset I was at the surveillance cameras I'd noticed all over the Village, especially in the parks." I worded my statement to see if he knew what I was talking about.

He responded as he came around the counter and reached for the elevator button. "I, too, am grateful to be working here. The Village is a wonderful corner of the world, important to all of us who love it." He paused. "I also feel like a shadow is lurking all around us and not just in the Village. It is almost like we are being followed. I'm not sure why I feel that way. Maybe it is our dependence on all these devices we carry around. It's something very real and seems to be growing more intense each year. Life in New York, as wonderful as it is, is far more controlling than I was used to back home."

I knew this kind man all too well. He was politely letting me know, without stating the obvious, that our lives *have* indeed changed.

"It's not only New York, Mr. Bonaparte. What you are feeling is a growing trend impacting the lives of almost every American. The same might even be happening in other nations." We held the elevator doors open, and we glanced at each other puzzled yet hopeful that life would go on, albeit very differently than each of us had known.

"Dr. Pryce, we feel different because the world we're living in is different. I do not know if I feel any safer. The only thing we know for sure is that privacy and freedom as we knew it no longer exist." He paused and waved. "Don't forget to call Ms. Anna!"

My apartment was smaller than the one I had once owned but would be more than adequate for my needs. It was on a high floor facing south, which afforded a view of the downtown skyline. In the mornings, I traced the path of light and shadows as the rising sun traversed dew-covered avenues at the rate of one degree every four minutes.

The apartment was furnished in contemporary Manhattan chic. Their library was not to my literary taste, which uncharacteristically did not matter to me. I have a 10% compatibility factor as my benchmark. If my host has at least 10% of the same books as me, I assume that we have the basis for a relationship. I brought enough of the books I would need for work, rendering this owner's library of no use to me.

After I put my groceries away, I poured a glass of Portuguese port.

I pondered again how all those businesses and shops, not to mention the street vendors and performers, managed to eke out a living in such a competitive and expensive place. I was acutely aware of the disconnect between what was happening on the street and what I was reading in these books as a student. I have always wanted to help these merchants and their families, but I had no idea how econometrics, differential calculus, and abstract micro or macro theories could possibly make that happen. I found no links between my social and humanistic desires and my formal studies as an economics student. I did, however, know that the answer was buried in what I was learning, and it was my job to absorb every aspect of this complex science that I could. My questions were somewhere in the minds of my professors and the textbooks and articles they required us to read. I just needed to be patient, diligent, and, most of all, committed to learn. I did just that, and time has linked what I learned in my classes to that which I still absorb from the streets. The brilliance of economics has never let me down.

I turned on the news before going to bed, ending an eventful day in the life of my city. I have been told by professionals that, given the disturbing political trends, we should not watch the news before bed. Screen time before bed does not make for a good night's sleep. Given the few hours each day that I do sleep, I tried to take this advice, but in these stressful months, I couldn't help but check out the news before turning in.

I called Anna in the morning and could tell right away that something was wrong.

"Benson, Dad is dead! He was delivering a sailboat to England and got lost at sea. I have been trying to get to you, but I didn't know where you were. It happened in October."

I was, of course, totally surprised. "Anna, this is terrible! Are you sure? You know how good of a sailor he is."

"Yes. A horrendous storm hit the area, and many small boats were lost at sea. He was never found. Even the large ships barely made it through. I cannot tell you how hard this has been. We met over the summer, and he told me about the trip. He gave me his will and made you his executor. I know he set up a trust fund for me with an enormous amount of money in it. How did he have all that money?"

"I'm so sorry. I was out of the country. Give me the lawyer's name, and I'll contact him or her first thing today. I cannot believe he was lost at sea. I cannot imagine life without your father. He was my closest friend. On the money, many years ago, I gave him an inheritance from my stepparents, who died in 1988. You know that I have no facility with money and your dad does. He invested it and made us both extraordinarily rich." I paused, and the reality just wouldn't sink in. "Oh, Anna, I have no idea how I am going to process this. I'm sorry I wasn't here with you."

We promised to get together as soon as possible. I guess I had just found out how Andrew decided to let her know that he would have to disappear. This was over the top, but he must have had a reason. I knew I'd have to contact him to find out how he wanted me to handle his death. I assumed, with no information, that he was, in fact, not dead. Economists make the wildest assumptions to deal with this crazy world.

I sent a text to Andrew on our burner. He would get right back if he was in Iceland.

★★★

CHAPTER 3

FEBRUARY 2020

I DID GET A TEXT BACK FROM ANDREW. We set a time to talk later that evening. He apologized for not saying anything to me. He wanted it to unfold exactly as it did. He was not aware that I would be away for so long. I was relieved, but not happy, with the burden of supporting such a lie to the one person in the world we both love and care about, the one person in the world we protect the most.

I woke just before dawn to a beautiful New York winter morning. The air was clear. The streets glistened with the first rays of sun dancing on the newly washed streets. The rattle of garbage trucks pierced the urban caverns as they collected 12,000 tons of industrial and residential garbage the city generates every day.

I stuffed everything I needed for the day into my aging leather brief, an integral part of my life for years. Around seven, I prepared three cups of strong European coffee and popped an almond croissant into the oven. I pulled up *The New York Times* on my iPad and browsed the headlines. Having shifted from my professional and technical work, which I prefer to do early in the morning when I am fresh, I then dedicated the next two or three hours to reading the news. I deliberately collate each source equitably across the political spectrum: Fox, Bloomberg, *The Washington Post, The Wall Street Journal*, and my favorite, the *New York Times*. I also download a conglomeration of news from *Huffington Post, The Daily Beast*, CNN, and *The Economist*. Key articles are stored in folders in a dedicated email address that is hosted by an almost completely unknown server. I prefer to keep my academic life and thoughts as protected as possible against the growing class of very sharp and excessively curious hackers. The internet and social media, despite many obvious benefits, have created a class of insidious invaders who want only to know our consuming habits, reading preferences, TV choices, and how we spend our time. All of this "collected" information is then sold to big data companies who compile it and sell it to anyone willing to pay the price.

The dominating story was the airstrike ordered by President Trump to assassinate Qasem Soleimani who was an Iranian military leader responsible for many deaths. He had been sanctioned by the U.S. for his support of Syrian president Bashar al-Assad. Several days later, the Pentagon announced that 34 US troops suffered traumatic brain injuries. President Trump said that they did not suffer any injuries as a result of the attack, which was clearly not true. Do we still condone assassinations? President Ford issued Executive Order 11905 in February of 1976. It was aimed directly at the CIA in an attempt to ban any assassination operations undertaken by the agency. This order was strengthened by President Carter in 1978 and again by President Reagan in 1981. Trump's airstrike represented a flagrant violation of law and presidential authority. In addition to the moral and legal issues, assassinations open the door for retaliation against our troops and dignitaries stationed on foreign soil. Unfortunately, Executive Orders have no teeth under the law, and short of binding legislation, little can be done legally when such acts are committed, even by our president.

UPDATED ON THE DAY'S NEWS, I showered, shaved, and got dressed more in the style of an entrenched, tweedy professor than a business school academic. I headed off to face the world. Locking the door behind me, I slung my aging leather brief over my shoulder. I had already planned my day at the Bobst Library, rummaging through volumes of scholarly publications. Academics must footnote almost every point we make. Doing so helps us remember what we wrote and where we got any pertinent information we have referenced and stored. It also helps other researchers duplicate our work and improve upon it with their own insight and perspectives.

I stopped in our lobby to greet Ramon, standing in for our morning doorman. I have known him for as long as I've known Mr. Bonaparte. I think they both were hired at the same time. Ramon and his family used to live in the ground floor apartment set up for our building super. Following the birth of his second daughter, Ramon moved his family out to Queens in a two-family house he shares with his in-laws. He stayed on as our super, much to the gratitude of every owner.

Ramon was born in Mexico and is a natural genius who can repair, restore, or reprogram any personal computer. He makes a decent living as a computer consultant and accepted the job of super for the steady income and health and pension benefits offered by the union. This decision was driven by his wife and three beautiful children. I have met few men who work as hard as he does, and I've often called on his unequaled skills with computers.

"Ramon," I smiled and said hello. I explained that I decided on the new XPS series from Dell. I hired him to transfer some of my files from my old computer. I also asked for his recommendation for the most current virus and hacking protection software. "I want an untraceable backup for all of my work and hope the Dell will do the job." Ramon was the only person I could trust on such matters.

"Of course, Dr. Pryce. How soon do you need it?" he asked.

"No rush. I plan to pick one up this weekend and can give it to you on Monday morning if that works for you."

"Great, I will have it back to you by the end of the week. Would you prefer that I buy it for you?

"Thank you so much, I would prefer that you purchase it yourself. Shall I pay you now?"

"That's not necessary, I'll let you know the cost later. I understand what you are asking for. I know that computer well and, after a few enhancements I can make, it will do the job for you."

THE FIFTEEN-MINUTE WALK to my office was direct, compared with my meandering path home the previous evening. Passing the *Forbes* headquarters on Fifth Avenue, I bought some water and fruit at Claudette's on the corner of Ninth Street and Fifth Avenue. I went under the arch and veered off to Mercer Street and my office.

As I turned the key, I noticed that the door was unlocked. To my surprise, my officemate was at his desk. He introduced himself as Arthur Ransom. Like me, Arthur was a visiting scholar whose specialty was economic history. I could not have been more pleased because I know of Arthur's work, even though we are in somewhat different fields.

I candidly expressed my pleasure that we'd be sharing an office. "Your research is wonderful and explains how economics plays such an important role in society," I said.

"Thank you so much, Benson."

"Are you teaching a course?" I asked.

"I might at some point, but right now I just want to work on a book I've been thinking about for years. I'll also be traveling over the next few months giving speeches on my last book."

"I just finished that book on how economic policies have impacted the postwar American economy—a true masterpiece of insightful research and commentary. It is frightening how much America has fallen behind as compared to economic and social performances of other industrialized nations. It is understandable that the average American would not be aware of this decline, many of the international indicators are not the least bit obvious, especially since Americans do not travel as much as people from other nations. I do, however, fault our private and public sector leaders who should be more up front about how much we have fallen behind in several key growth economic and social areas. Their issue might be due to the fact that those at the top of the economic scale are not as impacted by our weakening as is the general population. You document this with a strength that will hopefully be obvious to your readers."

"Thank you. I've received many kind comments from colleagues like yourself, which always makes an author feel good. I also appreciate the comments from elected officials. It's good to know that at least some of them actually read," he joked.

"How true. I've heard that many of the recent laws implemented and speeches given by elected officials are often written by lobbyists. How scary is that?"

I really wanted to learn more about the book Arthur was working on, but I could tell that he needed to get back to his goals for the day. I shared his time constraints. I went to my desk, turned on my computer, and began a search for journal articles I needed to download.

It was late afternoon by the time I finished, and I desperately needed a change of venue. I had not managed to get to the library as planned. I left a note to my officemate to have dinner next week. I decided to go to the Film Forum on Houston Street. Clearly one of the pleasures of being retired is not having a fixed schedule. The Film Forum shows films that tend to be more of an art than most studio-generated flicks. I know of no better way to reduce the pressures of a cluttered mind than to let it become totally absorbed in the action on the silver screen. If I could have a second life, I would be a movie director.

I had not been to a movie theater for months and, while waiting for the feature to start, I was subjected to the usual advertisements. Slipped into this afternoon's showing was a short news clip, the likes of which I had not seen over the many decades I had gone to the movies. It was highly professional in full color and covered the recent accomplishments of the Trump administration. Even though it only went on for a less than a minute, I was deeply annoyed at this interference into my private time. It was clearly a political advert and not intended to inform. I looked around, and most of the other viewers were totally unfazed. I let it go and was relieved to see the previews.

The film was great. I don't remember what I saw, which is often my best gauge of how tired I must have been. I was still annoyed at having to sit through the political message. I texted Anna as I walked home and asked if we could meet for dinner on Friday. She accepted right away, and we set a time and place. I was nervous to see her. We both know I'm a terrible liar.

WE MET AT A TIO LUCA COCINA on Lenox Avenue in Harlem, a few blocks from her apartment. My suggestion: I thought a good cocktail would make the evening go smoothly. I was early and ordered two margaritas to be served as soon as she arrived. I could tell from her face and body language as she entered that this was not going to be an easy evening.

"Hey, you, I can't tell you how sorry I am that I wasn't here for you," I said as I embraced her.

"It was a bummer. The news of Dad's death came so suddenly—I honestly didn't know how to react. I really wish you'd been here." Her eyes teared up. And she answered the question I had on my mind. "I got the call from his lawyer who was on his emergency contact list." She paused to wipe away her tears.

"It's still so hard to believe," I said, looking her in the eye. "He knew just what he was doing and planned everything down to the finest detail, especially when he made a delivery of someone else's boat. How are you doing? Do you have friends to help? What a time for me to disappear on you..."

"Where did you go?" she asked.

This was going to be the hard part. I needed to be believable and leave no room for doubt. She had stopped crying but her body language displayed pain and more than a touch of anger. "I had decided to retire and needed to get away," I said. "I borrowed your dad's boat for several weeks, then took off for Europe. I was pretty much out of contact for about four months. Your dad and I met in June to talk about some research we wanted to do together, but that was the last time we talked. I did tell him I was taking off for several months." I was very matter of fact, using as few words as possible to bring her up to date.

"Now I remember," she said. "Dad and I had dinner in July, and he said that he was making a delivery of some guy's boat. I think he was going to take it to Ireland or England, I forgot. He did mention that you retired and were going to take our boat for several weeks. I didn't remember that you were going to Europe."

"I might not have even known yet when he and I met," I said. "Getting old is beginning to show on me. This is really impossible to process. He was such a good sailor—I just can't image him ever getting into a jam like this. Tell me how you are. What can I do for you at this point?"

"I'm as good as I can be," she said. "I'm glad you're back and living near-by. Some days are more difficult than others. I just go to work and classes and go home. I am still in touch with some of my high school friends but, I am too busy to see them right now. Most of them are married and having kids

"I thought that you had finished your studies, what classes are you taking?"

I decided to get a master's degree and applied to and was accepted by Columbia School of Social Work. I figured I would need the graduate degree if I wanted to work as a professional social worker. I am also auditing some classes at NYU where you and dad went. They are not offered by Columbia. I have met some really nice students there and we get together as an informal gathering on current events. They are really smart and involved.

"I am glad you are doing that. As you know your dad and I are big fans of education, we cannot have too much education or love in our lives. I am also glad to see you getting involved with what is happening all around us. My biggest regret, before the loss of your father, has been how badly my generation messed up. I don't envy the effort it will require for your generation to get the planet back on an even keel. Do you need any money? I'm living in my old building on Thirteenth Street, and plan to spend time at NYU. They gave me an office."

"No. I don't need money. I am working part time in a clinic and dad left me a whole bunch. I can't believe how successful he was. I am working on a masters to help me set up my own practice," she said.

"That is good news! Your dad set up a trust fund for you as soon as we both cashed out. I suspect you will be comfortable for the rest of your life. I would recommend investing what you do not need. Retirement comes a lot faster than you can possibly imagine."

"Dad took care of that for me. It's almost like he *planned* this whole thing. I'm really upset with him."

I was not sure what she was saying. Did she think he deliberately killed himself? I needed to hit this straight on. "Anna. Do not think like that for one moment. Your father loved life and would never even think of such a thing. That trust fund was set up years ago. He also set up a retirement fund for me at the same time. He knows more about these things than you and me, and he knew if he did not handle it, we'd never get to it."

"I did not know that... We never really talked about money. I'm sorry if I upset you, it just seems weird that he would die at sea--the one place he felt totally safe."

"You are right on that. It is puzzling."

We studied the menu, drank our margaritas, and tried to settle into the evening. Anna was not in great shape, and I knew that I had to be around for her. We got through the meal, and I could tell she was tired. I offered to get her a taxi.

"No. I want to walk home. I need the air."

"Want me to join you?"

"Yes, please. Let's just walk and not talk."

"Okay. Last words—call, text, come over any time. I do not want to leave you ever again."

We walked the ten blocks in silence. I held her hand and hoped that I'd succeeded in re-creating the bond between us that she desperately needed. I felt as though I'd handled the evening well and only hoped that this charade did not have to go on too long.

I decided to take the next day off and enjoy the many benefits offered to those lucky enough to live where I did. I also needed to transition from the pain I felt knowing how much Andrew and I hurt Anna. Totally strange territory for both of us.

The life and culture of almost any nation on our planet is a subway ride away in this city. You can just walk into any of the hundreds of ethnic neighborhoods and feel as though you are physically in a new country. Eat their food, listen to their language, watch their street games and community activities, visit their stores, parks, temples, and galleries. The world is there for those willing to hop on a subway. Leave your passport home.

It was such a beautiful day that I changed my mind and traded Harlem for Central Park. In winter, parks are often perceived as dreary, though not to me. I think of trees as nature's finest gifts. I had recently learned how much of a mutually supportive community each tree creates and provides for all that exists within its domain. Watching them during their long winter sleep, knowing they are daily storing up energy, preparing themselves for the coming spring and summer has been a lifelong pleasure of mine.

Walking through the grays and browns of the park's 843 acres, meticulously designed and landscaped by Olmsted and Vaux, a legendary landscape design team known for working around nature with every one of their many urban creations. One cannot help but feel nature's omnipresent power. The drab wintry trees made the stylistic strollers, magicians, musicians, and poets gathered along the well-traveled paths look brighter and more colorful.

I noted that like Washington Square, Central Park was filled with surveillance cameras. What in the hell was going on? Had the Parks Department suddenly gone into the spy business? Did the orders come down from

City Hall? Is what I was witnessing an initiative from the post 9/11 Department of Homeland Security?

SUNDAY WAS A DAY TO REST, READ, and watch some news. I also went back to the Forum to watch Federico Fellini's *La Strada*, a self-indulgent masterpiece starring Anthony Quinn. I endured another political advertisement, different from the last, but still an unbelievably preposterous message on Trump. It was shown right before the previews and, as before, totally ignored by everyone but me.

By Monday, I was fully rested and ready to hit the books. As I entered my office, I saw a note on my desk. It was from Arthur, my officemate, accepting my invitation, which pleased me very much. He offered to meet me for dinner on Tuesday evening and had chosen Osteria 57 on Tenth Street. The day went productively.

I decided to work in the morning on Tuesday and took a long afternoon nap to be as sharp as possible for what would surely be an informative evening. I had many questions for this learned man, key to the research I wanted to do on the history of economic thought. I was not, however, ready for the wide-ranging questions my dinner partner had prepared for me.

I asked for the quietest table they had. I also let the maître d' know that we might be there for a while. I sat at the bar, and Arthur entered as I was about to settle in. "I hope you've not been waiting long," he said as he shook my hand.

"No, just got here. You're right on time."

We were directed to a table that was perfectly out of the way. I have a problem with loud restaurants and refuse to scream at my dinner guests over unwanted music or boisterous diners at nearby tables. I've been known to leave a restaurant after drinks if I can't comfortably hear those at my table.

We settled in quickly, exchanging a few comments on family and our living arrangements while at NYU. We ordered drinks and talked a bit before looking at the menu. We were both about the same age, though Arthur was several inches shorter and a bit stocky. He had dark, curly hair and was wearing a suit that didn't quite fit. He'd gone to Berkeley for his graduate work and knew that I had gone to NYU. He had taught in California for most of his career. We both had public sector experience and a respectable list of publications. The credentials dance successfully completed, we picked up our drinks and acknowledged each other's accomplishments.

Arthur asked, "When were you at NYU?"

"I finished my degree in 1974 and defended my thesis in early 1975."

"So, you were there during all that turmoil that the department of economics was going through?"

"Indeed! I was! That period was difficult for everyone. I've never since seen anything like what the department and university went through. Even my tour in the Navy could not prepare me for what I would experience at NYU."

"Please tell me about it. I only heard from colleagues who knew some of the actors. I've never met anyone who was actually there."

His comment surprised me since the economics profession is small, and I assumed everyone knew about the travails of NYU during that historic transitional period. Furthermore, my closest friend while at graduate school was also at Berkeley. I justified Arthur's lack of familiarity thinking that he was a West Coast guy who probably did not know my friend Richard. Not wanting to dwell on the history of my time at NYU, I formulated a reduced version in my mind of the more than five years of mayhem and suffering that, at the time, seemed like it would never end.

"Almost from my first day of classes in the fall of 1970, there was considerable tension in the department. Apparently, Professor Netzer, a well-liked faculty member from another school within NYU, had been asked to take over as chair. He lasted only a year or so before the faculty battles became more than he could handle. He was appointed dean of the School of Public Administration. I got to know him well and found him to be a pleasure to work with. He never hesitated to express his glee over no longer being in the department of economics.

"The president brought in a new chair from Princeton who sought some major changes. The president wanted our economics department to be ranked in the top ten as soon as possible. We were ranked around forty-fifth at the time. Such changes are always upsetting to the old guard, and NYU was no exception. Many new and universally recognized economists joined the faculty and pushed the old guard aside in the name of education, professionalism, and research. The students benefited from the education side of the equation, but the constant tension took its toll on everyone. I was really glad to have finished and be able to move on."

I cut the story short because I wanted to hear more about what Ransom was working on. But apparently, he wanted to talk about mine. Changing the subject, I said, "I attended your paper at the last American Economic Association meeting. I was mesmerized by how beautifully you wove a host of economic factors into twentieth-century American history. I have long had this feeling that America, within my lifetime, became the dominate postwar power, reaching a zenith around the mid-1970s. Since then, I've witnessed a gradual decline in almost all standard measures that we use to gauge a nation's economic, social, and political success. All I had, however, was a feeling that was void of any solid empirical evidence. Your paper outlined that rise and fall, event by event, and made the cycle I perceived crystal clear." I could tell that I had really captured my new friend's attention. He just stared at me waiting for my next words. "I mean, Arthur, you really nailed it. I watched the reaction of the audience as you systematically laid out how America prospered like no other postwar nation in history. The Marshall Plan, Bretton Woods, the baby and housing booms, Eisenhower's national highway construction program, the transistor, TV. Except for the endless Korean War, we lived through a period of relative peace and prosperity over most of the '50s into the early '60s. Rock and roll, cruising around in our cars on Saturday nights with our radios blasting, school dances, saddle shoes, tight t-shirts, and pleated poodle skirts filled the bulk of our carefree, teenage lives. The only hint of conflict at the national level was from Senator Joe McCarthy's misguided threat of Communists invading American institutions. As horrendous as that man was, most of us teenagers did not even understand or know what he was trying to do."

Arthur nodded and stated, "The '60s opened with the election of Kennedy and the age of Camelot. His assassination, and those of Martin Luther King, Bobby Kennedy, Che Guevara, and Malcom X reset the tone of the decade. The Civil Rights movement, the war on poverty, Vietnam, and President Johnson's decision not to run in '68, followed by the disastrous Chicago convention, made us feel like the world was turning upside down. The election of Nixon, the Kent State tragedy, the expansion of the Vietnam War into Cambodia, Agent Orange and the constant bombing... all precipitated even more violent protests. Watergate and the fall of Nixon, the rise of OPEC and the oil embargo all left us dumbfounded as to what was happening to our nation, indeed the world.

"You are right on all this, Arthur. So much was happening at one time that it seemed like the world was crashing down on us. The sixties actually took on a dynamic of its own that culminated with President Johnson refusing to run again for president, which did not lessen the unrest as witnessed at the 1968 Democratic Convention in Chicago."

Arthur agreed. "You're right, Benson, and all of this became more confusing by the emergence of China, and later by conflicts throughout the Middle East, 9/11, and, finally, the Arab Spring, which was primarily a revolt against oppression and a cry on the part of the youth of each of those nations. Young men begged for jobs and the right to marry and have a decent life within the confines of their culture. The lack of economic security and declining remnants of a normal life were part of a worldwide sea change that was not healthy. Each of these incidents also contributed to a breakdown in how most Americans saw their lives. America and the Middle East were not the only regions witnessing major disruptions. Other nations were experiencing the same frustrations—the fall of the Berlin Wall, the rise of China, and the collapse of the Soviet Union are among the most notable. The world was experiencing a major shift and America was not among the nations that were moving upward."

I interjected. "It is hard to pin down exactly when the post-WWII period of prosperity fell apart, but one thing is certain, we as a nation were, and to a large degree still are, clueless that we had peaked and were entering a decades-long slide from the top in terms of economic and political power."

This was when my dinner partner really opened up. I could tell that I had hit the Go button by redefining the conversation to the postwar rise and fall of America. Arthur expanded on this point stating, "Many nations rise to great heights only to fall. Ancient Greece, Portugal, Italy, Great Britain, China, and India are only a few examples. The Roman and Egyptian empires each lasted for more than five hundred years. The United States can legitimately claim World War I as the birth of its rise as a world power. America was later to become the only major nation in the world to come out of the Second World War unscathed by the ravages of the battlefield. And that was when the country really came into its own. Our economic growth, productivity, innovation, and democratic values established an American presence and global respect as a legitimate world power."

I could not have agreed more, I offered to defend his position by looking at why all this was happening. "The more subtle trend to the political right over the past three or four decades morphed us into a new and well-defined global environment. The global movement to the right began with the elections of Ronald Reagan and Margaret Thatcher. Both were popular, hard-right politicians who led their nations away from the prosperity and success of the liberal democracies of the postwar period. The fall of Russia was precipitated by Reagan's hatred of Communism. That event alone represented a major turning point. I even think it created an unsustainable model for world stability. The trickle-down philosophy of Reagan and Thatcher failed. It had been tried before and Trump is calling it back once more. It is a failed policy and one that only benefits the upper class.

"Arthur, this has really been a sticking point for Americans. It is hard for us to believe that, while we are still a world power, that role is gradually being taken away from us. I've long agreed with those who felt that it was Reagan's big mistake to go after the Soviet Union as he did. Having two strong countervailing forces in the world is the best deterrent to the many wannabees out there who dream of power through might. The fall of Russia put America in an unenviable position. Every potentate with oil money or sufficient financial reserves thought they could now build a military presence, get access to the bomb, or strive for world recognition."

"Yes," responded Arthur, "we could have handled Russia more intelligently. As costly as it was to Russia, Reagan's Star Wars program also broke the bank. The US national debt entered the trillion-dollar bracket for the first time, a surprising outcome from a conservative, balanced-budget Republican. I do not however, think that the Reagan/Thatcher Supply Side economics was at the cause of the problems we are now living with."

I could not have disagreed more. "Arthur, I strongly feel that the collapse of the Soviet Union was the tipping point for the rise of the radical right, which actually started with the defeat of Goldwater in 1964. I believe that was a signal to the far right that they could reshape the country in their image. Goldwater lost that election, but I believe that the extreme right saw his campaign as a bellwether that, despite the fact that they were clearly a minority, they just might be able to become a major force in American politics. He lost the election, but for the first time since the Civil War, a Republican won all seven Southern states. Republicans immediately launched a successful campaign to take control of as many state governments as they could. This was the birth of the Southern Strategy capitalized on by Nixon in '68. The Goldwater campaign enabled the right wing of the party to seek control over much of the local agenda nationally, including voter participation and determining who, when, and where citizens got to vote. The right wing-controlled tax policies, school curriculum, and much more in a growing number of states. Remember that the successes of the post-WWII period ended with the election of Nixon, which represented the beginning of the end of the New Deal, and the beginning of a trend away from the partnership of government and business that contributed to the prosperity of that period.

"The election of Reagan in 1980 tipped the country away from the successful postwar liberal agenda. The left gained a temporary reprieve under the center-left Clinton years. I do, however, think that the prosperity of his administration was due largely to the launch of the PC computer, which initiated a renewed economic growth in virtually every sector of our economy. Surely you recall that Clinton left office in 2000 with a $236 billion surplus, the largest since 1929, a surplus that was immediately destroyed by the GW tax initiative."

Arthur reluctantly supported my arguments. "I agree, the controversial Supreme Court–determined election of George W. Bush in 2000 cemented the Reagan/Bush I legacy. I will never understand why the court got involved or why they made the decision they did on that Florida election. I do, however, recall that Chief Justice John Roberts and a young Brett Kavanaugh both were involved in bringing that decision to the court. One of life's fascinating twists."

"Thank you for reminding me," I said. "The reaction to the 9/11 attacks precipitated a major shift in political focus, and it destabilized our nation. The Bush II administration did just about everything they could under the leadership of Dick Cheney, Donald Rumsfeld, and others, to destroy any compassion towards America following 9/11. In hindsight, we now know that we could have handled our response to this attack differently. It could have become the impetus to bring the world together. America had the sympathy of the entire world. We could have used our victimhood in that attack to wake up the world to the need to come together and find ways to bring more nations and their peoples into better, more secure participation in world prosperity.

"Instead, the Bush II administration emboldened a radical Islamist fringe. We invaded Iraq, which had nothing to do with the 9/11 attack. We also invaded Afghanistan, a nation far more culpable, but one that has historically been subjected to seemingly endless and unwinnable wars. One deficiency in our otherwise great nation is the persistent and apparently incurable urge to go to war rather than the diplomatic table.

"We then passed the Patriot Act, which basically took away most of the fundamental liberties that America was founded on. Some might cite this as the opening salvo against our civil rights since it overtly challenged many of those privileges embedded in our Constitution. Michael Moore's documentary, *Fahrenheit 9/11* revealed that none of the senators who signed off on the Patriot Act had even read it. We are left bewildered as to how such laws get past."

Arthur noted, "That act was in direct response to the fact that we were attacked by foreign terrorists and needed to establish safeguards to protect Americans against another such attack."

"The problem, Arthur, is that the Patriot Act was not a document directed at those who attacked us, it was a direct attack on the part of our government to dramatically increase the ability of our government to invade the privacy and civil rights of American citizens. Similar acts had been resoundingly rejected by congress. This one passed only due to the bullying of the Bush II administration and the 9/11 attack. How does that even address the threat of foreign terrorists?"

I paused to let him think about that. He had no response, which frankly baffled me since I knew that he was fully aware of the truth behind my argument. I continued, "The political negligence of the Bush II administration might have helped give us our first African-American president. Obama's intelligence, decency, and clear family values came along at the right time. Clearly, his winning the presidency was a total shock to some, like Kentucky Senator Mitch McConnell, who was frankly outraged that a black man had won the presidency. He made it clear at a Washington luncheon immediately after Obama's inauguration that he, Senator Mitch McConnell and eleven other Republican senators at that luncheon, were revolted. They publicly vowed to prevent Obama from winning a second term. Moscow Mitch, as he was eventually called, and his arguably racist associates also promised to do everything in their power to stymie any legislative initiatives from the Obama administration. Political scientists will probably give Moscow Mitch a win on that promise. He managed to stymie Obama from implementing the agenda he was elected to execute, most notably his judicial appointments."

Arthur added, "The one thing we all agree on is that America is becoming more polarized every election cycle. Not since the Civil War have we been so split between those on the left, who still think government can solve all our problems, and those on the right, who feel justified in redefining the role of government almost out of existence. There is fault on both sides, and the danger is that dialogue and compromise have become negative concepts. I fear for our future."

I tried to read where my new colleague was going with all this. I was beginning to think that he leans more to the right than I originally thought. I respect his working knowledge of the condition and knew that there was much to learn from this man. I countered with, "You are totally right. We have had a dysfunctional congress for more than twelve years now, and that has cost us dearly. It started as the nation began to see the folly of the Bush wars.

"The election of Obama added fuel to that simmering fire. Almost every idea from the Obama Administration had to be done as an executive order since McConnell made it clear that nothing coming out of that White House had the slightest chance of getting to the floor of the Senate for a vote. The ultimate disgrace on the part of the Republicans, led by the senator from Kentucky, was the total humiliation and blatantly unconstitutional behavior of blocking the Obama nomination of the eminently qualified Merrick Garland to replace the deceased Associate Justice Antonin Scalia. Moscow Mitch continues to take full credit with great pride for this despicable act on his part."

"You are right about the Garland appointment," he said. "McConnell's primary objective was to reshape the courts in America. The Trump administration has proven to be a holy grail for him. I do not think Congress has been that negligent, but it is hard to not recognize the growing lack of comradeship in both houses."

Interesting choice of words. I wanted to hear his perspective on Obama. "Many have disparaged McConnell and the Republicans for all that they did for the eight years of the Obama administration, and they were right to do so. My beef was with Obama himself. I was extremely disappointed in him for letting McConnell and company run roughshod over his administration for his entire two terms in office. Obama might have been the most decent and eloquent man ever to occupy the Oval Office, but I began to resent his passivity toward all those who managed to control his agenda. A smart, beautiful family man who, unlike most politicians, managed to live an exemplary life, free of scandal, was nevertheless a failure as our president because he never learned how to use the biggest bully pulpit in the world. He never should have let his agenda be managed by a bunch of racist old white men. Lyndon Johnson would never have let such a thing happen to his presidency. Look how well Trump manipulates everyone, including the media and the press, with his mastery of the bully pulpit. It does not seem to matter how many lies he tells, or how outrageous his actions are. He is the true Teflon president, not Mr. Reagan."

"Arthur, McConnell and the Senate had no respect for the fact that Obama twice won election, the voters spoke clearly and decisively. How could the leader of the Senate ignore that and choose to set up his own government, outside of the will of the people."

Arthur agreed. "Obama's failure to neutralize the Republicans in general and McConnell in particular will unfortunately be part of his legacy. Fortunately, Trump has found it possible to work with McConnell, especially on judicial appointments. History will be hard on Obama for not being able to do so."

I was not sure how much of what I had said was accepted by Arthur. He had listened carefully. His comment on Trump was so out of place, and there was no need to say what he did unless he was baiting me. Unfortunately, I often express myself on issues that I care about with more passion than good judgment would recommend. I made it a point to be more circumspect around this man until I got a clearer picture of his objectives.

We kicked the issues back and forth for quite a long time before we were both exhausted and decided to call it a night. We settled our bill and walked outside for some much-needed fresh air. We thanked each other and agreed to meet again soon.

Arthur walked south and I headed west for a walk to think about the evening. The streets of the city were made for thought and reflection.

Was I so single-minded with my distrust of Trump that I was unwilling to cut him any slack? Arthur was an educated man in a field I admire. Could I trust him as a colleague, or would we end up on opposite ends of the political aisle, too far from each other to form a constructive union of ideas?

★ ★ ★

CHAPTER 4

FEBRUARY 2020

THE NEWS OF THE MORNING WAS DEPRESSING. The World Health Organization declared that a new virus originating in Wuhan, China, had spread to the point of a global emergency. President Trump just announced that we would restrict foreign nationals from China from entering the U.S. That decision was met with a lot of criticism, as it did not make sense to restrict one nation when the problem was worldwide. Most nations did not understand the nature of the Coronavirus, but many were on guard to prevent it from spreading too widely. February 8, 2020 was the day that the first American died of the virus.

Trump had been impeached by the House for abuse of power and obstruction of justice, and was acquitted by the Senate, led by McConnell and the Republican majority. The TV pundits on the left were proclaiming that the Republican party was now the party of Trump. Those on the right were relieved that justice prevailed, thinking that maybe Democrats would back off of Trump and let him run the country he was elected to serve.

I saw vindication of my dinner discussion with Arthur in our shared conclusion that the U.S. was becoming more polarized. I could not help but wonder how all those Republican senators managed to ignore the testimony, statements made in the phone conversation with President Volodymyr Zelensky of Ukraine, and the transcript released by the White House, in which Trump clearly stated the quid pro quo. I decided that it was a vote based on fear more than the merits of the case. History will have to be the judge.

I got myself ready for the day and headed to NYU. It was cold, but the cloud-free sun beat down on the city's pavement, making the air feel warmer. I approached Washington Square on my usual path. Having already prepared my tasks for the day, I decided to sit on a park bench and indulge my fascination of watching people go about their day. No matter how pressing my work is, I try to take a moment beyond the madding crowd. In my ten years of jiujitsu training and learning Zen Buddhism, I learned the importance of taking a step back to observe and relax. Life takes on a greater importance whenever we let our minds and bodies be at peace, even for just a moment.

A street vendor I once knew told me that one does not have to walk around to experience New York—just find a comfortable bench or an outdoor café, sit down, and the city will eventually pass you. I chose an empty bench facing the early afternoon sun and relaxed into this favorite pastime.

Young people huddled in corners on the grass, others walked around looking for the meaning of life. Two women with strollers stopped in front of me to talk. I tried to figure out if the babies looked like their mothers. They did not even seem related. It is inevitable that everyone will carry some family traits—a nose, ears, eyes, but I prefer to think of each person as an individual unburdened by association with their gene pool. Studies have shown that most of us come from a highly diversified, multiethnic lineage. If one's heritage is European, there will be eight to ten genetic footprints lurking within their DNA

It was a cold afternoon, so only a small number of performers were doing their thing. Children filled the playground with their universally recognizable sounds of joy and play. I do love to hear children at play. I was reminded of an experience I had after visiting a Zen Temple of meditation in Kyoto, Japan. I found a park bench and sat down to let the experience of total peace granted by the temple sink in. I soon heard the sounds of children at play. For the briefest moment, I could not remember where I was. I have heard children at play all around the world and the one constant is that they all sound the same regardless of where I am. What is it that we do to these innocent youth that life's journey puts some on a path of kindness and others on one of hate and anger?

I turned my mind back to the discussion Arthur and I had over dinner the previous night. We agreed on the broader aspects of our discussion. Some scholars argue that the American Century began around the end of WWI. Others situate it at the beginning of WWII, when America was recognized as a world power, capped by the Marshall Plan and other postwar support for war-torn nations. Starting dates notwithstanding, America enjoyed a steep upward climb after the war, and has been on a perceptible slope of decline since the mid-seventies. A quick and positive action is needed if we are to recover.

Arthur and I only scratched the surface of what we referred to as the rise and fall of America. I was trying to pull together the various issues in my mind when Arthur appeared and sat down next to me. "Hello, Arthur, where did you come from?"

"I was on my way to our office, when I noticed you here, so I thought I'd join you for a while."

"Are you stalking me?" I joked.

Arthur's face twisted for a brief moment before he caught himself and laughed with me. "Not today. I did think that we should finish up our discussion, if it's even possible, given the complexity of the subject matter."

"Actually, I was just thinking about your comments. I was wondering if you have any specific thoughts on what might have precipitated America's fall. Was there a smoking gun that pulled everything down, or was it just a slow unfolding demise?" I asked.

"Interesting. I think we need to look to the beginning to answer that. The Bretton Woods fixed dollar rate placed the United States at the center of international exchange. Also, the invention of the transistor, the construction of our vast national highway system, and our leadership in education at all levels that we discussed, precipitated our solid increases in productivity and output, along with strong unions that gave rise to a vibrant middle class. We can surely include the accomplishments of NASA, science and business innovations, and entrepreneurship, in addition to our nation's New Deal and global generosity. All of these factors contributed to a sustained period of phenomenal postwar economic growth. Each is recognized as a source behind the rise of the American presence on the world stage."

I expressed my agreement. "So true. On the downside, I personally think that the fiasco of Vietnam represented what could be called the smoking gun. That war drained us economically, and more importantly, socially. The constant stream of antiwar protestors, many of whom gathered right where we are now sitting, split our nation like no other single event, with the possible exception of the Civil Rights movement. Not to mention the assassinations of so many strong leaders. Two other events, surrounding two specific individuals, had, in my opinion, a lot to do with a sea change in America," I asserted.

"Really, what are they?" asked Arthur.

"You'll be surprised. Firstly, the resignation of Sandra Day O'Conner from the Supreme Court. She resigned during the Bush II administration, and she had to know that he would appoint a conservative to replace her. John Roberts was both very conservative and young. We are going to live with him and his politics on the court for years. Secondly, Ralph Nader, a man of impeccable accomplishments whose ego came out in full color during the 2000 election. He was never going to win, and all he did was take votes from Gore. He threw the election into the Supreme Court, which refused to let the Florida recount take place. Why would they stop a legitimate recount, other than to place a court decision above the people's right to have their votes matter? American democracy got screwed and Bush got the White House. Think what 9/11 would have been if Gore had been president. I think each were major events that contributed to the post WWII American decline." I paused. "More recently, I could blame Justice Kennedy resigning, which gave Trump two nominations, both of whom are not only conservative, but also arguably believe in the absolute power of the presidency. The court is now pretty much exactly where Senator McConnell has wanted it to be for decades. Justice in America has been redefined with the appointments of Roberts, Gorsuch, and Kavanaugh. Those of us who lament these appointments live with hope that RBG stays healthy. I personally agree with those who think that Kavanaugh's questionable temperament, more than the accusations placed against him, should have disqualified him from the bench."

"That's pretty heavy," Arthur replied. "Whether I agree or not, the Supreme Court is what it is, and will be as such for some time."

I wondered if he actually supported the Kavanaugh appointment. "I also think that the inordinate amount of money we spend on our military has sucked our public coffers dry, so that a host of critical public sector investments never even got started. It's important to recognize that military spending does preserve national security. It does, however, precious little to support the multiplier effect on earned income as compared to that which we enjoy with private sector spending. Military spending had gone from just under $80 billion in 1970 to over $700 billion in 2019, far outstripping the rate of inflation. Our military spending each year is more than that of the next ten largest nations in the world combined. Every dollar spent on guns means less available for investment in the environment and our infrastructure which are also important to our national security. Some policymakers think we can have it all, but we both know that's impossible."

Arthur interjected, "The private sector also had serious problems. The 1970s saw a growing wealth gap between management and their employees. By the early 1980s, our once-vibrant middle class that used to support the consumption and productive sectors of our economy began to be left behind, despite solid improvements in labor productivity." Arthur continued, "Economists have proven that the degree of social and economic unrest correlates to the income gap between the top five percenters and the middle class. The average corporate executive earned twenty-four times his workers on the assembly line in 1965, and two hundred sixty times the average worker in 2005. That gap has continued to increase."

This gave me a chance to explain one of my pet peeves. "It won't take long for the average worker to see that the growing pie is not being shared with them. In fact, I think that this issue is the major reason so many of these folks voted for Trump. Real incomes in American households have not appreciably increased since 1970, even though during that period, many married women entered the labor force. This has caused a dramatic reduction in the spending power of the middle class. When the rising costs of healthcare and education are added to the equation, it does not take a Ph.D. to realize that the quality of life for middle America has suffered a drastic and sustained nosedive over the past fifty years.

For as far back as written history goes, labor, even in feudal economies, has been recognized as the source of all output value. It is labor that has historically generated the surplus value or rents that landowners and capitalists have selfishly drawn down forever. Yet the working class, the only organic component of the production process, has consistently been subjected to what has been called a 'subsistence wage,' basically just enough take-home pay to clothe, feed, and put a roof over their heads. It has been assumed for centuries that they need no more than subsistence. Even today in America, the federal minimum wage is $7.25. That's indentured servitude—as shameful as any federal policy on the books, and considerably below the returns given to land and capital, the other prime inputs to production."

Arthur took issue with that by stating how well labor has done in the post WWII period, in terms of earning, benefits and job opportunities."

"Arthur, you know that those advantages ceased in the early seventies, and when the wealth and income gaps began to diverge at unconscionable levels."

"You can blame the corruption throughout the unions for that."

"Corruption was certainly part of the problem, but far from the leading cause. We both understand the issues. The average American who lacks the knowledge you and I have cannot possibly see the problems we are facing from an informed base. We have failed to find the words and the means to properly inform voters. Economists fail because we do not use the right language. Politicians fail, I'm sad to say, because their primary objective is to get elected. All too often, truth and facts get in the way of elections, forcing politicians to bend truth to suit campaigns over policy. Our obsession with taxes is the most blatant misunderstanding on the campaign trail. Promise to lower taxes, and you get elected. This is true despite the fact that taxes are the least of our problems.

These issues are simply too difficult for hard-working families to absorb. We tend to drone on when speaking to people we want to enlighten on how important income inequality and racism are to them. We fail to *show* how government can be the single biggest agent of positive change, if we would only let it work as intended. We need to create a better message if we are going to rekindle our progressive, productive, and responsible growth path."

Arthur interjected, "As Reagan said, government is not the solution, it is the problem."

"Arthur, that is only true for bad government, and we the people and those we elect are the cause of that happening."

I continued. "The 2008 Great Recession exacerbated the wealth gap to the point where we are now witnessing an actual diminishing of our once-vibrant middle class. The gap continues to increase despite full recognition of its existence. Citizens United paved the way for corporations to funnel money into campaigns at unprecedented levels. For decades now, Congress and the courts have launched a subtle but effective attack on unions and organized labor. We can expect serious social, economic, and political problems to increase if the gap in the earnings of senior management and working-class people continues to grow. Even the most patriotic blue-collar workers in America have a breaking point and another factor leading to Trump's election. It was a matter of timing. Hillary's campaign mistakes, and four decades of neglect of our middle class. Trump had a marvelous opportunity to make positive changes for America. He appealed to the frustration of a large sector of our economy that has been ignored for decades. He could have been a major positive agent for change. He blew it because he is simply too focused on himself and incapable of understanding the needs of our nation."

I could see that Arthur blanched at the ferocity of my statements, especially those about Trump. I took note and decided that if I wanted to continue our friendship, I once again realized I should be more circumspect with this man, something that does not come easy for me. I hoped I was wrong about my new colleague but, I was beginning to think that he had an ulterior motive. The danger Trump represented to our nation should have been obvious to any thinking person. I also needed to go back to what I learned on my cruise. I just did not think I needed to be politicly correct when talking with a colleague. Life's lessons are certainly perpetually moving.

Arthur ignored my comments and called upon his extensive research, saying, "I am far too pessimistic and one-sided. We are still a world leader, and that is a fact."

I decided to give him both barrels. "Yes, we are but not one that is increasing its position, in fact we are not even holding on. Look at China, our most competitive economic trading partner. It grew from economic obscurity in 1979 to a $660 billion trading partner by 2008. Estimates claim that China will surpass the US by 2030, and possibly sooner, as an economic leader. In 1970, America produced 40% of the world's output. We are now down to 25%. In 1980, the U.S. owned about 24% of the world income, but by 2011, we were down to 19 percent. Our importance as a world leader remains strong, however, we must recognize that it is diminishing when compared to our trading partners, especially China.

"As all this was happening," I continued, "we were gradually losing ground in other important ways that are not as obvious to the average American. Infant and maternal mortality began to rise significantly. Deaths related to pregnancy went from 7.2 per 100,000 live births in 1987 to almost 17 per 100,000 in 2016. Deaths related to pregnancy puts America among the highest in the world. I saw a statement that a woman in America has about the same chance of surviving childbirth as a woman in Latvia or Ukraine, even though America has some of the finest medical providers on the planet. The problem is that they are only available to a small portion of our population."

"You're right," said Arthur, "we are ripe for a serious reform in our healthcare system. By focusing on the private sector, we have several layers of profit between the patient and the cure. Private sector companies deserve a profit. We need to decide whether the health of our people and our labor force is a right or a privilege."

I added, "The Affordable Care Act was not perfect. It was written as a positive change from a long-standing healthcare policy in America that was the most expensive in the world and yet, by design, excluded millions from access. The Republicans wanted nothing to do with healthcare reform. Healthcare in America is still among the least efficient systems when viewed in term of its impact on all Americans. If you are rich or have insurance, you get the best care; if not, emergency rooms, the most expensive healthcare delivery mechanism possible, are all you have access to. Rumor has it that Republicans fight any national health program because they do not want minorities to have access to it. The Trump administration has dedicated itself from day one to destroying ACA."

"Again, you seem to prefer further polarizing these issues, which does not produce solutions."

"Arthur, the Republican-led Congress initiated more than sixty failed votes over a twelve-year period to kill Obamacare without ever offering a single viable alternative. That inaction was a disgrace. That is all I need to make my case on that issue.

"I am, however, really glad that you see healthcare as an important problem," I continued. "I want to point out some other issues that are not as obvious but just as important. There is a perceptible decline of our underlying or core values: civility, kindness, love, friendship, and selflessness seem to be slipping away. As we have been losing ground, other nations have begun to pass us in a host of sociological as well as economic indicators, such as a reduction in infant mortality, success in reading, math, and comprehension scores. Crime, especially gun-related deaths, a problem that barely even exists outside the USA, has paralyzed our nation. Divorce rates have leveled off but remain high. That slowdown in divorces has been shown to be a result of the fact that people cannot afford to get divorced. This creates a lot of pressure on day-to-day family life.

"Travel to Europe, Asia, Latin America, and you will see similar equality problems, but you also see some amazing things that make our buildings, institutions, airports, and highways look run-down, dirty, and dangerous by comparison. You see happy children running around, lovers walking through their parks, and shoppers hustling from one store to the next in these lesser-developed nations. America remains a vital economic and military force relative to the rest of the world, but that force is much less than it was fifty years ago."

"Great points, Benson. We are clearly on a decline, but the average American is not even beginning to wake up to that fact. One of the most obvious frustrations to Americans is our Congress. We have lost faith in our elected leadership. The approval ratings of elected officials have continued a trend downward, sometimes hovering in the mid-teens. A democracy cannot survive a breakdown like this for our legislative bodies. I read a survey that stated that Congress has a lower approval rating than hemorrhoids and cockroaches. I hope it wasn't right. A recent Gallup poll showed that the approval rating of the Supreme Court, while higher than Congress, has slipped below fifty percent. This is our last court of the land. How can we function as a nation if we can't trust our most important judicial forum to make fair decisions?"

I agreed. "A big part of the frustration with our courts is just how politicized they've become. Have you noticed that every time a judge is mentioned in the press, it is an Obama judge, a Trump judge, or a Bush judge? Tell me that we have not politicized the most important branch of government that should never, ever, be associated with any president or party. I think that the Trump administration has approved more than two hundred lifetime federal judges. We can blame Moscow Mitch for compromising the objectivity of our courts and allowing several judges with strong rightward leanings. McConnell has proudly taken credit for a host of subpar federal judges nominated by the Trump administration, many of whom were not approved by the American Bar Association. The Trump appointments to the Supreme Court will only further polarize and politicize the court."

"Why do you call him Moscow Mitch? Is that not disrespectful?"

"It probably is. The title was given to him by Democrats when he refused to bring legislation that was passed by the House on Russian meddling in our elections to the floor of the Senate. There are about four hundred additional bills also sitting on McConnell's desk that have been passed by the House. This is not how a democracy is administered."

Both of us fell into a morbid silence. While we might disagree on causes and solutions, we knew what was really happening to our country. We both knew that the data showing the national decline significantly outweighed those indicators that showed us improving.

"This is not the America either of us grew up in," I said. "As children, we were sent to school or out to play, and our parents knew that we'd return. We were often late, dirty with scraped knees, but we always showed up. Parents now feel that they must watch their children 24/7. Helicopter parents are no longer just a *New Yorker* joke. This is a measure of how we have declined socially; we no longer feel safe on our own streets and playgrounds. We hate the fact that our elected officials seem to have forgotten the concept of debate, negotiation, and compromise. Legislative discourse is now an either/

or case, no middle ground allowed, not even on uncontroversial issues. We are shocked when a decision comes out of the Senate with a solid majority vote. Have you noticed how many elections worldwide end up without a clear majority? Our recent elections were won by razor-thin majorities, Gore/Bush had to go to the Supreme Court. Trump *lost* the popular vote and won by a total of 80,000 votes and won only through the peculiarities of the Electoral College. Israel, Germany, Austria, and France all had winners in recent elections that showed a definite lack of enthusiasm for the winners. It is notable that the 2008 election was won by Obama by 365 to 173 electoral votes and almost ten million popular votes."

Another silence fell between us. I decided to test his opinions of the overreach of surveillance of our citizenry. "Arthur, have you noticed a major shift in how we are living our daily lives? We are witnessing a huge increase in citizen oversight from our telecommunications companies and a significant increase in surveillance on the part of the government, especially since 9/11. There is also a loss of privacy from Google and Facebook and the rise of big data. Our privacy and values as a democracy are being stripped away."

"What do you mean?"

"Well, it is partially out of necessity, given the rise of terrorism worldwide. But it is more due to the information and technology revolution. An insecure government rides on the coattails of tech companies, as these companies expand beyond market transactions and monitor us in ways, we never thought possible. Cambridge Analytica created algorithms capable of monitoring up to five thousand data points a second on over two billion people every day. They sell these data to marketers and campaigns for public office. With those data, Amazon knows exactly what to promote to you, and how and when to do it. These companies might know us better than we ourselves do.

"A candidate for president can fashion an advertisement that addresses the interests or concerns of individual voters. Often these targeted ads are blatantly untrue and riddled with false statements. They are, however, exceedingly difficult to monitor outside the company that is distributing them. These ads do not go through established channels of public scrutiny and professional journalism. They are highly targeted and relatively inexpensive to distribute. Establishment ads close with a statement from the candidate that he or she approves this message. These highly questionable ads are edited to support or destroy a specific candidate and never identify the represented campaign. The Mueller Report made it clear that Russia played a major role in the 2016 election, yet Barr and Trump managed to control that conclusion right out of existence.

"Look for something you want online, and you are inundated with ads in your inbox on similar items, whether you wanted them or not. Facebook, despite minor efforts by legislators, has refused to monitor the accuracy of the hate-filled, completely inaccurate advertisements they publish, knowing that they are false and misleading. Some of these ads are known by their creators to be outright lies. A lot of people get the bulk of their information from social media. All of this misinformation is having a negative impact on the viability of our democracy.

"In the name of public safety, private sector companies and the government are putting hidden cameras everywhere. Facial recognition is the latest invasion of our privacy. Your credit card purchases, phone calls, Google searches, and downloaded news sources are constantly monitored. A recent report leaked to the *New York Times* showed how sophisticated these efforts have become. The *Times* gained access to the data system of a company and was able to identify a specific phone number, which happened to be that of an FBI agent. The *Times* isolated its owner and then monitored his every move for an entire day, second by second."

I could tell that I was making my colleague uncomfortable. He began to squirm in his seat and was probably wishing he had never sat down next to me.

"It's taken years to get access to Trump's tax returns, despite legitimate subpoenas and requests from Congress and several states' attorneys general. The truth is we're living in a world that George Orwell himself could not have imagined. His concept of Big Brother is only one or two steps removed from what a moderately technically savvy parent has in the way of cellphones to safely monitor and keep in touch with their children. Technology, as we are now witnessing it, might be defined as the most productive tool ever invented to serve the public. It might eventually also be recorded by historians as the single largest invasion of our privacy and personal freedom ever."

"Come on, it could not be that bad. I think you are seriously overstating the problem," responded Arthur.

"Look around you as you walk home tonight and count the number of cameras on poles and buildings. There are currently an estimated nine thousand surveillance cameras linked to the NYPD. As you leave the park, look at the number of cameras here alone. They are posted in stores, lobbies, and offices. Do you think they are just local installations for the merchants and block associations? You know that the government and law enforcement are monitoring almost every phone call we make. The Patriot Act and its revisions have made that a fact. The camera on your computer and phone can record images and voice at will. Amazon's Alexa hears, stores, and sends sound and text.

"The Obama administration attempted to eliminate invasive oversight. The effort was not successful, and the problem is ongoing, often in the name of national security. One cannot overestimate the amount of data any merchant, government official, police precinct, lawyer, or private detective can get on you in seconds. You and your life are an open book to a vast number of people and institutions, most of which you do not even know exist. That disgruntled employee you fired last week can track you, your wife, or your children. That colleague you snitched on because they were dropping dope on the job will find you.

"Europe is lightyears ahead of us in protecting people. They have passed legislation curtailing the ability of these companies to invade the privacy of their citizens. They have also successfully sued both Google and Facebook for bad business practices. Do you know that a law is currently working its way through Congress, at the behest of AG Barr, that will allow the government to override any, I mean *any*, encryption software on your phone or computer? It just seems like we are always being watched, and that makes me nervous."

Arthur blurted out, "I do not believe what you're saying is all that prevalent. You need to chill and start looking at the brighter side of life. I think you are paranoid."

Frankly, I was surprised at his reaction. Nothing I said was new to me or to any of my professional friends. Most of it was published in the *NYT, Washington Post, WSJ*, and elsewhere. I found myself questioning his responses. Why was my new friend taking this position? I knew that he was more informed than the average citizen.

"Arthur, do you see that man over there in the funny hat?"

"I do, why?"

"What do you see about him that is strange?"

"Hmm... Nothing comes to mind."

"I see a person totally out of place in this park, despite an obvious effort to fit in."

"What do you mean? He's just a guy like us, enjoying the park and the people in it."

"No. Look at his shoes, they have a purpose. Take a look at his haircut—professionally done. His clothes are appropriately ragged but not off a discount rack. He is purposely unshaven, yet stylishly so. This man is not from here. He is here to observe."

"You really are paranoid. Why did you pick him out? In fact, why are you picking anyone out? Can't you just enjoy sitting in the park?"

"Oh, I can enjoy it. Been doing it most of my life. This man, however, is on a mission, and it's not an innocent one. He's not like anyone else here. Notice how often he rubs his face. He is speaking into a recorder or mic. Take a look at his hands, smooth and manicured. He is also left-handed and a guitar player, probably either classical or Flamenco."

"How in the hell can you possibly see all that? I am beginning to think that *you* are a spy."

That was the reaction I was afraid of. I never once mentioned the word spy. What made Arthur say that? I realized that I really did need to be more circumspect around him. That realization deeply saddened me. I value his knowledge and incite, but I was concerned and beginning to think that he did not come to NYU by accident or professionally. I wondered who he works for.

"You're right, maybe I have read too many Le Carré novels," I said.

"How do you know that he's left-handed and a classical guitar player of all things? And what about his shoes?"

I decided that my friend was not just asking questions; he was interrogating me. Asking himself if I was professionally trained or just an obsessive-compulsive citizen who needed to get a life? I strategically took the bait.

"His shoes are standard-issue police--or other law enforcement. Comfortable, fast, and even though they are scuffed up, awfully expensive. His hands are soft and manicured, not those of a working person, nor the vagrant he is disguised to be. His left-hand nails are completely filed down, and his right-hand nails are much longer than the left, and both are carefully manicured, as needed to play a nylon string guitar preferred by classical and flamenco guitarists. His watch is on his right hand which makes him most likely left-handed."

"Maybe he's unemployed, or on vacation," Arthur said. "You're either paranoid or training for an undercover job at the CIA."

Okay, if he really suspected me, he would not have said it out loud. He is either very smart and well-trained or completely innocent of anything subversive.

"Right again Arthur. I've been marveled at for the things I remember and notice about people. It has been a lifelong trait and seems to come naturally. People often tell me that I would make a great witness. Maybe it all harkens back to a childhood spent mostly in survival mode and on the defensive. I agree that I tend to be more observant than I should, and maybe need to be. Do you think that man might be here to spy on us?"

Arthur did not respond to that and stared at me with a look of puzzlement. I wanted to trust this man. His credentials as a scholar are impeccable. He is a really decent guy who seems to have taken a wrong turn. I do not want to give up on him as a colleague.

I decided to test him one more time. "Arthur, what are your feelings on the impeachment? As you know, the Senate has acquitted Trump on all charges, even though they knew he was guilty."

"That was forgone from the beginning," he retorted. "The Democrats did not have the votes in the Senate. It was almost a pure party-line vote. They should have known that from the beginning and dropped the hearings."

"So, you think he was innocent?"

"I don't know about that, but the process was a waste of time and never should have happened."

"But he *did* make that call, and he *did* ask a foreign nation to help him get evidence against a political opponent. That is against the law and the Constitution," I said.

"Debatable. I do wish he had not done that, but he was never going to be impeached."

"If that action alone went unchallenged, it would have set a precedent for future presidents. The House had no choice but to impeach him. My regret was that they focused on only one infraction, when they had several others that could have been included as part of the impeachment. The acquittal does not take away from the fact that he was impeached. A significant number of senators knew he was guilty but did not have the balls to vote against him. That's not justice."

"Get over it, you lost."

"No, Arthur. America lost, and I'm sorry you don't see that." I decided to move on, since it was going no further, and I found out what I needed to know. This man is a lot smarter and informed than he was pretending to be, and that behavior on his part must have a purpose. "Did you hear the news this morning? An entirely new threat is only now hitting our shores. The

Coronavirus is not only a mystery in terms of its impact. We seem unable to understand how it's even transmitted. The first American has died. I am getting worried that this is going to be the big one that scientists have been predicting for years. I wish the president would get on it with some sort of a plan."

"He has. China is shut out, and he will probably prevent others as well."

"Arthur, he called it a hoax and a plot by the Democrats to deny him re-election. Besides, scientists have told him that stopping people at the border will not stem the virus. It knows no borders."

"I'm sure it will not be that bad. Like the president said, it will go away in the summer as the temperatures rise. It will behave like a flu and disappear."

"I do not think so and neither do the scientists who know about these things, but I hope you're right." My new friend was not passing my quizzes, he seems more comfortable denying the obvious.

"Benson, tell me about your childhood. What happened to you?"

"That's a long story, and both of us need to get to work. The short story is that I never really knew my father, and my mother was never home. I ended up spending most of my time at the homes of friends or on the streets of the suburban Long Island town where I was born. One develops a keen sense of situations and people when outside of a stable home or family."

"I'm sorry to hear that. You can put me in the category of people you know who think that you would make a good witness at a crime scene. And you're right—I'm off to Bobst, and I think you were on your way to our office."

We both stiffly rose from the bench. As I tried to gain my vertical equilibrium, I found myself quoting Bette Davis. "Getting old is not for the faint of heart!"

We shook hands and laughingly headed off in separate directions.

CHAPTER 5

MARCH 2020

DESPITE MY RESERVATIONS ABOUT ARTHUR, I wanted to continue our discussions, which were especially important to me. His professional arguments that showed how America was in decline in so many ways were an observation I had made but never formally studied. The problem was made more serious because we both knew that our decline was neither recognized nor accepted by the average citizen, nor by many of our leaders who should be more aware. Our efforts to increase voter participation would be harder to sell if most of us are oblivious to how much we are losing ground as a world leader.

I gazed out at the encroachment of dawn on the city's skyline before turning on the news. My quiet reverie was interrupted by an editorial special on how many nations throughout the world had been undergoing serious social unrest over the past few years. The French Yellow Vest protestors took to the streets with their frustration with climate change and their government's proposed tax increases. They had ground much of Paris to a halt in January. The streets of Hong Kong had for months been filled with citizens, sometimes millions strong, protesting Beijing's challenge to their treaty with Britain that turned over this vibrant island economy to the People's Republic of China. China sought to fold Hong Kong into their jurisdiction, ignoring the timeline of their joint treaty guaranteed through the year 2047. The people of Hong Kong had refused to accept these encroachments and made their frustration abundantly clear, as did mainland China. The PRC put an end to protests in Hong Kong by issuing a repressive set of rules, the sternest ever recorded by one nation over another. This represented a major defeat for democracy, the only form of government Hong Kong citizens have ever known. The global fear is that Taiwan is next on their list, an island not even a part of China that was under Japanese rule since 1895.

Furthermore, the formerly successful economy of Venezuela had almost completely fallen apart as thousands of its financially starved citizens migrated out to neighboring nations. Spain was forced to fight the Catalan independence movement's intense desire to secede from Spain. People in large numbers have taken to the streets in Lebanon, Iraq, Egypt, Ethiopia, Chili, and India. The underlying causes ranged from government corruption, burdensome taxes, lack of employment, and discriminatory policies. The lingering issues surrounding the subdivision of the Sudan have kept the region in turmoil for years, causing the actual and potential starvation of millions. As with the tremendous unrest in America, many nations throughout the world have been suffering under a yoke of political, social, and economic crisis.

It is not a healthy sign when the people of so many nations are angry. Over the past several decades, nations have moved dramatically toward the political right; so now, has the United States. This culminated with the election of Trump who claims to be conservative, but he is considerably further to the right than a traditional conservative would accept. Russia remains under the dictatorial thumb of Vladimir Putin. Austria, Hungary, Italy, Germany, Brazil, and India are now either leaning toward or become right-wing autocratic nations. Some of these political changes were ushered in by election, others by a series of questionable changes imposed on oblivious citizens by governments desperately trying to hold onto power at all costs.

The leaders of these right-leaning nations are grabbing ever more liberties and rights from their people as they strive to assume absolute power. China's president Xi Jinping has announced himself president for life. Putin has also received the right to rule through 2036. Trump has openly stated that he thinks the best thing for America would be to follow the Chinese way and make him president for life. Trump suggested this at a closed-door fundraiser in Florida in March 2018 when he praised President Xi Jinping, calling him "a great gentleman" and "the most powerful president in a hundred years." Trump suggested that he'd like to follow Xi's example and abolish term limits. Trump said, "And look, he [Xi] was able to do that. I think it is great. Maybe we'll have to give that a shot someday." At a Nevada rally, Trump said, "We're gonna win four more years in the White House and then we'll negotiate four more years, because based on the way we were treated, we're probably entitled to another four years after that."

I spent the day in a mild state of political depression. I did take a walk and grab dinner at a local Italian restaurant. I returned home, read some economic history, and agonized over all these struggling nations and their people, who felt that their governments no longer represented them. I felt similar pain for America. What other purpose does government have but to serve its people? Why have the people of the world allowed so many countries, America included, to come to a state of endless power struggles to the point of degrading human rights? How can we create an informed electorate that sees truth and their own best interests under threat of extinction? As current events are showing us, no one is fighting that battle for us. It can only be won if we vote and vote smart.

★ ★ ★

FOLLOWING A RESTLESS NIGHT, I awoke to an email invitation from a graduate school colleague to attend a reunion luncheon in Washington, DC with several other members of our class. We try to get together every couple of years. It had been many years since I'd been to our nation's capital. The luncheon was Sunday afternoon, so I reserved a Friday morning train with a Sunday evening return. I decided to splurge by staying at the Dupont Circle Hotel where I used to stay when I was a partner in an economic consulting company headquartered on K Street.

Exiting the elevator, the next morning, I was pleased to see Ramon standing in as doorman, something he would often do if someone called in sick. No one was in the lobby, so I asked if he'd gotten my new laptop. I decided to have him order it for me as a precaution.

"Yes, it was delivered this week. I should have it ready to transfer your documents by the end of the day."

"Thank you, Ramon. I can always count on you to help me out with all things technological. I need to talk to you about something that is particularly important to me. Can we go outside?" We walked up the short flight of stairs between the sidewalk and our main entrance. We stayed close to the entrance since Ramon was on duty.

"Is anything wrong?" he asked.

"No, not at all, but I need your special skills as we put this computer together. I need it to be totally invisible to the world. I'll be communicating with people who I cannot risk endangering. I could tell you what I'm doing, but that could compromise you and your family. I can only tell you that I'm working with some very bright people to make sure that as many eligible people as possible get to the polls this November. I'm also trying to reach Republicans to help them bring their once glorious and responsible party back to what it was. Does that help you understand just how important it is that you make this computer fully operational and my communications on it completely invisible? First question is how did you pay for it, and was it bought under my name?" I asked.

"I paid in cash. It has no receipt or name attached to it. I assumed you would want it that way."

"You're right, as always," I said. "Buy me another one exactly like it using my credit card. Take this red flash drive which has all my documents and programs. Load the computer you now have with the data on the red flash drive. Program the new computer as you would any other device. Should the other one be traced, I'll still have the new one to show. Load the new computer with the information on this *blue* flash drive. Give both flash drives back to me and do not copy them. Put the corresponding-colored stickers on each." I handed him both the matching stickers and the flash drives.

While we never overtly spoke about it, I knew that Trump's escalator comments about Mexicans hurt this wonderfully loyal immigrant very much. Ramon's tireless energy made it possible for each of his three girls to go to great schools and prestigious universities. They graduated with honors and have pursued successful careers and are now starting families of their own. They owed much to their parents' unconditional love and support, the hardest working, most loyal, and loving parents I have ever known. I will confess to having helped the girls on their college entry and career choices, but their success is theirs alone. Ramon and his family are a tribute to American values. Trump's comments used to announce his run for presidency in 2016, deeply hurt them and millions of other immigrants who have come to our country seeking nothing more than a better life.

Ramon understood my requests perfectly. He and I have never needed many words to communicate our intentions. He did say it would take several weeks to get it programmed properly.

"That's fine. Just make sure it will stay under the radar. I'll need instructions on how to use it and how to securely get rid of it if I must. Make sure that I'm the only one who can boot it up. Thanks again, Ramon. You are a prince."

We fist-bumped and gave each other shoulder bumps in recognition of how much I depended on him to get this job done right. I also knew that he took great pleasure in being a part of my work, understanding the importance it had for his family and friends.

I LOVE RIDING TRAINS. The Amtrak from New York to Washington has gotten more expensive, but it is still a bargain when compared to the time and aggravation of flying. Airports have become such uninviting places, and I avoid them at all costs. I prefer not to drive and use the time on such trips to catch up with my reading. I was glad that I'd accepted the invitation, even though I knew that I was about to enter a dog and pony show as each of us put our professional wares on display, while striving not to appear obnoxious. Recent appointments, publications, promotions, and ego fill a lot of the room when economists get together. Like most professionals, we economists are proud of what we do, especially when we create results that make a difference. Those of us in the public sector measure our success in terms of policy and legislation. Those who chose the corporate, finance, or banking worlds, titles, incomes, stock options, and golden parachutes are the indicators of accomplishment. Academics are measured by the ranking of the university where they teach and by earning tenure. Our publications and where they are published matter most to academics.

As my train raced toward DC, I knew that I had to have my story right for this luncheon to avoid lengthy discussions I simply didn't want to have.

My current top-secret political activities notwithstanding, I had nothing to hide. I spent my train time looking at how much the landscape of this well-traveled corridor had changed as I carefully rehearsed my unwritten presentation.

The ride was smooth, comfortable, and quick. I checked into my hotel, changed my clothes, and headed out to see how much DC had changed. After walking around for a few hours, I wandered over to the Kingbird on Virginia Avenue near the Watergate. It is a moderately priced restaurant with an attractive menu. Most of all, I wanted to see that famed building once more.

I spent Saturday morning at the National Gallery. This magnificent structure has probably the best Renaissance and Impressionists collections outside the Louvre. One can view excellent pieces by Degas, Van Gogh, and Monet—not to mention Raphael, all of which is more than this novice aficionado could possibly absorb in one day.

I had made a reservation to visit Arlington National Cemetery for the afternoon. It was a beautiful day, and I wanted to be outdoors. I signed up for the guided tour. The sheer size of the place was daunting. I gratefully accepted the discount offered to all veterans. I usually donate my veteran discounts back to them, but for this particular place, I decided that it was well earned. Several tombstones and the changing of the guard made the guided tour worth the time. Little did I know at the time that I was walking on the very paths that our bone spur–deferred president would soon use to denigrate every person whose valor and memory is emblazoned on these hallowed hills as losers and suckers.

My reaction to my visits to Arlington and Normandy could not have been more different from Trump's. The sheer numbers of young souls whose headstones stretched to the horizon overwhelmed me. So much potential lost forever. How many possible Beethovens, Einsteins, Hemingways, and

Lincolns are buried there? How many teachers, priests, firefighters, parents, and their children would the world never see because they lay there in front of me, lost to everyone? We will never share the joys and pains of life that these young warriors might have brought us, had they been able to live. The day walking among these graves increased my resolve to use all my skills and resources to prevent this, and all memorials to war, from expanding by even one more grave.

I decided to eat in the hotel restaurant and go to bed early. It was a trying day. I glanced over the headlines and found one featuring Trump's wish to be buried in Arlington. Bone Spurs Trump, who'd never served a day, alongside these heroes? This is similar to his initiatives to have him awarded a Noble Peace Prize. Not in my lifetime. I had to shake the grief that had enveloped me and find a way to shift gears for my Sunday luncheon.

The next morning, I chose a white shirt, classic blazer, designer jeans, and Bass loafers. Such dress made me feel comfortable. The open seating was for about twenty, and when I arrived appropriately New York late, most of the seats were already taken. I had chosen this strategy because it helped me avoid having to choose a place. I noticed for the first-time sanitizer dispensers on each table with instructions to wash our hands whenever possible. I was truly pleased to see so many who, like me, had successfully struggled their way through the politically charged and intellectually rewarding graduate program at NYU. Everyone in the room had managed to make a name for themselves in the various work environments of their choice. Stan was in finance and had published several well-received books. Steven was with the National Security Council and at the forefront of public and international affairs. Richard had carved out a strong position in healthcare; George was still at the IMF and looked as young as he had as a student. Eddie had bounced around a lot but had always landed on his feet and was currently working as an independent consultant. Stephen spent several years at the Fed before moving into banking and becoming an international name. Now retired and teaching at Yale, he is frequently called upon by the press for his insightful opinions. Dianne was working for a left-wing human rights organization. Carol was working for Brookings and still fighting to find her personal identity and purpose. David had a consulting company. He did not look well. No one has ever known exactly what he does or who his clients are. Chandra, who organized the luncheon, welcomed us with a short speech of his memories of our graduate years and his past and current work at the UN. Each of us then had a turn at the mic. We introduced ourselves and gave a five-minute précis. Some took a moment to talk about their private lives, spouses, children, the teams they coached, and where they lived. Others, like me, kept our time in the spotlight totally professional.

That was when I noticed about five people at the various tables who I did not recognize. They were definitely not in our class. Their dress and manner also indicated different professions than the rest of us in the room. I could tell that they were civilians, government-issue, and were paying awful close attention to our conversations and presentations. My paranoia tripped in, and I decided to be cautious.

My colleagues were surprised to learn that I'd retired. I did not mention the econometric model I had built for the City of New York. I did mention my more current research on art theft and fraud, entrepreneurship and cloud computing—studies that I knew were unfamiliar to them. None of my colleagues knew that I had published in those areas. They were most surprised to hear that I was retired and back at NYU as a visiting scholar.

Everyone there knew that I was close to our classmate Andrew, who they knew had recently died in a boating accident. I decided to mention him and how much he was missed by all of us. I suddenly realized that I had forgotten to mention this ruse to Ari at our dinner. I made a note on my phone to do so as soon as possible. After our introductions, we began our meal. The conversation was lively and diverse. Two of the interlopers were at my table, and for the longest time, they said nothing. None of them had introduced themselves or offered comments. As the conversation turned to political and current events, one of them asked pointed questions about our thoughts on domestic terrorism, Iran, Trump, AG Barr, and NATO, and they avoided stating their own opinions.

I chose to be circumspect and sufficiently vague. I could tell that these government plants were fishing, and I was not taking the bait. I was not sure that they believed that I was apolitical. In fact, they gave each other passing glances when I mentioned it. I decided to check out the credentials of one of the men at my table. I asked Richard about my suspected trespasser. I was not surprised to hear that Richard did not know him. Richard had spent several years in DC and knew everyone. I decided that a respectful, thankful, and early exit from this event was my wisest choice. This was just one more example of the government's insecurity, and the level of surveillance that has become the norm for the Trump administration. My only real question was what specific agency did they work for, and who assigned them to our innocuous reunion? Did my presence have anything to do with why they were there?

I respectfully announced my early exit to catch my train. I bid goodbye to each of my colleagues, expressing anticipation for the next time we can get together. I sincerely hoped that I was not disrespectful leaving early. As I boarded my train, I was glad that I had attended. I enjoyed catching up with colleagues and seeing them for being healthy, happy, and successful.

Reclining in my first-class seat, luggage stored, I began to reflect on what I had just experienced. I tried to think positively. Perhaps they were recruiters? Maybe they were unconnected guests interested in what a bunch of older economists thought about the pressing issues of the day. However, I had noticed that the room had cameras in each corner of the ceiling. A microphone in such a small space opens the possibility that the entire luncheon was taped. Was my mistrust being stretched too thin? *No.* My experience told me that whenever I denied my natural instincts, I was usually wrong to do so. Often, it did not matter—but this time I thought it would.

As the rails clicked to the beat of an iambic pentameter poem, I recalled a recent documentary that had revealed just how sophisticated surveillance algorithms had become. It focused on Cambridge Analytica, the British company that used their platform to, among other things, target voters in the 2016 election with dubious information and outright lies. Ads were directed at specific individuals based on the massive amount of information they had in their data banks. Ads and messages directly focused on the primary concerns, weaknesses, or strengths of the target. They were never explicitly approved by any candidate they supported. Nor were they vetted by an official source, which had been typical for political and campaign propaganda. Instead, they were produced by offshore entities deliberately organized to distort the election. Decisions like the Supreme Court's Citizens United and its reduction of the 1965 Voter Rights Act made it impossible to determine who had paid for these professionally produced, unattributed efforts filled with lies and deception. The social media platforms that carried them, notably Facebook, had no interest beyond the money they were making in truth or fairness.

Cambridge Analytica, Google, Amazon, and Facebook have admitted that they store and use our data, even those retrieved through our personal files. Our online searches, purchases, and personal data from our birthdays to our Social Security numbers, and anything else they can collect, go directly into several big data efforts. Our privacy and constitutional rights have no play as these companies strive to better serve their big data hungry clients. Their algorithms were relentless, omnipresent, and intimidating. Each of these firms deny that they sell our data to third parties, but suspicions to the contrary abound.

Our nation's telecommunications companies also collect an enormous amount of data on each of us through our activities on our smartphones. They also sell these data to anyone willing to pay. We like to think that we're the customer of these various companies, but we need to begin to recognize that we are their product.

Companies like FourSquare, Oracle, and Salesforce strive to be invisible but are very sophisticated data-hungry creatures. These companies track us and our activities and do so by name, address, phone number, and more. The fact that they can do this has been revealed by investigative journalists. If we have a cellphone, these companies can digitally watch us, one by one, second by second, as we go about our days. Many cities in the name of public safety are placing cameras wherever they want. We have no way of knowing who is monitoring this network of surveillance systems and for what purpose. Long-trusted agencies are trying to find ways to circumvent legal wiretap procedures.

Many respected reporters, scientists, and researchers have warned us about what we are now witnessing. Even Orwell could not have possibly foreseen just how sophisticated governments and corporations, not to mention the individual genius programmer sitting in their bedroom, would become. Overseers can zero in on anyone they choose: a jealous spouse, a disgruntled employee who wants your job, or even the undetected domestic or foreign terrorist. This technology is constantly being improved. Numerous reports by traditional journalists indicate that the invasion of our privacy is a given fact in our lives.

I began to wonder if it mattered. It does not seem to be a problem to most Americans. Arthur Ransom even blew them off as insignificant when I mentioned them to him. Our often-rebellious streets are relatively quiet and submissive participants. One fact that no one disputes is that the trend toward oversight is a fact of our 21st-century life and will only become more invasive over time.

The full extent of how sophisticated current surveillance capabilities is not known by the average American worker. The fact that trackers are out there watching us is known and apparently accepted. Maybe this is the price we must pay to catch the assault rifle –toting anarchist, hell-bent on releasing his anger or misplaced sense of social justice. Armed with cartridges stacked on military-style belts, these domestic terrorists come loaded with unlimited rapid-fire potential all designated and aimed at completely unsuspecting children, shoppers, or worshippers who have asked only to live their lives. If there is any doubt, just talk to any of the Sandy Hook parents who want only their massacred children back. President Obama put his presidency, and the office of the president itself on the line when, after meeting with Sandy Hook parents, he initiated legislation to responsibly curtail such events in the future. His bill had something like ninety percent public approval according to polls that were taken. Despite the tragedy, and overwhelming public approval, congress denied passage of the legislation. The NRA prevailed once again.

We might be better advised to focus on professional terrorists who are able to evade broadly cast nets designed to monitor us all. Does a broad-brush approach to surveillance allow the one in ten or one in a hundred thousand, or that one in a million, to slip through the cracks? The effort required to monitor all of us must detract from those who represent a real threat. Surely, we have the technology to place those who represent no possible threat to society in a passive holding bin.

Statistical inference, when combined with AI and algorithms, could readily identify within any acceptable range of error those who do represent a threat. Should such an objective, non-partisan, approach be taken, it is my guess that those profiled would be quite different than the demographics often touted as representing a real and present danger to our nation. Professionals who study these things have made it abundantly clear to all of us that the biggest threat to our safety is from domestic terrorists, such as the growing number of alt-right, the white supremacists, and well-armed fanatics who have shrouded themselves in a clear misguided degree of patriotism.

My last thought before succumbing to the rhythmic clicking on the rails was a comment I either heard or read many years ago. Policy initiatives taken by governments against any demographic, especially governments leaning toward absolute control, often find a way to expand their designated victims beyond those originally targeted. I slept most uneasily until the conductor announced our arrival at Penn Station.

★★★

CHAPTER 6

MARCH 2020

I KNEW THAT ARTHUR AND I adhered to different politics. But he was an accomplished scholar, and I did not want to walk away from him simply because we live in different worlds. Remembering my reaction to the other Americans on my cruise, I learned more by listening than by trying to convert. I needed more information and invited Arthur to meet me at the Metropolitan Museum of Art. He accepted. I asked him what he would most like to see, and to my pleasure he selected painters of the Renaissance through modern artists—"Rembrandt to Picasso" was how he phrased it. These were sprinkled throughout the museum in different galleries. Using the Met's website, I plotted out our day to see as much as we could in the time allocated. We planned to meet on Friday at 2 p.m., and I also made reservations for 6 p.m. at the Met's fourth-floor dining room.

I felt that would give us the time to view the galleries and grab an early dinner without being too tired to enjoy it. After our last discussion, I was determined to see if Arthur and I were really that far apart on the politics of the day, specifically as they related to Trump. COVID-19 was making more headlines every day. The virus itself was being outstripped by the administration's lack of leadership on how to safely navigate the virus. I checked with the Met, and they were open but advised all visitors to keep distance and wash hands frequently. Masks were not required, but I bought two as a precaution.

I arrived early and had purchased our tickets online. I also rented two audio sets. Arthur was right on time. We surveyed the grandeur of the lobby before heading up to the European paintings from the thirteenth through twentieth centuries, all on the second floor. I have probably visited these galleries a dozen times, each at a different phase of my life. I never get tired of these masterpieces. I do, however, wonder how so many archaeological and historical treasures of other nations and times end up in museums far from where they were created. I studied the art world as an economist for several years and was astonished by how much theft, forgery, and outright illegal activity were the industry norm. I could, however, still appreciate the gifts these artists have left behind. We slowly worked our way through each of the galleries and took the time to hear the descriptions of each piece. I was enjoying our day, and I think my guest shared my joy.

After several hours of viewing, we headed to the café and settled into our table for dinner. I knew scheduling our dinner early would benefit us; the restaurant was relatively quiet. "Thank you, Benson. This was a great idea and a wonderful way to spend an afternoon. I must plan to do things like this more often," Arthur smiled.

"My pleasure. I often like to engage in activities that have nothing to do with my day-to-day life. I have learned with age that downtime is as important as our working time. How have you been spending your time since we last met? I have not seen you in the office," I observed.

"I've been traveling. I went home to San Francisco for a funeral and to catch up with family and friends. I have also been lecturing around the country. It gets a bit boring but pays the bills. How have you been spending your time?"

"Exploring some of my old haunts around the city—that's been fun. That is, when I'm not in the library. I did meet a few colleagues from grad school in DC for a luncheon. It was great to see them and catch up."

"That must have been fun! What did you guys talk about?" he inquired.

"Who we're working for, what we're working on, our home lives, and what's next. No one knew that I'd retired and was back at NYU. We all mourned the passing of a dear friend, Andrew Lawson, who disappeared in the North Atlantic while delivering a boat to Europe. He was a close friend of mine."

"I'm so sorry. That must have hurt. How old was he?"

"Thank you. He was in his early seventies. He and I published several articles together and were working on a study comparing voter participation rates in different countries. Andrew left behind a daughter. I kind of watch over her, even though she's fiercely independent. I think I need her more than she needs me, and she knows that." I wanted him to become a friend, and he was not biting. Where have you been traveling? I suppose you are still lecturing on your last book?"

"Typically, on campuses. I also gave a talk at the Hoover Institute when in California and another at the American Enterprise Institute in DC. I was invited to speak at Brookings, which I suppose rounded me off politically. I had hoped to gain some insight into what these groups are thinking, so I found myself spending more time asking questions than answering theirs. What were the basic feelings at your luncheon?" he asked me.

I listened carefully, and as he waited for me to answer, I asked, "Who are you working for? These trips can be very expensive?"

He was clearly not prepared for that question. After several moments adjusting his napkin and silverware, he said, "I was awarded a one-year grant to write my next book. I took a leave of absence from Ball State University where I have been teaching for many years and moved to DC."

"Wow, nice to have a benefactor, who gave you the grant? Will they publish your book?"

"It is with the Claremont Institute in California, and yes they will publish the book, and we will share the royalties."

"Good for you, it is nice to take time off and do something new. Congrats." I knew the Claremont Institute to be a conservative think tank that was started around 1979. Their original publications were geared towards vindicating several forefathers for the fact that they were slave holders.

"The main feeling at our luncheon was despair." I had no reason to be dishonest with the man. "Trump has been a big shock to us. There was a consensus that it was an American version of the Arab Spring. I think the middle class, especially throughout the Rust Belt, finally gave up on sharing in our growth. After more than fifty years without an appreciable increase in their spending power, they got fed up with both parties and the establishment. Once Hillary was chosen as the candidate for the Democrats, they knew it was going to be the same old, same old. She was, at least in my opinion, the most qualified person ever to run for president, but she was not a particularly good candidate. She is definitely not her husband. Her message was stale. This was surprising given how strong and experienced she is. It appeared that the group considered the late-October Comey letter to Congress as the final blow that did her in. There was simply no time before the election to clean up after it, even though Comey pretty much denied that the content was worthy of debate. I have often asked myself why he released it in the first place. The FBI is supposed to have no influence in our elections. What Comey did was a violation of that long-standing policy."

Arthur agreed. "I think you're right about Hillary. The election was hers to lose. She should have cleaned up the email and Benghazi issues before declaring her candidacy. The Comey letter and the 'deplorable' gaffe gave us Trump. I'm not sure she accepts that responsibility, but many Democrats blame her poor performance on the campaign trail, and a growing dislike for her, for their loss. Trump was the 'accidental candidate' who was in the right place at the right time. The Republicans could have chosen a basset hound as their candidate and won."

"You're right about that, Arthur. There was also a well-orchestrated social media campaign against her. The Mueller Report blamed that campaign and the email leaks on the Russians, who've become very sophisticated at destroying reputations with innuendo and outright lies. At some point, Facebook and the other social media platforms are going to have to accept that they had a part in destroying our electoral process. I am concerned that the Russians will be even more sophisticated in this year's election. In any case, we got Trump. Many agree that he's the most dangerous man on the planet."

"Yes, but the Mueller Report was pretty clear that there was no collusion. I doubt that the Russians were anything close to a game changer," said Arthur.

"That's one opinion, Arthur. Remember that Mueller objected to the way Barr released his findings and to the lack of importance the report gave to the interference of the Russians." Arthur was not giving any credence to the Russia/Trump collaboration. "A lot of the report was redacted," I added, "and the investigators had been instructed not to look into any financial issues. Mueller did, however, show unequivocally how the Russians meddled in the election on behalf of Trump."

Arthur launched into a long monologue on how the Democrats had harassed Trump since he first announced his campaign. "They gave him no slack and no chance to prove himself as president. Trump was adamant that Obama had spied on his campaign. Trump felt disrespected at his meeting with Obama right after winning the election. Trump also hated the comparisons made about the attendance at his inauguration. The Women's March was an insult to him, and the impeachment was a hoax and never should have happened. There was no collusion and no obstruction," he concluded, parroting Trump's own denials.

This was the first solid statement from Arthur that unless he was baiting me, he was a Trump supporter. I watched his body language to determine if he really believed what he was saying or was merely trying to get a reaction from me. All I could observe was that he was uncomfortable with what he was saying even though the words came out convincingly.

I decided to take the bait. "Arthur, I'm surprised at the positions you have taken here. First, it was clear that Trump knew nothing about being a president. His record as a businessman was spotty at best, and it is a rare businessperson who understands how vastly different managing a public sector entity is from one in the private sector. The Democrats got on Trump's case when they realized that the man was totally unprepared to be president.

Without solid experience running a city, a state, or having actually been elected to the House or Senate, it is almost impossible to know how decisions are made in the public sector. Trump has consistently tried to run the nation like he ran his companies. Within twenty-four hours of his inauguration, a president has to make as many as six thousand political appointments. Many of them must go before the Senate for approval, so they must have lots of public sector friends and experience. Trump didn't even know six people. Those he chose for his cabinet were pathetically unprepared. Loyalty was his prime qualification for choosing staff and advisors, and that simply does not work. There's no evidence that Obama directed anyone to spy on Trump's campaign. There was a credible threat of Russian meddling that Obama quietly asked intelligence agencies to check out. Russian meddling, because if it proved to be real, would endanger our election—and our democracy. Mueller found evidence that the Russians did indeed meddle, and not only in U.S. elections. On the attendance at the inauguration, it was his lies as to the numbers that set that discussion off. The Women's March might have happened even if Hillary had won. Women are not going to sit back and follow the old model. That period is over and will not return. On the impeachment, he *did* violate the Constitution and his oath of office, and the House proved that beyond a doubt. Over time, it has leaked that many Republican Senators knew he was guilty, and that the offense was serious. They were not, however, going to break with McConnell. Their vote to acquit was a vote of fear and not one of justice."

I watched Arthur's reaction to my comments and could tell that he was observing more than dissenting. I honestly did not think he cared that Trump was a con man and a fake. He only wanted me to go on record as thinking that he was, and I complied. I decided to add one more point. "Arthur, even assuming that all those things we just covered were not true, can you possibly deny that Donald Trump is an exhausting liar? His base follows him and his platform of lies, and either they do not care or do not know that he lies all the time. How can anyone trust someone who has lied as much as this man? The truth is that his followers have legitimate complaints that the establishment has not followed through on their promises, a condition that has existed for fifty years. Many of these people were desperate for a leader who cared about them, and Trump convinced them that he was that leader. They did not want to believe then or now that he was and is a habitual liar and really not in their camp."

"We do not know how serious that issue is," Arthur said, "and besides, all politicians lie." It was clear that Arthur wanted no further part of this discussion, so I shifted the conversation. I decided that whatever he wanted to get out of me, he got it, and there was no reason to go further down that road.

"Getting back to my DC luncheon, we agreed that we are experiencing Trump fatigue. The endless news coverage has worn us out. His stupid trade war with China and his unwarranted attack on some our closest trading partners is hurting only us. It's going to take decades to clean this up, even if Trump were to leave office tomorrow. One colleague said that a second Trump term would pretty much close us down forever as a participatory democracy. That pretty much sums up our luncheon. Incredibly depressing, to be sure. What did you learn on your travels?"

"I found pretty much the same on the campuses I visited," Arthur admitted. "I was impressed at how engaged the students are. There are those who think Trump is the best thing since sliced bread and others who think he's the worst president ever. There's an enormous gap between them, and little constructive dialogue between the pro- and anti-Trumps, which is unusual for students who, I thought, love to debate. Their behavior is miles from how our generation dealt with the problems of our times. The think tanks were quite different from the campuses with almost unanimous concern about the direction of our nation, Trump, domestic terrorism, AG Barr, and NATO. Even those who declare themselves Republicans think that Trump is extremely dangerous. Like the Republicans in the Senate, however, none were willing to publicly say anything against him. He has them all scared, and, in private, they candidly admit it. Aside from Trump, I think that the issues weighing on their minds were climate change, the Supreme Court, and the number of marginally qualified federal judges being chosen and appointed. There is a general disbelief that nothing is happening to protect our voting rights in terms of Russian meddling. There was also a concern about how the press was under attack. The new focus on Fake News was seen as a deliberate attack on the Fourth Estate. Republican-led voter suppression was a topic of concern as well. Concern on these issues were very much on the minds of those at Brookings, not so much at Hoover or at the American Enterprise Institute." Arthur suddenly got serious and seemed to be defending Trump even more. "Trump's presidency is being watched closely by each of the professionals I met with. Most think that the chaos is Trump's way of distracting the press. There was a general attitude that he was being subjected to a lot of criticism not normally given a president."

It did not hit me at first, but I suddenly put together the list of issues he mentioned that concerned the think tanks and those brought up by the Feds at our reunion luncheon. The coincidence of that was far too unreal, and I took note. I then asked, "Do you think so? He does seem willing to run the nation via Twitter, which is unorthodox for a world leader."

"He's uncomfortable in front of the press and feels that they do not respect him. Did similar issues come up at your luncheon?"

"Only tangentially."

"Have you given them much thought?" he asked.

"Of course, doesn't everyone?" I decided on the spot to tell him about the Feds who crashed our DC meeting.

"What made you think they were Feds?"

"I do not know. Our group's pretty tight, and no one recognized them. Why were they asking such pointed questions?"

Arthur didn't respond. I could tell that he'd just put two and two together and figured out that I was onto him. I decided to change the topic again. I asked him what he thought about the art we'd just seen. I asked about some journal articles we had both read and our plans for the weekend.

All I wanted was to end our evening so I could consider the strangeness of our conversation. I was upset because I felt uncomfortable with him and did not want to be.

I suddenly without thinking looked Arthur in the eye and asked, "Have you met Trump?"

He had trouble finding a quick answer. He said that he did at a White House meeting that he and some of his colleagues were invited to. I just looked at him and we both knew that our meeting was not random. I really want to find out what agency he was working for. I knew that Ari could find out, so I did not ask.

Arthur was suddenly about as indifferent as a person could be. If he was fishing for insight into my thinking, I was offering nothing in return. It was apparent to me that he had gotten all he needed. We finished our meal, split the bill, and said polite goodbyes.

The Met is a long way from home. But even still, I decided to walk and clear my head.

Why was Arthur checking me out so carefully? Why did I feel the same as with my DC overseers? *Whose payroll is he on? Was he funded only by the Claremont Institute, and if so whose money was it?* Why should I be on anyone's radar? I decided to ask Ari to check him out for me, maybe I am just getting too suspicious.

⚓ ⚓ ⚓

FOLLOWING ANOTHER RESTLESS NIGHT, I awoke with a sense of urgency, but also optimism. If anyone could help me, it was Ari. I contacted him and we met at the Bluestone Lane Café, a nondescript coffeehouse in the West Village, on Greenwich Avenue.

"Good morning, my friend, thank you for meeting me."

"Of course. I know you only contact me when you have to."

"No insult intended, of course," I smiled.

We never use names in public, even though we have always met in and at a time and place of his choosing. I knew he had had the place thoroughly cleaned for bugs of any kind well before our meeting. "I think my office and possibly my apartment are bugged." I gave him a piece of paper with Arthur's name and contact information. I also told him that I needed this person checked out; his sudden appearance in my life felt like more than a random event.

Ari never questions me. He put a pad of paper in front of me with a pen. I wrote down the addresses and offered times to meet. He studied the information and accepted my schedule. We finished our coffee and bagel, and without another word, Ari quickly got up and left the café. Ari is a wanted man who will never be caught. Those of us who need his services have learned how to protect him because he is the best at what he does.

He is indispensable to those of us who live more than one life. Intelligence services worldwide know of his skills. No one knows who Ari has worked for. He is as discreet about his customers as we are about him. If I have a problem, it will be known as soon as Ari has finished checking out my spaces for bugs.

✦

I GET A CALL FROM OUR DOORMAN the next morning that the TV repairman was in the lobby. I asked to have him come up.

"Good morning. Thank you for coming. I am not sure what is wrong with my TV. The picture has just disappeared."

"Okay, let me take a look."

I stepped back, and let Ari do his thing. He's always prepared and can scope out and clean a space in minutes. He has to work fast since he prefers to be in and out as quickly as possible.

Ten minutes later, he was finished. "Your TV is up and running. Somehow the cable connection was damaged. I have repaired it, and you should be set." Which was Ari-talk that let me know that my apartment was bugfree. I saw him install a special detector under a bookshelf that would warn me should anything be installed in the apartment. I thanked him, and we nodded agreement for our next meeting scheduled for my office early Monday morning, when the building was the least crowded.

My office was most certainly *not* clean. Ari found that fairly sophisticated listening devices had been installed. There were no cameras, but the voice receivers were both expensive and extremely sensitive. Later, over coffee, he explained that the university could not have had access to such equipment and that they might not even know the devices were there. This system was government-grade and very professional. He was not, however, sure *which* government it was.

As we walked outside, Ari said that he left the one in my office in place. He knew that if he were to disable the devices, I would be found out. We decided to leave the system alone, and I would be careful about what I talk about. Ari would check out Arthur Ransom to see who he really was. He then disappeared stealth-like into the city streets, but not before telling me that he would try to track down who might have bugged my office.

I had a lot of thinking to do and decided to take a few days off.

TRUMP'S 2016 VICTORY WAS a surprising event for most of the country. Word on the street is that the most surprised person was Trump himself.

Many thought that he had no expectations of winning, he just wanted to run. He won on electoral votes alone—the fifth president to do so having lost the popular vote, Trump was the only one on the planet to consider his victory an unprecedented landslide.

This narrow margin emphasizes just how important every vote is. If we do not as a citizenry vote, we must accept the government we get without complaint.

But Trump's election was not all that surprising to me. It happened because large demographics, mainly uneducated, blue-collared white workers were finally beginning to see that their share of our nation's prosperity was dwindling. Those who watch the data could easily conclude that America was on a dangerous path. Middle class incomes had been flat for decades. It had become hard to find meaningful jobs, especially without a college degree. Artificial Intelligence and the personal computer had eliminated many office jobs, hurting even the college-educated. Health costs were rising beyond reasonable levels for those whose health benefits no longer came with a job. The cost of a college education had already soared past the means of most middle-income families. Bottom line, there was a degradation in economic and social conditions that had been festering for decades, and they were not going to take it anymore. Trump was there at the right time, and anyone not connected to the establishment would have won that election. One trait that must be afforded Trump is that he is a master at seeing a vacuum and filling it with his priorities. He did not win as much as America lost.

It is not difficult to evaluate Trumps' presidential performance. Almost four years into his administration, Trump has the highest turnover of key appointments of any sitting president. Most of his remaining high-level appointments were "acting" and unapproved by the Senate; others have resigned in shame or have been fired for lack of loyalty. Trump has created an unrelenting sense of tension and anxiety for Americans. Our nation was divided like never before.

Amidst all that has plagued us—from systemic racism to climate change, from poverty to income inequality, voter apathy and suppression rank above the rest. None of our problems can be fairly addressed if we do not elect a responsive government to make things happen. Trumps agenda for his administration has consistently been geared to serving his base and only his base.

Studies have shown that voter restrictions and suppression in America are overwhelmingly Republican initiated, a defensive action on their part. Trump has explicitly stated that Republicans have to restrict voters as much as they can because without doing so, Republicans would never get elected. They apparently find it easier to suppress their constituents' right to vote than to create a platform that would fairly win their votes. We are further away from "one person, one vote" than ever. The battle for voter rights, fought decades ago, once again was at the forefront of our election process.

Biden had just won the South Carolina primary in a major turnaround, since he had not been doing well. The highly respected black Representative Jim Clyburn had given Biden an unqualified endorsement which turned out the black vote for Biden. Several prominent candidates dropped out, and the race for the Democratic nomination became a two-man race between Biden and Bernie Sanders.

All of this caused me to rethink with greater importance, the project that I had been working on with Andrew. Our original intent was to help American voters increase their participation in elections and to enter the voting booth more informed. Our motivation was based on the historically low turnout of eligible voters. Many surveys have shown that a general lack of knowledge of the issues and the candidates are why most people do not vote. They also think their vote does not matter. I was beginning to think that maybe the project Andrew and I started needed to be greatly expanded to deal with the disruption and danger the Trump administration is fostering. I just did not know how to proceed. I needed time to figure out our best strategy.

★★★

CHAPTER 7

MARCH 2020

OLD, LASTING FRIENDSHIPS BRING BACK memories that fill the soul. Andrew Lawson and I hit it off from the first day of graduate school. We had never met prior to NYU and were surprised at how similar we were in terms of our backgrounds, personalities, and most importantly what we wanted to do with our lives. We've been there for each other since and through all the ups and downs. We had quite randomly sat next to each other at orientation. We immediately recognized our similarities in backgrounds and professional goals. We quickly formed a friendship that survived almost fifty years. Over that time, we were both torn between the pleasure of being educators, researchers, and scholars and the obligation to address what we both considered to be the post-WWII rise and fall of America. We also strove to understand the economic decline and what we both considered the dangerous slide to the political right as the same problem. Subtle at first, the movement away from the center left was stripping our country of the democratic fabric that had made America a respected, albeit imperfect, force in the world.

After high school and the Navy, I started a business that I later sold to pay for college. Andrew was about ten years younger than me. We both grew up at the very bottom level of middle class, bordering in outright poverty. We were both from seriously dysfunctional homes. Andrew went to Fordham and I went to C.W. Post on Long Island. Despite having little formal background as academics, we both graduated with honors. After college,

Andrew worked on Wall Street before working for various liberal think tanks over the years, mostly in DC

Our passion for truth, justice, and fairness was influenced by how we grew up. Without the guidance of our own families, we each benefitted from the kindness and generosity of wonderful people who, despite not knowing anything about us, entered our lives when we most needed them. Andrew and I each felt a strong desire to pay that kindness forward.

We shared a very liberal social and political leaning, built during our formative years. Bachelor's degrees in hand, we knew that we still lacked sufficient knowledge to carry us along the socially and personally productive road we each chose to travel. The realization that we needed more education if we were to make a difference drove each of us to NYU's graduate school of economics.

We spent our graduate school years discussing how the term *liberal* has different meanings to different people. We sought to define what it meant to the two of us. We were not what conservatives often call "bleeding heart liberals," categorized as those who want government to take over their lives at the expense of private sector initiatives and entrepreneurship.

A liberal democracy has best been defined as a nation that recognizes an individual's civil rights, and elected representatives serve within defined branches of government that establish a separation of powers. These powers are defined by a constitution that respects private property, equal protection, and political freedom for all of its people.

Andrew and I concluded that a liberal democracy demands a responsible government, one that provides fundamental rights to enable every citizen an opportunity to explore their passions, constrained only by the limits of their capabilities. A responsible government is a facilitator, established to serve and protect its constituents. It protects its citizens' rights and obligations and provides a safe place to grow up and to thrive. National security, education, decent housing, and affordable healthcare should be made available to all citizens. We came to that conclusion because we found through our research that to do otherwise ends up costing more, and a nation would be denied the full potential of its citizens.

Our definition also posits that a government that takes on tasks best accomplished in the private sector will fail. It would mire the nation in expensive and unproductive departments, agencies, and programs. A misguided government that does not assume responsibility for its citizens will also fail. An accountable government is structured to provide critical services that are best provided by a responsible public sector structured to serve its constituents. Government should then step back and let its people do whatever they do best within the constitutionally determined laws and established social and moral customs. That was what America's postwar liberal democratic government achieved, as did most of the governments of Western Europe.

Many Americans fail to understand their responsibility as citizens if they want to live in a representative democracy. Some are good people who just need to be better informed about their responsibilities; others feel entitled; still others are indifferent. Andrew and I began to resent those who built bubble-like communities of privilege for themselves. After a lot of empirical study, we found a strong correlation between those who lacked a social conscience and those who claimed allegiance to rightwing, conservative causes. There are always exceptions, but these folks tend to be comfortable in gated or protected communities, designed to keep others out. When they are asked why there are so many people outside their economic group who are suffering, they attribute it to laziness and entitlement and blame the less fortunate for their own suffering. When specific demographics, usually people of color, are refused access to basic rights, those who created those roadblocks rarely take responsibility for having done so. Our financing of education, discriminatory healthcare policies, narrow job opportunities, and redlining by banks that prevent people of color from purchasing homes of their choice, are the most obvious policies that have deliberately denied equality to all. Possibly the biggest problem with these discriminatory attitudes on the part of our institutions is that those who suffer them are officially prevented from ever being able to accumulate wealth. This means that every new generation must basically start all over with none of the basic assets we all need to prosper.

Allowances are hardly ever made for what happens to people who suffer indignities generation after generation. I was once at a party and heard a man telling his friends that we had made a serious mistake by allowing every citizen the right to vote. It was his conviction that most Americans do not know enough about the world to vote intelligently. I found out that he was born into a wealthy family and had gone to good universities and made a good living as a gambler. I listened to him for some time and concluded that his narrow perspective actually prevented him from any realistic understanding of the world outside of the sheltered world in which he lived. I gave a lot of thought to how I could convince him that most middle income and even many poor people have a much broader understanding of life than he will ever have. I decided as a new guest and a person not known to most of the people at that party, I was better off walking away. The buffet was infinitely more enticing and gratifying than would any discussion with such a person ever be.

Conservatives often fight for small government, thinking that the private sector always provides better. They argue that a lot of public money and effort went down the drain during the 1960s and '70s without solving any problems. Rather asking why these programs failed and correcting them, conservative politicians often chose to shut them down and blame either the oppressed or the government for the failure. They need only look at our success during the postwar private sector-government partnership to know what can be accomplished.

President Reagan was the father of this negative attitude toward government. It is always easier to blame than to take responsibility. It takes clear thinking, empathy, and hard work to change a broken policy, especially when considering difficult social and political issues. That is what a representative democracy is structured to do. The solutions, as Andrew and I saw them, were found in our economics textbooks and our study of the ancients through the rich and revealing history of economic thought.

Andrew and I individually chose economics specifically because it is the one science equipped to answer such questions. Economists define a private good as one that is best and most efficiently, in terms of resource utilization, provided by the private sector. It is exclusionary and rivalrous, meaning that only one person can use it at a time. An automobile, a pen, a book, or a parking space are examples.

For the same reasons, a public good is best supplied by government, and it is neither exclusionary nor rivalrous. Typically, one cannot be excluded from it by having another person use it. If one person uses a public good, it is still available to someone else. Should a person neglect to pay taxes that would ensure the availability of that public good and still decide to use it, that person would be called a *free rider.* National defense, highways, lighthouses, airports, and parks are examples of public goods. If I use any of them, that will not limit you from using them as well. Like many economists, I consider education and healthcare public goods. We think this way because we know that without them both being made available to everyone as a right, we as a nation cannot survive nor successfully compete against our trading partners. Treating both as a public good and as a right is both practical and efficient, assuming we are as a nation capable of creating and administering them properly.

Air pollution and traffic congestion are also public goods, usually created by excessive use, producing what we call a negative externality. Negative externalities would need a public-sector initiative to remediate them because a private sector company would rarely have the profit incentive to do it. If the negative externality can be identified with a specific polluter, a user tax can be imposed to put the responsibility of the cleanup on whoever or whatever caused it in the first place. PVC pollution in a river or lake is an example. A public sector entity decides on a resolution and finds the best provider to take it on. The government sector responsible for that problem must tax or fine the polluter to discourage a repeat offense. All cleanup costs and opportunity costs must be accounted for as part of the reimbursement to society for having polluted. An example of an opportunity cost might be payback to commercial or private sector users of the lake who were denied access as a safety matter.

We have learned that it is usually considerably more expensive *not* to solve problems such as the wealth gap, extreme poverty, or ignorance, than it would have been to find an economic solution before they became problems. These issues were brought to the fore with the trend toward populism and nationalism which began around the 1964 election when Senator Goldwater ran for president. Despite losing, that election made it clear to right-leaning people, usually Republicans, that with careful planning, they could take down what they saw as an ultraliberal, New Deal, government-controlled nation that wanted to take away their guns and their right to be "free." This movement was not designed to deal with costly social disparities like the income gap, racism, or generational poverty, each of which were becoming more problematic at that time. That election was also the genesis of the Southern Strategy for Republicans.

Andrew and I, along with many others, saw what was happening, but only a few of us felt the urgency to act. We wanted to turn this movement that was distancing us from the equity and fairness America had enjoyed in the postwar era when middle-income families were prospering and vibrant. The differences between income levels and the quality of life for average workers and the captains of business was significant back then, but it was nothing as dramatic as it is now.

Our personal and family circumstances meant that Andrew and I had never gotten to enjoy the prosperity of the 1950s, '60s, and '70s, but the majority of Americans did. Middle-income families had decent, livable wages, and the poor had safety nets that, for the most part, protected them from starvation and homelessness. The rich were very well off then, but not nearly rich as they are now relative to middle class workers. Poverty levels in the postwar period were unacceptably high and comparable to that of less developed nations. President Johnson's Great Society programs reduced them. By 2020, our middle class was once again disappearing as more families sink into poverty, partially COVID-related. The last four decades have not been financially kind to most Americans. One of every five children goes to bed hungry.

As graduate students, we knew that America was heading into a dangerous era for everyone except those at the top. We also knew this would lead to a lot of social disruption that will be costly to resolve. We agreed to take this problem on and knew that if we worked hard on our degrees, we would have the tools to make our dreams for America come true. We had just the right amount of idealism to believe that together we were going to make a difference.

★★★

IT IS VERY MUCH LIKE ME TO take time out of my day to ruminate like this about days gone by or about the many problems we face. I find myself returning to my past to relax and cope with life. Doing so also helps me keep in touch with issues I have cared about for many years.

I decided to make today a day to relax and reflect. I walked downtown to the Battery and hopped on the Staten Island Ferry for the first time in years. The service dates back to 1817 when it was owned by a private company, the Richmond Turnpike Company, until it was bought by Cornelius Vanderbilt. The service went through many private sector hands until 1905, when it was taken over by the City of New York and made a part of the MTA. The Staten Island Ferry has been free to all users since 1997. The service runs 24/7 and takes about twenty-five minutes to make the trip from lower Manhattan to Staten Island. Taking the ferry at night was one of the city's cheapest dates. It felt good to be at sea again, if only for a short while. I no longer had a sailboat. The sea has always called to me during stressful time. I have never been as dedicated to the sea as Andrew and we both have known for years that there's no better means that being at sea to connect with life.

I decided to continue my mini-vacation and took off the next morning just to get out of town for a few days. I had not made reservations. I just hopped into a rental car, inserted a CD of Eva Cassidy's favorite songs, and drove north, ignoring all that I left behind on my desk. There was nothing that pressing, and I had to remind myself that I was retired.

Time plays a strange role in our lives. More than a hundred years ago, Einstein showed us a completely new way to look at time. When we are young, time was a non-issue, and everything seemed to go so slowly that there would always be enough time to do what we wanted to do. I remember how long it took for every high school class and day to end.

As we age, time becomes our most important asset. At eighty years of age, entering my ninth decade alive and well, I think of time as second only to my health in importance. There is so much left to do and statistically so little time to get it all done. Is time really relative? If so, relative to what? Is my time left on earth relative to others in my current age group, ethnic background, or to smokers, marathon runners, or vegetarians? Is our time on earth genetically determined? All I know is I need to minimize my risks because I need a lot of time to finish the projects on my desk and in my mind. Maybe I should not have been driving?

On the fly, I decided to head toward New Paltz, a quaint college town about an hour from the city. I was sure that I would not be able to find a room at the famed Mohonk Inn. But I was confident that I could find something for a few nights. New Paltz is about as typical a New England town as one can find. It is an interesting and peaceful place to walk around. I assumed that I would find enough to do over my lost weekend. Why did I need to think of things to do on a getaway weekend initiated for the purpose of chilling out? I would have to give that some serious thought.

The weekend was perfect. I drove up to the Mohonk Inn and sat on the front lawn, remembering times past. I relaxed into the serenity on a timeless lake beautifully surrounded by the natural world. Then, back in town, I visited some galleries, hoping to see examples of the Hudson River School of Art, a long-time favorite of mine. There were only a few pieces in the Samuel Dorsky Museum of Art, none of which I recognized. I did get to see the historical sites surrounding the Delaware and Hudson Canal museum. I went on the walking trail with its old locks. I drove back to the city on Sunday evening, returned the car, and went straight home.

The time away had done the job. I was rested and refreshed. I slept unusually well and awoke at my usual time. After finishing my morning chores and reading my newspapers over coffee, I decided to visit another special place that I had not seen in years. I cleaned up, shut down my computer, and headed out to the New York Public Library.

After a quick trip on the 2 train, I walked up the grand steps leading to the entrance of the library on Forty-Second Street and Fifth Avenue. I immediately headed for the reading room. Its vaulted fifty-two-foot ceilings are painted with splendid murals of summer clouds surrounded by magnificently carved rosettes and gilded cornucopias. Frolicking cherubs playing their flutes provide cover for the thousands of volumes that line the walls of this recently renovated landmark. This room has been a sanctuary for renowned writers, journalists, scientists, Nobel and Pulitzer laureates, and students, all of whom have purposely sat under strategically placed reading lamps as they gather their thoughts and get lost in the endless resources found throughout this splendid institution.

Like many of the city's landmarks, the library was almost destroyed to make room for a more contemporary structure. Public outrage against the planned destruction of Grand Central Station down the road set the stage to save this historic site. A grant from Sandra and Frederick Rose, who were trustees of the library in 1998, saved the room from certain destruction. It was fully restored in 2016 and renamed the Rose Main Reading Room in honor of their children. Kudos and unbounded thanks to all who fought to save this magnificent structure. We can thank Jackie Onassis for stepping up to save Grand Central Station.

I did not want to read or research anything in particular. I wandered around the reading room and admired everything about it. The library is still an easy place to read and find just about anything you can imagine. Many of the resources are now digitally available, and the staff is as friendly and as incredibly informed as ever. I finished my journey, gathered my bag, and headed out through the main entrance. That was when I saw the notice on the front door that the library was closing as of tomorrow due to the COVID-19 virus attack. The press had reported that despite the protestations to the contrary coming out of the White House, the cases and deaths were beginning to rise at unconscionable rates. As a major international entry port for tourists, New York was getting hit particularly hard. Governor Cuomo had begun to hold daily televised briefings on the virus in early March. His urgency and pleading for New Yorkers to take this crisis seriously was beginning to take hold.

I stood in front of this notice and read it over several times before I managed to leave the library. I knew at that moment that we were entering an entirely new phase of life in our city, indeed the nation. This virus was not simply going to disappear like a miracle as the president has stated many times. We needed to accept the fact that serious adjustments were about to be made for us and by us. I pocketed my metro card and walked back to the apartment, thinking all the way what I needed to do to protect myself from this killer virus. All I wanted to do was to get home and figure all this out.

★ ★ ★

CHAPTER 8

APRIL 2020

THE PANDEMIC HAD BEGUN to take over almost every aspect of life in New York as well as the entire nation. The president had gone public with a series of injections and other absurd cures for COVID that astonished the scientific community. Trump's main concern was his reelection, and he wanted nothing to interfere with that goal on the front pages. Schools were closing. Public spaces were serving only takeout if they were even open for business. Sports, health clubs, and small businesses everywhere were getting hit extremely hard, and many were on the verge of going out of business. I used the imposed confinement as motivation to get our databases compiled and added several new series that I thought would be helpful to our project.

I did take a daily walk just to get some fresh air and think away from my computers. I returned home one morning after a long walk on the city's deserted streets. I was reminded of the late-50s, post-apocalyptic masterpiece by Stanley Kramer, *On the Beach,* where every living thing in the northern hemisphere was annihilated by a nuclear war.

I walked down a dark and cavernous Sixth Avenue and turned onto Thirteenth Street toward my building. Something was not right. I saw Mr. Bonaparte opening the door for me. I could see anxiety on his face, even behind his surgical mask. He told me that two men were waiting for me in the lobby. I glanced over and pegged them right away as Feds. They all must have the same tailor! I found myself wondering if they change out of their "uniforms" before they go home at night.

I walked over and sat down opposite them. They were both wearing black professional COVID masks. They introduced themselves as FBI agents, but offered no evidence. The first offered his hand out of habit. We both pulled back and standing in front of me at a safe distance, Special Agent Dean Watson introduced himself. He was a bit taller than me, his head was shaved, and he had a strong handshake. He was an African American in his mid-fifties.

His partner was about to introduce himself. I asked if his name was Holmes. He said no but admitted that he gets that a lot. He introduced himself as Special Agent Dennis Sanders. He was also about six feet, trim, with cropped brown hair. He could easily have been cast as a lead in *Law and Order.*

Dean said that they had a few questions and asked if we could go upstairs. I informed them that I was subletting the apartment and that it was not mine to offer. I suggested our community room, which they rejected. Their next option was for us to go downtown to Federal Plaza, which I said was not convenient for me just then. Due to the virus, I was avoiding large buildings with lots of people.

"What, may I ask, is the purpose of this meeting?"

They were circumspect and said they only needed an hour. They hoped that I could help them on a case they were working on.

"Am I a suspect?"

"No, not at all. Would you be able to come to Federal Plaza tomorrow morning?"

"Can you give me some idea as to what you want from me? Will I need a lawyer?"

"No. There will be no need for that. We just have a few questions and are asking you to come downtown tomorrow morning, say about 10:00 a.m."

I asked if we could meet in my office instead, which they agreed to, after glancing at each other.

We set the meeting for the next morning, and they got up to leave. The fact that they did not ask for the address to my office convinced me that I was in the presence of the people or agency who had bugged my office. Almost all classes and the university were closed down due to COVID, but we had received a notice that Tisch Hall will be open for the next two days so that faculty can gather anything they needed to work with students to finish the semester. Strict rules on social distancing, masks, and hand cleansers were posted.

Needless to say, this was not the way I wanted my day to end. I called my lawyer as soon as I entered my apartment, after taking a long hard look around to see if anything had changed. I checked out the anti-bugging device Ari had installed, and it indicated that no one had been in the apartment since I had left.

My lawyer was surprised to hear what had happened and decided not to go with me. Doing so, he said, would be a red flag to the Feds that I had something to hide.

I asked if they could arrest me in my office.

He said that they could, but that it was unlikely. His suggestion was to meet with them and answer their questions as succinctly as possible. He reminded me not to offer anything they did not ask for. He told me to take notes, get business cards, and ask if the discussions were being recorded. He suggested that I ask them if I could record our conversation. He indicated that they would most likely say no.

Taking a deep breath, I poured myself a single-malt scotch with a twist of lemon and one cube. I sat down and gazed at downtown Manhattan and pondered what I had been doing that would cause my office to be bugged. Why was the FBI knocking at my door?

Finally, I ordered Chinese takeout and spent an uneasy evening watching movies on Netflix until early in the morning. I sent a text to Anna just to check in. I also contacted Ari.

I woke up the next morning, later than usual, but not so late that I had to rush out for my inquisition. I took notice of the fact that it was April Fool's Day. I needed time to think, so I decided to stop at a coffeeshop on Waverly Place for breakfast. They were only serving takeout, which was fine. I walked over to Tisch Hall and sat down on a bench to think. I tend to stay off the grid in terms of my more sensitive searches and online activities, knowing vulnerable citizens are like open books to anyone interested. I have, however, recently Googled white supremacists, alt-right, and antifa groups. I've checked out their press coverage and followed their gatherings, speeches, and meetings. It's been surprising to see how much these groups have grown over the past five or six years, and especially since the Charleston riots. I learned that many of them have connections that span the globe.

I'd been pretty active against the Vietnam War, as were many students during the '60s and '70s. How could I not be as an NYU student at the time? This had to be a fishing expedition. I had nothing to hide and planned to take my lawyer's advice. Ari had not returned my call, which was unusual.

I asked Angelo, the guard at Tisch Hall whom I knew well, if I could get into a conference room for a short meeting. We both took great pride in our shared Brooklyn heritage and always had a story to tell each other about our respective hoods. I explained the urgency for meeting. He confirmed that the building was open for only the next two days and as long as we had masks and social distanced, I could go in. I informed him of the two federal agents who will be coming to see me. I asked the guard to let them in and if they asked to give them my office number.

He jokingly informed me that he had a few friends from Bay Ridge who knew how to handle themselves if I needed them. "They each weigh in at around 280, no necks, and are always packing, you know who I mean."

We both laughed. I thanked him and said that I did not think it would be necessary this time. I added. "Do keep them on call for me, however."

Angelo reminded me that the building was being disinfected and we would have to leave before they got down to my floor."

"We can do that." I thanked him and decided to walk up the three floors to my office. I arrived a bit early and used the time to straighten up and decided that we could not meet in such a small space. I was glad that I had reserved the conference room. I was not surprised to see that all evidence of Arthur Ransom had disappeared—his job was apparently done. I felt bad for him—what a waste of his true talent.

My unwanted guests arrived right on time. I repeated to myself their names, Dean Watson and Dennis Sanders—I wanted to be sure to remember them. I stood outside my office to wait. When they arrived, they were both wearing their black professional COVID masks. I suggested that we retire to a conference room where we could socially distance ourselves. They looked at each other knowing I was right but probably regretting that we would not be meeting in my bugged office. Well-deserved speculation on my part. They finally agreed and I said to myself, let the jousting begin. I walked them down to a large conference room and opened two of the windows. I then offered my guests two chairs at the opposite end of the long conference table.

I asked how their evening had gone, and they mumbled something inaudible. Had that simple question taken them by surprise? This was going to be fun!

"Why did you retire only to come to NYU to teach?" Watson began his interrogation.

"I wasn't happy with the academic standards where I was and decided to retire. That decision was made well before I was offered a visiting scholar chair at NYU."

"Had you planned to come to NYU?"

"Yes, but not to teach."

"What are you researching?" asked Sanders.

"I am interested in the economics of Reconstruction and the post-Lincoln period. I also have a few papers I am working on; one looking into the history of economic thought and the other on business ethics."

"Is there such a thing as business ethics?"

Okay, this was game-playing. Were they really interested in my research? I tried to gauge their body language. These guys seemed uncomfortable, maybe they were not pros. I reminded myself to take my lawyer's advice and be as brief and to the point as possible. "Yes, especially after the Enron case. Ethics as a strict and separate field of study has been around for many centuries. Surely you know that there is even a US Office of Government Ethics. It was started by President Carter in 1978. Imagine that it took that long to recognize the need?"

"So, you're an economist?" I knew they knew that. Were these questions meant to break the ice? If so, they were doing a very primitive job of it.

"I'm sure that you know that I am," I retorted.

"Tell us, professor, are you currently active in any political groups?"

"I'm afraid that you are asking me something outside your purview. I think we need to stop tap dancing and get down to why you've asked to meet with me. I'm willing to cooperate, but only if you have legitimate reasons to be here."

I clearly hit a raw nerve. Watson started fumbling with his papers, taking more out of his brief and carefully organizing them on the table, more to gather his thoughts than an expression of his OCD. "Dr. Pryce, we are authorized government investigators, and we have been both polite and respectful of you and your position. We are gathering information on activities that have been brought to our attention and we need your cooperation."

I looked straight at him and could see beads of sweat beginning to form on his forehead. I just stared at him for as long as I could to increase his discomfort. "Mr. Watson, you most certainly have *not* been polite or respectful. You have failed to show proper identification. I don't even know if you actually work for the government. You could be Russian spies for all I know. Are you representing the administration, the CIA, FBI, NSC? You do know that you are obligated to identify yourselves, and frankly if you can't or won't do that, this meeting is over."

Intense glances back and forth between my two inquisitors. Much shifting around in their chairs and glances back at me. They look at each other and ask to be excused. They needed to make a phone call. Why did both of them have to leave? I was reminded of several double dates I had been on when, at some seemingly pre-determined point, both women would suddenly stand up and have to go to the bathroom. Together? As my guests left the room, I stood up and wandered down to their end of the table to see what was on the papers they had removed from their briefs. Nothing was showing but a White House logo was on the folders. That told me a lot.

After about five minutes, they both entered the room and asked me to take my seat. "I am going to stand for a while, if you don't mind." I walked over to the open window and stared out at the street at nothing in particular. Angelo was still on duty.

"Okay, Dr. Pryce. Dennis and I are part of a federal intelligence consortium trying to get ahead of some radical groups that, we think, are trying to take us back to the sixties. We see activity of concern on both the left and the right. We're reaching out to anyone who might be able to shed some light on what might be happening."

"And you're interrogating me because...?"

"We're not *interrogating* you. Your name came up because of your activities in the sixties and seventies, and we thought you might be able to help us."

Sanders had yet to say a word, he was clearly the junior man in this team. Watson's voice did get stronger and more assertive, but I still sensed a hint of hesitancy as to how this was all playing out.

"Hey, I'm eighty years old, and I'm not involved with either right- or left-wing radical groups. What made you think that I was?" I was baiting them. "Could you please show me your badges?"

Watson reached into his bag and produced an envelope that he said contained some photographs of me while I was a student. "Interesting! Do you have baby pictures of me, too? I have none and always wanted to see what I looked like as a child."

"Dr. Pryce, we don't need sarcasm. We're only trying to get ahead of the curve on potential violence, especially as it might impact the upcoming election."

"I wasn't being sarcastic. I really have no pictures of myself as a child or of my mother. What did you want to show me? And really now, I need to see your business cards and badges, both of you." Watson stood up and reached for his wallet. I looked hard to see if he was wearing a gun. None was evident. Sanders also stood up and reached for his wallet. He also did not have a holster or gun evident. They both flashed their wallets displaying their badges and handed me cards with their names and the FBI logo.

"Thank you. Why was that so hard? I get the feeling hear that you guys are hiding something." As I was talking, Sanders opened one of the folders and spread out several old eight-by-ten black-and-white photographs.

Watson responded. "As I said, we are a part of a federal investigative consortium. These photos are of you from around the 1970s. Do you recognize them?"

They really were pictures of me. They were dark and grainy. My hair was exceptionally long, and I had a full beard, like every other student at the time. "Where were these taken?"

"This one's from 1971 or '72 during a student takeover of the Courant Building at NYU," Sanders responded. "This was taken earlier, around 1970, and it shows you on Eleventh Street in the Village, about a month before the building you are looking at was blown up by a radical student group. There are a few of you and others at an antiwar rally in the park, and this one is of you at an SDS meeting that was held at Columbia University."

Sanders pointed to the photos Watson was mentioning. I could tell that his hand was shaking and that he was uncomfortable. Something was terribly wrong here, and I needed to figure that out. These guys could not be that green. I sat there dumbfounded. I could not believe that my activities from almost fifty years ago had been kept on file in some obscure government office, probably deep in the bowels of a storage unit next to the Holy Grail. I turned to both of them and asked, "What is the lead agency of your team? Are you working out of the White House? Is there a principal investigator?"

Watson responded, "That has to remain confidential for now. You need to realize that we are asking the questions here. We can wrap this up very quickly or we can spend the whole day here going back and forth."

"Mr. Watson," I said, "unless you have cuffs and are prepared to arrest me, we are going to stay here as long as I am willing to put up with this BS. Who do you think you are? What country do you think you are living in? Everyone in this room knows exactly how irregular this is, and I am losing patience with both of you."

Watson began to pace the floor and worked his way over to the window, hands gripping the ledge. I suggested that he not jump.

That really pissed him off. He turned around; his eyes were red with anger. He then leaned into me, standing barely six feet away, gripping the table so hard I thought it was about to split in half.

"Dr. Pryce tell us about these photos!" he demanded.

As I glared at the pictures, thinking about how I wanted to respond, my mind drifted back to that iconic image in the last scene of an Indiana Jones movie where a government functionary is pushing a large crate into the obscure depths of a storage unit the size of Rhode Island.

"Wow, and *this* is why we're sitting here?"

"We have reason to believe that you are, in fact, still active in antigovernment activities. Conversations we have monitored have revealed that you harbor a significant dissatisfaction with this administration. We have to follow up on all leads if we're to avoid another series of violent street-level activity."

"I see. Might I ask what comments I have made, as well as when, where, and to whom? Did you have a warrant to tap my phones? I would, of course, like to see it." Images of Arthur and our time together were suddenly bouncing around inside my head.

Watson responded, "For the time being, that must also remain confidential. I can say, without specifics, that you seem to have strong feelings on many topics that relate to where America is heading politically. Your current stance mirrors some statements you made in the seventies. Can you please comment on these photos and why you were at these places?"

"Actually, I can, but I'm not sure I want to. You must have been scouring some pretty obscure files to have come across these. I suspect you listened to some even more obscure conversations that I'm sure were obtained illegally. Don't you have more serious work than to track down the activities of a bunch of aging counterculture students, whose only objective was to get our country out of an uncalled-for war? Do you know what that war did to our reputation as a world leader? I deeply resent you being here as you have brought all those terrible memories back to me.

"As we sit here, there are thousands of uneducated, disaffected, angry, and psychotic people all over this country who are stashing military-grade weapons in their closets. Do you have children? Are you sure they're safe at this moment? We are in this room social distancing with masks on, people are dying everywhere and ICUs throughout the land are filling up faster that a Super Bowl game. The World Health Organization had just declared COVID-19 a full-fledged pandemic yet you guys are comfortable spending two days in New York waiting to interrogate *me*? I hope you realize that by being here with me you cannot possibly be anywhere near the real dangers that facing our nation at this very moment."

"Please, just answer our questions so we can all go home," directed Watson., growing more impatient as evidenced by his increasingly flushed cheeks and the sweat forming on his brow. Somehow these guys were way out of their comfort zone and unable to hide it.

The problem now was that I was also getting angry. This is not the way our government functions. I do not believe that these guys were working with others. Their cards were either fake or they were sent here by the White House. Maybe that is why they were uncomfortable, given the little respect Trump has shown to our intelligent agencies.

I decided to pause. I looked at the photos, then back to my inquisitors, then back to the photos. Was this all they had on me? I stood up again and turned back to the window.

Watson was at the end of his rope, exactly where I wanted him. "Please tell us what was going on when these photos were taken, and why were you there?"

"Okay," I ceded, "I'm going to play your game, but before I do, I want you and the FBI to know that I resent you tracking me down. I also want to know if you are recording this meeting."

"Please, just answer the questions." I took out my phone and indicated that I intended to tape it myself. "Please, sir, that will not be necessary."

"You're here in my space when obvious threats to the integrity of our intelligence organizations are out there planning to shut your agency down. As we speak, you and your organization have serious internal enemies banging at your door, and you apparently don't even hear them. You work for a president who despises everything you stand for. You report to an attorney general who's entire being is focused on redefining our constitution and extending the limits of the presidency as far as he can. It's been his goal to establish the president's complete authority over your agency and our nation. He wants to turn us into some kind of autocracy, and he's doing everything in his power to neutralize us all. And you are focused on fifty-year-old photos of a patriot fighting to get us out of a war we not only lost, but one we never should have entered. Do you guys know of Mohammed Ali and what you did to that man's career?

This administration has done nothing but humiliate you and invalidate the oaths you took to carry those badges—which you have yet to show me. Yet you spend valuable resources on a concerned citizen when you have people who want to shut you down tomorrow. The mission of any idealistic radical students from the seventies has been put to rest. Actually, the greatest threats facing us today are from domestic, not foreign, sources.

You might think that we were unpatriotic radicals in the seventies. We were not. We did successfully help force an unfit paranoid president out of office and stop a horrendous war. Your presence is giving me an idea. Maybe I should get another bunch of idealistic students and get them back on the street to join the Black Lives Matter, and all the others out there."

Sanders spoke for the first time in a while. "Sir, please answer the questions so we can all go about our business."

"Does that mean that what you are doing here is *not* your business?" I was now convinced that this was not anything authorized, and these guys got roped into dealing with a deeply insecure president who cares about nothing but his reelection. The president wants no student or street protests of any kind to interfere with his goal. I could tell that I'd struck a chord with these guys, who were only doing what they were told. I also thought if my lawyer had come to this meeting, he would certainly be disappointed in me. Are you recording this conversation?" I demanded.

"Sir, please..."

"Okay, sit back and make sure the voice recorder's on. You might want to take notes as a backup." I took out my iPhone again and pushed the record button. As I did, my guest approached and tried to take it from me. "Do you really want to do that?" I asked.

131

"Professor Pryce, there's no reason for you to record this conversation. Just answer our questions, and we will be gone."

For the first time, I really believed him. All he wanted to do was get out of this room and far away from me. "If there's no reason to record our meeting, there must also be no reason *not* to record it. Kindly return to your seat." Watson did as I asked, and I pushed the record button and sat back for a moment. "About the Courant building," I began. "I was asked by the provost of NYU, Dr. Alan Carter, to try to enter the building that had been taken over by Black Panther sympathizers. I was a student, but older than most, and he thought that with my military experience, I could manage to find out what they wanted to accomplish."

They nodded and Watson pointed to the photos of me on Eleventh Street. "On the Eleventh Street brownstone, I was getting married in the fall of 1970, and my fiancé and I wanted to find an apartment near NYU. Tenth and Eleventh Streets between Fifth and Sixth Avenues were my favorite blocks in the entire city. There's a great diner on the corner of Sixth and Eleventh that you should try. Classic 1950s atmosphere. Red vinyl stools and booths with a jukebox on each table. The bacon and eggs will take you back to your hometown Sunday morning breakfasts. Do not leave town without going there."

"Dr. Pryce!"

I paused, looking back and forth at both of them. "Yes, I looked at all the buildings on Tenth, Eleventh, Twelfth, and more. Unfortunately, students and artists are not able to live where they want to in this town. We typically end up happy to find an affordable space where we feel safe. I searched for several days but found nothing we could afford."

They looked at each other and seemed to accept my explanation.

Sanders pointed to the next batch. "And these?"

"Yes, I was at the SDS meeting at Columbia University. Do you have any idea what that meeting was about? Do you also know that I was auditing classes at Columbia because they had some pretty cool professors up there?" I wanted to know what they knew. "Have you ever heard of Kelvin Lancaster? He wrote a book on mathematical economics. Every economics graduate student studied that book, mainly because it was beautifully written, but we knew that it contained several mistakes that became a challenge for us to find, and we made a contest out of the effort. I could never understand how this book got published with all those mistakes."

"Dr. Pryce!"

I waited once again for a full theatric pause. "I finally figured out why, as I audited his class one semester. Professor Lancaster was a really smart and funny man. His lectures were to the point, and as I got to know him, I decided that he deliberately put those mistakes in his textbook as both a challenge and a joke to future students. I was never all that good at math, but I did find a few of his teasers. Do either of you have any idea what it is like to be a lowly struggling graduate student and manage to find a mathematical error in a textbook written by one of the world's leading economists? I think someone actually published a paper on all the errors as a further test of our creative thinking. Professor Lancaster was simply playing with us."

"Dr. Pryce, please answer the questions."

I knew that I had pushed just about all the buttons these strait-laced goons had in their arsenal. I also knew that if these photos were all they had, they had nothing on me or on any of my current activities. That was a major relief since the new project was far more important to me than these photos. I had to protect that project and my colleagues, and one way to do that was to be as much of a pain in the ass as I could. I wanted to show them that I am a patriot, not a revolutionist. I also wanted no lingering thoughts that I could in any way be a threat to this administration. They would then need significantly more incentive to come back to me.

"Mr. Watson, you came to me. I did not come to you. You asked me some questions on my activities from fifty years ago. I am reluctantly answering your questions, which frankly I do not feel that I have to do, and as a veteran and a patriot, I resent having to. I will, however, answer them as fully as I can so that you and your agency will leave me alone. As a taxpayer, I would prefer that you use your time and talents to go after people who really represent a threat to your agency and our nation's security."

"It is Special Agent Watson, not Mister!"

I responded, "Sir, that is a very important title, and you have shown me no proof that it is one that you are qualified to own." We entered another stare-down, until I relented.

Pointing at the Columbia University photo, I continued. "About the time that picture was taken, I had formed a study group with a few of my fellow graduate students. We each had different skills and decided to share what we knew to help each of us do better in our classes and on our exams. We would meet in a coffee shop and pour over the Lancaster text for no other reason than to find as many of the errors as we could. What fun that was. Professor Lancaster got the last laugh, and we gained nothing short of complete respect for this man as an economist and an educator."

"That is all interesting, but not the least bit informative. What were you doing at that SDS meeting? You know how violent this group was and how much damage they caused." Watson was about as pissed as I was amused.

"Actually, they were significantly less violent than our government was—and probably still *is*. Go talk to some Vietnamese families still struggling from the Agent Orange we dumped on them. Take a walk through the killing fields in Cambodia but be careful of the craters and watch out for unexploded American bombs and mines—they're everywhere. If you don't see how vicious we can be, you need to take a step back and do some research. How about the ongoing violence of our militaristic aggression in the Middle East and Afghanistan? These, gentlemen, are actions we define as violent, and they should not be compared to broken windows and a burning car."

"Professor Pryce, the photos, this is all interesting but, please just tell us about the photos."

"The SDS were the Students for a Democratic Society, and except for the few outliers, they were nothing more. Other groups like the Weathermen splintered off and were more aggressive. SDS violence, however, was rare. It originated from the establishment that was unable to understand what they were trying to accomplish and by the mid 70's it hardly even existed as an organization. The students rightfully felt that what our government was doing in Vietnam was criminal. Many young people tried to draw attention to the amount of damage being done by our country. How dare we think America had the right to do such things to other human beings!? Mohammed Ali had it right, and his long overdue exoneration by the Supreme Court proved it. You do know that our government destroyed his career, but not his integrity or his lasting reputation."

"Professor Pryce, whatever you say, we were at war and many considered the actions of groups like the SDS were treasonous. Were you a member? And again, why were you at this meeting?"

"You guys were not even alive at this time. Those of us against this war, considered those who got us into it as treasonous. No, I was not a member, but I was very much against that war. You need to understand that many students and young people who saw these atrocities knew that peaceful protests would never get your attention. The SDS was formed by a group of idealistic students with the sole purpose of waking up the administration.

Can you think of a nobler goal? Do you even know how widespread the antiwar movement was at that time? You probably weren't even born when all this was happening, yet you are sitting here in judgement of me. Have you read about this period in our history? Have you seen *The Deer Hunter*? *Apocalypse Now*? *Born on the Fourth of July*? Have you read *Matterhorn*? *The Sympathizer*? *The Thirteenth Valley*? Do you know about Kent State? Shame on anyone who felt justified in killing all those poor Vietnamese people and damaging the good name of America forever. More than 58,000 young American soldiers, barely out of childhood, were listed as casualties, not to mention the millions of civilians we murdered. You surely know how many veterans from that war came back to an ungrateful nation."

Watson was flushed and ready to strike. "You're stalling and wasting our time. All this is beside the point. Please answer the question. Why would you spend time at an SDS meeting if your studies were so important to you?"

"Why was I at that meeting? Is that what you want to know? Well, first, you tell me what that meeting was about. Are you familiar with Professor Joan Robinson?" Blank stares barely hid their frustration. "You should have done your homework before this meeting. You should know about her because she was the guest speaker at that meeting. I was there to listen to one of the most brilliant and unheralded economists of the twentieth century. She taught at Cambridge with another twentieth-century giant, John Maynard Keynes. Do you know anything about the many gifts this genius gave the world? Professor Robinson made significant contributions to Keynes' book, *General Theory of Employment, Interest, and Money*.

"Much later, around the 1950s, Professor Robinson was once again challenged on her working knowledge of capital theory. Her understanding and clarification of the role of machinery and equipment was a major contribution to our understanding of almost everything the world produces.

"Two eminent Nobel Laureates, Professors Paul Samuelson and Robert Solow, both at MIT, entered into a long debate with her that was carried out in writing. These giants of economics eventually conceded and gave Robinson her due. The world gained valuable insight into capital theory from those debates, insight that every economist since has appreciated. Professor Robinson was a powerhouse and highly respected throughout the profession. She also wrote the first textbook on microeconomics, in which she clearly laid out the intricate workings and behaviors of households and firms. That book was published in 1933 and defined microeconomics as never before."

Watson took over, displaying his already worn-out patience. "We really appreciate the lecture in economics, but you have yet to answer the question."

I was really enjoying myself and committed to making this invasion of my time and space as uncomfortable for them as possible. I was glad my lawyer had stayed home. "Thank you, Special Agent Watson, for recognizing it as a lecture. By the way, I usually get $3,000 a day plus expenses for my lectures. I would send you a bill if I knew your address. I'm not, however, able to give you a passing grade for this class. If you'd done your homework before you bothered me, you would have figured out why I was at that meeting.

"Professor Robinson was invited to speak before the SDS. She was going to talk about her research and the war. I had never met her and nothing, and I mean nothing, could have kept me from the opportunity to hear her speak. It was extremely hard to hear anything at an SDS meeting, as the noise and confusion is truly deafening. Before our honored speaker was due to arrive, the volume in that lecture hall would have drowned out a B52 bomber landing on the roof."

"Professor Pryce, *please* answer the question."

I was meeting my goal: to annoy this starched shirt, uptight bureaucrat. I continued, "When the door opened and Professor Robinson entered, followed by the person who was to introduce her, the entire room became so quiet. Everyone stood up and maintained a total respectful silence as this tiny woman walked to the podium. No one else said a word. She was far too respected by everyone in the hall and needed no introduction. We remained standing until she gathered her notes and looked up at us. Then and only then did we take our seats and remain totally silent as this beautiful person talked to us about how important morality and decency is to those of us who have chosen economics as our life's work. We were reminded of Adam Smith, the father of economics, whose PhD thesis on philosophy and ethics, *On the Theory of Moral Sentiments*, is the actual bedrock of our profession.

"Yes, I was there, and so was every graduate student and working economist in the City of New York. Do you know what it's like to be in the presence of a true genius? Do you know what it's like to have total respect for a person who has dedicated her entire life to making the world a better place for you and your children? I don't think either of you have ever even given a thought to such a gift." I paused. "I now hope that I've answered your questions."

The silence in the room was deafening. I think I made my point, and I knew that I had managed to neutralize my inquisitors. As they were leaving, Watson turned to me and said that he did have one more question. "What do you know about the work of Dr. Andrew Lawson?"

I looked at him for a long time. I wasn't sure how to answer, especially because I knew exactly why he asked it. I tried my best. "Dr. Lawson was a dear friend of mine. We were students together at NYU. We published several articles, all of which are available on the public record. Dr. Lawson was lost at sea two years ago, may he rest in peace." I knew it was last fall. I was testing their evidence.

"He was reported missing last year. His profile came up with yours."

Okay, they were tracking Andrew. "That would hardly be surprising. We were close personal and professional friends for almost fifty years. What do you mean my 'profile'?"

"It seems he had a passion for ultra-rightwing groups, white supremacists and anti-fascists. for example."

"Have you ever looked at how many online hits there are for those groups?" I asked. "They range in the millions. I look at them as well. There is a frightening rise in white supremacy in our country, and we should all be concerned. These people hide behind our flag. They pose a serious threat to everyone outside their ignorant, uninformed, and violence-prone cults. Of course, Andrew was interested as a citizen and a professional social scientist. My real concern here is that maybe you and your vast body of intelligence agencies aren't. It's abundantly clear that you have no idea what economists do for a living, and you have no idea who Andrew and I are. I'm wondering why you'd ask me about the hypothetical fifty-year-old activities of a well-respected published professional who, unfortunately, is dead? I think we're done here." I picked up my recorder, just for effect, and threatened to hit the off button. "I would appreciate a copy of whatever report you write up from our meeting and sincerely hope we never meet again."

Watson responded that the report would be confidential. "You can FOIA it if you wish."

Both men stood up and offered their hands, which I refused, reminding them of the pandemic that was ravaging our county. "I sincerely hope that you find as much time as you have wasted on me to tune into the pain and suffering of this pandemic and the many white supremacist groups who are the true threats that should be demanding your attention." I could tell that they had more questions about Andrew.

Before they turned their backs to me, I blurted out. "You might consider sending Dr. Ransom back to spy school. He has much to learn before coming back out into the field. You might suggest that he get off your payroll and focus on his considerable knowledge as an economic historian."

Watson ignored me. Sanders could not help acknowledging the value of my humor and observational skills. He looked up slightly as he left the room.

I nodded.

I sat in the conference room after they left, and I asked myself what the takeaway from this meeting was for them and for me. I think I effectively diffused the issues behind the photographs. My lawyer would be proud of that, but he would be terribly upset by the amount of information I disclosed. In any case, I think that the whole exercise was a ruse to get me to the table. I think their only point for meeting with me was to get my reaction to their question about Andrew. That was a problem for me, and I wasn't sure if I'd handled it well. Maybe I should have been a bit kinder at that point, if for no other reason than to deflect any further action on their part. I also knew that they were going to continue to watch everything I did. I had to factor that into my plans.

These guys were good, but somehow, they acted uncomfortable around me and, I felt, less than professional. Was it a low-level team effort? I knew that a first-class FBI team would never let me get away with dismissing them as I had. Maybe they weren't really FBI. I also knew that I wasn't the only person on their worksheet. They would spend a lot of time trying to tie us together as some kind of national conspiracy to take over the government. I hoped they would try, since I work alone, and that search would be a great distraction for our work. I needed to think about all this and how I could become better at watching my own back. I needed to talk to Ari.

More importantly, I had to protect the one person who I knew must remain unknown and invisible at all costs. I placed a code urgent call to Ari and asked for a meeting.

I waited a reasonable amount of time, left my office, and headed toward the Film Forum. It didn't matter what movie was showing. I felt a strong need to cleanse my body and mind from the stench of what I'd just gone through. Films are the perfect remedy to meet that need. Sadly, the Forum was closed due to COVID-19.

★ ★ ★

CHAPTER 9

MAY 2020

EVERYTHING WAS BEGINNING TO MOVE extremely fast. Joe Biden had won the Wisconsin primary and Bernie dropped out soon after. This pretty much locked it up for the party and for Joe. One major difference over 2016 was that Sanders did not linger and threw his weight behind the candidate almost immediately. Protests surrounding the killing of George Floyd spread throughout the nation and were gaining traction world-wide. Some were concerned for the health of protestors in the wake of COVID-19. Trump slammed the protestors in DC and threatened military action against them as local police were pepper-spraying peaceful protestors. Trump also withdrew from the World Health Organization, causing disbe-lief everywhere, given the rising pandemic, which was beginning to have a major impact on our economy. House Democrats had more unredacted sections of the Mueller Report released, and those pages indicated definite Russian meddling in the 2016 election. History will marvel at how deftly the administration blew off that report and its damaging conclusions. As a result of all this distention and political chaos, the American voter no longer recognized the nation they grew up in.

I took a walk and found myself in front of the Café Bohemia. I walked in and sat down in an obscure corner as is my habit in jazz clubs. The place was almost empty—customers could only sit in staggered tables placed no less than six feet apart. I ordered a beer and settled into my head. A lot was happening, and I wasn't processing it very well. I was embarrassed that I had not been keeping up with the coronavirus as much as I should have. It had been marching, Sherman-like, through almost every community in America, indiscriminately contaminating everything in its way. Unlike Sherman, whose march stopped at the sea, the virus let nothing like an ocean stop its dedicated path to human misery and death.

I knew that the events that had concerned me for decades had reached a crescendo since Trump's election. My preoccupation with America's very survival had firmly taken over my life, leaving precious little room to think of anything else, clearly dictated how I missed the importance of the virus. Trump inundated us with his daily chaos, creating distractions that methodically and effectively deprived Americans of all the gains we have painstakingly made on so many key issues. Could we wake up on just one morning without drama or another outrageous Tweet?

The whole world was also under attack by COVID-19. The main difference was that many other nations were handling it much better than we were. Trump had been caught completely flat-footed. Unlike the way he usually dodged his business creditors and successfully wove himself around political blunders, he could not BS his way out of this one. He was probably ignoring it, hoping it would go away and not throw a stumbling block under his reelection. Trump repeated his lies so many times that he and his followers eventually believed them, despite all evidence to the contrary. The virus was bigger and more lethal than him, and he could not take it to court.

I should have been more on top of this virus earlier. I should have been alert to its potential to wreak havoc across the earth. For months, I had been laser-focused on our project and the 2020 election. I now believe, more than ever, that another four years of Trump, McConnell, and their Republican legislative lap dogs would move America irretrievably closer to a political autocracy or worse. We were all concerned. I was convinced that the future of our nation was at risk.

The problem was that the rapid-fire Tweets coming from the White House did not give us time to react to any single one before another, even more unbelievable was released. The country was being manipulated by Tweet, which of course was Trump's way of marginalizing Congress and the press. Temporary appointments were made to head the EPA, Homeland Security, the Department of Defense, or FEMA, avoiding Senate approval, mainly knowing that those appointed were either unqualified for the post or hostile to the agencies they were asked to manage, or both. While some might still have been confirmed in the Republican-controlled Senate hearing, I suspect Trump did not want inevitable objections from Democrats on the record.

The EPA systematically removed protective environmental regulations. We woke up one morning to an executive order to reduce automobile emissions standards that were already accepted by the industry. After declaring that it would keep the Obama-recommended standards, the DOJ sued California. Anyone with a scientific orientation was pushed off the podium or out of a job. Trump was convinced that his gut instincts had more validity than science. He had explicitly stated that he knew more about war than his generals. I guess being a draft dodger provided him with all the military experience he needed. Trump's prognosis was that COVID-19 would disappear like a miracle and prescriptions could be easily filled in the cleaning aisle of the supermarket. Trump continued to tweet out his skepticism about science, and he was dismissive of Dr. Fauci, a highly respected professional.

The hundreds of Tweets and policies via executive order shocked people, even some of Trump's most loyal followers. He once explicitly stated that he and he alone had total authority to demand when states would reopen from lockdown. This was quickly denounced by governors as simply not within his authority to mandate. Trump genuinely believed, with the active support of his AG, that there were no limits to his authority. In the end, he decided that it was not his responsibility, and he shifted the ramifications of the virus from him to the governors, most notably "blue state governors." He refused to accept that being president he should executively administer for the entire nation, not just his base.

I found myself backing off from my own thoughts and concerns, Was I overreacting to an administration that has a completely different political agenda than I do? Was I exaggerating the dangers of what Trump was doing on a daily basis? Was he making America great again? Was he functioning as the people's president? Calling up my most objective, fair-minded self, I could not find one shred of evidence that my concerns were unfounded or that he was in any way a responsible and competent president.

Everyone agreed that our government is broken. The problem was deciding exactly what was broken and how to repair it. The lack of agreement had made it possible for our government to flounder, squandering time, money, and resources without reaching solutions. We were living in the classic "divide and conquer" strategy traced back to Machiavelli's 1521 *The Art of War*. Trump made no effort to bring his opposition to the table, not even as a condescending display of collegiality. He had no desire to hear from anyone who was not loyal to him or not part of his base. He never intended to be a president of all people. Congress shut down attempts to reach across the aisle. This was not accidental. Dialogue stopped and any Trump loyalist could walk through the gap to either destroy or create the dysfunctional world they chose to occupy.

These thoughts rattled around my brain as I turned my attention back to the music. A young horn player was trying desperately to sound like the legendary Miles Davis, who was often called "The Prince of Darkness." I closed my eyes and drifted into the soothing, muffled sounds of his horn. I managed to put all things Trump and political out of my mind. I knew I would have an easier week ahead, and I needed freedom to focus. I also knew that my favorite pastime in New York was about to come to a, hopefully, temporary end. COVID-19 had entrenched itself into almost every corner of our lives, and our president had yet to recognize the problem, much less develop a plan to help us survive it.

I paid for my beer, left a ten-dollar bill on the piano, offered full appreciation to the musicians, and headed home.

THE NEXT MORNING, I went out for breakfast and lingered for more than an hour over scrambled eggs and bacon, several cups of coffee, and a book of poetry by Edna St. Vincent Millay. I sat at one of the temporary tables set outside. Most people were wearing masks, but not everyone. Somehow, Trump managed to politicize the wearing of masks. He refused to wear one and did not press his team to do so, in fact he insulted them into not wearing one. His game plan was to ignore COVID and the fatal numbers we were seeing daily. Deny it often enough and people will soon believe that it is a hoax. His irresponsibility on this issue alone should have forced him to resign. So many Americans sick and dying just to feed his ego and election obsession. I then headed back home. I needed to focus. I returned to the apartment, prepared to put in a full day gathering information for our project.

I found it impossible to ignore the multitude of injustices that were wildly circling around us, controlling every aspect of our daily lives. I missed Andrew. We'd always managed to figure out exactly how to proceed, no matter how complicated the task before us. Our database showed just how far America had fallen behind as a twenty-first-century, global power. Our job was not easy back in the '70s when we first started to build our files. The computers and statistical capabilities we had back then were really primitive. All data had to be collected and loaded into a borrowed mainframe computer by hand. All the basic national economics series, including labor force, wages, hours worked, census, and financial data had already been collected and stored by others. It was the fringe data that many people didn't know about that took considerable time and effort to collect and put in computer-readable form.

Andrew and I had published a lot of papers on policy using our data banks. We attended seminars anywhere we considered the content important to our objectives, which were fluid and ever-changing. We felt that America as a participatory democracy was moving into a whole new and uncharted realm. Higher education and healthcare had become prohibitively expensive. The demographic gap in both income and wealth was increasing at a phenomenal rate. I recently read a study that showed that the fifty richest people were worth about the same as our poorest 165 million people. That is not the sign of a healthy, robust economy.

America's long-standing, vibrant middle class was being systematically shut out of the steady economic growth path the nation was on. The economic classes in our nation were growing more distinct, as witnessed by the growing income and wealth gaps, now firmly weighted at the top. Corporate mergers meant that vital consumer products were put in the hands of fewer decision makers and distributors. It has been estimated that almost everything the average consumer buys is now distributed and controlled by only twelve corporations: Kellogg's, General Mills, Kraft-Heinz Company, Mondelez International, Mars, Coca-Cola, Unilever, Proctor and Gamble,

PepsiCo, Johnson and Johnson, and Nestle. This trend represents an unacceptable concentration of buying power and market control that is not representative of a functioning capitalistic economy.

Our political system was rapidly becoming less accessible and responsible to the voting public. Special interests and lobbyists had taken over the legislative agenda. Our already low participation in voting had not improved, and in most cases, fewer eligible voters were coming to the polls. Some states were actively subverting voter participation, and their methods had become more sophisticated. Estimates of suppressed and restricted voters have ranged from the thousands to the millions. These repressed voters are mostly poorer black and brown people who tend to vote Democratic, but who may no longer vote because of the restrictions they face. Many people think that their one vote does not matter. This is a most dangerous condition for many reasons, all bad.

Andrew and I saw all these things early on, and we were not sure how to address the problem. We knew that they were a result of the seismic shifts in how the economy and political systems were functioning. We were heartened by the increase in institutes as well as publishing efforts, designed to make the population more aware of what was at stake in each election. These have been effective, but the governing problems and excesses were expanding faster than the solutions. Despite news reports, documentaries, testimony before national and state legislative bodies, books, and peer-reviewed articles, the concentration of power and money in the hands of a few continued unabated.

Yet there were some organizations that have had an enormous impact on critical issues: MADD, started by a grieving Long Island mother who lost a child to a drunk driver; The Southern Poverty Law Center; Earth Day; the Sierra Club; Greenpeace; Doctors without Borders; the MeToo movement;

Black Lives Matter, Greta Thunberg; and various other civil rights groups and individuals have each changed the world. Andrew and I wanted to contribute to that positive change as well.

Gross inequities as well as greed and corruption plagued our nation. The blatant overselling of subprime mortgages and the violation of traditional financial checks and balances that brought the world to its knees in 2008 were particularly heinous. Thousands of decent people were sold mortgages that never should have been written in the first place. Many went bankrupt. Professionals from the financial industry blamed those who bought these mortgages claiming that they never should have accepted them. But these people just wanted the American dream of owning a home. They also trusted the professionals who were putting these mortgage packages together. Why shouldn't they have trusted these salespeople? After all, they were the professionals. The problem was that their loyalties were with their quotas and not their customers.

When banks bundled subprime mortgages as marketable securities, that only threw gasoline on the burning fire that went global. When the smoke finally cleared, we knew exactly where to lay responsibility. We knew which banks had directly benefited from the incredible loss of wealth that impacted low- and middle-income families. A controversial, yet reasonable, bailout program was pulled together to prevent a total meltdown of our financial institutions. Inexcusably, not a single executive was fined, arrested, tried, jailed or fired. Shareholders lost out and paid billions in fines that were later levied against the perpetrator institutions. Decision and policy makers at these institutions were held harmless, the shareholders and homeowners were not.

Homeowners lost their homes and savings, while only a few companies suffered. Lehman Brothers went bankrupt. Merrill Lynch, AIG, Freddie

Mac, and Fannie Mae, among others, were dramatically reorganized, more for their protection than for their victims. Many individuals and companies actually made fortunes on the losses of others. It was estimated that U.S. households, mostly poorer families, lost up to 25% of their wealth. Something like $22 trillion in wealth, almost all from low- and middle-income families, was lost because of the actions of a few financial people whose greed for money seriously outstripped their profession's traditional operating standards.

The social costs continued to plague the housing market for years. Adding insult to injury, many of the same financial institutions that wrote those irresponsible mortgages and received the TARP bailout, proceeded to unconscionably foreclose on those same homes, profiting once again from their resale. Who should have been held responsible: the homeowners? the banks? Congress? Capitalism? The courts?

Was that wealth really lost? Or did it merely shift upward on the food chain, adding to our growing income and wealth inequality? Remarkably, some of the actors who participated in the creation of the problem were actually brought in to make decisions and find a solution. The 2008 TARP, The Troubled Asset Relief Program, consisted of over $700 billion in tax-payer money that was given to the financial industry to prevent its collapse. It was offered without any constraints as to how it should be spent. Not a single executive was held legally responsible or sent to jail for this *second round* of sanctioned corruption that contributed to what had become our most disastrous financial collapse since the Great Depression. This disastrous event and its self-serving solution represent one of the most important reasons why we need to create a more informed electorate if our democracy and our economy are to survive as originally designed. The financial crisis of 2008 is probably the clearest example of how the political and economic systems are enriching the wealthy and powerful and are not serving the public. The lack of accountability did nothing to prevent the same behavior from happening again.

ABOUT THE TIME ANDREW AND I had turned our attention back to our voter awareness project, Trump had been elected president. Anyone who lived in New York knew that this con man, a would-be emperor with no clothes, could not possibly understand the responsibilities of the presidency. His string of bankruptcies, outright theft from contractors and small businesses, his legendary dalliances with women while married, and his grossly overstated impact on the New York real estate market made him a laughing-stock.

Trump had declared his candidacy from the lobby of his Fifth Avenue building, using a multitude of false and obnoxious insults about immigrants from our valued neighbor, Mexico. He then bullied his way through a bevy of Republican candidates, all of whom were far more prepared to become president that him. Trump assumed the posture of a braggard and populist with a nationalistic slogan. Trump's bravado appealed to people who had begun to realize how marginalized they had become by our political system. Trump won the Republican nomination and was pitted against Hillary Clinton, probably the most qualified and experienced person ever to run for the presidency.

That election was further complicated by the popularity of Senator Sanders. He appealed to young and black voters because of his progressive stance on social programs he rightly felt needed to be more inclusive and affordable. The battle between Sanders and Clinton became extremely heated and did not help the Democratic party. Many feel that Sanders' attempts to hide his programs as socialistic by calling himself a "Democratic Socialist" hurt him. This is unfortunate because the good senator is anything but a socialist, which Republicans have successfully redefined as Communists. More importantly, the concept of socialism is grossly and hopelessly misunderstood by the American voter. A nation like America and most of Europe who have active participation of their government in their respective economies are socialistic, and not even close to being Communistic. National healthcare, Social Security, food stamps, highway maintenance and construction, environmental programs, the military and many other programs are representative of government responsibilities that are social programs best managed by government. Those who like to call government participation in our economic growth fail to understand how a capitalistic economy and democratic government work to the benefit of the people. Those who fear government are usually the same people who think that free markets, as defined by them, will solve all the problems of society. It is unlikely that the election would have turned out differently if Senator Sanders had been the Democratic candidate in 2016, but we can reasonably assume that the rift between Clinton and Sanders did not help the Democratic cause. Many democrats still feel that if Joe Biden had been encouraged to run, he would have handily beaten Trump in 2016.

Hillary was a vilified candidate who ran a flawed campaign. Despite her positive ratings as President Obama's Secretary of State, as well as her popularity as a senator from New York and First Lady, Hillary became a widely disliked candidate. Some of this feeling was justified as she had failed to get the Benghazi mess and the email issues behind her before declaring her candidacy. The truth was that the Benghazi affair had been subjected to a $7.8 million investigation that went on for more than two and a half years. One of the longest and most expensive congressional investigations, it concluded with a sharp indictment against the military for not being better prepared. It could find no culpability on the part of Clinton.

The email problem plagued her entire campaign and continued on, despite the fact that Congress and the FBI found carelessness but no direct violation of law. Both of these issues were endlessly harped on by Trump for the entire campaign without an effective counter from the Clinton campaign. Trump publicly asked Russia to undertake an investigation to find the missing 30,000 emails, which many political pundits' thought was against the law. Additional evidence from the Mueller investigations revealed that Russia did in fact interfere with the 2016 election. Trump was, of course, the favored candidate by the Russian hackers of DNC emails. The relentless and unchecked social media spread of false statements about Hillary in several key delegate areas did more damage than her campaign could counter. Ultimately, these issues did impact the campaign and contributed to her Electoral College loss. There were FBI investigations and relentless attacks often based on false or misleading statements. This damaging barrage of misinformation was capped by the infamous, later retracted, Comey letter issued eleven days before Election Day, leaving no time for correction or rebuttal.

The mood of the electorate itself was probably the single biggest political enemy facing Clinton. Through forty years, and at least six administrations, the middle class in America had witnessed continual economic erosion. Republican and Democratic administrations alike continued to ignore the fact that since 1970, most blue-collar workers had been at largely the same level of real spendable income in 2016 as they were in 1970. At the same time, those in the upper classes were enjoying unprecedented increases in both their income and their wealth. The Economic Policy Institute revealed that real wages for the top 1% rose by 138% from 1979 through 2013. The bottom 90% of wage earners grew 15% for the same period rendering them essentially flat.

Andrew and I both knew in 2016 that Trump was not going to drain any swamp. As shocked as we were by his win, we decided to let time pass before we took action. After all, who were we compared to a throng of far better connected Trump antagonists? It did not take long to realize that we could never have imagined the damage Trump would do. He bore out our worst fears and went much further. His appointees to key agencies, EPA, Commerce, Housing and Urban Development, National Security, and Education, actually disdained the agencies they were taking over. They were loyalists, dedicated to the diminution if not outright elimination of the agency they swore an oath to protect. Most appointees, like many of the 200-plus federal judicial appointees, were not the least bit qualified. Their conservative vitae were the only qualification Trump and Senator McConnell needed to put them forward.

Trump's relentless attacks on the "fake news" became a daily event. Anything written or broadcast that was not favorable to him was immediately labeled "fake." Trump was a climate change denier who insisted the Paris Agreement was a threat to our economy. As promised, he eventually pulled out of that important agreement and cancelled the hard-fought anti-nuclear agreement with Iran. He found himself more ideologically comfortable in the company of notorious dictators than with our allies and trading partners.

Trump launched a massive trade war against China and many other long-time trading partners, designed to shift the balance of trade. He imposed heavy tariffs without any attempt to renegotiate our trade agreements. Despite claiming to be the best of negotiators, Trump resorted to tariffs, trade-destructive weapons that have rarely if ever worked. Tariffs are a weak and ineffective tool to right a trade dispute.

BACK AT HOME IN MY APARTMENT, I made myself another pot of coffee and sat at the dining room table writing notes on these points as they came to mind. It was almost noon when I looked up and realized that the problems Andrew and I had been concerned with for many years truly paled in comparison to the Trump presidency. Three years after his election, his popularity among his base had solidified, despite numerous blunders and outright treasonous acts. He was systematically dismantling advancements in pollution control, consumer protection, international relations, and healthcare. He did nothing to reduce the cost of education, raise wages, strengthen women's rights, or promote fairer tax policies.

With the aid of his hand-picked Attorney General, William Barr, Trump managed to get the entire Mueller Report neutralized that there was "no collusion and no obstruction," despite numerous statements and entire sections of the report stating the contrary. Trump's impeachment in the House was sabotaged in the Senate, even though his guilt was generally accepted by even Republicans who voted to acquit him. His irresponsible quid pro quo conversation with the president of Ukraine led to his impeachment. Yet he was acquitted. This victory was so definitive that the press and political circles drew the conclusion that the Republican Party was completely and possibly irrevocably now the Party of Trump and McConnell.

During McConnell's entire six-term Senate career, he has moved the courts toward a radical right-wing posture. McConnell is the personification of power over the people. He had no vision for America outside of his obsession to bend our judicial system to serve a power base that also lacks a democratic vision.

By eventually installing three conservative Supreme Court justices, Trump and McConnell have accomplished more than even he had thought possible in less than one term. No matter how ridiculous or outrageous his Tweet, statement, appointment, or action, Trump has never been effectively challenged by the press, the public, or the now marginalized Congress.

Trump has been calling the shots. He never had to answer to the many legal charges against him, flouting both the Constitution and accepted norms. He continued to profit from his businesses, a constitutional violation. He never released his promised taxes. He protected all financial aspects of his life because revealing them would compromise his stated wealth and expose his fraudulent behavior. The "law and order" president was anything but. He also suffered the highest turnover in major appointments of any recent administration. Many of those appointed were in jail, under indictment, resigned in shame, or had their careers and distinguished reputations damaged by a man who demands total loyalty and offers none.

Andrew and I knew firsthand just how much of a con artist Trump was. He has masterfully used the legal system to his benefit, no matter how egregious his behavior. That same bravado got him the presidency, a goal he flirted with for years. His timing to run was impeccable. He won the required electoral college votes, but not the popular vote. The middle American blue-collar worker had grown tired of waiting for the establishment government in Washington to accurately represent them. They are still waiting.

These voters, like their counterparts throughout the Middle East, Asia, and Europe, finally recognized that their governments worked for anyone but them. The Arab Spring started in Tunisia in December of 2010 and spread to other North African nations. These governments eventually fell, and the revolutionists took over. Several nations have since moved to embrace populist, right-wing leadership. America is among them.

Trump was welcomed by the disenfranchised voter as a populist who promised to shake things up. Hillary Clinton, who purposely represented the very establishment they wanted torn down, misjudged the anger toward that establishment. Biden was an establishment candidate, but not toxic to the voters and as stated, might have carried the day in 2016.

Trump used his hyperbolic rhetoric to sway just enough voters to beat his more qualified adversary. The fact that he vilified anyone in his way meant nothing to his base. He was the bold face of their future, and nothing was going to stop him. Even losing the popular vote by more than three million was dismissed and declared as voter fraud by our new president.

Andrew and I successfully put together a series of statements to get the American voter to realize how much their earnings and constitutional rights were being taken away from them. This information was ready to go.

Could our efforts prevent Trump from winning another term? We already had a lot of information to put out there. Maybe it wouldn't take any votes from his base; they were unmovable. There is nothing Trump could ever do that would prevent them from voting for him, and he knew that. Trump also knew that his ace card was distraction. Keep his opposition angry at him. He did that well, assisted by a press and social media that seemed powerless to stop him.

Trump was a zero/one candidate. About 85% of the voting public was either for him or against him. That gave either side about 15% of eligible voters that needed to be persuaded. We identified a few voting blocks that were either on the fence or leaning away from Trump. Another block of potential voters was comprised of those who chose not to vote in 2016, the millennials, and Gen Z'ers.

The DNC and RNC each knew who they were, and each was courting this block. My job was to figure out how our organization could be utilized to make a difference. If we couldn't make a difference, should we step aside and let it just happen? Neither of us were stand-back people, we had to give it a shot and hope that we might be able to make a positive contribution.

IT WAS A BRIGHT SUNNY SATURDAY MORNING. I walked over to Sixth Avenue and hopped on the downtown D train to Brooklyn. I had decided to take some time off and visit Coney Island, where I hadn't been for years. The best part was that I could get there by subway. They were still running with dramatically reduced ridership. I decided to take the chance and hopped onboard mid-morning. I was the only one in the car, and I kept my mask on for the entire trip. This virus has dramatically changed the way we live. As much as we all must be careful, it is inexcusable that the president shuns wearing a mask and his followers listen. This behavior is destined to not bounce off him as the election gets closer. His strategy is to deny and ignore, hoping that it is either a Democratic hoax, or a danger that will by some miracle just go away as the summer unfolds.

I took my notebook to write down any ideas I might come up with for the project. The trip took about an hour on the train which, given the time of day and my direction, remained empty. The New York subway system with its 850 miles of track is the largest in the world. It logged about 5.6 million rides each workday, hitting a record of 1.7 billion rides in 2017. People often complained about it. We nevertheless have a truly massive public transportation system that actually originated as a private sector investment until the city took it over early in its construction phase. It finally opened as an important part of our public transportation system in 1904. Construction and new lines were continually added to eventually serve the communities of all four boroughs for several decades. Staten Island remains a mass transit stepchild.

I got off the train at Stillwell Avenue and decided to walk as far west as I could on the 2.7 miles of boardwalk, rebuilt in 1938 under the authority of then City Parks Commissioner, Robert Moses. Moses was a master planner and had great designs for this recreational jewel of the city, the Great Depression notwithstanding. The first park ever built on Coney Island was Luna Park. It was filled with many fun attractions from when it opened in 1903 until was destroyed by a fire in 1944.

Steeplechase Park, the only remaining amusement park at that time, was first built in 1897. It was destroyed in 1964 when the land was auctioned off by the city. It was bought by Fred Trump, father of Donald and a rising developer in Brooklyn. Trump had a series of grand plans for the area that were rejected by the city, but not before he organized and publicized a ceremony for the destruction of the famed and loved Steeplechase Pavilion of Fun. The Parks Department did not like what Trump had in mind for Coney Island and launched a campaign to stop him. Trump Sr. initiated a series of lawsuits against the city as he tried to implement his plan. He won the lawsuit but was blocked by the Board of Estimates from participating in any further development of Coney Island. Therein might lie the seeds of resentment on the part of the Trump family, and how Donald Trump learned how to use the legal system and the courts to wear his adversaries down.

★ ★ ★

REACHING THE WESTERN END OF THE BOARDWALK where it borders the Sea Gate section of Brooklyn, I turned around and walked back on the beach, one of the most beautiful stretches of pure sand along Long Island's south shore, which stretches from the southwestern tip of Brooklyn to Montauk Point, more than a hundred miles to the east. You haven't lived until you have dug your toes into the soft sand of Coney Island.

The eastern end of Coney Island is bordered by the New York Aquarium and Education Hall. I have a problem with zoos and aquariums that keep animals in an environment unlike their natural habitat. I fully respect all that dedicated professionals do to save endangered species, but marine tanks and artificial landscaped cages do not do it for me. I walked past the aquarium and headed toward Brighton Beach, now known as Odessa by the Sea, since the area has largely been taken over by Russian immigrants. For a $2.75 subway ride, or half-price if you're over 65, you find yourself in a bustling Russian village filled with Russian culture in the form of great restaurants, shops, and night clubs. I had lunch from the Kashkar Café and spent the rest of the afternoon walking along Brighton Beach Avenue. I felt like I was in a small Russian village on the Caspian Sea.

I had decided to stay the night with a Brooklyn friend who manages his Bed and Breakfast on Prospect Park West in the heart of the Park Slope section of Brooklyn. One cannot help but meet some of the most talented and interesting people at Don's home away from home. Walk through the front door, and you immediately find yourself surrounded by the charm of this quiet Italian sanctuary far from "the madding crowd." Those sitting around the large table will be discussing politics, literature, art, or music. The topics are ever-changing, and the level of discussion is always top notch. If music is on the unplanned agenda, prepare yourself for a marvelous cello, piano, or violin recital, often with accompaniment.

My evening did not disappoint.

I got up early Sunday morning wanting to take a walk around nearby Prospect Park, first opened in 1867. It was the last park to be designed and built by the partnership of Olmsted and Vaux, America's most famous urban park designers and landscapers. Prospect Park's 526 acres are a magical sanctuary bordered on the west by the bricks and mortar of Park Slope's glorious late-nineteenth-century brownstones, one of which I owned and lived in for thirty-five years. The park was originally designed so that no matter where one strolled, not a building or manmade edifice was in sight. While joggers and dog walkers dominated the park on weekday mornings and evenings, on the weekends, a multi-ethnic explosion of picnickers, cricket matches, softball and ultimate frisbees games, and frolicking children enjoy Long Meadow. Long Meadow has claimed to be the longest uninterrupted green space in any urban park in America. It is also where the Battle of Long Island took place in 1776 when the Continental Army was defeated by Hessian mercenaries hired by the British.

I walked around the full 3.6 miles of the park perimeter, exiting on the Grand Army Plaza with its monument dedicated to the Civil War. I headed up Eastern Parkway, also designed by Olmsted and Vaux, toward the Brooklyn Museum. The team of Olmsted and Vaux were the inventors of the concept of a parkway. They designed a four-lane, two-way highway, bordered by a wide strip of green grass, lined with benches where nineteenth century Brooklynites could watch the horse-drawn carriages pass. Built before air conditioning, these benches and green spaces provided socially active escapes from hot Brooklyn apartments. What made a parkway unique was the one-way service street built on the outside of the green space, allowing local residents to park and enter their homes. Eastern Parkway, finished in 1874, runs for more than four miles and was the very first such Parkway ever built.

Entering the Brooklyn Museum, I found myself wandering among the many wonderful exhibits and the new and unrecognized monuments of art and culture. As my time was short, I decided to visit the galleries dedicated to Rodin, one of my all-time favorite sculptors. I wanted to end my Brooklyn weekend in the Botanical Gardens and the Japanese Hill and Pond Garden, a majestically serene slice of nature designed for meditation and thought. I have spent hours in this area of exquisite homage to Japanese culture, handsomely carved out of the Brooklyn Gardens.

Sitting by the pond, I let myself drift back to my team and our project. The world had changed since Andrew and I had first conceived of our idea. We needed to look at it from an entirely different perspective.

Using the best contemporary technology, we wanted our message to be directed to the average American and not tied to educational or economic levels. We wanted truth and clarity, without any political or profit motive getting in the way. Over the years, Andrew and I had already saturated professional journals with research. We considered it our job to get our message out to as many people as technology allowed. We needed to use every tool available to reach those who get the bulk of their information from social media.

Most adults grew up thinking that America was the best, most modern, and strongest of nations and do not see how far we have moved off the superpower highway. The most visible aspect of our decline is witnessed in the increasing income and wealth gaps and in our persistent racism, both of which are rapidly becoming flash points of social unrest. It is not too late, but we must first recognize that much needs to be done if we are to return to the envy of the world for what we do domestically and for our foreign trading partners. That recognition must first be cemented in the hearts of the voters.

We knew that the information we had compiled was readily available and not from any illegal or dubious source. In fact, most of it was published. Our problem was our audience. We were not going to exclude anyone from accessing our message. It was that simple. However, getting to those who do not normally vote, or who are committed to a way of thinking that has prevented them from other, factual information is not easy.

We realized that we would need to employ some sophisticated search and hack programs, much like the Russians and others had done during the 2016 election. Despite the fact that we would be spreading nothing but true, verified, and properly vetted data and information, the means to reach our target audience would stretch normal methods to their limit.

To protect our team and message, we would have to operate below the radar. Authorities would be doing everything they could to find us, and I needed to protect us from arrest while we kept our message flowing. Hacking, regardless of its purpose is a felony and the penalties can be far more severe than anyone, except me, on our team are prepared to endure.

Our project was designed and ready to be rolled out. We knew that we were at a critical point and had precious little time. What we had not understood was that the 2016 voter saw the problem differently, and much sooner than we had. They saw Trump's presidential campaign as their opportunity. Those who had felt left out of the growth equation knew it and did not care how crude, unprepared, or brash a candidate he was. In fact, that is what they loved about him. They loved that he was going to clean the swamp and bring government back to the people. His loyalists believed he alone was going to "Make America Great Again," a clear message that everyone could understand and rally behind. He did neither and some say he never intended to. It was that inevitable betrayal that would, once recognized by these voters, cause them to once again feel that the system was rigged against them. We wanted to get to them before Trump dumped them like he has done most who hitch onto his wagon.

As I sat at the edge of the Japanese garden, gazing over the beautifully landscaped hill and pond, I came to realize that our nation has two major problems: our deterioration and the rise of a classical dictator hell-bent on serving those with invisible wealth and power. It did not take long for many to realize that Trump duped the 2016 voters with tremendous help from the Russians, all-powerful social media, and a market-share driven press. Most importantly, the wealthy power grabbers saw him as the key to their long-held goal of conservative domination.

Did the nation have enough responsible people to stop this juggernaut? Would professionals who saw the danger be able to stop the path toward a dictatorship? Those who have seen the larger picture noticed a pattern of behaviors that centered on getting away with outrageous actions and consistent untruths. Human history is riddled with such dictatorial leaders that have left a well-defined anti-democratic agenda in their wakes. Does Trump have a political sword hanging over his head that would eventually bring him, like all tyrants, down? These are the reasons Andrew and I need to take on the challenge of our project to encourage and inform that misguided voter. We want to join those who recognize these dangers we face and are willing to confront them.

Republicans and Democrats alike were beginning to think that 2020 would be among the most contested elections in history. They also knew that every illegal, unethical, and possible trick in the books would be put into play by the Trump team to keep their man in the White House. They have no shame, and any objective observer of Trump sees this to be true, the evidence was overwhelming. Trump was reshaping the Republican party into something unimaginable.

The shift further to the right was being orchestrated by the president. I recognized the fact that we all live in "a bubble." Bubbles are set by birth, wealth, race, education, luck, and sometimes by choice. Human nature, and who we become as a person, has as many divergences as we have people. Statistical norms were, however, defined and created because they exist. There are some broad-brush attributes that set the left comfortably apart from the right. These are observable tendencies and do not apply to everyone. Broadly speaking, lefties are more in touch with the Social Contract that seeks to create a good life for everyone.

This is not the philosophy I observe with most conservatives. Conservatives equate being well off as testament to their personal effort. Generally speaking, in their view, America offers equal opportunities for anyone with traditional family values who is willing to work hard. Ultimately the reason for these class and income differences begins with the experiences that each of us witness as children and the world we are born into. There are those on all sides who, for a host of reasons, do not fall into that mold and do think differently. While not impossible, it is hard to be born into a level of comfort where all basic needs are there and available, making it impossible to think that life could be otherwise. If you were not lucky and born into a life of perpetual deprivation, it is equally hard to focus on anything other than a daily search for basic needs. Life is experienced as a perpetual struggle to survive. Some days you succeed, others you do not and go to bed hungry.

My purpose was to gauge reactions and not seek conversion. I gave up on that a long time ago, especially when it comes to Trump followers. Political conversations differ greatly than those of a generation ago in that dialogue today is a four-letter word. People are not comfortable talking to others of a different political persuasion. We are living at a time when many of us have little patience with those who do not think like us. It's easier to say, "Let's not discuss politics," or "We never talk about religion. We will never agree on abortion." Such attitudes solve nothing. I wish I could follow along but knowing that as long as we continue to leave large segments of our people behind, we will never again be the glorious nation we only think we are.

"**WHEN I FIND MYSELF IN TIMES OF TROUBLE,** Mother Nature comes to me, speaking words of wisdom..." Why did that song enter my mind at this moment? Why did I hear Mother Nature and not Mother Mary? Why did I not hear "let it be?"

It is not in my nature to let anything "be" if it's not working. Mother Nature is my creator, my symbol of divinity, my go-to spirit for wisdom, relief, and peace. At this moment, in this inviting natural space before me, I realized that I was looking at the political, social, and economic problems we were facing all wrong. People blamed the crash of the stock market for the Depression. People blamed Bin Laden and 9/11 for our going to war with Iraq. Some people say climate change is merely the earth going through its normal cycles. People have blamed the Chinese for Covid-19. I have been blaming Trump for the mess our nation is in. None of these things is to blame; they are just warnings. We have been confusing cause and effect. The market crashed largely because investors could see something was wrong with our economy and they needed to preserve their cash. 9/11 happened because of huge cultural and political differences and a lack of tolerance for a people who think differently than we do. A pandemic has been predicted by science for decades, although not due to eating bats or unclean markets. Climate change is nature fighting back for its land and space that is being taken away as a result of our disrespect for the balance between nature and mankind. Donald Trump is not the cause of our problems; he is, however, the result of a nation that has lost its way.

The election of Trump was our Arab Spring wake-up call to get back to basics as a nation in terms of policy and dealing with the more dangerous attack by nature. We've ignored our workers. We've sacrificed fundamental services that are a right for every citizen for the primary goal of profit and market share. Education, healthcare, national defense, communications, and transportation have become profit centers that do not focus on planning for our future and serving our nation's needs. We have allowed social media giants to create wealthy entrepreneurs at the expense of our democracy. Domestic and foreign enemies distort the institutions we have built to protect and preserve our constitutional democracy. We cannot put the blame on Trump, the rise of white supremacists, corporate greed and corruption, China, Russia, or the coronavirus for these troubled times; we have to blame ourselves. A representative democracy cannot survive, much less thrive, if we the people are not engaged with what is happening every day. We can, however, blame Trump for using these serious problems to his political advantage.

When less than 40% of our eligible voters go to the polls on off presidential years, and only around 60% come out on presidential years, we have deliberately abdicated our responsibility and our obligation as citizens. We deserve the government we never wanted but have.

We love to complain about a multitude of issues we see as unfair. We fail to recognize that unless we choose leaders who are of like minds, these issues will never go away.

So much needs to be done. We need to take a hard look at our tax and regulation laws and reshape them to foster economic growth, but with an eye to eliminating the insidious inequality that has reduced us to a nation of haves and have-nots. Black lives do matter as does the respect we show each other, regardless of our race, religion, or culture.

I believe that the better informed we are and the larger and more inclusive we allow our bubble to grow, the more we will understand each other and appreciate our differences. I do believe, generally speaking, the bubble of an educated liberal is a larger and more socially inclusive one than that of a diehard conservative. In Plato's cave, one can choose to live a life in the comfortable darkness of the cave or choose to crawl our way to the top and suffer the blinding conflict of enlightenment. We have all made many choices. I no longer want to talk only with those who live exclusively in my bubble. I yearn to find a way inside the bubbles of those with whom I disagree. I now want to find out why I disagree.

My unconscious state was broken by the laughter of children. It needed and took a moment to figure out where I was and where my mind had gone, I had somehow entered a world of active meditation, assuming there is such a thing. This level of introspection has happened to me before and it never ceases to enlighten. To a Zen Buddhist, this is a moment of Satori. I knew one thing. Our tiny team might not matter one bit. Having put all these thoughts together in my mind, I knew what we had to do. I decided, at that moment, on the banks of that serene pond, that I have the means to join this fight. I must do everything I can to make the opportunities for the next generation at least as bountiful as life was for mine. We had a lot of work to do, and I needed to get to it.

CHAPTER 10

MAY 2020

As I ENTERED MY BUILDING, Mr. Bonaparte handed me a small parcel. There was no return address, which made me suspicious, so I asked him who'd dropped it off. He replied that it was on his desk when he came back from a break. I waited until I was in the apartment to open it. Remembering the anthrax letters a few decades ago, I put on one of my COVID masks with goggles and rubber gloves and held the package as far from my face as possible. I kind of laughed at myself for my rising paranoia, but given events throughout the world and at home, much less to me, one cannot be too careful.

Nothing exploded, but the contents were a total surprise. There was a burner phone and a short note: *Watch out. You are on a 24/7 watchlist.*

Okay. That scared me. I immediately went out to find an increasingly rare pay phone. They are slated for removal, and I found one of the last ones in my neighborhood on Fourteenth Street. Given all that has been happening to me, I was afraid to use my personal cell to make this call. I phoned Ari to request a code red meeting. Surprisingly, he picked up on the first ring. After my brief description of what had just happened, he gave me an address and time to meet the following day. He reminded me to proceed with caution and bring everything that came with the package.

I looked at my watch and looked around to see if anyone was hanging around the phone booth. I could not see anyone, but I thought there could possibly be an electronic tracer somewhere on me. I waited a few more minutes, looked at my watch again, and walked toward a local diner I used to frequent. It was now only open for a few hours a day, like so many restaurants. I sat down at an outside table, took out my paper, and ordered coffee and dessert. I needed to be sure that I was not being followed.

It was getting so hard to keep up with the news. I was drained from Trump's constant tweets and rantings, the COVID-19 data, and daily crises. The Floyd protests began at the end of the month and were beginning to spread worldwide—and they were heavily attended by white people. The *New York Times* released a story on a bounty Russia put on American soldiers in Afghanistan. The president denied that he knew about it despite confirmation offered by those who managed the president's daily brief. Trump gave no warnings or threats to the Russians once the story was verified. The economy was beginning to tank as Wall Street numbers increased towards record levels, giving proof that Wall Street is not the economy, as many who know better tend to think.

Both Trump and McConnell made statements that there should be no stigma for not wearing masks. This position created a strong reaction to those who are on the front line of the pandemic. Science and the professionals have stated in no uncertain terms that wearing a mask and respecting social distancing is our only defense against this airborne virus, at least until we have a proven vaccine. All but nineteen states held their Democratic primary votes, and Biden was marching through them unopposed.

By the time I finished the paper, I saw no one lingering, so I paid up and headed home. I had to prepare myself for my meeting with Ari.

Not surprisingly, I slept restlessly. For some reason, my actions had made me a target. Maybe I had not fooled the Feds after all. I could not imagine what I might have done that would have made me a suspect. I dressed in clothes that I had not worn for months. I worried that my clothes might have been bugged. I left my apartment carrying only my wallet, the burner phone, and the package I received. I carried none of my own electronics in my briefcase, as Ari had instructed. I took the downtown 2 train, which was empty, watching carefully for a tail. Seeing nothing out of the ordinary, I got out at Chambers Street and sat on a bench as two uptown trains passed by. It was after rush hour, and I was alone on the platform. Maybe the tail had not been set up yet? Maybe the warning was a hoax? No. The burner phone made it real. Ari would know what to do. I took the next uptown train, having already reversed my jacket and put on a hat.

Switching to the 1 local at Columbus Circle, I got off at 116th Street and walked to Amsterdam and the Columbia University Student Center. Ari had chosen to meet outside, and, if necessary, leave separately in any direction. Most importantly, we could easily spot anyone who did not seem to fit into that location. Students and academics of every generation on campus have a certain look, not easily replicated by someone assigned to follow citizens around. I chose a bench, sat down, and opened the *New York Times*.

Ari showed up looking more academic than me. So much for my theory about being followed. I think he has a credible disguise for anything. As he sat down next to me, I placed the package with the note and phone on the bench between us, under my newspaper. He looked it over, pushed several buttons, put it in his pocket, then handed me a device about the size of a pack of cigarettes along with another phone.

"This is another burner for you to use when you need to call me. Do not use it for anything else. I will activate the one you received with an untraceable email and text address. I will extract the unit's phone number and set it up with two individually coded speed dial numbers: one for whoever sent it to us and one for me and you. We will be able to call or text without worry. I will also try to ID the sender." At least I would now be able to call or text Ari any time. The other device he gave me was a tracer used to locate electronic bugs anywhere on or around me. If the light blinked red, it would show that I was bugged. If it was green, I was safe. To function properly, the device needed to be fewer than six inches from any item of concern.

"Do not even try to disarm anything you find," Ari said. "Just leave it behind and replace whatever it is attached to with another item. If you want to be more secure, put anything bugged into your oven, that will help hide it from surveillance. I will try to figure out who gave this to you but, I am sure that it will be untraceable. This person is scared and vulnerable. We must protect their identity as well as we do our own. We do not want whoever is onto you to realize that you know this person even exists."

Ari told me to move the device he just gave me all around my body. I did so, and the light remained green throughout the exercise.

"Let me know if you find a bug," he said. "What else did you want to talk to me about?"

"Well," I said, "you know that I've been building a database with information on the state of our nation. I want to find social media sites to reproduce these data in an entertaining format that would appeal to the average American—including graphic art and animated video. My goal is to help folks understand the depth of decay in our social, economic, and political systems. While nothing I plan should be considered threatening, I know that releasing this information in such an accessible way will upset a lot of important people who would prefer that it remain out of reach. We will also have to do some hacking to reach many of the voters not on the normal grid. The team I've set up, thanks to you, can take care of the technical side of things.

"I long ago decided to keep everything top secret so that our equipment, labs, and location couldn't be discovered. Those who might want to shut us down would love access to our databases and, I suspect, to learn how we've organized our files. I originally thought that the visit I got from the FBI was about this project, but how could they have found out about it? I've only told you and Andrew!"

"I kind of guessed what you were up to on my own," interjected Ari. "I was glad that my guys, Yosef and Lavi, were available to help you. They happen to share your progressive values, and I'm sure they can help with the presentation as well." Ari uncharacteristically gazed up at the clear blue sky. "It baffles me that you got targeted. From your description of the questioning by the Feds, I think they were only fishing and had nothing that could warrant a 24/7 tail. I assume you followed our plan to get up here without being followed. If they really are watching you, it means you must be bugged. Maybe...someone has been hacking into your web searches and downloads. But that's a stretch since they'd need some intensive priors before getting to that level of surveillance. I should know more once I've checked out this phone and the note."

"Thanks, Ari. I 've recently been engaged in more searches than usual. I'm also following Trump's tweets, trying to figure out how he comes up with all these initiatives. I honestly don't think he's that smart—he must be getting help from someone. I have no proof, but I suspect that a few of those far right think tanks are feeding him ideas. There are plenty of Trump followers out there wanting to help him succeed." I began to recite all that had been bothering me about Trump's dictatorial and outright fascist behavior. I admit I got carried away, ranting on for five minutes, when I noticed that Ari was laughing.

"What's wrong with you?" I asked him. "I know this president and his henchmen get under your skin, too. Why are you laughing at me?"

"You're just like all liberals. You can't imagine how such a man even exists, much less how he got to the Oval Office. The way that you feel about Trump is the same way McConnell and company felt about Obama."

"That was almost totally a racist reaction—they weren't critiquing his incompetence."

"Yes, Benson, I'm as angry as you are. I'm not really laughing at you. Trump continues to do so many outrageous things without anyone really caring or calling him out. We used to call Reagan the Teflon president, but he was nothing compared to this guy."

"Such titles need not be mutually exclusive."

"You, my dear friend, have fallen into the same trap as the media, his base, and most importantly, all those Never Trumpers who think that all their moaning and groaning matters to him. He doesn't care what's said about him. If his name's in the press, he's winning. How much free publicity did someone say he got in 2016? I remember hearing that he got two or three billion dollars' worth of print and airtime without spending a nickel of his own money. We might as well have made the media his campaign manager."

"You're right about that," I said. "I blame his craziness on the press as much as I do him. They cover every word he says, not because it's news but because they rely on advertising sales and market share is critical to them."

"Agreed," said Ari. "Trump's base is encouraged by every negative story. He simply denies it as fake news and finds a sound bite to neutralize any comment or question he does not like. If that doesn't work, he fires the person if he can, humiliates them, or devises an insulting nickname. That is the man you guys are trying to beat. And you are playing by his rules. Trust me, this will never work. Democrats have never confronted a creep like this, and frankly you do not seem to have a clue as to how to beat him."

I sat there humbled because I knew that he was right. You can't beat an enemy if you play his game; you need to create your own strategy. You must neutralize your enemy before he can neutralize you: *The Art of War* remains an eternal teacher. "You're right, Ari. The one thing I decided to do was to set up a sidebar to our original plan to educate and motivate voters. I'm thinking of adding an attack against Trump to our project. I've researched how the RNC spends its advertising money, especially for its online campaign. I also investigated the Russians' 2016 efforts on Facebook and Twitter. The experts think that they'll do the same this year. I've learned that it's not as hard as I thought it would be to tap into foreign efforts and match them point by point. Using the same social media platforms that Trump uses, our goal is to get *verifiable* and *truthful* messages out to the same people that the Trump campaign is courting."

"Well," chuckled Ari, "*now* we know why you're being flagged. Your searches on the Russians opened up some politically sensitive doors. The Trump campaign, and now you, and probably every intelligence officer knows how indebted Trump is to the Russians. You, my friend, are a marked man."

How could I have been so stupid? "Wait a minute. Do you honestly think that I'm the only civilian looking into all this?" I asked, stupefied.

"Of course not, but you were already on their radar."

"Okay, guilty," I sighed. "But I won't let that stop me. What I need to think about is how to separate our effort from the pack, how to take an entirely different approach. Some ideas are already coming to mind, but they are going to take some time. I think I need to sit down with the team and explain my plan. Do you think it's possible to set up an in-person meeting without being followed? I would prefer to be invisible and not have to clear customs on either side. I wish I could figure out who's onto me. If it is not the Feds or National Intelligence, who are they?"

"Look back to your book and journal purchases, your Russian research, and your monitoring of alt-right groups," Ari advised. "You mentioned that you've searched the Southern Poverty Law Center for a comprehensive list of rightwing groups. It would be simple for the government to monitor your search engines from their computers. Your computers are on their watchlist, and once you're there, you stay forever."

"I honestly don't think I'm any more active than the Feds themselves. As a published academic, I would think that any research I'm doing would provide more than enough cover. Do you think they have tapped into the secure laptop we set up?" I was referring to the one that Ramon got me.

"It's possible. I'll check it out. Your searches wouldn't stand out if you were publishing in the field, but you have not, at least to my knowledge, published anything from these searches."

"Right again. I should've been more discreet and use only the secure laptop and the university library computers. I have a completely different username and password at NYU. Maybe I should use their computers more? Would you see if you can get a corporate jet to get me to Europe? I can have the team set up a meeting point, unless you want to contact them yourself. I'd like you to come with me. I'll have to plan a stopover in Switzerland to pick up some cash as well. I'll also take your advice and redesign my approach to this project. Cooler heads need to prevail, and I do not want to go through this if we can't be successful."

"Okay, I'll see if I can line up a jet and get a price to you. I'm not sure I should be on that plane with you, but I'll think about it. If I could Facetime into the meeting, I think I'd be able to be more helpful on the ground. I'll get back to you on that. I do agree that if you go, no one can know you've gone."

"Okay," I said, "thank you so much. Don't worry about the price—our safety, especially from COVID, and invisibility are all that matters. You really are an incredibly special person, or shall I call you an asset?" I laughed.

"Call me whatever you want," Ari laughed. "Let's go. We have a lot to do. I'll get back to you. I should be able to get everything set up. I will have the burner delivered to Mr. Bonaparte with instructions on how to use it. Leave the laptop with him as well. Just remember, our new DC contact and I are the only outgoing numbers you will have on that burner. Use the other one I just gave you to communicate with Europe and me. I think it's best to keep them separate."

"You know Mr. Bonaparte? How the hell did that happen? I can't believe how naïve I am. Holy shit! Will you ever stop knocking me on my ass?"

"I've actually known him longer than I've known you," said Ari. "I had two particularly good operatives in your building who I worked with for years. Mike and Charles were a smart and talented couple. Unfortunately, Mike died of AIDS. Charles never got over the loss. He sold their apartment and moved away. I miss those guys a lot."

"I knew them both and admired them, too. They were so much fun to be around, and you are right, they were smart and devoted to each other. I had no idea that they were your assets."

"You were not supposed to know, and yes, they were very much on the right side of things. They even suggested *you* to me as a possible asset."

"Really? Given all that has apparently been going on right under my nose, I think I'd fail the snoop test. Ari, the virus adds another complication to our plans. The last thing we need is for one of us to get sick. Time is moving fast, and now that we are going to participate in the election, we only have a few months to get everything online."

Ari agreed. "I need to be careful since I am on the run most of the time. I have a driver on call 24/7 so I can stay out of public transportation. It is so helpful that I can now legitimately wear a mask anywhere I go. Life is strange! Take care of yourself, professor. I'll get back to you. I will contact the team myself and set the meeting; you might be too hot."

"First time anyone has accused me of that," I laughed.

Ari disappeared as quickly as always, except this time he left laughing. As is our custom, I never leave a meeting at the same time as him. This time, I deliberately wanted to remain seated for a while. I needed to digest what Ari had just said to me. He was right. I was falling into the same trap as many of us who care about what's happening in our country. Getting angry at Trump is exactly what he wants us to do. Trump, like Giuliani, thrives on conflict. The angrier we get, the more attractive he is to his base, and the more energized they become. He's the kind of person who becomes depressed if he's ignored by the press. He might complain about the press all the time, but they are his go-to team as the purveyor of his "fake news."

I let the sun warm me. I knew that there was an answer, and I felt like a cat that's fallen into a rain barrel, clawing at the water, and unable to get out. I could see daylight, but it was beyond my reach. I took a deep breath and exhaled very slowly, closed my eyes, and let the sounds of nature fill my consciousness. My mind cleared, and I found myself in that fifth state of Zen, defined as nothingness, the place where much wisdom has been discovered. I deliberately give thanks to my sensei each time I move into that zone of enlightenment.

I do not know how long I ruminated there in my own private world in the middle of the quiet and closed-down Columbia University campus.

When I opened my eyes, I saw a cluster of young people walking by laughing and joking with each other. To my delight, they all wore masks. They were teenagers, seemingly without a care, enrolled in one of the finest universities in the world. They were smart and privileged, but still they were kids who had only a rudimentary idea of the world they inherited and are charged with fixing. And just then everything fell into place. These young people represent the single strongest reason why I'm doing all this, and they are the reason I cannot fail.

My anger, and that of a lot of "woke" people, ought not be directed at a Trump, McConnell, Putin, Kim Jong-un, or any of these dictatorial types. We must direct it at ourselves. We are the citizens who haven't been active players in our democracy. We, the American people, are the only agents of change still standing, and we very well might be our democracy's last hope.

Memories pop into my head at the oddest times. As I watched those students, I tried to see myself as an undergraduate. Traveling back to my student days, I was never that free, not for a moment. I was much older. I was jealous and admittedly a bit sad, knowing that my student days were filled with doubt about my own abilities and anxiety over the social unrest of that time. I had little time to reflect, and none whatsoever to party or hang out. I remembered something I should have told Ari. When I was a graduate student at NYU, I was approached by someone who said she was a lawyer and asked if I'd be willing to help in the case of a Brooklyn and Queens landlord who'd been charged by the government with racial discrimination. He had his brokers tell black or brown applicants there were no apartments available in the buildings he owned. They were also told that the rentals were double the actual rate, a tactic used as a further discouragement. The building was owned by Donald Trump's father. Fred Trump's brokers had been instructed to code applications of minorities with a C or 9.

One of the tactics the DOJ used to prove their case was to have a black applicant go undercover to apply for an apartment. He was told that nothing was available and to go to some other building, usually another Trump building where they did allow minorities. Soon after, usually on the same day, a white person, also undercover, went to the same broker and asked about the same unit. He was invariably shown several choices. I did this as the white applicant a couple of times for the government. They paid us for our time and expenses.

Eventually, the DOJ filed a lawsuit that Trump decided to fight. The family hired Roy Cohn, of Senator Joe McCarthy fame, to defend them. Trump and company eventually lost the case but did not have to admit to guilt. That was proof to the Trumps that they had won, despite a series of legal constraints. I honestly do not know if my name was in the court documents. I think that I conducted about three or four interviews for the government, all in Brooklyn. It was soon after this case that Donald took over his father's company.

Another Trump incident unfolded in 1974. It involved two huge lots in Manhattan over the Westside Railyards. One stretched from Thirtieth to Thirty-Ninth Streets and another from Fifty-ninth to Seventy-Second Streets. Trump decided to break from his father's real estate holdings and make a name for himself in Manhattan. He was twenty-eight at the time and becoming a well-known gad about town in his gold, chauffeur-driven Cadillac with vanity plates. Trump had secured an exclusive option on the Thirty-fourth Street parcel and put it in contention for the proposed New York Convention Center. Ed Koch had just been elected mayor and was setting up his administration when the foreclosure of the Railyards was scheduled for bid. The decision about which of the tracks would be the best location for the Convention Center was to be made by a special commission. Trump was negotiating to have his land chosen and pressuring everyone involved. A lot of money was to be made by the winner.

Soon after he was elected, Mayor Koch had asked me to take a pro bono seat on the board of a group of retired executives who provided free business advice to budding entrepreneurs in the city. I remember a discussion on the yards at a meeting chaired by the mayor and some of Trump's legal team. Trump and his Thirty-Fourth Street property came up. I reminded those at the meeting about the racism that had plagued the Trumps. Everyone was aware of what had happened, so my comment was not news, but I'm sure I was right to remind them of Trump's unsavory dealings. I have no idea if my input ever got back to Trump. In any case, he eventually won the bidding when his track was chosen. He made a lot of money on that deal.

I was far from a major player in this game. Not being a politician, I freely accepted any position with an administration if I thought I could help the city I loved. Having watched Donald Trump for many years, I know that when he sets his sights on a goal, he will leave no stone unturned. He hates to lose and will hound anyone he thinks is not on his side, especially if he thinks they could prevent him from a win.

I have no reason to think that my current problem with the authorities is related to my interactions in these Trump-related affairs. Maybe I did piss someone off who wanted to make my life difficult.

I do, however, know that these young people bouncing down the path toward Broadway, are too young to grasp what's been happening to our country over the last forty-plus years. They were likely unaware of just how much was going on at this moment that could change their lives, depending on how the election would go.

These students most certainly knew that our system is broken. What they probably did not yet know was that it was up to them to fix it. They lacked only guidance and a working knowledge of what was happening. Then and only then would they be on the right track to recapture our nation's core values. At this point, I trust no other sector to get the job done. I wanted to reboot the system. I particularly wanted to energize the students; I had concluded long ago that our future as a democracy rests in their hands.

I stood up, happier than I had been for a long time. I needed to get home and to completely redefine my mission. My spirit and mind have not been this clear since I first experienced the beauty of learning as an undergraduate student. The world suddenly looked a whole lot more hopeful. I gave an invisible thank you to these students for my memories.

★ ★ ★

CHAPTER 11

JULY 2020

I'D BEEN WORKING AT HOME since early morning. Around 3:30, after a short nap, I took a walk. I wanted to find a quiet place to grab a hamburger and think. I also wanted to see if the warning I'd received had any merit. I made a point of being as obvious as possible to anyone hovering in the shadows. Maybe the package was sent to me by mistake? As dedicated as I am to being an agent of positive change, I am truly a tiny fish in a big pond. Nothing I've done should warrant anyone wanting to follow me around.

But the reality was that we were living in a period of tremendous social and political discord. People should have been working together to deal with COVID -19, recognize the severity of our country's racism, and harness the economic power of our nation, but we were embroiled in senseless, self-serving political battles over power and money. These conflicts were draining our potential and creating a cloud of suspicion intended to set us against each other. Were we really willing to accept an Orwellian world that pitted one group against another where only one winner can prevail, and the loser is relegated to obscurity? Compromise, trust, and hope have been usurped by greed, corruption, power, and money.

I found myself on University Place in front of what is now the Reservoir Bar, a sports bar on 70 University Place. The owners know me well since I have been going to this place since I was a graduate student at NYU when it was called Bradley's. Bradley Cunningham was a major Big Apple jazz enthusiast and Bradley's was the go-to place for all Jazz musicians after their gigs. The Big Apple was a name given the City of New York by New Orleans Jazz musicians. Some would come in just to have a drink, others to practice together and go over new tunes, some just to chill until the sun came up when they would drift out and go home. I would often drop in around two in the morning just to listen to them and be among the greats. Bradley died in 1988 and Wendy, his wife tried to keep the place going but finally had to sell it in 1996. She would only sell to another bartender. The Reservoir looks pretty much the same as it was back in the seventies, and a favorite go-to place for me when I need to think. Tonight, was one such night. I chose a table next to the legendary bay window that has been there since the bar was Bradley's. I ordered a single malt scotch, one cube, and a twist of lemon and took out my steno pad. I knew I was in for a rough night. Tony, the owner was on duty and tending bar. There were only a few customers, properly disbursed throughout the tables of this venerable establishment. Tony brought my drink to my table.

Reflecting on our nation's past, I could not help but wonder how the vitality of the peaceful and prosperous postwar period had morphed into the America we were now inhabiting. Back then, we could not get enough of Detroit's creativity embodied in the swept back, winged, gadget-rich cars that filled our streets and the parking lots of our factories, malls and schools. It was a period when working-class men labored in a wide range of factories where backroom engineers were constantly pouring out a bevy of new kitchen appliances, televisions, and electronics all focused on making our lives better. The best part is that they were made in America and affordable to Americans.

This prosperous, peaceful time was ripped apart by Vietnam, Watergate, political and racial assassinations, the civil rights movement, and, later, the oil embargo. Any one of those events could have easily brought our nation down, but none of them did. There was a lot of anger, protest, and social upheaval to be sure, but our roots as a nation somehow held everything together, and we managed to pull through. Our country was wounded, but not broken, and most importantly, we found a workable path forward. That was a time when all sides were still at least talking to each other.

In private discussions over the years, I could not help but notice that very few people had perceived the level of national disfunction I saw so clearly. How was it that most of us simply went about our days barely paying attention to the fact that our government and our nation was under a massive attack from within? More recently Trump, the Distractor-in-Chief has succeeded in pounding us into numbness with his relentless tweets? His reelection obsession has denied the levels of human suffering we were witnessing from COVID-19? That strategy denial has largely been accepted by millions of Americans who, despite the number of cases and deaths, are willing to not wear a mask. Who else would or could politicize such a minor safety mechanism, and why would rational people accept such a thing? Are we so confident in our system that we know it will survive and rebound? Do we just not care?

What most of us had failed to notice, especially since 2016, was that the seeds for a vastly different Orwellian world had begun, decades ago, to creep into almost every aspect of our lives. Technology gave industry and government a whole new basket of weapons with seemingly unbridled capacity to reshape who we were and would become as a nation. 9/11 and the government's reaction to global terrorism convinced the public that oversight was necessary as it fundamentally altered our civil and human rights. The Patriot Act in 2003 gave the government and industry license to watch civilians with unprecedented oversight and surveillance. This power created a whole new technological gateway of control and potential abuse over our privacy.

This represented a structural shift in how we would subsequently function as a representative democracy.

The data our team had been compiling showed how economic and political power had become more concentrated into the hands of the few and taken directly from the pocketbooks of the many. The price in dollars and lives showed how pervasive these changes were. The Bush/Cheney years were absorbed by a hugely expensive unnecessary war that cost us our standing in the world, especially when viewed on the heels of Vietnam.

Wars are paid for by taxing the people. Bush/Cheney knew that their war had to be financed differently so they borrowed begged and stole funds from anywhere they could grab them, including, unauthorized appropriations from the military, debt-based loans from China and borrowing against our Social Security surplus. It was a war that benefited Halliburton, Cheney's company before he joined the Bush 2000 ticket. Haliburton earned close to $40 billion in Iraq-related federal contracts. Blackwater Worldwide security firm was the recipient of a $350 million contract, hired by the State Department during the Iraq War. Their contract was revoked following a September 2017 incident that resulted in the killing of fourteen Iraqi civilians.

The people who benefit from war are rarely those who are sent to fight it. Estimates on the cost of the Bush/Cheney wars run from eight hundred billion to $2.3 trillion. This money was borrowed against future national debt, since, as the Bush administration realized, there could be no traditional war tax to pay for this highly unpopular war. That was a massive off-budget debt that Obama inherited from his predecessor and not generally known by the public.

Since his inauguration, Trump's actions on any given day would have been considered censorship and possible impeachable offenses had Hillary held the office and committed such acts. Why was the bar lowered for him? How did these egregious acts get a pass?

The whole world was experiencing the impact of climate change. The droughts, fires, floods, and violent storms were pounding the South and Gulf Coast states as never before. The Philippines, Japan, and other nations in Southeast Asia were also being battered; Australia and the West Coast of the US were on fire. All of these things leaving wide swaths of devastation, death and destruction in their wake, and the climate deniers, encouraged by our president, continued to move forward as if nothing was happening. 2019 was declared the hottest on record, and it looks like 2020 will prove to be even hotter.

America mourned the death of Representative John Lewis, an icon of the Civil Rights movement. The Black Lives Matter movement increased an awareness of the number of military bases, monuments, and plaques we have scattered about the country honoring Confederates who committed treason against the Union all in support of maintaining slavery as a valid economic model of their success.

As I sat sipping my scotch, my increasingly upset mind began bouncing from one crisis we were living to another. I began writing down notes as these thoughts came to me. They were violently ricocheting off the dark paneled walls, through my head and onto my rapidly filling steno pad. My body was suddenly beginning to feel very heavy and the events that have dominated me for the past several years were randomly falling onto the pad. I felt as though I was being whiplashed.

I have always questioned and studied the forces that drove our lives. Years ago, the questions and problems were difficult but manageable. Working with colleagues, we were always able to help decision makers formulate solutions that worked. Lately, the intensity and depth of the problems are far more complicated and life threatening. The game had changed, and solutions were far more difficult to define. Chaos was winning and reason had no place on the board. I was feeling the pressure like never before.

America was suffering a pandemic of global proportions. To date, more than 119,000 Americans had died from COVID-19, which Trump labeled as a hoax created by the Democratic party to deny him reelection. When he was not encouraging Americans to inject household disinfectants into their bodies, he was ranting that Obama left the cupboard bare of medical supplies inside the agency that Obama himself had set up to meet the challenges of such a pandemic. That would be the same agency that Trump abolished soon after his inauguration.

Our COVID-related deaths had begun to level out somewhat, shifting from blue to red states such as Texas, Florida and the Carolinas. More than a thousand Americans were dying every day. Scientists were warning us that we must prepare for another wave of cases as the fall emerged. Dr. Fauci, the most respected of Trump's ineffectual COVID team, warned us that we were making a serious mistake by not protecting ourselves with the simplest of masks and social distancing policies. Violating these actions was only going to keep that airborne virus alive as it continued to spread. We had just learned that $1.5 trillion of the CARES money allocated to help COVID suffering people and businesses had yet to be distributed. In addition, CARES money found its way into the coffers of some large companies that were already cash rich. After more than six months since the administration was first made aware of the virus's danger, we had no plan in place to protect and contain this true enemy of the people. Of note, the economy had just taken its biggest drop in recorded history, due to the impact of this rampaging and unchecked virus.

The photograph of Trump at the 2011 White House Correspondents' Association dinner suddenly slammed into my head. This was an annual affair where everyone gets roasted as part of the event, all intended to be in good humor. Obama went after Trump, who was in the audience, starting with his unfounded birther campaign which he managed to keep on the front pages for several weeks. Trump has no sense of humor and the anger in that photo of Trump should have foretold us what was going to happen. That was the moment, I think, when Trump decided to run for president. He was going to bury Obama, and nothing could stop him.

I sat back a moment and gazed out at the street. I watched New Yorkers pass by, some sauntering, others in a New York rush, all of them considerably more at ease than me. I could feel the anger welling up within me as a multitude of events since the 2016 election began to crystalize in my head.

The very day, as I sat in the Reservoir Bar, professional public health officials had testified before the Republican Senate that the president's orders to open our nation for business while the pandemic continued to rage would represent a catastrophic action on his part. Also, on this same day, the Supreme Court heard two arguments where Trump was challenging Congress's right to exercise proper oversight of the executive branch, he considered that power was his and his alone. These restraints were designed to protect the office of the president and all elected officials from undue pressure and possible blackmail on the part of a foreign nation. A second Trump-initiated court challenge concerned the president's alleged campaign payments in the form of hush money to two women who accused candidate Trump of having an affair with them.

One of the arguments offered by the administration was that the president did not have time to devote to every DA who might choose to subpoena or charge him with criminal acts. The Supreme Court was also hearing other arguments to determine the limits to presidential power. If Trump were to win any of these cases, we would have an imperial presidency, the very form of government our nation was originally set up to avoid, and exactly the stated goal of Trump's attorney general. The court split: it did not hold that grand juries could harass a president and concluded that current controls over how they proceed with a case would prevent that from happening. The court did rule 7-2 that the president did not enjoy immunity and that certain cases, including that of the Manhattan District Attorney could move forward. The president did have to comply with subpoenas requesting tax records. The court did not give the same blanket to Congress's demands for those identical documents. The court also decided that a president's actions of a personal capacity, completed while in office were not liable, however this did not extend to criminal cases where presidential immunity would not prevail.

I thought about our "longest day," when AG Barr and the DOJ suddenly announced that they had vacated the guilty plea of former NSA Director General Flynn. The fact that Flynn had already pleaded guilty on two felony counts no longer mattered to Barr. President Obama uncharacteristically came out vocally on this one and stated very clearly that this one action on the part of the attorney general was tantamount to stating that we were no longer a nation of laws. Never before in the history of the DOJ had a guilty plea been reversed. And these actions represent only what our self-absorbed, crude, thin-skinned president has done to dismantle and destroy our country in the past two days alone.

Trump downplayed the decision on his sequestered tax reports. He had been accused of creating two sets of books, as reported by many sources, most notably in a Pulitzer Prize–winning article published in the *New York Times*. One set allegedly claimed a robust value of his assets to potential lenders which were themselves in dispute as to who actually owns them. Another set establishes much lower values claimed on the very same assets when filed with the IRS.

Given his track record, my guess was that he would stall some of the arguments before the court, given how well he and McConnell have stacked the courts against the people, also given how he successfully muscled his way through impeachment, Trump's deviant behavior will not be exposed. He took his wins as a right to continue. Many of his critics feel that it's only a matter of time when someone will get a hold of his taxes. Then and only then will the world know firsthand the lengths Trump has gone to manipulate his holdings.

Tony replaced my drink with another and asked if I was okay. I looked up at this kind man and had to admit that I was not. "I am more concerned about the future of our country than ever in my life. I cannot imagine how we ended up in this rabbit hole"

"You are right Dr. Pryce. I will have to shut down in a couple of weeks if we do not get some relief. I am paying the staff from personal savings and operating at twenty-five percent capacity. If I did not own the building, I would have closed weeks ago. My tenants upstairs can barely pay their rent and I cannot kick them out because I have known them, and their children for years."

Tony brought all the drama of Trump down to the street level for me. I realized that all that I am suffering is nothing compared to what was happening to this man , which only pulled me further into the pit of despair. "Tony, I cannot imagine what you are going through. Every merchant on University Place is in the same boat, as is every American as we are all being bombarded by the COVID and Trump viruses both of which strike without pity, without shame, and without mercy.

"Doc, how did all this happen to our country? My grandparents moved here from Italy with nothing in their pockets but hope and the desire to live a decent life. We all grew up knowing that if we worked hard and were good citizens, our lives would be happy. I was not able to go to college, but our three children were, all from the success Martha and I achieved from working this bar. What happened, what did we do wrong?"

"Great question Tony, you and I and most Americans have done nothing wrong but, we must take the blame. We were all working hard and doing the right thing but, the game plan changed under our feet. The good life we had after WWII began to morph into something, we did not see it coming. During the 70's we suddenly couldn't pay our bills and our wives went to work. The cost of basic needs, housing, health care, transportation and education were killing us. Over the last several years we began to see how much more those at the top were earning than we were. Unless you closely watched changes in the courts, our tax code, and legislative initiatives, favoring lobbyists and key industries over the last forty or fifty years, you had no idea how wide the income and wealth gaps had become. Racial tensions, the destruction of unions and the labor movement, along with the removal of health care and pensions, all historically shared with our employers were no longer available. Working class families were suffering and those at the top were living the high life. The entire job market, wages, benefits, and rash of social and political changes drained the middle class of all the gains we thought we had achieved. We took our hands off the wheels as those at the top built cars that drove themselves. We are where we are today because a lot of greedy powerful people took over and we let them do it by not watching what was happening and not voting. Ultimately the voter and the consumer are king, but only if we keep our eye on the ball and protect our interests.

The pain we are suffering under Trump is not really his fault. He is a terrible person who saw an opening and took it. A lot of people who voted for him just wanted someone to believe in. They knew that they were being screwed by the system and that the system was not listening to them. Millions of decent working-class families wanted someone to care about them and Trump convinced them that he was their man. He lied and manipulated his way into our lives, and we are only beginning to see the dangers he represents for our nation."

"You might be right but, I am not giving up, I am going to keep this place open for my customers and I am going to keep them safe, no matter what the cost." I could only watch in awe as Tony walked back to the bar to take care of another customer, strong and resolved albeit with bent and heavy shoulders, this was a good man.

I took another sip, picked up my pen and let my mind drift back to the battles of the day. Has this president ever honestly reached out to the opposition to find a compromise? Never. Has this president ever apologized for any of his many lies, gross misstatements, actions, mistakes, or humiliations? Never. Has this man who lost the popular vote ever embraced all Americans and not just his loyal, fear-driven base? Never.

I could not tell if the heat I was feeling from my chest was anger or despair; I only knew that I was letting my own thoughts drive my emotions beyond my control. I needed to put my pen down and chill, but the force driving my words was stronger and had taken over.

President Trump has spawned a cottage industry of fact-checkers who listen to every public statement he makes. As I sat with my scotch, they had already recorded 18,000 lies and counting. Who behaves like this? All leaders stretch the truth and often evade it, but what leader takes pride in a record of lying to his constituents so many times over a three-year period?

What president has ever had to admit that, since taking over his father's extraordinarily successful business, he had been in court more than four thousand times? Estimates vary, but it's been shown that Donald inherited over $400 million, mostly tax-free from his father, which may or may not include funds he diverted from other family member's. He explicitly stated that he only received a million-dollar loan from his father. One thing about Trump that has to be admired. He is not necessarily what he says he is but, he is definitely exactly what he does. He is not what most of his followers believe; a man who speaks his mind. We must learn to listen carefully to his endless volume of lies, which are hidden beneath the populist rhetoric and are consistently and diametrically opposed to what he does.

That puts the shame on us and most importantly professional journalists for letting him continue lying, cheating, and getting away with each infraction that would have brought anyone else to their knees. Donald Trump is incredibly believable in front of a mic and at his rallies, and that is what appealed to the base that voted for him. The problem is that he is a habitual liar and does nothing that will not enhance his fortune or fame. We, the public, should have known better and not allowed the media to laud his absurdities. We chose to ignore the facts, just like he does.

Was this the president who promised to hire the absolute best, only to suffer the highest turnover in key staff of any administration in history? Many of those who left did so totally frustrated with his behavior and actions. Others resigned or were fired because of Trump's humiliation and relentless criticism of them for telling the truth. Several past appointments and loyalists were either indicted, jailed, or awaiting imprisonment. Active indifference to the safety norms demanded by health care providers caused many members at all levels of the administration to suffer the consequences of becoming COVID infected, it is of no matter, like everyone who tees up with Trump, they are expendable.

We e had in Trump, a man of unprecedented incompetency and ignorance. A man who has no respect for the office he holds, other than the power it gave him to protect his fragile image, and to obscure his lifetime of untoward behavior. We had in Trump a man who had no idea how to do his job, part of which required him to find a way to fairly represent every American and not only his loyal base. Trump even threatened to withhold federal COVID aid to blue states and their governments, aiding only those who voted for him.

How did we allow all those helpless and vulnerable children to be jailed in pens on our borders and separated from their parents? What kind of a nation are we to let such a thing happen to these desperate people? There was certainly a more humane way to deal with that problem. The stain on our integrity as a democratic nation will not go away soon.

The visual thought of all those children in cages without their parents did nothing to reduce the increasing anguish I felt, now being stimulated by Tony's soothing scotch. I can only imagine what I must have looked like to anyone in sight of me.

How do we square our abandonment of the brave Kurdish fighters who fought on our side for years? Trump woke up one day and, without any discussion with his own military advisors, withdrew the only military protection these people had from two armed tyrants. The Kurds were forced to defend themselves without our help on their northern and southern borders. What impact will this decision have on America, should we need to align with another nation's military? Will we be a trusted ally?

How do we reconcile what he has done to diminish the reputation of each of our intelligence agencies and authorities? Trump was perfectly comfortable destroying the most trustworthy sources of information in our nation. Even COVID and its horrendous destruction to our lives had little impact on his actions or concerns. How would we rebuild after the complete destruction of our fourth estate by Trump claiming any story, fact, or topic that does not agree with him is "fake news?" Trump will go down in history as the president who leveled an actual war against professional journalism as he totally ignored the real war, he faced with COVID-19.

Tony exchanged my drink again and could tell that I was not in good shape. Not only were the words flowing from me, but the table and my pad were filling up with my uncontrollable tears that were flowing all over the place. I felt like I was being waterboarded by a mob of irresponsible elected officials who cared only about being reelected. I was losing it emotionally, but the thoughts I needed to record were coming from every direction, through my brain and onto the foggy pages of my notepad, I could not stop them even if I wanted to. The clarity of how we got into this mess had become more obvious than ever to me. I was also identifying with the personal agony of all the Tony's, families, and first responders who get up every day not knowing if they will make it through COVID and Trump alive. The pain was becoming unbearable and I hurt all over. It did not have to be like this.

The scotch had become the mediator between these two worlds I was suddenly battling. I no longer felt anger, empowerment had taken over, but I did feel helplessly whiplashed from one event to the other. I knew that I had the resources to weather all this, and I knew that most people walking by on the street did not. I knew that Tony would make it through but, not without a lot of pain. Neither of these enemies of the people were created by us, yet we were the victims of both their armies of evil and pain. I needed to find a solution in my understanding of how this war was being waged. I had to leave COVID to the scientists, at least for now. I had to focus on the politics of the situation because that is where I could make a difference. I could feel myself drifting further from reality as a lucidity of what was happening to our country surrounded my every thought and being.

In what way did Trump make America great again? What policies did he put forward that served us better? His obsession with Obamacare, his destruction of our global relationships, his relentless attacks on the Democrat-controlled House? Each of these represent major steps backward for the country. He most certainly has not drained the DC swamp.

There are people who honestly believe that Trump could, as he has stated, stand in the middle of Fifth Avenue and shoot someone and not lose a single vote. He would probably deny he was the one who took the shot. He might claim his innocence and then blame the previous owner of the gun. Just think of what all this craziness says to us, our neighbors, our children, and our trading partners. Can we really afford another four years of this persistent disregard for everything we, as a nation, have held dear for so long?

Citizens United has become a money pit for those seeking public office. He sent militarized police forces and National Guard into our streets, against legitimate protestors to protect his agenda. He found a way to disengage from the international community, leaving us to fend totally for ourselves. He made no effort to raise the middle and lower classes to financial and social independence. The rapidly growing income and wealth gaps moved toward even greater disparity under his watch, leaving others on the outside of what became a series of heavily guarded communities. The courts are already compromised and of little use to anyone below the ninety-fifth percentile in wealth. Social Security, not in any way an entitlement program, is on the cutting-room floor for the 2021 budget. Healthcare coverage is in jeopardy. The ACA is continually in the courts and slated for republican led elimination. After ten years of relentless threats by Trump and the Republicans, not a single page of a viable upgrade or measure of a replacement has emerged. It has Obama in its nickname and therefore it must go. I have not pulled these points from thin air. Most of them are already in motion and an emboldened second term Trump will most certainly accelerate them as much as possible.

Those who are part of Trump's base and think he is doing a good job must know that he will throw them under the bus as soon as he realizes that their loyalty and vote are no longer needed. That has been the fate of literally everyone around him even before he sought and won public office. That is the way he will treat you; he has a long history of doing so. He has no loyalty to anyone, least of all the blue-collar, middle-income voter who is rightfully fed up with the establishment. His base might be willing to take their chances once again a on a con man rather than trust an establishment that has ignored them for four decades running.

Okay, if Ari were here, I would be getting another earful that I have once again fallen into Trump's pit. He would look at me with those all-knowing eyes and tell me that as long as I stayed on this path, I would lose because Trump loved to play the victim and wallow in self-pity because of people like me. How do we, in this toxic environment, encourage rational discussion of what is wrong with our country and acknowledge our own role in bringing us here? What must we do to pull it all back together in a way that allows each and every American to live a decent life, free of fear, uncertainty, and drama? Michelle Obama told us to go high when they go low. Sounds great, but will it work? Despite having nothing short of total admiration for Michelle, her words reminded me of Nancy Reagan's "just say no." I do not know how to reconcile that solution given the tens of thousands of people who have overdosed since she said that to us. I have the means and the drive to counter this threat, yet I'm not sure how I can best design an effective counterattack. That will be my main task when I meet with our team, hopefully soon.

Our democracy is hanging by a thread. Who is left to protect us? The Congress who impeached the president only to have our senators cave almost eliminates them as a candidate? They could not do the right thing, even though many knew that the president was guilty. Can we look to our religious leaders? The Catholic Church has lost congregants and valuable real estate due to forced closings of churches and legal debt. The church has had to pay out vast sums in reparations for decades of child abuse. The Evangelicals have completely succumbed to this non-Christian president, mainly because he promised that he will deliver a reversal of *Roe v. Wade*. A promise not kept. Muslims have totally and rightfully, given up on any compromise with Trump on any issue. All those bridges had been completely burned.

Can we look to the police? Maybe if we are white. One of our nation's greatest tragedies is the daily fear a person of color feels from the police. This reality belies the fact that many police officers do in fact honor the code to protect all Americans. Sadly, unless we can identify and remove racist and violence-prone officers, our trust in our police forces will remain under a dark cloud. Police reform, demilitarization, and reorganization must be given serious consideration in light of what has been happening for years in our communities across the country.

Emotions were flowing through every pore of my inner self. Thousands of Americans dying every day from presidential neglect, a once honored political party prostrate at the heels of its own self-serving leadership void of even a hint of moral fortitude, children still in cages separated from their parents—possibly forever. Just knowing that eight million hard-working Americans will slip into poverty this year as generations of entrepreneurs watch their family businesses crumble before them and the persistent fear of not being white as supremacists and conspiracists gather freely across the land rumbled helplessly in my gut. Is this who we are as a nation, or is all of this just passing through as we seek to rise above this carnage before us?

Despair took over and as I looked out at the street which was only a couple of feet in front of the window, I saw a young girl in a party hat looking directly at me. Her mother was next to her, holding her hand as they looked at a tired old man with his pen writing furiously on a tear-soaked pad. The little girl was holding a small potted jade plant that was probably a party favor she had just received. Tony was standing next to them. It was obvious that they knew each other and were talking about me. I drifted slowly back into my thoughts and notes until I felt Tony standing next to me with the jade plant in his hand.

"Her name is Kathy. She wanted to know what was hurting you. I told her that the weight of the world was on you and that you were going to save us. She wanted you to have her jade plant."

That act of kindness suddenly obliterated everything that was pouring through my body and mind. I remembered something an Australian friend once said to me. Bush had just been reelected and neither of us could imagine how we could have made that mistake twice. I apologized to my friend who put his hand on my shoulder and said, "Benson, we have never judged the people of America by their leaders, we know your goodness and your generosity as a people." This little girl, Kathy, and my friend were the shock I needed to realize that there was a much more powerful force out there that was going to prevail, and my team was going to pitch in to help make it happen.

I sat back to reflect on all this drained of life itself. I am not sure if it was the scotch or the bevy of thoughts scratched out by an emotionally drained professor. Everything around me became very fuzzy, and I could not focus my attention or my eyes. I did not see the sports posters or the flatscreen TVs that dominated the dimly lit walls, or the tinned ceiling and pre-war tiled floor of times past. My mind's eye saw Miles Davis and Chick Corea huddled in a corner poring over a crumpled-up score on the table in front of them. I saw Herbie Hancock, Gary Burton, and the famed drummer Tony Williams across the room laughing over a beer. Frank Zappa and Wayne Shorter were at the bar, and the shadow of my younger self was between them just listening to the sounds of life and hope that filled the room. Empowerment returned, and I knew that we would overcome. Right is might.

I knew that it was time to leave and that I could not do that on my own. I took out my burner, texted Ari where I was, and asked for a driver. He responded right away, and I took out my checkbook and wrote a check out for a thousand dollars for Tony. I put my pen and pad in my pocket as I desperately tried to pull myself together. Ari showed up in less than five minutes, walked into the bar, and nodded to Tony as he pulled me out of my seat and into the car. Tony held the door open for us, and I handed the check to Tony as we headed for the car. My jade plant was cradled in my arms. I asked Tony to thank that little girl for me, I have loved jade plants all my life and deeply appreciate this gift."

"Will do, Doc. You take care of yourself for us, please."

THAT WAS THE LAST MEMORY I HAD until I woke up the next morning still fully dressed and in pretty bad shape. I have never been able to hold much liquor. Ari had apparently just dumped me on my bed and left. I was alone and definitely needed a long hot shower during which I recapped everything I had gone through the previous evening. As complicated and upsetting as it was, my mission was made abundantly clear to me and I knew better than ever what had to be done.

There was a package on the table, with my name on top. The package contained the burner phone with a note that our contact was in DC and working in the White House Security detail. Another note with instructions from Ari:

Code 72 for you and Ari, 39 for our mole. Find a name for him/her. Flight today leave apartment 17:30, carry nothing but flash drive and this phone. Walk to 14th St. subway, wear jacket and hat, jeans. Stand by uptown entrance, change wallets and apartment key. A man your height will ask you for a light. Say that there is no smoking in subways. Contact confirmed, give him your jacket and hat, give him your key to your apartment and put your wallet and the flash drive in this bag. Take the uptown subway to 23rd St. and walk out on the northwest exit and look for a limo with Smith on the front windshield, get in. Burn this note. Bring a couple of masks and disposable gloves.

Ari had apparently secured a corporate jet, and I needed to get everything ready for the trip. I booted up my secure laptop, which Ari had checked out and downloaded everything I wanted protected to a new flash drive as backup and put the drive and phone into my insulated waist belt. I went down to the lobby and asked Mr. Bonaparte for a safe place to store some things when needed. He handed me a key to 102. We nodded at each other. I knew that he knew that someone else would be staying in my apartment as me while I was away. I packed all my sensitive papers into a nondescript garbage bag and, together with the computer, and got it ready to give to Mr. Bonaparte.

I wondered...if the Founding Fathers were alive today, would any items on my project's to-do list be taken off their agenda as too radical? Too expensive? Impossible to implement? Not politically correct? My answer to each was an emphatic *no!* They would only need to have lived in America for the last ten to forty years to see how far the rights and privileges of living in the democracy they envisioned for us have deteriorated. It is also safe to assume that the great social and political thinkers and economists of the past, who were dedicated to the clarification and understanding of the systems they were living under, would react negatively to what was happening. They couldn't have imagined the degree to which a few individuals, one in particular, could possibly have commandeered broad sections of our nation as they have.

I honestly do not think that the average American family is asking too much of their leaders. We are all willing to work for what we want, and most of us do live within our means. We are not, however, willing to support a government or other powerful organizations that only want to empower themselves or its friends at our expense. That is not the nation we were founded to be.

Our team's job would be to see our nation as it is and to let the voter know how far we have drifted. Economic and social policies, quality of life, national security, rule of law, and justice for all are the ideals we have fought for since before 1776. Now, it seems, we are no longer doing so. We must reclaim the freedom to be ourselves, including respect for one another and for the laws that make us the free and prosperous nation we fought so hard to preserve. Trump tells his followers that they have to fight if they want to win. We need a champion to tell us that we will have to fight them if the America we know is to survive.

With the presentation tasks completed, I took a moment to consider Ari's position on the election. I knew he was right, but I was unable to let that divergence of purpose slip out of view. I needed to find a way to be both clear and succinct to our team, the hard-core Trumpers, and those on the fringe, all of whom might well turn out to be the very voters we need to win back our country.

I loaded all that I'd just written onto the flash drive I had filled with the data from the secured laptop that I had given to Mr. Bonaparte, who will store it for me. I had also downloaded the presentation for our meeting. Nothing had been saved on my regular laptop, except for the random papers stored in a to-do file. If this computer were confiscated, our projects would not be compromised. As instructed, I packed nothing except the burner phone and the flash drive, both well-hidden as was my now dry steno pad. I was ready to meet our team and decide how we could best use the resources and talent I gathered.

I decided to take a late morning walk.

CHAPTER 12

JULY 2020

THE STREETS OF NEW YORK always inspire me. I need only turn the corner to see children playing, skateboarders practicing, or to hear folks talking in a myriad of languages. I wanted to pick up some groceries for the stand-in who would be staying in my apartment while I was away meeting our team. The virus had abated a bit toward the end of July and the governor and mayor opened the city, but only partially. It was good to see people on the streets and the shops again, virus protected, but out and about.

I walked for about an hour, and an idea came to me about how I could meet all my goals. I needed to get an idea from our DC mole on how close he was to the Oval Office. Did he have inside information about the president? Against Ari's wishes, I decided to make contact before leaving on my trip that evening. The information this person had for us and his willingness to keep us informed would determine how deep our inroads to the Trump campaign could be. I knew that the phone DC sent to us has been proven secure, and as Ari said, I can phone or text with confidence.

I casually walked toward a park bench in Washington Square Park, sat down, and sent a text on the DC dedicated phone Ari gave me:

How close to POTUS and advisors are you, and how much inside information are you able to get to me?

I waited, not knowing how long it would take or if I would get a response at all. Nothing came, so I headed to the grocery store and then home. As I shopped, I began to pull together my thoughts on this new aspect of our project. I didn't want to let Ari know what I was planning until I was sure it could be done. If our mole could accomplish what I needed, it would increase both the value and success of our project. My thoughts were interrupted by a text buzzing in on the burner.

Fairly close. Recently transferred to WH security. Position very risky, worth the effort if you can do your job.

That was exactly what I wanted to hear, especially since I knew that any tracing for these text and voice messages was secure at both ends. Now I needed to think of a code name for the mole. I have never been particularly good at naming things. I let my mind wander as far as it could while I walked three more city blocks. As I turned the corner of Sixth Avenue and Thirteenth Street, the perfect name came into view. Our mole would be code-named Agent Orange.

I immediately responded, Bilboa to Agent Orange: Great! How often and when to expect messages from you?

Every Saturday morning. Text is best. Agent Orange. Love my name.

Mission accomplished. Now I needed a secure way to transmit messages to the team, free from any possibility of them being traced. Ari would deal with that while we were at our meeting. I needed to ask Ari how we could verify Agent Orange's authenticity to make sure that we were not being set up. I decided that I would not contact AO again until Ari and I were sure this contact was reliable.

After gathering my things, I left the apartment at 5:15 p.m., walked toward the subway station, and waited at the uptown gate until, as planned, I was stopped and asked for a light. We exchanged the code exactly as instructed. I handed him my coat, hat, and keys to my apartment. The stranger was my height and build, maybe ten pounds lighter, which made me jealous. I was supposed to take the uptown 1 train to Twenty-third Street exit. I had time, so I walked up Seventh Avenue past the Joyce Theater and several great Thai restaurants that are among my favorite in the city. My car came almost immediately. I hopped in and found myself next to Ari, who had apparently decided to join me.

We greeted each other. I was glad he'd be with us. I asked if he'd been able to get the case of wine I had asked for. I had bought a case of New York State's wine of the year, a product of the Six Mile Creek Vineyard located near Ithaca. This 2016 Cabernet Franc had won the Governor's Cup as the best wine of the year, as well as best in show at the celebrated New York Wine Classic at Watkins Glen Harbor. Nothing but the best for my Swiss friends and bankers, honorable protectors of my assets.

"Got it!" said Ari. "I had to stake you for an unexpected cost increase. I got a bargain I could not refuse on the 2018 vintage of the same one you ordered, which was more expensive, even though it didn't win any awards. I was told it's even smoother than the 2016. I hope you don't mind. I bought a case of each. They are stowed up forward."

"Thank you, Ari. We will give both cases to our Swiss bankers. I wanted you to know that I activated the burner with a text to our DC contact whom I have named Agent Orange. My code name is Bilboa and yours is Raven."

"Agent Orange! Perfect. I like being Raven as well. Good job," he said.

I was relieved that he was pleased. "I sent a text to Agent Orange to get an idea of what kind of information to expect. He said that he had recently been transferred to the White House on security and was pretty much free to move about. He requested a once-a-week transmission of information early on Saturday mornings."

I could feel Ari's brain going through the options as we sped north on the West Side Highway. "That's no good. Saturday is slow, and any communication would be easier to trace. Ask for Friday around 4:00 p.m. when a ton of data is being transferred. It's the end of the day at the end of the week. It will be harder to track any single message."

"I will try. It might be a bad time for him for the same reason. Text is okay?"

"Yes, your line is linked to an out-of-state phone that would be difficult to trace. These phones have a device-specific key which prevents any information from being stored anywhere not on the device. Information *is* stored on the SIM, though, which must be removed if the burner has to be destroyed. If anything should happen, I can give him a safe house and contact in DC if he needs it. I will pass that on as soon as I clear it through my DC sources."

"I want to find a way to check this person out before we go too far with him," I suggested. "I just want to be sure that we have not been set up."

"Good thought. I will think about it and come up with some ideas."

We rode in silence through the Bronx and into Westchester. About an hour later, we pulled into a small private airport, off the highway. We drove right into a hangar, got out, and boarded a very fancy jet that could hold about fifteen passengers and crew. This flight had only Ari, the pilot, co-pilot, and me. We took off with only the briefest of communications with the tower and ground crew. We were soon flying at 25,000 feet heading northeast, all in less time than it took me to walk nine blocks to Twenty-third Street. "Where are we going?" I asked.

"Iceland," Ari answered. "We should be there by midnight our time. The team is meeting us at a private airport. Because of the virus, we will meet in a secure, well-ventilated office. We'll have to wear protective clothing, which we have brought on board. We also have enough meals on board for two days. I made the arrangements to land in Switzerland without going through customs. You can use my phone to call your contacts there."

"I have to wonder what it would be like if we were doing something really threatening and of interest to national security," I conjectured.

"You might say that you *are*," said Ari. "We know someone's onto you, and I doubt it's because your ex has filed a lawsuit against you for an increase in support. You have been visited by two Feds, you know your office has been bugged, your NYU reunion was infiltrated, and now we have a contact from inside the White House sending you warnings. How much more do you need to know? They are worried about something, and we have to be at least three steps ahead of them. The DC phone I left for you with Mr. Bonaparte is as secure as anything. That alone tells me that it's from a high-level government source. We just do not know which one."

"I forgot that I told you about that lawsuit," I chuckled, remembering the ordeal of my divorce. "I discounted my ex as nothing but a disgruntled woman with no life of her own. Most of our data is public, nothing from secure sources; it is just not widely distributed unless you are a professional. I have logged into dozens of websites that could have raised suspicion, as you said. I think I'll use Duckduckgo.com from now on. Sounds like my Russian forays must have rung a bell for someone."

Ari agreed. "This isn't a stretch if they're working for the campaign. Trump will track down any threat, however obscure. We can also expect this to be one of the dirtiest elections ever. I hear he's working up a host of fake stories about anyone he can, just to divert attention from the pandemic, the economy, and his other problem areas. He's also doing everything he can to reduce voter participation. He has a plan to disrupt mail-in ballots and is even trying to control the ballot boxes wherever his people can gain access. He is suing a bunch of states for their vote-by-mail programs and forcing any and all gerrymandered districts to double down on voters not in full compliance with their excessive voter restrictions. He's even trying to get more liberals to run as third-party candidates, hoping they'll take votes from Biden. We also know he's relying on the Russians, and maybe the Chinese. Iran might be meddling as well, though I doubt that they'd support Trump. The campaign even has a plan to use misinformation on the coronavirus as a distraction. We can be sure that Hillary and Obama will continue to be targets whenever possible. We can expect several releases about dirt on Biden and his son Hunter to hit the headlines later this summer. He's only doing what will further his campaign—presidential duties be damned."

I was listening to Ari in total disbelief. Where did he accumulate all that information? Was he actually coming around to my way of thinking on Trump and this election?

As I listened to Ari and his thoughts about the way Trump was twisting his way to a victory, he suddenly interjected, "If that man had only put half as much energy into trying to be a responsible president, he would've been unbeatable. As revolting as he is, he can electrify an audience. If he'd only figure out how to use all those persuasive skills, to capture any of those on-the-fence voters, this election would already be over, and he'd glide to the finish line. He is most certainly his own worst enemy."

"Absolutely. I responded. "The problem is that he's so used to being behind that eight ball that he doesn't know how to win without releasing sleazy initiatives coupled with a bunch of marginally legal machinations designed to cloud everything beyond recognition." I remembered that I had to tell Ari about my Trump encounters so that he was aware of that history. "Ari, I want you to know that back in the early '70s, I was part of an operation to take down Trump and catch him for discrimination in his apartment buildings." I also told him about the Thirty-fourth Street Railyard incident with Mayor Koch. "I honestly don't think that my name could have reached

Trump's defense team, but knowing how paranoid he is, I could not say for sure. What do you think?"

"He's paranoid and will do anything to win. He hates to lose. But I can't imagine his suspicions running that deep. You were certainly not on the front line of either of those incidents. I forgot, who was his lawyer on the discrimination charge?"

"Roy Cohn."

"That changes things—Cohn was beyond lethal. If your name is on any of the papers submitted to the court by DOJ, he would've seen them, and had you put on a hit list when he hooked up with Trump."

I thought this would be a good time to let Ari know about my short tour of duty with Rudy Giuliani. "I think you should know that I was recruited by the Giuliani transition team in 1994."

"Ha! I can't imagine you working for him."

"It was a problem, but I'd never turn down an opportunity to help the City. Actually, I've worked with every mayor from Lindsay to Giuliani, mostly pro bono. Rudy was always a strange dude and not nearly as successful as District Attorney as he would like us to think. Check out his reversals on appeal when you have a chance. He was more interested in sensational arrests than solid convictions. He was also not as bad then as he is now. I honestly don't know what happened to him. In any case, I served as Assistant Commissioner of Business Services for about a year until he fired me about six months after he asked me to take over the Office of Economic Policy and Marketing. We had a staff of about thirty-five people, mostly economists."

"What did you do to get fired?"

"We were asked to look into the possibility of creating gated communities on the Upper East Side. I thought it was a crazy idea, but I was asked to evaluate the concept."

"Why would they want to do something like that?"

"I'm not sure. I think someone read about gated communities in Houston, and they thought it would be a good idea to keep 'certain' people out of specific neighborhoods. I honestly didn't think it would work in New York. We did the study and wrote a report that looked into all the possible impacts of implementing a policy like that in Manhattan. That is what economists do; we lay out the options and implications of each choice, and the decision maker decides which works best to meet their specific objectives.

"At a meeting with the administration, , we were told to remove the section that showed some possible negative impacts. We were told that the mayor did not need to see them, that he understood all sides of the issue. We said that professionally we could not remove the section. Economists are basically researchers, and we are professionally required to look at all of the possible implications of any decision. They can ignore whatever they want to from our report, but we're obligated to include all of our findings. We were asked repeatedly to remove the section.

"I told the administration that I understood and would take the report back to my team to figure out what we could do. I pointed out that my team was comprised of long-time civil servants and professionals. We had to be sure that we didn't violate professional standards just to meet the demands of any one administrator. I was reminded that we work at the pleasure of the mayor, and that was that. I called a staff meeting. We agreed that we couldn't eliminate our findings, but we would be willing to remove our names from the report. They could then do whatever they wanted with it. I took their suggestions back to the administration, who rejected the idea. I walked back to my office, and there was a message letting me know that I was fired, as was my entire office."

"Wow," said Ari, "that was a bit extreme. What did you do?"

"I requested a meeting with the deputy mayor who was in charge of our office. I told him that he could fire me, but not anyone on my staff. They were career civil servants who were only doing their jobs. That did not seem to matter to him. He told me that we all had to clear out our desks and leave immediately. I had an ace up my sleeve that I decided to use on the spot. I let the deputy mayor know that I would make his proposal and his reaction to it into a public incident if he refused to give me time to find everyone on my staff comparable jobs elsewhere. I knew he had the authority to close down the office. I also knew that Giuliani had no respect for research, that he trusted his gut on all decisions."

"Where have I heard that before?" Ari smiled.

"I can't imagine. It must be someone with a noticeably big gut."

"That must have been a tense moment for you."

"Not for me. Remember, I was on leave from my university and was scheduled to go back the next semester. I told the deputy mayor that unless he agreed to my terms, I would have a story in the *New York Times* within forty-eight hours. He could expect to be interviewed.

"We stared each other down for a few minutes, and I could tell that he was not going to blink. I asked to use his phone. He handed it to me. I looked up the number of a graduate school colleague in my address book. Ray was recently hired by the *Times* as their Director of Corporate Planning. His office was right next to the publisher's. I gave the number of the *Times* to the deputy mayor and asked him to dial the number and ask for the publisher. When the receptionist for the publisher picked up, he hung the phone up and agreed to my terms.

"I returned to my office and let the staff know what was happening. They said they weren't surprised. That was when they told me that they had had an inkling before I took on the job that their positions were on the line.

Knowing the mayor's disdain for research, they thought I was brought in to close down the office. I reassured them that if that had been a condition for taking the job, I would have turned it down, and I would have found a way to make that go public. I have too many friends in this town to ever get mixed up in something like that.

"I told them about my plan and that it worked to give me enough time to get everyone placed. I was not going to let these dedicated civil servants be hung out to dry."

"How did everything end up?"

"I managed to get everyone placed in about three months. Some of them had contacts of their own. Others decided to just leave government. I closed down shop and left. Before all that, I tried to reason with some other higher-ups in the administration but could tell that the word had come down from the top— Giuliani has never liked research or official reports. He prefers his own instincts. It was clear that our department was history.

"I returned to teaching and, regrettably, that was my last public sector appointment. One takeaway for me was that working in the public sector provides the opportunity to do great things. I take a lot of pride in what we were able to contribute over many years of public service to help small businesses in my city."

"*Your* city?"

"Yeah, I get possessive of our town. For a long time, I hid this incident and never talked about it. I think I was embarrassed and probably could have handled it better. Given all that Rudy has been doing since leaving City Hall, especially his role as Trump's lawyer, I have to admit that getting fired by him has turned into a badge of honor. Maybe I should put it at the top of my CV..."

Ari then began to say things that I never thought I would hear from him. "I'm beginning to think that I was a bit hasty at our last meeting when you went off on Trump. Trump's just like Giuliani, shoot from the hip and damage control later. They both love to create a major problem so they can come in and fix it. Hero status claimed and credit taken. They're both autocrats who thrive on chaos. With this new information you have shared, my guess is that your visit from the Feds was not random. This message from Agent Orange is somehow connected with that visit, and the Trump administration has your number. You are no longer a stealth enemy."

"I agree, Ari. I've always wondered why Giuliani and his people would care about my desire to place my staff. It's really hard to figure out what really matters to politicos."

"That's because politicians have no loyalty to anyone, unless it will push them further up the ladder," Ari continued. "I still think Trump is a bungler and not a serious politician. Like you, I also wonder where he gets all his ideas from. I doubt he knows anything about Homeland Security, immigration, the EPA, or the DOJ, other than doing his best to destroy them with all his devastating initiatives. The appointments he makes for these agencies and the policies he comes up with are off the charts and must be coming from someone else. Trump is only making the swamp wider and deeper."

"I know I tend to get overheated when I talk about all that Trump is unraveling," I said. "I don't think I'm wrong—he's dangerous. I've watched that man do the craziest things over the years, and one overriding trait is that he never loses—whatever the cost. There is a good reason that he always has cases on a court docket somewhere. There have been thousands of cases either initiated by him or leveled against him. He knows that losing this election will put him in the path of a dozen indictments waiting for him, most of which can't be pardoned. What bothers me is that I was unaware of the fact that a president is immune from prosecution while in office."

Ari agreed. "It was news to me as well. Seems like the jury is out on that decision for everyone but him."

"An apt metaphor. The Supreme Court has just come down on that decision. A president is not immune from criminal acts, but the jury is still out on other infractions he has committed."

I was surprised that I'd somehow managed to turn Ari around on most things Trump. I also knew that we had to tread lightly, especially since we knew that Trump loves a battle and controls an awful lot of resources, far more than do we. As Ari said, we needed to keep our eye on the ball and not get deflected. Our message on voter participation was much bigger than Trump.

The flight was incredibly smooth. I was able to settle back and rest a bit as I thought about what was to come. I was eager to meet our team and work out what we needed to do to go public. But I felt more confident than I had in a long time.

I took a look around the plane for the first time since we boarded. The appointments were in light cream leather, with mahogany trim. The carpets were designer grade, as were the overhead liners. The galley was not only well stocked, but each appliance was also top grade as were the heads. There was a separate cabin aft, it was loaded with the most contemporary electronics and communications available. I was also suddenly aware of how quiet it was. Despite the fact that we were slicing through the air at just under five hundred miles an hour at 35,000 feet, our cabin was as quiet as an empty cathedral. Thinking about how unpleasant airports are, and how passengers are treated like cattle, I could really get used to this. As I drifted off to sleep, I was reminded of the carboard boxes that were my bedroom for so many years as a child, when I wondered whether I would even make it through the day. Maybe I have done something right after all.

★ ★ ★

Chapter 13

July 2020

THE CHANGE IN AIR SPEED and the banking of our jet woke me. It was still too dark to figure out where we were. I let my mind and body slowly awaken before hitting the head for a quick shower and shave. The executives who get to ride in these planes really are privileged. I got back to my seat as we started our descent. I had two major goals for this meeting: Informing the team about our commitment to get as many eligible voters to the polls and get them as informed of the issues as possible. My second goal, which would be new to the team, was to ensure that Donald Trump was not reelected. In addition to traditional right-wing media, we needed to gain access to as many of the non-establishment, unconventional platforms that have access to fringe voters. I have also targeted several specific demographics who have not voted. Gen Z, Hispanics, and disenfranchised uneducated working-class people, all of whom have the most to lose in this election, were on my A-list.

Our jet taxied toward a row of hangars. We stopped just short of one that was open. We exited the plane, and the ground crew guided us into a small conference room. Ari immediately and thoroughly checked for bugs. I was now even more pleased that he had decided to come. The two of us sat down to a great breakfast which, though unexpected, was most appreciated. I made sure that the flight crew was also fed. The door opened about ten minutes later, and our team entered. There was Andrew, looking thin and tired, but otherwise great. We were genuinely happy to see each other and painfully remembered to maintain a proper social distance. It had been more than a year since we were last together.

Ari introduced me to Yosef and Lavi., two long-time Israeli associates of his. Ari had told me that they were at the outer limits on the knowledge curve for cybersecurity and communication systems. They are part of an international team of sophisticated technicians focused on protecting the privacy of individuals and companies who hire them. That's all Ari would say. He made it abundantly clear that we could trust them and that the less I knew about them the better.

Andrew pulled me aside and asked about Anna. I filled him in on how well she was doing but admitted that she really missed her dad. I showed him a picture of her that I'd taken during our dinner. Andrew took out his phone, and I air-dropped the photo to him.

"You know, this deception is without a doubt the most difficult part of this entire exercise for me. I had no idea how much I was going to miss her," sighed Andrew.

"I know, Andrew, but we need to keep her safe. As it turns out, that might become even more important as we get deeper into this project. Have you been able to keep up with what's going on in the States?" I asked.

"We do, Benson, we get all the news. In fact, we probably get more than you guys do. I really do not like what's happening, and I hope we get to talk about it."

"We will! In fact, I've put some ideas together and added them to our agenda. Let's sit down and accomplish as much as we can. I 've planned for us to have some time together after the meeting."

"Great, thank you for doing that. She does look great. Does she have a boyfriend?"

"No, and she blames you for setting that bar in her life beyond the reach of mere mortals."

Following our introductions, we all chatted over hot coffee and a variety of European cheeses and cured meats brought in by Andrew. We then launched into the tasks at hand. I wanted us to be efficient, as we were pressed for time, and I wanted some time with Andrew before we had to leave for Switzerland.

I opened the meeting. "I want to thank everyone for all that you have done to get this project online and ready to go. I also thank you for coming out at this ungodly hour to meet with Ari and me. It is my understanding that all of our data are finally collated and stored. That leaves us free to focus on critical areas of distribution, security, and the systems we need for our communication with each other.

"There is an additional focus to our mission I want to introduce. Given the political atmosphere in the States, we can't think of distributing a voter awareness campaign without dealing with the possibility of Trump's reelection. Who better to build a case for a more informed voter than a candidate who lied his way into office? A candidate who runs counter to everything we stand for as a nation. We need to deal with the election this fall, and I have some ideas about how we can do so without interfering with our primary goal of getting more people to vote intelligently," I declared.

"Whoa, we agree that Trump might be the worst president ever, but what you're putting forward was never part of our plan! This puts us in a whole new realm in terms of our mission." Andrew was clearly upset.

"I know, Andrew, but I'm convinced we can make a difference, and everything is really heating up. Trump's made it clear that there's nothing he won't do to get reelected. No limits on the cheating, stealing, Russia meddling, or encouraging white supremacy groups. Most importantly, many on the front lines of this election think he just might pull off a win, and we all know the consequences if he does."

"Benson, we're not set up to add this to our mission," Andrew argued.

"We're a lot closer than you think. The biggest challenge is to figure out how to distribute our work so that it gets onto the desks, into the living rooms, and on kitchen tables of all those who need to see it most. The life these folks will get to live depends on how successful we are. Our posts, which I think should be daily as we approach the election, need to be entertaining, on point, and informative. Many can be sent more than once. Trump has shown us that repetition works to promote his lies. We are going to use this technique to solidify our message.

"I'd like to add a graphic artist to our team. I'm also thinking of a cartoonist. "I have here a proposal that includes images for the voter awareness project that will use the cartoon character I have in mind. If it can be animated, the reader will stick around our site longer. The time commitment will be intense from now through the election. After that, tasks will continue with much less intensity since time will be on our side. The artists can work from anywhere. I would like to hire only one or two artists , so that we can keep our team as small as possible. Do you have any recommendations?"

"My brother is an illustrator," Yosef said. "I'm not sure he does cartoons but I can ask."

"I have a cousin in Paris who is familiar with the software we will be using," contributed Ari. "He works for a publishing house where he designs graphic layouts for promotional materials. He could write a program for our format, install it on our computers, and work from home on any follow up as needed."

"I know someone, too," said Lavi. "She's a really good cartoonist—not a professional, but always drawing and giving her creations away, mostly to neighborhood children. She works at a university in Brussels on admissions and student relations. I think I could get her to work for us."

"These are great suggestions," I thanked them. I have some thoughts for the cartoon character. I will leave them with you to help them understand the look we want to create. We should also be open to their ideas. Our presentation on the election material needs to be completely separate from our voter awareness effort. I want both campaigns to be simple and easy to digest. My thinking is to have a banner on each post to create familiarity. We need to make sure that our readers see that we're legitimate and nonpartisan, definitely not radicals."

I handed them the proposals. They were short and to the point. I wanted us to reach an agreement at this meeting, so that we could avoid going back and forth remotely. I could tell that Andrew was not on board with adding a Trump offensive. I tried to reduce the tension. "Since the presentation and artistic tasks were so different, I thought it might best to use two creatives who we can trust to keep us invisible. I don't care if they live in different countries. If you trust them, reach out and see if your contacts will work covertly, an objective second only to their skills. If possible, send Ari a site where I can see some samples of their work. If not, I'll depend on you to make the right choice. Ask them to set a budget, and I'll transfer funds directly to them. I'll have Ari set them up with secure communications. Content will be communicated to them through a system that Ari will set up for us. It might turn out that he will do the communicating. I would only like to see the proofs after you guys have gone over them. I would want them only for the first set so that I can approve the basic look of the illustrations. I prefer to leave the rest of the decision up to you."

I could tell that Yosef and Lavi were fine with what I was saying, Andrew was still skeptical. He offered no rebuttal, at least at this point.

"Ari, how do you think we can send and receive files between these artists and the team without any security risks? Maybe I can send the content to you, and you will forward it to each artist? I would like to avoid having them communicate directly with me."

Knowing the risks, I was facing, Ari had already thought this through. "I can set up a Virtual Private Network for each of you. It will communicate through an anonymous email account. If you get nervous about the account, let me know, and I will set up other VPNs and email addresses."

As Ari was explaining his systems and how they would work for us, I focused on Yosef and Lavi. They were in their early thirties, and both were handsome and confident. They were comfortably dressed, clean shaven, thin, and athletic. They were definitely not nerdy, and it was obvious that they could easily focus on everything that was going on. Like Ari said, these guys are smart, and this was not their first rodeo. I needed to test them on technical skills..

"Yosef and Lavi, do you both take care of the distribution of finished content?" I asked.

"Yes, we share it. Lavi's better at finding new sources for content distribution, so I tend to focus on input and programming specific to the sites and distribution channels."

"Great. Facebook and Twitter are key distribution vehicles for us. I'd like to repost what others are doing as well. I just heard of a new site that's getting more popular—I think it's Tik or something? Do you know about it?" I asked.

Lavi interjected, "Tiktok. It's shot to the front of the line with more than 1.5 billion downloads. It's most popular with young people. It is currently based in China, though they are trying to establish a presence in the States, which makes a lot of people nervous. New sites like this come up all the time. We constantly check them out and decide whether they are worth our time."

"That's great! Millennials and Gen Z are major voter demographics who did not vote in 2016. We want to get to them as a sympathetic group for our goals. I am sure the majority of these young people do not like Trump, and we want them to vote. Have you guys heard of Twitch.com? I have also just heard about another social media App, Parler."

Lavi said that he'd have to look at Twitch to see if it would be worth the effort. "They offer a lot of viewing options and their total views run into the billions. Parler is popular with several radical right groups like Proud Boys who do not want to be on Google. We have already started exploring these and many other search engines, in anticipation of what you would want us to do."

I continued, "Okay, Lavi, our strategy is to have our posts act as free riders. Every time these political groups send anything out to their followers, we'll automatically be tagging along. The kinds of institutions we will also be hacking are colleges and universities, we want to attract these young voters. Also, the DNC and RNC, Trump's Facebook and Twitter accounts, AARP, open news services, religious sites, and individuals. Once linked to a page, we can post and encourage them to like and share our content separately or as an uninvited guest to the host. AARP has over thirty million members, all of them seniors, another critical demographic for us.

"There's a group of Republicans who are fed up with what Trump is doing to their party. They have formed an advertising group called the Lincoln Project. These guys are well-funded and are making a difference. We should connect with them somehow. We also need to reach voters who might not want to follow us. Our job is to put a bug in their ears and hope that they will listen to what we have to say. I am referring to those on the alt-right. We need them to at least consider our message."

Ari found it necessary to let me know that my metaphor usage needs to change—*we* are the bugs.

"I agree, Ari, my point exactly. You're still not used to my sense of humor." That got a few desperately needed laughs.

Returning to my agenda, I added, "I think it's best to launch our current output and see where it leads. We want friends out there—like Occupy Democrats or the Southern Poverty Law Center—but we don't want to compromise them in any way. We can monitor them to see if our materials are being utilized in other ways. We are more than okay with them doing so.

"Feel free to add any other websites or search engines of interest. If it works for you, it works for me. We'd like to reach as many rightwing news sources as possible: Sinclair, Blaze, Hannity, Beck, *Drudge Report*, and Fox. I'd love to find a way to tap into Rush Limbaugh. He has a huge audience that is totally dedicated to him. But I'm not sure it's worth the effort. We know that we represent a hard sell to some of these voters, but unless we try to inform them, we'll never know if there are some who might consider the issues from our perspective.

"I recently learned about a few White House–based rogue Twitter accounts who have stirred up a lot of concern through the Trump years. Remember Anonymous? That Op-Ed piece really got under the president's skin as did the book they just published with the same title. There is a slew of anti-Trump books being published this year. He hates even the thought of a disloyal staff member, as we know all too well. There was a group of rogue employees within the White House in 2017 that were posting several negative stories about the administration. I'm not sure they're still around, but they were effective. Facebook killed the account as fake, but Twitter did not, and a few are still online. These accounts share Trump's true nature with the public and rattle Trump's cage, causing him to show his true colors."

"We are on it Professor." interjected Lavi.

I continued. "Even if these outlets repost us with negative editorial, we will still be reaching people otherwise unavailable to us. Remember, everything we send out is open-source and free for anyone to use as they choose. We have not copyrighted anything or placed any other restrictions on use and distribution by third parties. This is the exact model the Russians used in 2016. It worked for them. We can only hope that it will work for us.

"One reason we want to cast as wide a net as possible is for our own protection. My research has shown that readers love to repost and forward things to friends and family. My hope is that the classic exponential path such things usually take will work for us as well. And, if several sources are distributing our content, it will be harder for any intel group to identify us as the originators. We also want our content to go to as many people as possible. We should not care what their politics are. What we are producing is information for everyone to consider and hopefully adopt.

"Lavi, how can you identify fringe channels out there with wide distribution and how can we convince them to add our content to theirs's?

"This is difficult because of the way they work," said Lavi. "Facebook likes to distribute content based on what their readers want to see. Point of View content appears to person X because they have shown an interest in that kind of content. Most important is how long they have stayed on any given site. Getting our content to others is not impossible, but difficult. A lot depends on the language we use in our headlines. Making our message appear as general as possible helps keep it from being blocked. We need to find language that excites but does not threaten either a reader or Facebook's monitors. If people don't click on our content, Facebook will stop publishing it. Their model is based on numbers and time spent on a site. The more likes coming out of their systems and the longer the target stays on their site, the wider our distribution. Also, if a particular POV likes or agrees with the content, it will get an even wider distribution to other POVs."

Yosef broke in. "We need to keep in mind that Facebook wants content that produces clicks. That's their model. We should also post off-peak hours while others are not posting. Remember, time in this world is measured in nanoseconds. We need to build a following that might not agree with what we are saying, but that is engaged enough to like or dislike our posts and pass them on."

"How would you link to a major Twitter feed?" I asked.

Yosef jumped in. "One nice thing about Twitter is that if you respond to someone else's tweet, your response automatically goes into a replies and mentions column to everyone on their feed. People can add our content to their contact lists, which as you know rapidly becomes an exponential expansion. We will collect as many as we can and add them to our next posting."

"This is good, but we'll need to set up new identities and accounts every day or two so that our posts don't get muted or blocked." I then asked. "Lavi, maybe you can set up an algorithm so that our content links to that reboot and routes itself freely."

"How about a Facebook feed? Facebook is changing its posting procedures in response to all the flak they are getting about fake news, especially regarding how Russians and others are trying to manipulate our elections."

Lavi interrupted me. "Dr. Pryce, we thank you for all this input, but you need to know that the reason you hired us is that we do this all the time. Just leave the search and distribution tasks to us. The less you know about the specifics, the better. Many of these tasks cross the line and need to be handled very discreetly if they are to succeed. I mean no disrespect, but your job is to get content to us, and our job is to get it out there. I know that you know your job, we need you to feel confident that we know ours."

This was exactly what I needed to hear. "Thank you, Lavi. No disrespect taken. I appreciate you both for your expertise. Let me be perfectly clear: if you ever see us drifting off-course, call us out. We do not have the time to make repairs and even less time to mend wounded egos. Everything must be done right the first time. You're right, the less I know about the details, the more convincing and uninformed I can be if questioned.

Ari is leaving a bunch of burners here for each of you. We need to re-program these frequently. Ari will work out a new burner distribution plan for us. Keep the old ones and plug them in to charge at 1:00 a.m. every Sunday morning, your time. Ari will reprogram them and get the new access codes to you. Remember, we're not breaking any laws, only bending them. We must, however, remain anonymous. We don't want to come face-to-face with the Communications Assistance for Legal Enforcement Act that requires companies like Verizon or AT&T to make all data for any given number traceable. We need to start slowly until we have enough traffic and feedback from our visitors. Remember that the more traffic we get, the more our content is downloaded and shared by others. This makes it harder to trace the posts and protects our identities.

"I will supply content and data that you guys will recast as specific posts. I'd like our team character used as the person of record for spreading the word. His name will be Professor Mike."

I held up a couple of comic strips for everyone to see. Pogo, an extremely popular syndicated comic strip that ran in most papers from the late 1940s through the mid-70s. We loved reading it every week. Pogo always had an important message for us kids. "Lavi, I'd like you to show these strips to the artists, along with this photograph of a man I'd like our character to resemble. I want our character to be similar to Pogo, who projects objective confidence and is both wise and informed. He has no party affiliation, he is up front and direct, no fanfare, sticks to the facts. Our messages are going to be wrapped in the flag, but neither maudlin nor condescending. Mike will be the narrator of the content. If possible, I'd like Mike to eventually be animated. Each clip should include audio, if possible, and no more than twenty-five words. Any questions on this? Andrew?"

"No, we're pretty set from this end to start up as soon as we get the word from you. Every message we send out for distribution will go through a randomly generated, global list of different central transmission stations so that it will be impossible to trace where our posts originate. That path will also be random."

"Right," I said. "We'll work through normal posting channels and monitor our progress to learn how our content is being received. If we do not automatically get linked to the more obscure sites and platforms we want to get to, we'll have to find more creative ways of hacking into them. Remember, we are not regular viewer or followers of these host distributors. We want to infiltrate the host sites so that our posts automatically get linked to their posts or messages. They will surely figure out what is happening at some point and block us, hopefully we will have reached enough potential voters by then to not care. Remember, exposure and clicks are at the heart of our success. I plan to make the first several posts straightforward and non-controversial. I thought it best to start out like that and post more provocative texts as our exposure and clicks expand. That will also give the creatives time to design the audio and animation phase.

"One addition: This component is a short-term effort, ending on November 3, and to deal with the 2020 election. I want us to be an alternative voice that exposes the many lies, cheats, and outright subversion everyone expects from this administration. In fact, they've already started. For many reasons, Trump cannot afford to lose this election.

"I want you all to know that I was recently visited by two FBI agents who asked a lot of questions, but nothing about what we are doing. They seemed interested in my activities as a graduate student during the Vietnam War. They had some photos of me that were laughable. I believe I countered them convincingly enough so they will not be back. The only disturbing question from them was casually thrown in at the end. I believe it was the actual reason for their visit. They wanted to know about Andrew. I think they were questioning his unexpected demise. As much as I was involved with the war in the '60s, Andrew, as we all know, was much more active and maybe that was the source of the question.

"Andrew, I said you were lost at sea and that we do not know what happened. That has been our official line. I made them feel pretty cheeky for even asking. I think I was successful. They haven't gotten back to me.

"We have the capacity to throw a few monkey wrenches into the Trump juggernaut and hopefully convince a decent percentage of those sitting on the fence to come over to our side. Ari and I have decided it's critical that we not enter the fray with angry diatribes that would only put us in the same pack as millions of Never Trumpers. We're going to fact-check and counter the many lies and misinformation we expect this candidate to spill out. Their messages will range from his falsely claimed successes as president, to his relentless attacks on all challengers, real or imaginary, our posts and messages will go out to their followers with our message which will invariably counter that of the hosts."

I looked over at Andrew to gauge his response, since earlier he had expressed doubt about our added focus. He still looked skeptical. "This will take us off message. Why do you want to get involved in something as complicated as this election?"

"Because, Andrew, the vitriol has gotten out of hand and we have the ability, through the contacts we are making with the voter awareness campaign, to enlighten a key corps of voters. We only need to convince about half of the people who are undecided. There are about six or eight swing states that hold most of these influential electoral votes, the target audience for both sides. There are a lot of people who feel that our country cannot survive another four years under a Trump Administration, and I completely agree with them.

If it were an honest election and the will of the people were to prevail, I might be willing to let the system work itself out. The amount of illegal and manipulative actions from this president and the Republican Party forces us to get involved. Trump already wrote a series of Tweets claiming that the Democrats were going to steal this election, which turns out to be the very thing that he is doing. In fact, as I put together content, I first look at what Trump is accusing the other side of doing and that tells me *exactly* what he's planning. He'd make a lousy chess player. We have to do what we can to win our country back with an experienced and rational message. We will project ourselves as patriots who are connected to our nation's core values.

Andrew was clearly upset with me. "How do you plan to do this without contaminating our primary mission of getting people to vote?"

"We've been approached by a mole who says he works in the White House. His concerns are compatible with ours and the mole's purpose is to expose the more realistic persona of Trump, the man, and how disdainful of his so-called base he actually is. Our mole knows that he's not the least bit concerned with them or their needs. He wants only their votes and that is all. Our mole is convinced that another four years of this president would cause lasting damage to America and beyond. There are a lot of people taking big chances to get him out of office. We need to help them. Trump's actions and policies do not support his base, and we can show that to be the truth.

"Our mission will be to release the truth about the administration's policies and actions and let the voters decide. We know that there are a lot of biased news outlets out there that do not offer a truthful picture of what is happening in this administration. Fox News is the worst. It is the opinion of many in the profession that Fox has tied itself so closely to Trump that any hint of them as an objective source for news is no longer viable. They are a popular source for the voter we want to attract. Our job is to get to as many of that demographic that Trump and Fox call their base as we can and give them food for thought. My job will be to identify the best market to win the most votes. I have ideas on that, but they are not finalized as yet.

"We will be receiving messages from inside the White House on a weekly basis. Put that with the information I'm mining, and we're going to have a strong platform for his base to see the real Donald Trump. Ari and I are going to DC to meet with our mole and do some vetting; we cannot be too careful.

"I feel that this needs to be said. If this part of our project does not seem to be working as we get deeper into it, we'll drop it and move on. Please think about what it will mean for the election if we are able to make even a small dent in his base. Trump captured the electoral votes in Michigan and Wisconsin by fewer votes than the number of people who live withing fifteen blocks of my Brooklyn home. If we could persuade slightly more than half of those from Michigan and Wisconsin to our side, our impact on this election would be monumental. Are there any questions or comments? We must work as a team if we are to succeed, and I hope that I have convinced you that we are on a solid track."

"Benson," began Andrew, "I really hope that you've thought this through. We've been working on the voter awareness project for years; that alone will be a major effort. We're finally ready to go. I still feel that we do not have the resources for this extra project you seem committed to doing."

I understand and appreciate your concern, I don't think you're aware of just how successful Trump and his allies have been at subverting this election. At this point, the big money is betting he's going to win it. Not because he deserves to. People are afraid to vote because of COVID-19. Trump has taken over the Post Office to slow deliveries down; mail-in ballots may never see the light of day. He is trying to siphon off Democrat voters by recruiting left-leaning candidates to run in key states. Fringe candidates on the ballot is another reason he won in '16. Trump would not have won if Jill Stein, Gary Johnson, or others hadn't syphoned off votes from Hillary. There's no viable third-party candidate this time, and Trump knows that's a big negative for him. He also knows that Biden is not as disliked as Hillary was. Did you happen to hear that Trump actually stated that if the Republicans could not suppress the number of voters, then no Republican would ever get elected? Just imagine anyone else saying such a thing! If this is at all true, why would they not simply design campaign platforms that appeal to their constituents, rather than do everything possible to stop them from voting?"

"I actually have to hand it to the Republicans," added Andrew. "They have pulled themselves together far more professionally than the Democrats. They've managed to disqualify, gerrymander, and deny huge blocks of voters from ever voting. I recently read that more than 15 million registered voters who usually vote Democrat have been removed from the rolls in the past ten years alone." There were several nods of approval on Andrew's comments. I was beginning to win them over. This was a small team of highly motivated and skilled people. That made my job easier, but if any one of them does not buy into this goal of mine, it will sink under its own weight.

I had to be careful, not too pushy or defensive. This was their project as much as mine. I was pushing, but I could not diminish Andrew or his role. The team would follow him, since they all work together.

"Lavi, Yosef, are you on board with this? It is not going to happen without you."

Lavi looked at me and said, "Benson, we both know that Trump is not a person to be trusted. Biden is a known person and does not come with all the baggage of Trump. If this project of ours can bring a more responsible person into the White House, we're on board. We would, however, like to know what plans you have for the voter awareness part after the election."

"That's a great question and something I have given a lot of thought to. We know that anything we can accomplish over the next few months will not be enough to keep the American voter engaged. I will definitely want to do that but, not with all this anxiety. My plan is to keep the team together and try to find distribution channels that are above board and capable of luring as many eligible voters possible on an ongoing basis. Thanks for that and I look forward to discussing the possibilities after this election."

It looked like the meeting was over. I thanked them for their time and instructed them to keep in touch with Ari as often as necessary. He and I are in constant touch and there is no need to complicate our communications."

As we were walking out of the room and toward our plane, Andrew asked, "I want to hear more about Anna. How is she? Is she happy?"

"You won't believe what has happened, Andrew! She enrolled at Columbia University for a master's degree in Social Work, and she is also taking courses at NYU. She has made some great friends there and seems to be doing well. She misses you terribly, and not being able to be honest with her is one of the most difficult things I have ever had to do. Financially, she is doing very well on her own. Like many in her generation, she is taking full advantage of the city and all that it has to offer young people. In our day, we never had the time or money to do a fraction of what they get to do. They are super-careful regarding the virus, get tested often, and are gathering only in small groups of people they know well. They have been highly creative with masks, and it has become a designer-based competition. As we get closer to winter, this is going to change, and that's a problem. I have suggested that she keep the money you have left her in the Roth account you set up. She thinks I did it for her. She does not need the money now, and I know you want her to think of it as a retirement fund. She is beautiful and confident. Discounting the pain for having lost her father, she's really doing well. I do hope that we will be able to get you back together soon."

Andrew's shoulders sunk down and all the air came out of him. "This has been hard but given the events I have had to deal with from the Feds, we have both agreed that this is best. It will be over soon."

He collected himself. "I couldn't agree more. I never thought I'd have to do something like this to her. I counted on her strength when I did what I did to protect her. I only hope that the damage will not create a permanent gap between us. I want to bring us back together but can't as long as there is a risk. What has happened to you with the Feds proves that we're right."

"You know that Trump is pretending that COVID doesn't even exist, right? Scuttlebutt is that if he ignores it, does not wear a mask or worry about social distancing, his base will do the same and he will lose no votes."

"He doesn't really think that, does he?"

"Apparently so. In any case, no need to worry about Anna. She is being incredibly careful. I also hope that we can get you back together soon. My thinking is the best we can hope for is after the election. The voter awareness component of our project will continue, but that will not require this level of intrigue. We can only hope that Trump is defeated," I said earnestly.

"I honestly think that the information we will be publishing is going to set off a lot of people, especially the corporate and elected officials who are bleeding this system. We both know that we do not plan to publish anything that isn't already public. However, it will be new information to the specific audiences we want to reach who have no idea how much they are being ripped off. This will be especially true because of the initiatives the Republicans have taken to suppress voters. If Biden is elected, we really need to rewrite the Voting Rights Act and make it immune to any further Supreme Court actions. Once our message is out there, things should settle down, and we can figure out a way for Anna to come to you without revealing to the world that you are still alive. If she blames you, I insist that we put it all on me. It would be difficult not to have her in my life, but totally unbearable for you.

"You both know that no one in the world means more to me that the two of you, Andrew. I hope we can keep the three of us together. If not, I will have to be the sacrificial lamb, not you. But for now, I have to get out of here. We're flying to Switzerland this afternoon to replenish our funds. Ari and I believe that I'm under observation. I do not have a wide window to be out of the country, so we have to get back to the States before I am missed. I will clear it with Ari to see if we can use Skype or WhatsApp to talk." I wanted to know one more thing from him. "Andrew, do you plan to come back to the States at some point, or are you going to stay hidden?"

"I'm really not sure; a lot will depend on how all this turns out and what happens between Anna and me. I am not comfortable not being around for her. Frankly, I have no reason other than Anna to go back, but I have a lot of reasons to stay in Europe. I am more comfortable here, a fact that will really be true if Trump wins. I'll keep you posted."

"There you go, you just gave the best reason I can think of to attack his reelection effort. He loses the election, you get more choices for your life."

"That's not nice, clever but not fair. I can see that you are committed to the Trump offensive. I really understand and will back you totally, and you know I will."

I smiled and let him know that his loyalty towards this new twist was never really in doubt.

"Love you, big guy, do be careful," Andrew said. We did an offside hug. Which I have on good authority is acceptable if you know each other. "You're actually the most exposed member of this team. You need to be careful. I have a feeling you're not being up front with us about the extent of the surveillance on you. There are a lot of corrupt people out there who are going to be hurt by what we are doing. Your new wrinkle, as you call it, really puts you and this project at risk."

"We're all important. You know that I will do my best. Our biggest asset is Ari, he amazes me almost every day. I want you to calm down, we have this under control. I actually thought I was the most paranoid person on the team. Apparently not. I must go. Are you sure everyone is on board with what we are doing?"

"I do. This team is as dedicated as are you and I,, and they are incredibly happy to be a part of this effort."

I said my goodbyes with sincere thanks for everything. Ari and I boarded our plane and took off immediately. It seemed so strange to have entered and left a foreign country without going through customs. Now, we had one more stop to make. I could only hope that it would be as uneventful.

Two hours later, we were on the ground in Switzerland, at a small and obscure airport well outside of Geneva and clearly dedicated to small private planes. My banker was on the tarmac ready to hand off my package. I gave him both cases of wine, stating that I was not sure which one he would prefer. We shook gloved hands, and I got back on the plane. It was ready for takeoff before I returned to my seat.

The flight back was quiet. Ari and I were both drained and slept for the first half of the trip. Halfway across the Atlantic, we woke up. I took a long hot shower, and Ari prepared a great breakfast. This plane was really amazing. I want one. For the first time in what seemed like an eternity, we were able to talk.

I took a handful of cash out of the briefcase, folded it into my money belt, and handed the rest to Ari for safekeeping. I asked him to deduct the travel expenses, tip the pilots and drivers, and get home safely. I suddenly realized that I had no idea where he lived.

"Thanks for pulling this together for us, my friend. I hope you know how much I depend on you and our relationship."

"I do, Benson, I do. I now consider myself an integral part of the team, not just your security cop. I am glad that I came on this trip. We are doing something especially important and I love being a bigger part of it. I am looking forward to being more useful."

"Never doubt that you are," I said. "I think we're in fairly good shape. Lavi and Yosef will get back to you on the artists. Let me know how you want me to contact them—or if you want to do that yourself? Let's plan to meet next Thursday."

"Can do," he said. "I'll find a time and place."

"Ari, we talked about setting up a meeting with Agent Orange or their rep?"

"Yes, we should do it soon. We need to make sure that he or she is for real and not a double agent. Ask AO to meet in DC or NYC, their preference. You and I will go together. I will make sure that wherever they want to meet, that it's secure. Send me the time and place as soon as you find out."

"Will do. I hope he agrees," I said.

"We have to be careful. Who do you think we are dealing with?" he asked.

"I have been thinking about that, and I believe I know who he is."

"Really, care to share? You just let me know that we are dealing with a man," Ari said.

"Nothing gets past you, does it? I am not sure, but you will be the first to know."

Chapter 14

August 2020

I met my replacement in the subway and retrieved my clothes and keys with thanks and best wishes. I picked up my secure laptop from the studio apartment. I had never been in this unit, but I could tell that it was a wonderfully disheveled storehouse for the condo. It was perfect for my purpose. I also knew I was in for one of the busiest weeks of my life and would barely have a moment to breathe.

I had sent a note to Agent Orange requesting that we meet. I let him choose where and when. We could meet in DC or anywhere he felt safe. He got back to me almost immediately stating that he was about to suggest the same idea. He offered the following Sunday in DC at the Lincoln Memorial. He let me know that he would be in a white shirt with a MAGA hat and be at the top of the stairs at noon.

Got it. I'll be in a Boston Red Sox cap, tan cargo jacket.

I got busy pulling the text together for the voter awareness posts. The hardest part would be choosing which issues to put up first. I hoped that the prototypes I'd left with the team were sufficient. I knew everything would go smoother and be more secure if the graphics were done from their side of the pond.

After working for some time, I warmed up the Chinese takeout that I'd picked up and found a beer in the fridge. Then I sat down and gazed out at my familiar downtown view. It felt good to relax for a few moments.

My next state of awareness was when I woke up. It was midnight. I still had the chopsticks in my hand, and my untouched dinner was in front of me. I realized how tired I must have been. I find myself needing more sleep than I was used to getting. In any case, I was refreshed and knew that I had nothing on tap for the next day. I finished the sesame noodles and General Tso's chicken. I drank the warm beer and booted up the security laptop, inputting all the coded links Ari had installed to make it impossible for anyone else to use this machine. Then I inserted the flash drive with a copy of our database and the information that Andrew had downloaded. I'm still amazed at how much information can be stored on such tiny devises

This was the fun part for me. Andrew and I had been thinking about how we could wake up Americans to the fact that we were no longer the superpower we once were. Content and presentation were critical. We did not want to sound like doomsayers. We knew that our audience didn't read much, and time was in demand, which was why they used social media for their news. We needed to get our message to them in a format they would accept.

Traditional publishing outlets were all we had when we first created this idea. Fortunately, the unlimited power of the internet came along. The limits of our data collection capacity were only constrained by our ability to master how to use it and make it receptive to the audience we wanted to reach.

I decided to concentrate on non-controversial topics of interest to a broad demographic: employment statistics, the US infant and maternal mortality rate, and the differences between how black and brown people live in the US when compared to whites. Even when controlled for age and education, black and brown families suffer a shocking deficiency in America, the land of opportunity! I knew the sensitivity of this issue to those who really do not care about the lives of minorities, I also knew that there are a lot of people on the right in America who are not inherent racists.

I took a closer look at selected data on our health compared to that of other developed nations. On a per capita basis, the US spends almost three times more than other developed nations. Other comparable nations on average spend less than $4,000 per capita per year on healthcare. We spend almost $11,000 per capita each year, and we suffer considerably higher rates of ill health. Given that America also has a lower life expectancy, a higher obesity rate, and a higher death rate for treatable and untreatable diseases, one must conclude that we are doing something wrong.

Complicating the problem, we have some of the best hospitals and doctors in the world. But our healthcare system is only functioning efficiently for those upper income families that can afford health care insurance that used to be provided to most workers as a part of their employment. We must do better. The pandemic was most certainly on the minds of most Americans, whether or not they were listening to Trump's denial strategy. Twenty-five million cases worldwide were reported. America had just hit the six million mark with an average of 45,000 cases every day and a thousand deaths per day, but still no plan out of Washington.

I put all of these data into an accessible format to save our team the trouble of doing so and sent them to Ari. That was a good start. Our next purpose was to criticize our president and his administration, but to do so in a constructive way. We needed to ensure that the posts wouldn't be interpreted as spam. More importantly, we wanted our posts to be read and favorably absorbed by even the most die-hard Trump supporters. We wanted our posts to give them pause and change their perception of the man they chose to support. We wanted our readers to ask themselves if he was really the populist, man of the people, that he projected himself to be? Was he really an intelligent, thoughtful, informed, and capable president for America and all of its citizens? Did he have the experience and critical thinking skills to do the job? Was he dedicated to unifying our nation? Did he really understand America's responsibility in an increasingly volatile and competitive world? Would you want him to date your single mother? Our task was to convince at least 55% of American voters. I say 55% because anything less, and we would be stuck with a contested election that could get much dirtier than Gore/Bush. As disastrous as I think Trump has been, he had the advantage of being the incumbent, and he had the loyalist base of any modern-day politician. We also worked from the premise that he would do anything to win the election. The fact that he hated to lose has almost become part of American political lexicon. Trump knew that there were several district attorneys holding incriminating information on him. A second term would allow the statute of limitations to kick in on many of them.

Ari and I set up a time and place to meet. He chose Union Square. Neither of us had much time, so we had to make it short. He gave me a new burner for calling the team and a series of temporary email addresses that enabled me to send text messages. He already sent out the first batch of posts to the team.

"We can't be too careful on communications," he said. "They are listening all the time. Don't use any of these addresses more than twice, and never in a row. These addresses are linked to old ISPs that are not in use anymore."

I looked them over and chuckled. "Ari, you have several user interfaces under Pipeline."

"I know. That company doesn't even exist, but their interface is still active."

"You're right. The problem is that I have had a Pipeline address since the early 80s. That was when email was first introduced. They made it available to us academics, thinking that we'd be the most obvious audience for internet communications. A gross underestimate, one might say. Pipeline was started as PipelineNY, which was sold to Pipeline USA, and later to Mindspring. It's now folded into Earthlink.net's ISP."

Ari couldn't believe that. "What are the chances? Let's not risk it," he said. "Use the others for now."

"I would rather not replace my Pipeline address and if I did, it would surely be noticed." I let him know that we were set with Agent Orange. "He told me to come alone, which I don't want to do. I want you there at the Lincoln Memorial with me to prevent anyone from possibly photographing us together. Can you make it? I thought we could take an early morning train to minimize pandemic exposure. I have Amtrak reservations on the 6:02a.m. out of Penn Station."

"I can come," he said, "but we should travel separately on different trains. I might decide to go down the night before and check out the site. I could also check up on our DC safe house in case we need it. Here's an earpiece I want you to wear. If I see something, I can warn both of you. I want you to tell Agent Orange as soon as you feel comfortable with him that I am nearby. I want him to know that you have the piece, and that it's connected *only* to me. I don't want him to find it on his own before you tell him. Are you still going to keep me in the dark as to who he is?"

I could see that this was important to Ari. "Yes, I *think* my guess is right, but I don't want to second-guess him. Thanks for getting the voter awareness posts out to the team. I haven't heard anything about the artwork, have you?"

"No, do you have the new text with you?"

"Yes, on a flash drive. Do you want it now?" I asked.

"Yes, I did not store the data myself," Ari responded. "The team will text me if they have any questions. I can hide the drive. I'll complete the data with secure links to you and the team as soon as I know the system is clear and secure."

"I'm beginning to think everything will go smoother if they can communicate directly with you," I said. Also, as Lavi pointed out, I should be taken out of as much exchange with the team as possible. Remember that I'm on someone's radar. I would prefer that you communicate with the team and the artists. Is that okay with you?"

"Yes," he said, "you're right. We will work out a system where I get the content from you rather than having to meet. Maybe through Mr. Bonaparte. We set up a delivery and pick-up system with your building years ago through UPS. I've kept the account open, and it is folded directly into their normal deliveries."

"Okay. Just be sure that he's not compromised. Let me know what you want me to do as soon as you can. I am going to do the elections content tomorrow. I have decided to call those posts 'Enough Trump.' Do you think that will make it past the platform reviewers?" I asked.

"Given what's already out there on Trump," I said, "it sounds pretty passive. Leave an unlabeled flash drive with Mr. Bonaparte for now. He and I will work something out."

"Sounds like a plan. I'm still shocked that you two not only know each other but have worked together for so long."

"We connected many years ago when Barbados was having some pretty serious political problems. I was able to bug the government offices they needed to track. Barbadians don't like leaders who rip them off."

"I'm glad that you were able to help. Mr. Bonaparte is the only person from Barbados I know. He has been like a brother to me. Please give me some insight into how I should deal with Agent Orange. I want to walk away fully confident that he is, in fact, on our side. I don't know how he could have possibly figured out what we are doing."

"First of all, wear two shirts, and put another baseball cap in your pocket," Ari said. "Maybe wear cargo pants so you have a lot of pockets. Make sure the colors of the second shirt and cap are different from what you will wear to the Memorial. Don't wear flashy shoes—we don't want them standing out if you have to make a run for it."

"Good idea. I'm wearing a light cargo jacket which I have cleared with Agent Orange already. I do not even own a pair of flashy shoes. I do have to pick up a Boston Red Sox hat."

Ari got serious. "The best thing is to ask him, right off, what he knows about you and how he learned it. Follow his answers closely to be sure that what he says adds up. Don't ask his name; we don't need it and it can be threatening at a meeting like this. Try to find out about his career, education, family, and current position. Also, bring up the question on how he learned about you again. Ask him about his security systems to make sure that he's familiar with them. That'll show us how he is protecting himself. If this has been set up by a third party, he will not know about it and that would be problematic. In fact, if he seems hesitant on the workings of our phone and communications procedures, he's probably wearing a wire. I would leave immediately."

"Wow, that would be a shame," I said.

"It would, but you'd have no choice. If that happens, walk into a crowd as soon as possible. Work yourself as deeply into the crowd as you can and head toward the bus station. Buy a ticket to Philadelphia. Then go into the bathroom. Make sure you're not followed; you most likely will be. Do not waste time. Change your shirt and hat, maybe add sunglasses and change your mask, and come right out, as soon as possible, in your new disguise. Don't throw your old clothes away—they will find them. Stuff them in your pockets. Walk quickly and directly out of the terminal toward the south exit and go to the corner of North Capital and E Street. They will figure out that you slipped out in less than five minutes. Wait on the corner for me. Try to wait behind other people. I will have a black limo with a handwritten sign on the window reading *Smith*. Hop in and we'll drive back home. What hat will you have on at that point?"

"A green Sierra Club hat."

"Good."

"I sincerely hope we do not have to go through all that, but it is best to be prepared." I stated. "What else do I want to know about Agent Orange should things go well?"

"If you make it to this point, let him know that I'm here, but out of sight. I don't want to disturb him if he should get suspicious. Tell him who I am and that I am there only to make sure no one is hovering. Let him know that I'll already have checked out the location where you are meeting. He should be okay with all this. Once he's comfortable, ask why he's helping us. What's in it for him? How free is he to communicate with us? His answers to these questions will be critical. You will know if he is given prepared answers, and that's what you are looking for. He will probably also have a backup some-where nearby. Ask him how he wants his backup and me to know that we've been spotted? Does he have a second phone?"

I was furiously taking notes and looked up to see what Ari had to say next.

"You really are an academic, aren't you?" Ari smiled. "Make sure that sheet of paper does not get loose. I'll let you know as soon as our artists are onboard. I think you did a good thing to let the team pick them."

"Do I have to eat my notes?"

"Given your penchant for high end dining, I strongly suggest that you don't."

"Okay, I think we're done," I said. "Time for you to fade into that fog you manage to create every time we finish talking. It will be difficult for you on a day like this—" Ari was gone before I finished the sentence. I wrote some more notes on a separate piece of paper, opened a book, and sat for a while before leaving. I had a lot of work to do and wanted to get back to the apartment.

I KNEW THAT THE NEXT SEVERAL WEEKS were going to involve a lot of data input and writing. I needed to keep the security laptop hidden when it was in the apartment. So, I bought a large book on antiques from the discount shelf at The Strand on Broadway, my favorite bookstore. I cut out the pages just slightly larger than the laptop, so I could hide it in the book on one of my bookshelves. Even though neither Ari nor I saw any evidence of surveillance, that didn't mean I was in the clear

That afternoon, I started to build up a library of content for the election-related posts. It was my intention not to create a character for these. I would rely only on the headliner "Enuf Trump." I thought of using the original family name, Drumpf, which was changed to Trump by Donald's grandfather, Friedrich Drumpf who, like many immigrants, wanted to anglicize the family name. I needed to focus on the audience I wanted to appeal to. Some would never change their minds or votes. The diehard Trump base ignored even the most egregious of their hero's actions. Paying off a sexual affair with campaign money, bribing the president of another nation to dig up dirt against a political foe is, to them, apparently an acceptable act, and on and on.

Trump conveniently ignored the fact that his actions conflicted with the Constitution and the law. I wonder if he has even read our Constitution. He passed a major tax decrease that barely impacted his base, resulted in no increase in economic activity but, it did significantly increase our national debt. He fired anyone who won't break the law or their oath of office to prove their loyalty to him. He was known to offer none in return. If his base willfully tolerated this stream of behavior, it is unlikely that anything we said would move them off their alt-right soapbox. We *want* to win them over, and all we can do is try.

We must be credible. To gain their ear, and that of others we wish to persuade, we must publish the truth. It must also be something that directly impacts them. Anything less would be a nanosecond away from fake news. Our target audience was the 10 to 20 % of registered undecided voters. The secondary audience were the voters in the eight swing states whose electoral votes we would need. We also targeted millennials, Gen Z, and black and brown folks who did not vote in 2016 and/or 2018, and suburban working women, an important block that seems to be leaving the Trump tent in droves. It is truly incredible how micro we can now get on data collection and digital distribution. The opposition can, of course, do the same.

Most pundits felt, at this point, that the election could go either way. We had to deal with the power of incumbency and trust that there were enough voters in the middle whose desire for competency, decency, and a unifying voice would prevail in November. Biden's appointees would not suffer jail or indictments. An awfully low bar, to be sure.

After working on the Trump posts for the afternoon, I got a quick take-out delivery and comfortably sat looking out at the darkening sky.

⋆ ⋆ ⋆

I STORED MY COMPUTER AND THE FLASH DRIVE inside the book. I set an alarm for 4:30 a.m. on Sunday, allowing plenty of time to get to Penn Station. I needed to make this trip, and I did not want to drive. I had to hope that there would be few people on board at that time on a Sunday morning. My sleep habits are so established that I can tell myself when I want to wake up. That morning was too important to leave to chance. Surprisingly, I slept pretty well and was dressed and out the door by 5:00 a.m. I bought the paper and some snacks and headed uptown, discreetly glancing behind me as I walked.

I was ready with the Red Sox hat in my pocket, not something a New Yorker would otherwise sport. I also had a green Sierra Club hat as my backup, which was stuffed into a separate pocket. I wore my backup shirt underneath my other one with the collar turned down and a reversable jacket. I was ready.

There were two trains on the track, so I casually boarded the one I wasn't taking. The train schedule board in the waiting room informed me that it was leaving sooner than mine. I walked down a few cars, and as soon as I heard the beep of the doors closing, I hopped off and ran across the platform to my train. I saw that in a movie many years ago. I think it was *The French Connection*. I felt pretty cool and could only hope that I had lost any tail I might have had.

I took a window seat so I could see if anyone had also gotten off the other train. Now I had only to worry about a tail who knew where I was going and what train I was taking. Although I was getting used to all this subterfuge, I would be glad when it was over. My assumption on fellow riders was correct—I had the car almost to myself.

I settled in with my coffee, poppy seed bagel scooped-out with Nova lox, tomato, capers, and onion, and the Sunday *Times*. Trump continued to dominate the headlines. That week, he had once again asked the Supreme Court to abolish the Affordable Care Act. I lost track of how many times these suits made it to the courts and the floor of the Senate. He was also trying to get back on the campaign trail, given the lockdowns and spreading coronavirus. Justice Thomas hinted at retiring, which would give Trump an opportunity to place a third ultraconservative on the court. Thomas was probably trying to avoid public scrutiny, should Trump lose the election and the Democrats take over the White House and possibly the Senate. Trump continued to refuse to wear a mask despite the strong advice of his own health advisors. He has also fired two more inspectors general for not following his dictum. Like every other day, this one began with unfathomable drama brought on by Trump. The drama would inevitably be repeated the following day, only the actors would be different.

It was clear to me that the constant bedlam coming out of the White House on Twitter was a strategy to create diversions to keep the press and the public at bay. Each new initiative was designed to enhance his growing autocracy. Executive orders were issued most often before dawn each day. The "Distractor in Chief" was a master of this art.

I folded the paper and walked down the aisle toward the garbage chute, just to look my fellow passengers over to see if there was a tail on board. My job was easy since there were only three people in the car, none of whom seemed suspicious. I began to think that my White House snoop was wrong about me being under strict surveillance. I got back to my seat, shut my eyes, and started to go through what Ari had told me and how to handle the meeting. I had burned my notes as soon as I memorized them. I recognized that, should Agent Orange work out for us, he would make it possible to get closer to Trump and his behavior. We would gain credibility with the information we had against the administration, proving that it was focused on the destruction of democracy in America.

Soon I heard the announcement that we arrived at Union Station. I left the train, deliberately heading the wrong way before I turned around to see who was behind me. No one was visible, so I headed to the exit. I had a couple hours before my meeting, so I grabbed another coffee and sat on a bench outside the station. Mindful of everyone around me, I pensively enjoyed the warm August sun on my face. I stood up and headed toward the National Mall. I decided to walk rather than take a cab. Doing so was no sacrifice because I genuinely love walking by these venerable memorials and impressive flags and symbols of our nation's heritage. I'm a patriot and it makes me angry that the alt-right has taken over the flag as their own—how dare they! The sheer boldness of these sights deliberately overwhelms and impress. They each provide a clear statement that represents America's strength and resiliency. Our nation is in pain right now and walking past these symbols gave me confidence that we would once again, hopefully soon, regain the respect and privilege of being an American.

As I approached the Lincoln Memorial, I caught Ari on the lawn off the corner of the stairs. It was about 11:45, when I climbed up the stairs of the Lincoln Memorial and worked my way over to the designated spot to the left of Mr. Lincoln, at the top. I was in direct sunlight, so I put on my Red Sox hat. I heard a cough from a pillar behind me. I turned around and saw a MAGA hat on the floor next to a trim, clean-shaven young man in a white shirt. We both had masks on, which kind of made this whole exercise of discretion a bit humorous. We both laughed at the same time, moved a comfortable distance and removed our masks, having cleared the air between us in more ways than one.

I asked him for the time.

"Right on time—it's noon. How was your trip down?"

"Uneventful and quick," I said. "A cross-country trip on Amtrak is definitely on my bucket list when I retire."

"Sounds like a plan. I'm pleased that you're here and hope that we can forge a solid working relationship that will have no need to exist past November."

"I could not agree more. I'm really too old for this, but I feel that we need to step it up, as recent events have proven that another four years will not only wear us out, but leave our democracy struggling to survive." I looked at him and said, "You're much younger than I thought you'd be. Tell me a little about yourself if you don't mind."

"I am an FBI agent, temporarily assigned to the White House detail of the Secret Service. I am thirty-six, and my wife and I have our first child on the way. Uh... I was born in Virginia and I went to the GW School of Public Policy and Public Administration. I've wanted to work for intelligence since I was ten. I hope to get a master's degree, but the job has been pretty intense for several years, so that goal is on hold for now. I envy your PhD."

"Okay, sounds good. Congratulations on your child. But I have to ask—how'd you find out about me? I honestly thought I was going to meet someone else today."

"Dennis?"

"To tell the truth," I said, "yes. I thought you'd be either Dennis or Dean. I couldn't imagine anyone else figuring out who I am and what I care about. In fact, I thought I had kept anything substantive from both of them when we met in New York."

253

"Dennis told me about that meeting," Agent Orange said. "The White House ordered them to interview you along with a bunch of other former NYU students from the '60s and '70s."

"I was really surprised that they were doing this. They seemed extremely uncomfortable which confused me. Do they really think those Vietnam protestors are a threat? Their last question to me was about a friend and my takeaway was that he was the entire reason they wanted to meet me."

"They liked the way you handled yourself. They believed you. The deal was clinched when you went off on them for wasting their time on you when the real threat to the agency and all of our intelligence services is the orange man in the Oval Office. We all know it but can't say anything about it. Because of our positions and the oath, we have taken, we have to tread lightly. Talk of disloyalty, treason, and civil war are rampant. People are really scared."

I took the time to let the importance of what he was saying sink in for both of us. I sensed the anguish in his face and body language. These people are patriotic and totally devoted to the oath they each have taken. Just talking to a person like me with my purpose is not a task a man like Agent Orange is comfortable doing. I asked, "Have you cleared meeting me with your superiors? Does anyone outside of your team know what we are talking about and planning?"

"Yes, completely. I cleared this meeting with our director and his superior, in fact our meeting today was their idea." he continued. "We all met off campus and went over the meeting Watson and Sanders had with you. They had reviewed your profile and were both convinced and impressed with your patriotism, which was further verified by your academic and professional record. I might add that the meetings you had with Dennis and Dean were expunged from the record. So, for all intents and purposes, you no longer exist in our intelligence offices and files. Dennis and Dean were instructed to contact me, and they told me to contact you. We don't know *what* you're actually doing. We *do* know that Andrew Lawson is alive, and that you two have something going on."

"Wow, how'd you know about Andrew?"

"It's our job—simple as that. I'm frankly uncomfortable with this kind of meeting, but our director authorized me to work with you. Like you, he knows who our real threat is. We're constrained by our professional limits, and he knows what would happen if we violated them. I don't know how much further up the ladder this information has gone, but our team and directors are on record to support you. My goal today is to hear what your plans are and figure out how we can help."

"I'm as nervous as you are. I came down because I thought you may be of great help to us. I do, however, have to tell you something just in case you are suspicious of me. I have an invaluable tech guy who's been with me for years. I never make a move on security matters without his input. I have already introduced you to him on the burner you sent to me. I called him Raven for this project and while you probably can't see him, he's watching us and can hear us. Raven scanned our position last night to make sure no one was listening."

"Actually, I'm not surprised. In fact, I have a security guy as well. We should let them know about each other before one of us gets a dead hand throttle to bug out. Tell me something about him."

"He's wearing a red MAGA hat and he's dressed in black," I said. "He told me that if you were legit, you would have a backup close by as well."

"Ha, you know my guy, it's Dennis, also in a MAGA hat. ."

"Another MAGA hat? I'm beginning to think that we're a marketing team for Trump."

We both laughed.

"You get the word to Raven, and I will tell Dennis," he said. I took off my hat and brushed back my hair three times. Raven had been informed. Agent Orange muffled something into his wrist. I was glad we covered that. It would have been a total waste if they had spotted each other not knowing their roles.

"Fortunately for us, these guys do think alike."

I breathed a sigh of relief. I really thought Dennis was going to be my mole. I didn't for one second, think that we actually had the blessing of the agency. That was a surprise.

"Please tell me what you're doing so I can figure out how to help you. What's your primary objective?" he asked.

"Fair question. But first I need to ask you about the tail you said was on me in your first message. I haven't seen any sign of a 24/7 tail. Do you have anything new on that?"

"No, I was told about it during my initial briefing with Dean and Dennis that the White House had flagged you for 24/7. We decided to pass the intel to you. I'll have to get back to you on that."

"We thought that it would be better to communicate via text around five on Fridays. More traffic, harder to trace. Are you okay with that?" I asked. "Also, end your message with the @ if you feel you're in trouble and a thumbs-up emoji if you want to talk."

"Will do, and these are good ideas."

"Thank you. Andrew and I started our project to help American voters become more informed about the issues, with the hope that they would feel compelled to vote. We've monitored the low voter participation over several elections and consider that to be a threat to our democracy. We are now technically able to go really deep into these data and identify people by party, home ownership, profession, when they last voted, and more. We're committed to getting every viable voter to the polls and helping them be better informed. We'll be contacting them several times with similar messages.

"Our intention was to also infiltrate fringe, non-establishment, sources where periphery voters typically get their information. Many of these postings and broadcasts are actually libelous in terms of the information they distribute to their audiences. This was the strategy used against Hillary in 2016. We hope to offer a more believable alternative, backed by facts, and distribute them through their own media."

"Facts don't seem to have much value in today's political world," Agent Orange chuckled.

"You're right. We're creating a series of informational posts that highlight how America has been falling behind the rest of the world and what needs to be done to get our country back on track. I would rather not reveal how we plan to accomplish our goals...but suffice it to say that we want more people voting, and we want them better informed about which candidates best reflect their interests. This aspect or our project is long-term. The election-based releases were recently added and are temporary. They differ mainly in format and the audience we want to reach."

"This is certainly a major issue for the nation. Tell me more about the election related effort."

"Because of the Russian interference with the 2016 election and recent events that reflect a total breakdown in this administration's ability to lead, we've added this 2020 election component.. We will now highlight how Trump has created a serious vacuum of trust, not only nationally, but to our vital global interests as well. We feel that the election will be pivotal for the survival of our representative democracy. We will distribute only truthful information, and we're prepared to reach out to potential voters and citizens whose usual sources, based on our research, are more propaganda-based than informative. We have a sophisticated staff and are prepared to hack into the same channels as those who infiltrated the 2016 election. Russian hackers are also on our list. Many of them have been identified by investigative journalists, and that's where we started getting into their heads."

"That's not far off what we thought you were up to. We know about the expertise that you and Andrew offer through speeches and publications. We reached out because we felt that you were involved in something that could be of use to the agency. This has to be a very expensive operation, how are you funded, whose money are you using.

"Fair question and I am sure it was on the list of items given to you to ascertain. Everything is funded by me. We have never taken money from any outside sources for obvious reasons. Fortunately, I am able to do this and decided early on that we would remain financially independent. That decision was made by Andrew and me about ten years ago.

Thank you, that is important to the Bureau, as you know. It would be problematic if political money of any kind were on the table. How can we help you?"

I could tell that we had just crossed over a threshold. Agent Orange's face and entire body seemed to fold into the marble step we were sitting on. I could not tell if it was a feeling of confidence, relief, or joy. I knew at that moment that everything he and his team had discussed and hoped for in terms of who my team and I represented as a way out of a dilemma they were facing and could not resolve on their own. I gave him some time as we both looked out at the Washington Monument.

As soon as I felt that the air had cleared, I said. "Well, our job is to get the truth out in a clear, simple format and publish it where folks will easily find it. We hoped that your position in White House security might give us an insider's perspective into how this administration functions. How does it make decisions? What is the president like on a daily basis? Is everyone in agreement with him, or are they just trying to save their jobs? We can see that this White House is not an easy place for staff and executives, due mainly to the erratic behavior of the president. We are told that, at this point, there are few 'adults' in the room, and that those who have remained don't know from one moment to the next what he'll say, do, or proclaim in a tweet.

"I want to make a critical point. We do not want to print or broadcast anything that's not true or anything that could be traced back to you. We'd like to get a more open and honest impression of the workings of the Trump White House; however, it has to be done with no exposure on your part or that of the Bureau. Is that something you can do?"

I watched for his reaction. He was in deep thought and reluctant to respond, which frankly concerned me. After what seemed like an eternity, he looked up at the Washington Monument again, as though he needed its approval to continue our discussion. "I'm a third-generation agent," he said. "My father and grandfather served, as did my mother. My family is grateful for all that this nation represents. I've taken an oath to serve our president. I need you to know that my country comes first, and I'm prepared to die to protect our Constitution. You also need to know that the situation in the White House is beyond anything I've ever seen. The other agents and I live in fear that something terrible is going to happen—each and every day. Something needs to be done, and we have little power. Step even slightly out of line, and we'll be fired. We stay on just to keep things from getting out of hand. Our loyalty and oath are to the office—not the person. That won't help us deal with what many consider our national emergency. That's it in a nutshell, that's is why our group was formed and why we contacted you."

I responded sympathetically. "I suspected as much. You guys have to walk a fine line between your professional honor and the chaos all around you. We would never ask you to do anything that would put you in harm's way—we have enough to work with already. What we could use is evidence that displays how unhinged things are getting. We need a Watergate-era smoking gun to let the world know what's really happening. Not names or dates, but reliable evidence to help the voting public see that we are at great risk should Trump win another term. We want to show his base that he really does not care about them. His re-election is his only concern, and he's willing to go to any length to win. At least, that is what many of us are witnessing. Above all, we need to be credible. The truth is, as professional economists, we are sympathetic with those who have put their trust in Trump. Too many unfulfilled promises and their dwindling opportunities have driven them to anyone not connected with the establishment."

Agent Orange looked me straight in the eye, and I could tell he needed to hear what I'd just said. "The bureau and I can help, but we must be left whole when the dust settles, if we are to have the needed credibility to clean up this mess. We need to know that we will in no way be identified with this effort. How do I get information to you? We're clearly not comfortable with all this, but we feel it has to be done. Whatever was going on during Watergate—that entire exercise was trivial in terms of the danger this administration represents to us."

"I'll talk with Raven and get back to you. The phones we have are perfectly safe. You can text me, even call. If I have any doubts, I will @ back to you and set up another way to securely talk on this or another phone we will get to you. I will get a mailbox in the city set up so you can send anything you want us to have in hard copy. Raven has a safe house and colleagues down here and he will get that info to you.

"Do not remove any documents from the White House. Doing so would be far too risky. We will put our trust in you and assume everything you text to us is authentic and cannot be denied or challenged. Just be careful that nothing can be traced back to you. Focus on events and discussions also observed by others. Our objective is to portray a dangerous administration that must be voted out of office."

We both felt the air around us, and even the marble we were sitting on suddenly become agreeably softer. I felt a deep sense of respect for this young man who was clearly taking a huge risk just to meet with me, much less help drive a dysfunctional president from office.

"We also want to concentrate on how he is not a man for the people. We will present everything such that it could not have originated in the White House. If we succeed, we'll not only get rid of a clear and present danger to our country, but we'll also plainly show just how important each voter is to all of us, and how little this president represents us. I personally put more faith in an informed voter than anyone on the Hill or in the corporate boardrooms."

We both knew that our business was complete. I suggested that he leave from the rear. I decided to hang around a while and walk back down those venerable steps that held so much historical significance. As I left the Lincoln Memorial, I walked along the reflecting pool toward the WWII Memorial, which seemed a hundred miles away. I sat down on a wall facing Seventeenth Street. At that very moment, a black limo pulled up with a handwritten sign with the name *Smith* on the window. I couldn't have been more relieved. The driver handed me a bottle of water and opened the door. I fell in right beside Ari, who could tell that I was as spent as he'd ever seen me. I really would not make a good spy.

The last thing I remember saying was that I was glad not to take the train back. We really needed to be more careful until the virus was no longer knocking at the door. I didn't even remember falling asleep, but I woke up as we were crossing the Delaware Memorial Bridge into New Jersey. Ari handed me a cold bottle of water and a ham and cheese sandwich on rye. It was on a ceramic plate decorated with an image of the Lincoln Memorial. I really love this man and all he does for me.

"Did you hear our conversation?"

"Not fully. I could tell that you guys were getting along well, so I just let it ride."

"We were. I was surprised it wasn't Dennis. I was even more surprised to learn that the section of the FBI that he was attached to was actually behind setting up today's meeting. We were right about them, the discomfort I felt from Dennis and Dean was due to the fact that they were sent up by the White House, not their director. They didn't want to be there any more than I did. Agent Orange is assigned to White House security and pretty much has free reign of the place. What made this happen was a result of how I had laid into Dennis and Dean in my office. And I thought my tirade with them blew my cover!

"In fact, Trump's doing everything he can to discredit all of our intelligence agencies, and they know it. They believed I wasn't a threat. They had a good idea that I was up to something. They didn't know what, but now they do. Ari, they know that Andrew's alive,"

"Wow! Do they know where he is?"

"No, but they know he didn't die at sea. I was really floored when AO said that to me."

"Well, at least if this man gets booted from office, Andrew should be able to come back home, if he even wants to."

I looked at Ari. "Where'd you get that idea?"

"Just a hunch—Andrew never actually said anything about it, but I think he is tired of running so hard and needs to put his feet up," said Ari.

"I can certainly relate to that. I did talk with him about coming back to the States, and he was pretty ambivalent. I think he is moving towards not coming back. A lot will depend on Anna and her plans once she learns that her father is alive."

"I have the feeling that the Trump administration has set up a separate layer of intel that reports only to him," said Ari. "They don't talk to the traditional agents. I just received a phone call on your buddy, Arthur Ransom. It seems that he lied to you. He doesn't have a full-time teaching job at Ball State. He works out of an office provided for him by the White House. He does research and writing but is often sent into academic institutions mainly to check out individuals the White House is concerned about. You were on their list and they assigned Arthur to spy on you and to find out what you were up to. He did tell you the truth about the Claremont Institute, they are funding his White House assignment."

"Wow, so my suspicions were right," I said. "Right from the White House. I wonder if that's even legal, to have a private security and spy staff in house? I was also beginning to think that this was happening and if true, it represents a real problem for the nation. It also explains why the FBI reached out to us. That is going to make our job with AO extremely difficult. He is working in a hostile environment, and everyone knows it."

"Benson, are you comfortable with this guy?"

"I trust him," I said earnestly. "When he told me that he also had a backup to cover him and that it was Dennis, I accepted his story. I had been a bit put off by Dean, but I did like Dennis and could tell that he was a good guy. Dean and Dennis are a team. I could also tell that they knew that they shouldn't get involved with anything that we're doing.. I also decided to ask about the tail. I told him that we've seen nothing and wondered if his intel was still current. He promised to get back to us on it."

"Good point. Do you think he can be of help to us?" Ari asked.

"I do, but our man does not want to be an in-house spy. It goes against his values based on his family of three generations in the intelligence agencies. It's clear they want to help, but we will have to make sure that AO and the Bureau is protected from retribution."

"I can handle that. You have gained their confidence. What is your plan?"

"We're off to a good start. I think we need to proceed slowly. I did tell him not to give us anything that did not involve at least one other person. The more the better. We do not want anything we publish to be traceable to him."

"Good thinking. I am going to make a good spy out of you."

"Don't bet on it."

As we were talking, I could see how nervous Ari was. I was becoming even more convinced that we needed to expand our effort to the election. The plan to wake up voters was not enough. America has a long history of abuses at all levels—corporate, government, research and political operatives, and lobbyists. Remember the flack over the release of the Pentagon papers? Many Americans didn't even know about them. They still don't. Other examples include the Panama papers, Halliburton's Vietnam War role, Senator Joe McCarthy's hearings, Enron, Watergate, not to mention the Mueller Report and the impeachment of Trump. Most Americans might have heard about these incidents but are clueless as to how each impacted their lives. Income inequality, the wealth gap, corporate abuse of our tax codes, even Trump's refusal to release his taxes have had a disastrous financial impact on all of us. Some of these things have been deliberately presented so that even the best of us have trouble understanding their effect on us. I think we need to find a way to get the facts out to voters so they can better understand what's really going on at the highest levels.

"You're really setting us up for a possible failure. Aren't you biting off an awful lot with all this?" he continued.

"Probably. Let me think about it and get back to you. I left Agent Orange with a mission to focus on the actions originating from the Oval Office that generate discussion and debate throughout the White House. We want to focus on the president's erratic behavior, especially things that would shake up his base. We want them to know that he's not a person who speaks his mind, even though they think he does. We need to show the world that this president is unstable and ultimately a danger to them!"

"Okay, sometimes I think you are as far off the wall as Trump. I only ask that you not say anything to the team until you've worked through what you want to do. Make sure you know what to expect once we go public. The team is behind you, but, as you saw, they think these divergences are not going to be productive. We all know how your passion tends to take over your otherwise logical thinking," warned Ari.

"I promise to do just that. I'll run everything by you first. Actually, you'll be sending it yourself. Maybe we need to meet again with the team to reassure them?"

We were in the Holland Tunnel when we finally fell silent. Ari dropped me off at the Fourteenth Street subway. I was really glad we drove back. The sun was setting as the end of a brilliant summer day. It took only ten minutes for me to get home. Mr. Bonaparte was on duty, and we greeted each other as we have for years.

Once in my apartment, I opened a beer and sat down. I was exhausted, physically and emotionally. Trump wore us down, and I knew it was deliberate. I was tired of waking up each day to the drama. We knew that most of what he said did not necessarily represent his administration. He has an inspiration, and it suddenly becomes policy. Whether it was finding a signed copy of "Rocket Man" for the dear leader or pulling troops out of Syria with no input on the part of any military advisor. Policy by tweet had completely replaced the traditional presidential press briefings.

Trump had no desire to consult with experts. But I knew he must be getting advice from someone because I knew that he was incapable of thinking up most of what he tweeted. These ideas came from someone with an agenda. I suspected that that agenda was not born with the election of Trump but in the works for some time. When it came to votes, Trump was for his base, and only his base. He never made a single effort to reach out to anyone else for advice or support. He never once honestly tried to work with any Democrats. His comfort zone was dangerously narrow, not only for his administration but for the nation.

Ari might be right, I thought, Maybe I was too obsessed with the risk that this man brought to his position. Like AO, I considered myself to be a patriot deeply concerned with what this man was capable of. Unlike AO, I could do something about it.

I woke up the next morning with a text from AO. Trump was bouncing off the walls. He had just seen the first ad by the Lincoln Project. It displayed Trump as a doddering old man who was clearly neither physically nor mentally fit for the job. AO let us know that the entire West Wing had been up since 5:00 a.m. trying to temper his mood and moderate his bevy of tweets against this newest challenge.

AO said that he was stomping up and down the halls in his bathrobe and slippers. No one could calm him down. I passed the text onto Ari to let him and the team figure out how to deal with it.

I was suddenly reminded of Howard Hughes and how as one of the richest men in the world, he used to stomp around his penthouse apartment, also in a bathrobe. One difference was that Hughes walked around with his feet in Kleenex boxes in deference to his obsessive compulsiveness against dirt and dust.

★ ★ ★

CHAPTER 15

SEPTEMBER 2020

IT WAS THE FIRST WEEK IN SEPTEMBER. I received a note from Ari to meet at L'Artusi at 6:00p.m. According to our code, that meant we'd actually meet at 7:00, and that he had a reservation. Ari's choice surprised me—L'Artusi is one of New York's finest Italian restaurants and pricier than he usually prefers. They are in the West Village on Tenth Street, possibly my all-time favorite street in the city. They have outdoor service and have shut down their glorious dining room for the pandemic. Seven is also early for New York dining, so we would have the place pretty much to ourselves. The pandemic was really cramping our style.

I had no idea what Ari had in mind, so I turned off my cell, wrapped it in aluminum foil, and headed out in an indirect manner. I stopped occasionally to look around, and, satisfied that no one was following me, I proceeded to my destination. When it comes to exposing Ari, I'm at my most diligent; he needs to be kept safe.

He was more excited than I'd ever seen him. We sat near the last outdoor table so that we were only blocked on one side. I waited for him to let me know what was happening. He reached into his bag and gave me a flash drive, telling me to use it only on the secure laptop when offline. He could hardly contain himself, so I just let everything move at his pace.

"I got a message from the team. The designer finished the presentation. I copied the designs onto that flash drive for you. I think you're going to like them. The best news is that they've also completed all aspects of the distri-

268

bution phase. They did a test run on some of the more obvious hosts: Facebook, Twitter, and Instagram. They all ran smoothly and quickly. They were on and offline in less than six seconds. Most of the difficult, secure platforms the team had targeted have been successfully invaded. As expected, it took a bit more time to download our posts but it was completed well within our safety margins."

I was pleased. "This is genuinely great news, but remember these posts are as benign as possible, so that any red flags will not be unfurled until we hit harder. I also used the Office of Economic Cooperation and Development as our data source. This is a highly respected international research group that is the go-to place for such information by most heads of state. Remember, everything we put out must be documented and verified as fact. How long before we know when to strike will depend on how many clicks and likes we get from these posts."

"We should know within a week. I think they want to send the same series of posts a few more times before they analyze the results. For now, the team is set to go. Do you have more posts for them? They want to stay ahead of the curve in terms of content."

"I do," I said, "and I can get that material to you before the end of the week. They know to post the same text several times a day and every other day?"

"They do," Ari added. "They also said that the actual transmission originates from a different global location each time. This is a security strategy that they mentioned at our meeting."

"I don't remember it, but that's an excellent idea. This is really the best news I've had in months. Thanks for getting it to me so soon, I know you don't like spontaneous meetings."

"You're right, and that's why I want to leave right now. I'll get back to you for the new content. Leave it with Mr. Bonaparte. Keep yourself safe. I still have no evidence that either of us is being followed, but I do respect AO's intel. Has he gotten back to you?"

"Nothing beyond the occasional check-in, but I'm hoping to hear more Friday. I'll let you know."

"Great, get yourself home," said Ari.

"Actually, I'm going to order some dinner since I wasn't able to eat all day. They are serving an excellent *mozzarella di latte di bufala* tonight. The cheese is made from a special Italian breed of water buffalo raised in the Campania region and served with fresh-grown New Jersey tomatoes and their homemade balsamic vinegar, made from their own balsamic resins. It really complements their garlic and spice pasta. A meal to die for."

"Well, let's hope you don't die," joked Ari. "You do enjoy treating yourself, no matter how strung out you are."

"You're right about that; maybe it's an age thing, or maybe it is because for the first time in my life I can indulge myself. Or maybe it is my way of distancing myself from all of my self-imposed stress and anxiety so that when I need to focus, my mind is free to do so. I'm not one who likes being on the edge all the time. Life is such a gift, and as many country musicians have told us, we only get one go around."

"Enjoy your meal. I await your call." Ari was down the street before I could even look at the wine menu.

I took my time over dinner, even though I was anxious to see the posts. I also had to put the finishing touches on the new posts I had in mind.

I went home directly after dinner, eager to see the new content. I was pleasantly surprised with the images that filled my screen.

Prof. Mike says: Did you know?

Median US household income of black families with one child in 2018 was $36,300.

Median US household income of white families with one child was more than twice as much: $80,000.

Source: 2018 census data by the Center on Poverty & Social Policy

For United Sakes!
Every vote matters. Please vote!
We can and must do better.

Illustrations by Rob Zammarchi
www.zammarchi.com

Prof. Mike says: Did you know?

More American women die of pregnancy-related complications than in *any other* developed country. Only in the US has the pregnancy related death rate been rising!

Source: 2017 NPR and Propublica Report

For United Sakes!
Every vote matters. Please vote!
We can and must do better.

Prof. Mike says: Did you know?

> In 2018, about 72 percent of US white households owned their own homes.
>
> Only 41.7% of blacks, 47.5 percent of Hispanics, and 59.5 percent of Asians were home owners.

Source: 2018 American Community Survey

For 50 United Sakes!
Every vote matters. Please vote!
We can and must do better.

Prof. Mike says: Did you know?

> Our unemployment rate has recently receded to 13.3%. Great news... but if you are out of a job, you are 100% unemployed.

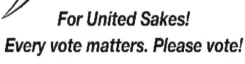

For United Sakes!
Every vote matters. Please vote!
We can and must do better.

Prof. Mike says: Did you know?

In 2018, the United States, at 16.9%, spent the highest percentage of its Gross Domestic Product on Health Care. The average for all 36 OECD nations was 8.8%.

The average per capita expenditures on health care for all 36 OECD nations was $3,994.
We spend $10,586 per person in the United States!

Source: OECD Annual Health Reports

For United Sakes!
Every vote matters. Please vote!
We can and must do better.

Prof. Mike says: Did you know?

The average life expectancy rate for all OECD nations in 2017 was 80.7 years.
Life expectancy in the US was only 78.6 years.

Only Estonia, Hungary, Latvia, Lithuania, Mexico, Poland, Slovak Republic, and Turkey had lower life expectancies than the United States.

Source: OECD Annual Health Reports

For United Sakes!
Every vote matters. Please vote!
We can and must do better.

Prof. Mike says: Did you know?

The OECD reported in 2017 that the average obesity rate for all 36 of its member nations was at 16.7% of their total population.

31% of total US population was obese, the highest among all nations. South Korea was the lowest, 3.4% of its population were obese.

Source: OECD Annual Health Reports

For United Sakes!
Every vote matters. Please vote!
We can and must do better.

Prof. Mike says: Did you know?

The average Mortality for all OECD nations was 133 per 100,000 people for preventable causes in 2017.

At 175 People per 100,000, the United States had the 7th highest mortality rate for preventable causes of all 36 OECD nations.

Source: OECD Annual Health Reports

For United Sakes!
Every vote matters. Please vote!
We can and must do better.

THE TEXT WAS SHORT AND TO THE POINT. I loved Mike's image as our resident philosopher. Most importantly, the message to vote was obvious, but not in your face.

I sent a text to Ari that I fully approved and encouraged our team to get them out on as many platforms as they could.

One concern about our project was that so many efforts had formed to counter the Trump campaign that we might not get as much exposure as we had foreseen. The Lincoln Project was well-funded. Evidence showed that some key Republicans who were up for re-election seemed to be backing away from Trump. The Never Trump groups from 2016 returned, as did several GOP related anti-Trump PACs. All were committed to defeating Trump. I even heard of a new group, "Rednecks for Black Lives Matter," not specifically an anti-Trump organization, but certainly an unexpectedly anti-racist effort out of the Deep South that would not be well received by the Trump camp.

All of this activity was making me feel very hopeful that we were going to succeed and that we will stop Trump's reelection bid cold. An interesting thought past my mind as I sat down to work. If he should lose, Trump is going to deeply regret ever running for president. He did it out of anger and spite and not in any way to make America great again. If he does lose this election, his ego will never recover. The man who hates to lose might end up losing a lot more than the election. I feel that he will eventually be exposed for the phony he is, and not only will he no longer have the presidency, but he will also find that the Trump brand as an entity will be in shatters along with his ego.

I decided to pull together the next generation of voter awareness posts for Ari to submit to the team. I created them from the latest available information we had in our data banks. They were more controversial than the first set, but not even close to what we'd be putting out in later posts. This later set would get more closely to how Trump has not served his base. I have thought about several initiatives on healthcare, with COVID trends. Maybe we would do an international comparison to show how badly the US was faring compared to other nations. Such information is plastered all over the establishment sources, and I am willing to bet a lot that those on the fringe have no idea how devastating this virus really is. I have friends and family who are convinced that it is only a variant of the flu and that the numbers on deaths and cases are "fake news." We also had a lot of data on voting rights, tax policies, and tons on his real attitude and policies towards his base that offered much fodder to make the case that Trump is no populist.

I downloaded a chart that showed how wealth and income in America have become concentrated to the top 20% of our population. It distressed me to learn how skewed the income and wealth gaps have become. We used the Federal Reserve Survey of Consumer Finances for most of these data.

No other statistic more vividly shows just how much the concentration of opportunities and economic power has shifted from the middle class to the upper 1%. Consumption makes up about 70% of our GDP. Prevent the working class from participating as consumers, and you drive your economy down and into a recession. Remove disposable income from middle-class families and you destroy our most important source of growth and employ-ment.

I passed these charts onto Ari with brief descriptions and let the team figure out how to best present these data to our audience. I trusted them to put them into a palatable format for those who clicked on our posts.

The distribution of income and wealth in the United States

Share of total income or wealth by quintile, 2016

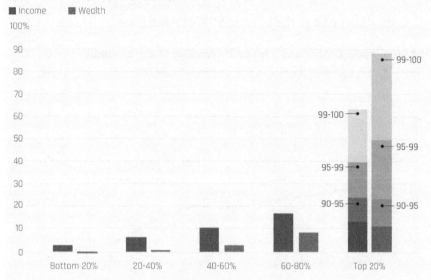

Source: Authors' calculations using Federal Reserve Board, "Survey of Consumer Finances" [2017].

Note: Income shares computed with respect to quintiles of the income distribution, and wealth shares computed with respect to quintiles of the wealth distribution..

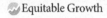 Equitable Growth

I LET THEM KNOW THAT the next chart showed how much the concentration of wealth has grown from 1989 for the top 1%. Again, it has been done at the direct cost to the bottom 90% of Americans.

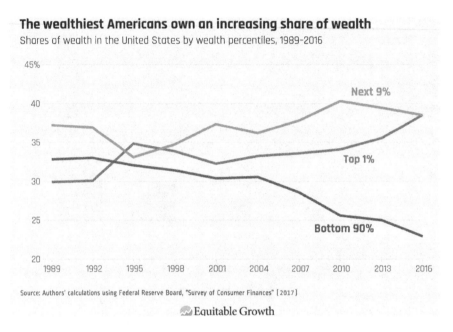

The wealthiest Americans own an increasing share of wealth
Shares of wealth in the United States by wealth percentiles, 1989-2016

Source: Authors' calculations using Federal Reserve Board, "Survey of Consumer Finances" (2017)

 Equitable Growth

THERE WAS AN INITIATIVE BY CONSERVATIVE LEADERS to convince the public that an education was not worth the time or money. This strategy has been typically followed by every dictator who realized that uneducated people are easier to control. I saw this strategy in action when I was in Persia in 1971. Now called Iran, the Persian government had a planned illiteracy rate of 75%. I was told that it was deliberate and intended to keep the masses happy but ignorant of what they were doing behind the scenes.

These data for the US, and those of almost every previous year, provide strong evidence that college-educated people live considerably more financially secure lives than their uneducated neighbors. We learned the value of a college education as more high school graduates in the 50's and 60's got college degrees. There is no empirical proof I have ever seen that college-educated people have a lower quality of life than do the uneducated.

College graduates have much more wealth than those without a college degree
Median wealth of U.S. households by educational attainment, 2016

Source: Authors' calculations using Federal Reserve Board, "Survey of Consumer Finances" (2017)
Note: Educational attainment classification based on household head.

Equitable Growth

I **DECIDED TO INCLUDE** the following chart. While it doesn't show the benefits, the public enjoys as a result of taxes, it's clear that at 24.3% of GDP subject to taxes, the United States ranks well below average in terms of our tax burden. The American voter complains bitterly about taxes during every election cycle, yet among industrialized nations, we are consistently at the lower end of total taxes. We need to focus more on what we get for our taxes, not what we pay.

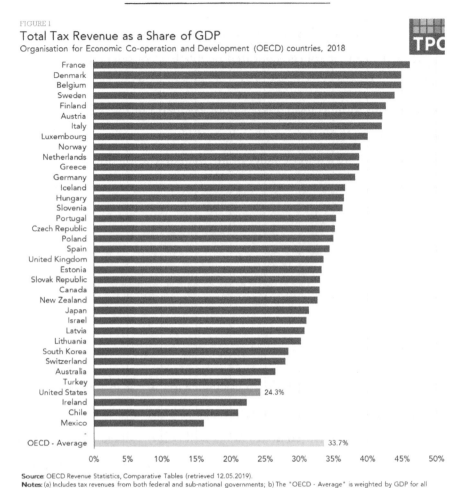

FIGURE 1

Total Tax Revenue as a Share of GDP
Organisation for Economic Co-operation and Development (OECD) countries, 2018

TPC

Source: OECD Revenue Statistics, Comparative Tables (retrieved 12.05.2019).
Notes: (a) Includes tax revenues from both federal and sub-national governments; b) The "OECD - Average" is weighted by GDP for all countries excluding the United States; (c) Data for Australia and Japan are for 2017.

OUR THEME WAS INCREASING the participation of American voters. The United States ranked dead last as a percent of registered voters in 2014. Although percentages of voter participation increased for the 2016 election, the US still ranked last in the percentage of eligible voters in the population who vote. I was hoping that these rates would increase for 2020.

I accidently found information on something I hadn't thought about. It was sad to see how badly America compared in terms of the number of seats in both chambers held by women in other nations. We are close to the bottom on that statistic as well, although the 2018 election pushed us closer to the norm. We really needed to do better if we were to continue to claim that we are a representative democracy.

Income equality has seriously deteriorated in America from 1970 to 2018. Upper income households have increased their share of income by 19%, while the share of middle-income households has ironically, decreased by the same 19% over the same period. Lower-income households have held steady, meaning the gain of upper-income households has been at the direct expense of the middle class.

The gaps in income between upper-income and middle- and lower-income households are rising, and the share held by middle-income households is falling

Median household income, in 2018 dollars, and share of U.S. aggregate household income, by income tier

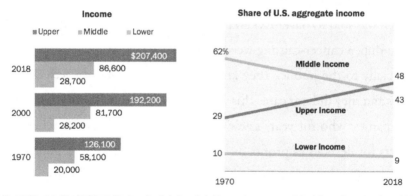

Note: Households are assigned to income tiers based on their size-adjusted income. Incomes are scaled to reflect a three-person household. Revisions to the Current Population Survey affect the comparison of income data from 2014 onwards. See Methodology for details.
Source: Pew Research Center analysis of the Current Population Survey, Annual Social and Economic Supplements (IPUMS).
"Most Americans Say There Is Too Much Economic Inequality in the U.S., but Fewer Than Half Call It a Top Priority"

PEW RESEARCH CENTER

THAT WAS ENOUGH INFORMATION for the time being. I now needed to compile the political statements I wanted to make regarding the 2020 election.

I had long recognized that our traditional institutions, such as Congress, the courts, and the executive branches, chartered to do the job of preserving our nation's constitution and values, have let us down. We no longer have trust in elected officials of our constitutionally framed institutions that they will live up to the oaths they have taken to protect and preserve our nation. No democracy can survive if citizens do not trust those who they elect to represent them.

Industry failed to observe professional standards, costing us trillions in lost wealth over the last several years. This added to the lack of trust we have as both consumers and voters. The 2008 Recession, largely due to an over-eager finance and banking sector, caused irreparable damage to the financial futures of millions of Americans. A lack of environmental awareness on the part of our energy companies, and the irresponsible distribution of opiates by pharmaceutical companies are additional and glaring examples of such corporate irresponsibility. I consider the horrendous behavior of Monsanto, which was sold to Bayer AG and had to assume much of the legal liability of Roundup, a cancer-causing weed killer that was sold to industry and commercially to the public. They knew that this product was lethal for many years and they did not care. This was exactly like the behavior of the cigarette companies, who for years knew that their product kills. They held up the courts for decades as profits on their product continued to pour into corporate coffers. The Monsanto case ended in a $10 billion lawsuit, which in terms of suffering and lives lost, will never be enough. We are not even sure that any of that money gets back to the victims. At some point, we will have to learn that fines mean nothing to these socially irresponsible companies— shareholders end up paying them one way or another. The only answer to such behavior is jail time for individual executives and the humiliating sting of living with a felony on their records.

More than ever, our democracy was almost solely dependent on citizen voters to make the right choices so that we could regain our trust in government. With the help of a more trusted government and of our power as consumers, we could make industry more socially responsible. An informed and participating American voter could bring back our core values and our sense of justice.

One of our biggest challenges to increasing voter turnout was a long-term, concerted effort to prevent African Americans from voting in the Deep South. This was not a new problem, and the Voter Rights Act of 1965 was written into law to prevent these restrictions. With the 2013 Supreme Court reversal on key clauses of that act, once again it became more difficult for many citizens to vote, and voter restrictions have expanded to northern states as well. It's hard to believe that the Roberts court could have been that naïve on this ongoing issue that was far from resolved. Estimates exist that more than twenty-three republican led states have instituted voter restriction and suppression policies since that court decision. This action alone, which is largely confined to Republicans, has led to a serious credibility gap within and for the republican party. Whatever the outcome of this election, republicans are going to have to find a way to undergo a major reorganization and re-evaluation of their current practices. America has always been a two-party nation. If republicans continue to legislate, and behave as they have over the last several years, they will soon find themselves outside of the political arena looking in.

My next data for the team was on our abysmal voting participation rates. The last two elections brought out a larger, but still unacceptable percentage of eligible voters. We could only hope that the trend would continue. One solution to this would be to impose penalties on eligible voters who do not vote. Eighteen nations currently do this. We needed a higher participation rate of our eligible voters, as much as we needed them to be informed so that they could vote intelligently.

IT WAS A LONG DAY, so I decided to put everything away for the night. I packed up and hid the laptop, put the flash drive in a safe place, and turned on my other computer to catch up on the news. I poured a brandy as my computer was booting up. I turned to cable news, and it was not pretty. The president was once again ignoring the COVID-19 catastrophe. He had blocked billions of dollars set aside to improve testing. His strategy was to continuously deny that there was a problem, asserting that it would somehow just disappear. No one else thought that was even close to a possibility. The president was focused on his re-election, while his COVID advisors were focused on saving lives.

I heard a text message come in on my regular phone. It was from Anna. I called her right back. "Hey girl, how are you doing? So nice to hear from you."

"Well, how about a news flash- phones work both in and out." She said admonishingly. "I was relaxing and realized that we haven't talked for a while. How are you and what are you up to?"

"Never been busier, I love being retired, even though it seems like my days are fuller now than when I was working. How are your classes going?"

"I love what I am learning, I am glad that I am at Columbia, but I can also see why you and Dad really appreciated being at NYU. This is such a great place to study. I have met some students who get together to just talk about things that concern them. They're really smart, and I enjoy being with them."

"I hope you are being COVID mindful. This virus is beginning to totally take over our lives."

"We are, we are. When can we get together? I miss you."

"Ditto. I'll take a look at my schedule and text you. What days are best for you?"

"Since we aren't having classes, any time works. Let's plan to meet for breakfast, since I am still working at the clinic."

"Great idea. I will get back to you on that as soon as possible. Great to hear from you, do take care of yourself."

Can't wait to see you. Bye."

"Bye. Love you bunches."

I knew that I was avoiding her and shouldn't have. I just did not want her to read my mind, especially regarding her dad. She knows me better than I do myself, and I fear she will see through me. I will have to set a breakfast date and do it soon.

The Coronavirus death toll was up toward six figures, and several Southern, as in red, states were feeling the pinch. Despite that shift, the president at his daily briefings on the pandemic was railing about it all being the fault of the radical left Democrats, offering nothing in the way of relief to his supporting states. Black Lives Matters protestors were also getting under his skin. He sent troops into Democrat-run cities to make his point. The major outcome of his actions was an increase in violence. He repeated that all of this, especially the virus, was not his fault and he would accept no responsibility for the number of Americans who died from the disease. He was trying to shift responsibility to the states or China.

His illegal use of the White House platform for his campaign shocked most of us who watch these things. Like his persistent lies, his irreverent behavior toward our political norms had become so commonplace that no one, not even the press, complained anymore. It is doubtful that a Democrat would have gotten away with such a violation of our political standards in this political environment. The battle of the day was about the first major spending legislation, designed to help those most financially impacted by the Coronavirus. It had passed months ago, but all kinds of problems existed getting the funds out the door and into the hands of the people who desperately needed help. Ostensibly this historic package was to help keep people solvent during a crisis not of their making. A second objective was to get the economy moving again as more establishments were closing down and unemployment rates had tripled. Sadly, it did not, largely due to administrative bungling. What made these problems more hurtful was that most other nations had developed a wide range of policies to help their people. They were working and the pain and suffering of almost every nation was considerably less evident than ours.

The South Carolina primary was history and a major turning point for Joe Biden, whose candidacy had been in trouble up to that point. Massive protests following the horrendous death of George Floyd on May 25, were still spreading throughout the globe. Almost every nation had thousands of people on the streets demanding police reform and justice for Black people. White protestors continued to participate, setting a new stage for the age-old problem of police violence against blacks and that of systemic racism in the United States.

In addition, Trump, who had insanely managed to politicize the wearing of masks, continued to defy science and logic on this simple protective solution. This set up a major battle between him, his advisors, and the scientists on his own COVID-19 team. Trump refused to wear one in an attempt to minimize the degree, if not the very existence, of the crisis. This action set the stage for a civil backlash against wearing the only protection we have against the spread of the virus. Science, like truth and facts, to this president, were nothing but an inconvenience.

I closed the window of the news, recognizing that the daily drama created by this narcissistic head of state was beginning to seriously impact my sanity. For the first time in my life, I found myself only reading headlines. I could tell what the story was going to be about without reading it. I could no longer commit the energy to be beaten over the head with political posturing from an enemy of the state who is actually the head of that state. He knows no boundaries, certainly not any political ones. He truly is the Chief of Distraction

CHAPTER 16

SEPTEMBER 2020

BIDEN WON THE PRIMARIES and was chosen as the Democratic candidate for 2020. Bernie Sanders reluctantly suspended his campaign and offered significantly more enthusiasm for Biden than he had for Hillary in 2016. The COVID-19 virus was still raging. The United States had recorded almost 25% of the world's deaths, even though we have only 4% of the world's population. Brazil, whose president took pride in mimicking our president's approach to the pandemic, was running a close second. President Bolsonaro, who like Trump disdained wearing a mask, had himself just become infected with the virus. Despite the fact one American was dying every 80 seconds from the virus, Trump continued to proclaim that the pandemic would soon miraculously disappear.

Biden was making headlines from a command station in his Delaware home basement, totally out of reach of the virus or anything Trump was throwing at him. The question of Biden's choice for VP dominated the political airwaves. All of these circumstances guided me as I formulated the posts I wanted to release before the election.

Russian interference in the election, and the news that Putin offered the Taliban a bounty for killing American soldiers in Afghanistan, bothered everyone except our own president who doubled down on his solid relationship with the Russian leader.

The Democrats had just held their virtual 2020 convention, establishing the Biden/Harris ticket. The Republicans, after several changes in venue, eventually decided to also hold a virtual convention because of the virus. Trump was upset, since this would mean he would lose the chance to host a huge crowd for his acceptance speech. American life was more drama-filled than at any time in my life. The nightly news burst with anxiety, uncertainty, and distrust of the election, all exacerbated, indeed orchestrated, by Trump. His latest salvo was aimed at the US Postal Service with its newly installed director who, like most Trump appointees, was hell-bent on destroying the very agency he was appointed to manage.

No administration had ever tried to sabotage the efficient work of our nations more than 600,000 dedicated postal workers. The USPS was being dismantled, ostensibly to improve the bottom line, but the accompanying propaganda that the election would be tainted by mail-in ballot fraud told another story. The USPS is one of the most reliable apolitical agencies we have. Numerous studies have shown that, unlike other nations, we have virtually no incidence of vote-by-mail fraud, a fact verified by several studies, including one by the prestigious Brennan Center for Justice at NYU. These findings, predictably, were completely discounted by Trump. I wondered if the incidence of mail fraud in America is lower than the probability that an alligator would die by lightening while attacking you in your bathtub. "The only way I can lose the election is if it's rigged," Trump loudly repeated at rallies and on Twitter. Of course, the very voting system that Trump so zealously degraded as rigged was the exact same system that elected him in 2016.

One fact that journalists and Trump critics alike were coming to recognize was that virtually every lethal, vindictive, and frequently illegal action Trump has accused an adversary of committing, was precisely the action that he himself had been engaged in doing. "This election is rigged!" was his refrain, and he was right. In fact, Trump himself was the Rigger in Chief.

Apparently, the only weapons he could imagine a political enemy employing were those he was using for his own campaign.

Our team knew that the consequences of not defeating Trump in 2020 were simply too great. While we definitely wanted a dog in this fight, we did not want to overlap or conflict with the strategies of other groups similarly dedicated. What approach would be both unique and effective? What would matter to voters whose minds we most wanted to open?

The perfect demographic suddenly came to me. We would focus on reaching the massive bloc of evangelical voters, which could, if successful, potentially win millions of votes for Biden, or at least fewer for Trump. It was also the most vulnerable segment of Trump's base. Estimates have been made that almost 25% of Americans, spread out over many denominations, identify with the evangelical movement. I can't for one moment understand the appeal of such an irreverent, ungodly, and unchristian like man like Donald Trump to a group that claims Christian values. *Roe v Wade* was of course, the reason. These folks tend to be one-issue voters.

The fate of *Roe v Wade* loomed in the court and hung heavy in the hearts of many people. Statistics show that, soon after the Supreme Court affirmed *Roe v Wade*, making abortions legal in 1973, the number of abortions in the US commenced a steady and precipitous decline. This created a lot of concern over abortions when the total number of under-reported abortions in the US went from 6,211 in 1968 to more than 27,000 in 1969. As the procedure was illegal at this time, actual figures were probably even higher. Once the law was passed, rates began to decline. Other factors played an important role as well. These included the wider availability of birth control, as well as information and counseling about family planning. The truth is that no one is pro-abortion. Being pro-choice is not even in the realm of being pro-abortion, arguably one of the most horrendous decisions a woman ever has to make. Give people planning options and the ability to make their own choices, and we will find that the painful decision of abortion will naturally continue to decline.

These steady decreases in both the rate and number of abortions occurred *after Roe v Wade*. The unacceptable rise in the rate of abortions in America had successfully been reversed. One could say, with statistical conviction, that *Roe v Wade* has been the most successful anti-abortion effort ever.

So, if single-issue evangelicals support Trump because of their determination to reduce and eliminate the number of abortions in our country, they should let *Roe v Wade* stand. And it follows that if the removal of *Roe v Wade* were off the table, evangelicals' major reason to support Donald Trump for president would no longer be a factor.

TRENDS IN ABORTION

In 2014, the U.S. abortion rate reached a historic low

Number of abortions per 1,000 women aged 15–44

www.guttmacher.org

291

BECAUSE ABORTION IS, WITHOUT DOUBT, a deeply troubling and painful topic, much controversy surrounds any discussion of it. There are two organizations that collect reliable data on abortion rates, demographics, and more. These are the Center for Disease Control and Prevention and the highly respected Guttmacher Institute, established in 1968 and headquartered in New York. This institute compiles and maintains a comprehensive global reach on reliable sexual and reproductive health. Many critics of abortion label the Guttmacher Institute "pro-abortion," which verges on libelous. All such organizations such as Planned Parenthood and others identify as pro-choice. None would ever claim to be in any way pro-abortion.

Except for relatively few statistical outliers, abortion is a decision that is never taken lightly. All studies on this topic show that the decision to have an abortion is closely tied to medical, emotional, and financial reasons and the life circumstances of the woman and her family. Studies have shown that the most successful anti-abortion policy is when women have access to responsible contraception and family planning information. Yet those who most adamantly fight to make abortion illegal often promote the abolition of such planning organizations. These same people are often those who make adoption extremely difficult especially for single parents and the LGBT community. They also often decry government subsidies for the poor. One could readily conclude that to the most vocal opponents of "pro-choice" are in actuality not "pro-life," they are only "pro-birth." It is ironic that the legislators who fervently campaign for less government intervention are the same people who find it both necessary and acceptable to disallow free choice.

With this in mind, I decided to design a strategy that would align with the values of the larger evangelical community. I hoped that a greater awareness of the real facts and figures about abortion and family planning would at the very least give evangelicals pause. At best it might provide a solid reason for them to become more compassionate and move towards the center on this one issue.

I pulled out my files on Trump and began reading through the multitude of actions, statements, and policies initiated by the president over the past four years that should, when objectively viewed, move any faithful evangelical closer to the political center. I chose the Seven Deadly Sins as the organizing theme for our posts. I pulled together background information for the team to use in designing our campaign.

These seven sins were defined by early Christians to show how in moments of weakness, humans can stray from a righteous path and give in to natural passions. The modern version of The Seven Deadly Sins can be traced back to a fourth-century monk, who was one of the "Desert Fathers." Ponticus attributed the source of his wisdom to Aristotle. Aristotle's *Nicomachean Ethics* were located at the extreme of each positive virtue we have. The Roman writer Horace also extolled life's virtues that were bordered by a list of potential vices that tempt us from a righteous path. Pope Gregory I in AD 59, released his list of the seven deadly sins; Pride, Greed, Lust, Gluttony, Sloth, Wrath, and Envy, The Church followed these soon after and released the seven virtues: Chastity, Temperance, Charity, Diligence, Patience, Kindness and Humility. It was believed that the practice of the latter would eliminate temptation for succumbing to the former. While it was generally accepted that all seven sins were destructive, most theologians focused on Pride as the most dangerous, since pride severs us from grace and represents the essence of evil. Greed has historically been viewed as a close second; all seven could easily be attributed to Trump's behavioral pattern.

Indeed, who was a better poster child for the Seven Deadly Sins than our perpetually self-serving president? He has never turned the other cheek, never offered empathy nor forgiveness. He thinks any humility is for losers and suckers.

I finished my text and sent it to Ari to be forwarded to our team. I asked them to take the seven behavioral examples I have included and do a characterization of Trump participating in each of the seven deadly sins. I mentioned that we will do other election specific posts later, but I wanted this one done right away and targeted to the evangelicals. I would like to see the illustrations before they are posted.

It was time for a break. It was still early in the morning so I decided to go for a long walk, something I hadn't done in weeks. As I left my building and walked down Sixth Avenue, I suddenly felt like I was being followed again. So, I changed my plans and went to my favorite diner. They were open for breakfast and lunch, with staggered booths and stools. There were lots of windows there to enable me to see outside. I chose a booth that gave me a view of the entire corner of the block, ordered a bowl of barley soup, a favorite of the chef, and waited.

My original concerns were soon confirmed. Two sleuths walked by the diner, their heads down, their glances furtive. I took out my burner and sent a Code Red to Ari with a photo of the uninvited sentries. Five minutes later, one of them entered the diner and took a seat at the counter. The other remained under an awning across the street. Ari was right, I might very well make a decent snoop. At least I would have managed to be more inconspicuous than these guys in their off-the-shelf suits, buzzed haircuts, and black patrolman's shoes.

I took out my paper, stirred my coffee, and pretended nothing was wrong with the world. My lunch was served. Before I knew it, a young woman entered the diner, walked over to me, and sat down in my booth, giving me a quick peck on the cheek. She took my hands and told me her name was Susan. I knew immediately that Ari had sent her, and we settled down to talk. She was about forty years old and dressed in a loose-fitting blouse and floor-length skirt with a shawl draped casually over her wide shoulders. She had short, unbrushed brown hair that was partially covered by a floppy Scottish golfer cap. It was obvious that this woman was extremely fit and not someone to take lightly. She'd clearly left wherever she'd been in jig time to come to me.

We leaned toward each other and smiled like we were the best of friends. We laughed and joked, and then got serious. We did everything two lovers would do over lunch. After a short time, my counter friend paid for his coffee and left the diner. His buddy followed soon after and I breathed a huge sigh of relief. I offered to buy Susan lunch which she declined. Now that I didn't need to worry about my tails, I decided that a movie was still a good idea, so I asked Susan if she wanted to join me. To my surprise, she accepted. I explained I needed to stop by my apartment to get something. I put a twenty-dollar bill on the table, and we left the diner.

Susan told me that Ari had instructed her to stay with me all day. I welcomed her company, knowing that, if necessary, Ari would have also stationed a few of his very capable associates close by. I remember thinking that life is really defined by who you know and who you can count on to always be there.

This whole experience was making me extremely nervous, so when I got home, I decided to return the laptop and flash drive to its second floor hiding place. As we entered my building, Mr. Bonaparte was there to open the door. He warmly said hello and greeted Susan with a knowing look on his face that his mask could not hide.

"It's wonderful to see you again, Ms. Susan. How have you been?" I glanced at Susan and then back at Mr. Bonaparte. He walked over to the elevator and winked at me, acknowledging my state of shock. I think he was enjoying his new role in my life.

"Okay, how long have you known Mr. Bonaparte?" I inquired as soon as the elevator doors closed.

"Oh, for years! I've been working for Ari since 2000 when I first came to the city to escape the suburbs."

"I guess I shouldn't be surprised by anything Ari does. I honestly don't think I could live without him."

"I feel the same," Susan agreed. "I also know that he has a lot of respect for you and keeping you safe has become his number-one mission."

"I just need to get my computer and hide it. It'll only take a minute. Wait for five minutes then meet me in the lobby. I retrieved the computer, flash drive, and the papers I had left lying around and wanted no one to see, should the apartment be raided. I stuffed them in a bag and went to meet Susan. When I left 201, I walked down to the lobby. With the key in my hand, I caught Mr. Bonaparte's eye and gave a slight a nod. Susan and I left the building together, mission accomplished.

I had forgotten that the theater was closed due to COVID, so we walked over to one of the West Side piers and decided to enjoy the afternoon there instead. The marque at the Forum showed a true classic, *A Man and a Woman*, released in 1966 and starring the incomparable Anouk Aimee and Jean-Louis Trintignant. The theme song alone makes this flick truly unforgettable. I can only hope that this movie will come back whenever we can go to a theater again.

On the way over to the Christopher Street Pier, always bustling with activity. I felt the buzz of the burner in my pocket. Ari had gotten back to me. I excused myself and went off to the side. I took out the phone and read the new message with the time and place I was to meet Ari. There was a second text from AO saying the tail on me was legit and to watch out. He also said that the president was really beginning to lose it and frequently lashed out everyone at COVID's dominance on the front pages and not on him. Stomping back and forth early in the mornings in his bathrobe. Trump was beginning to realize that COVID was diminishing his reelection chances and becoming the number-one issue on the minds of the voters. The president had wanted the election conversation to be on his successes with the economy and foreign affairs, nothing else.

I rejoined Susan and tried, without success, to enjoy the view and the people milling about.

"What is it?" she asked. "Is everything okay?"

I told her it was, but she realized I was upset. She took my hand to ease the stress. This was a sensitive woman. Her compassion put me more at ease.

We left the pier around 4:00. I invited her to have some sushi with me. Having eaten alone for months, it was pleasant to share a meal with someone. Susan walked me back to my apartment, where I flagged down a cab for her and entered the building. Mr. Bonaparte was not on duty. I got in the elevator and punched the button for the thirteenth floor. When I opened the door to my apartment, I found that I was not alone.

A masked man I didn't recognize stood in the middle of the room and signaled to me with his finger to his lips to make sure I did nothing stupid. I understood right away that he was one of Ari's operatives. He even looked a little like Ari. I looked around—no sign of anyone in the apartment other than my new bodyguard. Ari's security alarm was still activated, and everything seemed to be in order.

"Everything's cool," he said. "I'm Moshe. Ari told me to stay with you for a few days until he can figure out who's tailing you. He also told me about your meeting for tomorrow. I'll be going with you. Do you know how to get there?"

"Yes," I assured him. "We have met there once before. I even planned a circuitous route to get there."

"I will do whatever Ari tells me to do. I will need to stay the night if that's okay?"

"Of course! I'll set you up on the couch," I said. Any discomfort I had regarding my privacy was overcome knowing that I was safe.

"I'm sorry you have to go through all this. Ari has told me a little about you and clearly this is not your normal game."

"Right. It isn't even close to my normal but, I'm getting used to it. What can I get you? A beer? Scotch? Did you eat?"

"A beer would be perfect. I've had dinner, so don't bother."

"Okay, I need to do some work, if you don't mind. I can turn on the TV for you."

"Thanks. Will it bother you?"

"Not at all."

The meeting wasn't until 10:00 in the morning, so I wasn't anxious to get to bed early. Having submitted the first wave, I wanted to get a jump on the second phase of the seven sins campaign. The team would have the posts ready soon, but I had decided not to release them until we got an idea about how the first phase was received. I wanted to get online to see if there'd been any action. Moshe was watching the news, and I was buried in Facebook, Twitter, and online news releases, just to see if we were out there. I didn't see anything in my feeds, but given my general lack of presence online, I wasn't surprised.

I WAS AWAKENED THE NEXT MORNING with a text from Ari. He told me to have Moshe join me at our meeting and not bother to take the usual precautions. He had decided to see if we were tailed. I knew that if we were, Ari wouldn't be at the designated meeting spot, and we'd have to reschedule. I also knew that Ari had posted another detail to follow us as we made our way uptown.

Moshe and I left a little early just to be sure we'd be on time. We got the uptown 2 train to Columbia University. Moshe sat on a bench as I went into the Student Union. I picked up some brochures while I hung out for a few minutes. Then I looked out the window at Moshe, who nodded slightly to let me know that we hadn't been followed. I went back outside and sat down next to him. Waiting anxiously for Ari, we began a conversation about nothing at all.

I was nervous because I felt that Ari was taking a big chance coming up here. I watched a tweedy professorial type enter the building. He soon came over to us and gave me some brochures that he said I'd left on the counter. I looked up at the man and was surprised to see Ari standing in front of me, perfectly disguised. I took the papers and the professor walked briskly away. Moshe and I continued to talk. I pushed all the papers into my bag, and we both left for the subway.

As we headed back downtown, I didn't notice anyone following us. Once back in the apartment, we spread out the papers that Ari had handed us. They contained the drawings and posts for the seven sins release. We went over each illustration and were more than pleased. Our illustrator had captured each sin and the intent of each image. A picture really is worth more than a thousand words, but only when created by the right person.

Illustrations by Rob Zammarchi www.zammarchi.com

I SENT A NOTE TO ARI asking how it was possible that they got these out so quickly. "These artists are used to deadlines and they had already been working on caricatures of Trump. Ari included a note explaining that the team will post the seven sins as soon as I sign off on them, which I did right then. "Please let them know how pleased I am with these illustrations, they are perfect, and I know they will do the job, many Kudos. Ari wanted to do a follow-up investigation on the tail to figure out how much pressure was on us. Moshe and I went online to find our posts. I wanted to remind Ari to post them on all of our voter awareness lists, since these were specifically intended to show up repeatedly on all evangelical sites. That meant that we needed to get into Russian social media platforms, as well as those of the other countries that were meddling in our election by inundating the feeds of evangelicals. We hoped to create confusion by having divergent opinions of the president appear side by side on the same sites. We wanted our posts right alongside the president's disinformation.

I asked Moshe, "Outside *Roe v Wade*, why would any evangelist support a man like him? He doesn't go to church unless there's a camera on him. He doesn't know scripture. Remember how he publicly destroyed his reference to the Corinthians? Trump has pretty much violated every basic Christian value, especially those relating to Christian faithfulness and women. I've collected a dozen more incidents, each of which defines his lifestyle as one that personifies the Seven Deadly Sins and most certainly does not reflect the beliefs and practices of an evangelical."

I continued, "The way the president speaks to people was most insulting, and unchristian, especially to those who've challenged him or posed a question he can't or doesn't want to answer. His business practices, subject to more than four thousand lawsuits, can't have been honest and ethical. There must be an awful lot of guilt in his life. He is known for his bankruptcies and for stiffing contractors who have worked for him. As president, Trump was proud of his refusal to compromise or negotiate with anyone from across the aisle. He devised insulting names for anyone who called him out or stood in his way.

Moshe, why would Trump block nearly everyone from testifying before Congress? He knew that he was guilty and afraid that anyone asked to appear before a legal forum, or a congressional committee might be forced to reveal his guilt under oath. An innocent person has nothing to fear from questions that might be asked. A guilty person has everything to fear

The polls were still showing that Trump was going to win in November. After 2016, we no longer trust the polls. "He's already begun to implement an array of executive orders to control who gets to vote and who does not. He's even sent some of his administrators out on the campaign trail, which is a direct violation of their positions as public servants. The Director of National Intelligence has stopped briefing Congress, another violation of standard practices, and probably the law. The president had launched a major attack to diminish Biden's reputation via his son, Hunter. So much more is sure to come. This man is relentless."

I saw Moshe's eyes begin to glaze over as I rambled on. "I know that I'm over the top on this issue. I also know that my concerns are shared by millions. I'm encouraged by the number of books criticizing the presidents that are coming out this fall, many of which have been written by ex-Trump loyalists. Michael Cohen, his lawyer; Mary Trump, his niece; John Bolton, his national security advisor; the journalist Bob Woodward, and so many more. Many Republicans are supporting Biden but, most were still solidly in Trump's corner. They would agree that Trump does not deserve to be president and that he represents, in the words of one former Republican, an 'existential threat to our nation.' Each author also states that one should never discount Trump—he'll do anything to win."

In the end, I thought, our project might not have a significant impact on the election, but it will give us peace of mind because we weren't just sitting on our hands and complaining. Each of us feared for the very survival of our country.

★ ★ ★

CHAPTER 17

OCTOBER 2020

I HAD BEEN SO IMMERSED in my writing, posting, and meetings with Ari and Agent Orange that I had all but forgotten about the rest of my life, mainly keeping in touch with Anna. We had talked a few weeks ago and agreed to get together, but I had failed to get back to her. So, I took a chance and speed dialed her number.

She actually answered which is not usual. We talked for a few minutes and I was about to set a day to meet when she let me know that she had a better idea. She reminded me that she had been meeting with a few of her NYU all of whom were graduate students in different fields of study. "I mentioned you to them and they said that they wanted to get together with you to talk about the election and about a few things that we have been discussing. They asked if you would come to our next meeting. We worked up a list of topics that we have been discussing, and I will email it to you."

She had assumed that I would accept, and she was right. "I would be delighted, Anna. I'll look for a place for us to meet, given the restrictions on indoor dining. How many are in your group?"

"Our group has grown to be more than thirty. There are only about five of us who will be coming. Let me know when, and I will pass it on. Would you mind if we taped the meeting so that we could share it with the rest of them? See you soon!"

"Of course, I hope I can meet with all of them at some point. I am looking forward to this and to meeting your new friends." I was really pleased with this invitation, I get to see Anna, meet her friends, and avoid a one-on-one conversation. I cannot believe I am even thinking like this when spending time with Anna has always been a pure pleasure. I do hope we can get past this deception soon.

A few minutes later, the list of discussion topics arrived. I printed it out and looked it over.

CONCERNED STUDENTS, 2020
List of Priorities in Need of Action
Baby Boomers through Gen X: Get on Board or Step Aside

1. TRUST
2. JOBS AND CAREERS
3. CLIMATE CHANGE
4. INCOME AND WEALTH
5. GOVERNMENT ACCOUNTABILITY
6. AFFORDABLE EDUCATION
7. PUBLIC HEALTH CARE OPTION
8. GOVERNMENT REGULATION
9. RACISM
10. NATIONAL SERVICE CORPS.
11. SINGLE PARENTHOOD
12. DRUG OVERDOSE OR SUBSTANCE ABUSE
13. PERSONAL DEPRESSION
14. STUDENT DEBT
15. SEPARATION OF CHURCH AND STATE
16. REGULATION OF SOCIAL MEDIA
17. ABORTION AND CIVIL RIGHTS

IT WAS CERTAINLY A WELL-THOUGHT-OUT LIST of issues. I doubt if I could have made a better one. It also showed me how practical they were. Their generation is focused, socially oriented, and with an important quality-of-life perspective. There was also a certain amount of idealism, fully appropriate given their age. These were topics that belonged on the front burner of national debate, although some of them had not been given attention for years. I looked forward to meeting with these young friends of Anna's. I also thought I would add a few of my own comments to her list, and then book a place for us to meet.

I made reservations for 7:00 p.m. at Salon de Tapas on Sullivan St. I had gotten to know this small restaurant and its owner from my walks around the area. They had a large open room in the back that was screened in and perfect for social distancing for a group of up to fifteen diners. I reserved four tables for eight and a separate one for myself. The tapas and sangria would be on me. I was looking forward to meeting her friends and being with students again. The biggest loss in my retirement was that I was no longer around young people whose energy and perspective I always found invigorating. The second biggest loss was that we could not mingle as a group thanks to the lack of any plan to protect Americans after nine months of living with this invisible enemy. Why can we not put Jacinda Ardem, New Zealand's marvelous, smart, caring and competent prime minister on our presidential ticket? What a breath of fresh air this woman was, and I mean that literally since her country knows nothing of the COVID pain and presidential neglect we suffer every day.

If Prime Minister Ardem is not available, we could ask the leaders of Japan, Taiwan, South Korea, Finland, Norway, or say, Australia to take the reins, all of whom have stellar ratings protecting their people. America is practically last in the world on the list of responsible handling of the virus. Beyond 200,000 deaths to date, someone should be held accountable and responsible.

I had learned through my teaching over the years to really appreciate young people. I see them as our best hope for the future, especially since my generation has left a horrendous mess for them to clean up.

As I walked to the restaurant, I was excited about our evening together, even more so because of their connection to Anna. I was impressed that they are concerned enough about their lives to have come up with the list Anna sent to me. Her friends were already there when I arrived. I could hear the animated chatter surround me as I entered the room, added proof that these young people were indeed engaged and passionate about their concerns.

I brought Carlos, the convivial owner and bartender of the Salon de Tapas, in with me and introduced him to the group. He kept every glass filled all evening as he spread his usual good cheer among us. His tapas are among the best I've ever had. I was sure my guests would enjoy the food as well. Carlos imports his wine from Spain and prefers Garnacha, an authentic Spanish blend for chilled sangria. I learned firsthand that he uses apples and pears after Labor Day to embellish his in-house sangria, strawberries and peaches as summer additions. A small, sliced lemon with a touch of brandy to sweeten it is added. He makes his sangria early in the morning so that all ingredients can properly soak and blend in a refrigerator for at least eight hours before serving.

Tapas are very seasonal and typically reflect the personality of the chef. I do have favorites; pincho de tortilla, a Spanish omelette, calamari, croquettes stuffed with mushrooms, crab, squid or cod depending on the season. Carlos recommended his pan tumaca and his homemade paella, a favorite of his regular customers. I added beer and a white wine for those not interested in the sangria. I had Carlos distribute his menu, should the students not prefer my choices. They were all graduate students, so I assumed the were over 21, the drinking age in New York.

Once we were seated, Anna asked me to introduce myself. I did so as briefly as possible, stressing my long personal and professional relationship with Anna's father having first met him at NYU's Graduate School of Arts and Science.

As soon as I sat down, a young woman introduced herself. "Good evening, Professor Pryce. I'm Angela Towers from Chicago. I'm doing a masters in African Studies. Thank you for coming here tonight. Anna has told us about your work. We talk among ourselves about a lot of things that are happening around us that concern us, but we do not have the experience or knowledge to go beyond complaining and wondering. As soon as you agreed to meet with us, we each picked a topic from the list Anna presented to you to get your thoughts. We hope that you will be able offer some insight on how these problems came about. To tell you the truth, we're scared. Most of us are finishing our studies and going out there to face a world we don't understand.

"My family and I have been activists for justice and fighting systemic racism that I have personally faced my entire life. Growing up where I did, I have always lived with the humiliation of racism and the pain of poverty. West Garfield has one of the highest crime rates in Chicago, and the nation. Per capita income is less than $12,000 per year, and we have a 1 in 8 chance of being a victim of a crime. This is my reality. Our inability to earn a living contributes to the crime we suffer. My family has been robbed more than once, and I have lost family and friends to street violence and now to COVID.

"George Floyd, who was murdered outside of a Minneapolis pawn shop earlier this year, was just one of the one thousand unarmed black men who are killed by cops each year in America. Most of us in Chicago have had to get used to our streets being dangerous. What made the Floyd murder different was that it was caught on tape, so the whole world saw it happen. People all over the world expressed their anger over the total lack of justice for black people in our country.

"I've traced America's racism back to 1619, when the first boat filled with African slaves landed on our shores. Slavery is no longer legal however, we have yet to escape the vicious cycle of crime and poverty—we still live with that curse. We learned that the current federal minimum wage in America is $7.25 per hour. How in the hell can a single person live on that, to say nothing of a family of four? Where is the justice for people of color in America, supposedly a nation where all men are created equal?"

What I appreciated with Angela's presentation was her professionalism. She was intense and serious but, without the rancor and anger that does not work. I could tell that this woman had her facts and thoughts in order. "Thank you, Angela, for sharing your very personal perspective on an important age-old problem. You mentioned the year 1619. May I assume that you've read Nikole Hannah-Jones' *New York Times* piece that won a Pulitzer last year?"

"Yes, I did. I even made copies and handed them out to our study group."

"Great idea, that report was professionally researched, thorough, and at the top of my list on the subject of slavery in America. The *Times* piece clarified any lingering doubts that slavery was not only a massive system of human depravity, but also a successful economic system. Slave owners built a thriving economy directly on the backs of their slaves.

"You're right, no one, especially a family, could possibly live on an hourly wage of $7.25. Economists have questioned how labor has moved from purely agricultural economies, dependent solely on the land, to the birth of the Industrial Revolution in the nineteenth century, and now to the digital age, without ever being fairly paid. We have historically called their pay a subsistence wage, providing only the barest of income to clothe and feed the working class and put a roof over their heads, yet labor is the only input to production that is a living, breathing, organic component. Machinery, equipment, factories, money, in fact, everything other than labor and land that is used to produce whatever the market wants are all human creations. One would think that the worker would be first in line for a fair return. Wages and benefits were once fairer from just before WWII and for about thirty years after when labor could rely on strong unions. This was only a brief moment in the history of working-class prosperity. Real wages, meaning the purchasing power, of working-class America, as well as in many other nations, have been essentially flat since around 1970.

"If you add systemic racism to the mix and attach the traditional economic multiplier effect, you will capture the extent of the wage gap for people of color who have not shared in the prosperity of our nation. That gap is not confined to wages, the wealth gap is even more important. Because of discrimination in housing, healthcare, education, and transportation, black and brown people have never been able to accrue a wealth base that could be passed on to the next generation. This has forced each generation to start with nothing and work with the opportunities they are given within their lifetime. All of this is why the battle for reparations continues, although I doubt that it will sadly, ever be carefully considered or resolved. Some feel that the single biggest reason that America is the only industrialized nation without a universal healthcare system is that those who have power to make laws simply do not want to support people of color with public money.

"Don't forget that our Constitution considered Black people as only three-fifths of a person. This was to justify slavery while excluding them from the otherwise inalienable rights of life, liberty, and the pursuit of happiness offered white people. Article 1, Section 2, Clause 3 affirmed the three-fifths status of former slaves. This was specifically designed to increase the population count in participating states so that they would have more votes in Congress and more electoral votes in presidential elections. They were added to the census counts but, since they were officially designated as less than whole persons, they were denied the right to vote. Regrettably, voter suppression continues today in all its many ugly forms.

"So, Angela, the answer to your question which I believe is taken from our Declaration of Independence:

We hold these truths to be self-evident, that all men are created equal, that they are endowed by their Creator with certain unalienable Rights, that among these are Life, Liberty and the pursuit of Happiness.

Even still, we continue to live with prejudice and discrimination all around us. Some movements and progress have made important advances toward leveling the playing field. The Civil Rights movement of the 1960s, Reverend King, Bobby Kennedy, and school desegregation all strove toward equality for African Americans. Educational and job opportunities are also better today for minorities than they were forty years ago. But until black mothers no longer have to warn their children each morning how to behave in front of 'the man,' we have much left to do on this front. Recent events in the year 2020 have made that clear to all of us."

"You do know that those words were written by Thomas Jefferson, a founding father and a slave owner!"

"He was one crazy dude. Didn't he have a black mistress?" asked a young man at Angela's table.

I responded, "Yes he did, her name was Sally Hemings and she had four children with him. Her role in Jefferson's life has become well known. She's often referred to as his concubine and apparently was able to negotiate unusually favorable conditions for their children. I do not know whether he was cruel to his many slaves, but the fact that he owned more than 400 is telling. Jefferson was not the only president who owned slaves, as I am sure most of you know. Thank you for your question.

"Angela, one can build a legitimate argument that race has no basis in biology. We are all of one species, Homo Sapiens. Our skin color only means that tens of thousands of years ago, your ancestors turned left and mine turned right. In fact, the only real genetic difference between you and me is my blue eyes. Blue eyes are a recessive trait, making me blood-related to every blue-eyed human who lives now or has ever lived. My eye color is an authentic genetic difference, not my skin color or yours."

"Well, our genders are different," Angela laughed.

"Now that's true, and by my life experience, that gives you the upper hand," I replied smiling. "I'm encouraged by the effectiveness of Black Lives Matter, mainly because of the number of people of other races who've joined the protest marches. We can only hope that the day will come when we judge people by who they are as a person. Are they kind and caring? Are they responsible citizens, parents, siblings, friends? These are among the traits that make us good people and good neighbors. Whether they be gay, straight, black, white, old, or young, none of those things should matter to a functioning community. We each determine who we are as a person; we have no control over who our parents were, the color of our eyes, our height, and most definitely not the color of our skin."

"Thank you, Professor. But what can we do to change these laws and beliefs? I don't want my children to have to live with the same oppression that I have had to endure."

"To start with, we need to pass a new Voter Registration and Eligibility Act. We need to realize that racism is both a cultural and social phenomenon. We have fairly good laws on the books to prevent discrimination, but they're not uniformly respected nor enforced. We should start with the BLM call for police reform. It would help to demilitarize our police and retrain them to once again be our guardians and not our militaristic overseers. We need stronger regulations against all forms of discrimination. This is a moral argument. But it is also an economic problem. When we discriminate against any minority, we reduce the opportunity for our nation to prosper. Deny a young black girl the ability to study music and we might be denying the world of the next Itzhak Perlman, Aaron Copland, or John Lennon. By not allowing full educational and health services to everyone, we will surely be denied the next Bobby Fisher, Pablo Picasso, Steve Jobs, Stephen Hawking, or Ernest Hemingway. Genius knows little about gene pools; heredity matters, but so does access and opportunity.

I continued. "If we can't find it in our hearts to eliminate discrimination and institute equality and justice for all, we need to be bold. If we cannot open our doors and communities to everyone, we need to rethink the model. One idea, should these discriminatory trends continue, might be to set up separate minority economic zones. Fund them as we would any new business and do it like the many economic zones already established in many states that are financed by government and based on a well-drafted business plan. Let a black or brown community have its own banks, schools, hospitals, and police force, and my bet is that they will prosper. Once a level of confidence and prosperity has been achieved, the walls of color that surround that community should be opened for anyone who wants to contribute their skills and efforts. The point here is that all opinions of inferiority are unjustified and would not exist if equality and justice prevailed for everyone. If people of color are systemically denied equal access to a white man's world, creating the means for them to form their own communities under the laws and rights of other peoples is a second-best alternative. My bet is that these communities will prosper and become beacons of light.

"I'm sure you know about the 1921 Tulsa Massacre. A group of white men, jealous of the solid economic success of an area of Tulsa known as the Black Wall Street, viciously attacked the entire area, destroying everything those folks had built. If our society remains unwilling to let people of color share equally maybe Blacks need to build their own self-managed and owned communities like Tulsa. I don't favor this a solution because I believe assimilation and integration are the best answers to our social differences, but we cannot continue to let generations of citizens have their rights and opportunities denied. This has become ever more urgent as we suffer the rise of white supremacy groups, especially since the election of Trump."

"Thank you so much, Professor. You have given us a lot to think about."

"You're welcome, Angela, but do not think too much. We need action to put this horrible stain on our nation far behind us."

"Hi, professor. I'm Richard Greenblatt, from Brooklyn, and an MBA student majoring in business marketing with a minor in economics and finance. I want to talk about the economics of the political movement that I think is taking over our nation. I went to Erasmus High School and spent a year at Brooklyn College before transferring to NYU. Our family is Jewish, and my great grandparents escaped from Poland in the late 1930s. They lost family members and close friends who I'll never know. Their memories will never fade. We commemorate them on holidays. My parents and grandparents only reluctantly talk about Nazi horrors, Hitler, fascism, and authoritarianism. Antisemitism really hurts—they say it is the oldest hatred, and they're uncomfortable talking about it. I have always been glad to have grown up in a family that wanted me to know about these things. But here in my lifetime, I don't think white Jews have suffered as much overt prejudice as people of color have. Maybe my experience is a result of living in New York, where we speak hundreds of languages and where ethnic and cultural diversity have evolved differently. The fact is that any kind of racial or ethnic discrimination is harmful no matter who it is aimed at.

"New York has managed to capitalize on the diversity in our city. Little Italy, Chinatown, Odessa by the Sea, and Black and Spanish Harlem have all managed to be welcoming to others. Restaurants, music, shopping, and cultural centers are very often gathering places for tourists and New Yorkers from other communities. Jews are comfortable in New York. But like for all ethnic minorities, discrimination is always in the air when we find ourselves in certain social or professional environments. It is a level of discomfort we feel that should have no justification but, sadly, antisemitism and racism in all its forms not only still exists in America, but they also seem to be on the rise of late.

"Income and ethnicity dictate how certain groups live compared to others. Different political systems impact living conditions, especially if any ethnic group is excluded. This becomes clear when representative democracies are compared to totalitarian systems. Nazi Germany was horrendous, and brutality toward Jews, gays, and the Romani is well known. Most of the world considers capitalism and democracy the best of all systems in terms of the opportunity and freedom it offers. History has shown us that despite their touted opportunities and freedoms if racism and discrimination are in the minds and hearts of a citizenry even the best of legal and constitutional systems will not be strong enough to overcome. Authoritarian rule, by comparison, gives basic rights only to those at the top, who determine and benefit from all political, social, and economic decisions. The lower classes and working people in such nations are not treated much better than chattel and have precious few rights as citizens."

Richard paused to catch his breath and look around the room. He was saying things in public for the first time and wants to make absolutely sure that we realize how important his words and thoughts are to him and need to be for us. Continuing, Richard said, "I'm focusing on this because I sense that America is moving toward authoritarianism. I'm not sure exactly how we have managed to drift away from the long-standing liberal government that was so successful for many years. I think the country is falling away from the representative democracy our founders envisioned. The very existence of many of the hard-won and respected social advancements including civil, human, and women's rights; environmental protections against climate change, racial justice, healthcare and educational opportunities are all being threatened. I worry about where our country will be in five years. If we continue as we are, we may no longer be a representative democracy. Professor, do you see what I'm saying as real or am I overstating the problem? Angela mentioned that we are all scared. As graduate students, we are entering a working world that is not functioning within the legal or moral values we cherish. We do not know what to do to change it, and we will not live in a world that seems to be driven by greed, corruption, and hate."

A pall descended over our group. We looked at Richard and then at each other. I knew that this young man was hurting. We all newly sensed that our basic rights were threatened. "I feel your pain, Richard. There is one simple solution: get informed and vote. The citizen voter is, at this point, the only line of defense against those whose self-serving policies are undermining our great nation. Sadly, America has one of the lowest voter participation rates of any developed country, especially in off presidential years. Your family, like so many who found their way here to escape oppression, understands why we need to vote to prevent anything even remotely resembling a fascist takeover of our country. I have personally and professionally made the importance of being informed and active as a voter a lifelong goal if America is to survive and thrive as a representative democracy.

"One of our most important sources of being informed is a healthy, free, and vibrant Fourth Estate. Unfortunately, some of our professional news outlets have neglected their responsibility as a force for responsible governmental oversight. Social media, which is not a professional news platform, has nonetheless assumed the role. Let me offer an example. We all know that Trump is an incessant liar. While I'm sure there are some exceptions, when was the last time you heard a responsible journalist actually question him on his lies? We call them misspoken, falsehoods, untruths, or just ignore them. This negligence leads to confusion on the part of the voter. We cannot discriminate between truth and fake news if those responsible for doing so fail to meticulously keep us informed. Trumps cruelty, incompetence, and lies have become accepted as normal. Until the press and the social media call him out on his lies and cruelty, he will interpret that as license to be even more so. This feeds directly into his misguided and misinformed base, who lacking any challenge, believe his lies. This is how nations fall into autocracies. We have a free press that is not acting like one."

"Richard, I have looked hard at the issues you have raised tonight and in your list. While there are and always will be exceptions, for the most part, I am no longer able, especially under the current administration, to put my confidence in the leadership of our nation to deal with these real problems in a just and fair manner. Like so many great civilizations of the past, Rome, Greece, The Ottoman Empire, England, and others-- all have fallen. The reasons are complex but, a softness in resolve, greed, corruption, and injustice tend to top the list. Richard has alluded to a similar path he feels that America is on, and I agree with him. Having tried to find trust and faith in our leadership, I have concluded that I trust the will of the people more than any other factor at this point. We know what we want for ourselves, our families, and our communities. What we lack is the necessary commitment to get informed and involved and vote. These are all basic requirements and obligations for all those who live in a democracy. It truly does not matter to me what side of the political spectrum any of you might fall. What does matter to all of us is that we vote informed of the issues and the facts. Raw emotion and anger absent of any reality to the facts will never create a fair and just nation for all.

"Richard you are right on, America is rapidly moving away from its roots toward a totalitarian state. As a Jew whose relatives have personally witnessed this path, you have due cause to worry. The whole world is watching. If you care, and are unhappy with our direction, I repeat to you all: vote!"

Another heavy silence hung over the group, and I decided to let it linger. I signaled to Carlos to bring us more sangria. He came over carrying two pitchers. He was followed by his wife, who carried two platters of the most amazingly creative tapas I'd ever seen. Both wore masks and gloves.

To my surprise, Carlos spoke up. "Could I make a comment?"

"Of course!" I responded. "This is actually their meeting though."

Getting no objections, Carlos began. "I want to thank you for coming to our restaurant. Professor Pryce first walked in about a year ago and told me that he had his first tapas in Madrid with a group of students who were participating in some kind of an international competition. It was the Taberna el Sur, right in the heart of Madrid. Professor Pryce told me that he had been to Spain several times and had somehow never been to a tapas bar. He grew to love the way Spanish people enjoyed their time together over the wonderful tapas that were passed around. I told him that my cousin owned that very bar and we could not believe the coincidence. I am so pleased that you have chosen our humble restaurant for your meeting. You are all most welcome."

"My parents lived through the reign of the Spanish dictator Franco. I was too young to understand what was going on, but Franco, like many other dictators, claimed he was a man of the people. Fascists always promise that, if elected, they will raise the standard of living for workers. Of course, they lie, and once chosen to sit on their self-styled thrones, they quickly forgot their promises to the people. Hitler decided to conquer Europe and wanted to control the world. Franco was dedicated to staying out of the war and continued to rule Spain with an iron fist. It is said that Franco ordered the execution of 200,000 people. I might point out by comparison that as of today, that is about the same number of Americans who have died so far this year from the virus.

"We know firsthand, just how brutal dictators can be. I do not know how they can call themselves populists as they tend to be everything but." Carlos pulls up a chair and sits on it backwards as he looks intensively at each of the students. True to his heritage, he is a man of great passion and that begins to show as he brings his story to a conclusion. "I am grateful for the opportunity to live in this wonderful country, but, like Richard, I see something happening to our country that should concern all of us. If we do not get involved, as the professor has said, we will come to deeply regret allowing it to continue. The right to vote is not something available to the peoples of all nations, and those are the very nations that almost always live under a yoke of oppression and poverty. Voting is not a privilege; it is an obligation."

"Thank you, Carlos, I said. "I didn't know about your family's history. I think subjects like these are so much easier to understand when they are linked to personal experiences like those of Angela along with Richard's and Carlos's families," I added. "What was shared here tonight will stay with us all for a long time. I see a young man over there who looks like he has something to say," I said, turning my attention his way.

"Thank you, Professor. My name is Darius Brooks. I'm a music theory major from Alabama. I studied music and political science in college and like Angela, I grew up with racism. It was different for me in Alabama. In fact, Angela and I have talked about the differences we faced as children. In the '60s and '70s, when my parents were kids, I heard that racism was understood by Black folks differently in the south than in the north. In the north, they were told that racism was only a Southern problem. The only people who believed that, however, were white. I know that things are better for us now, but in the South, black people have seen evidence of our perceived inferiority a thousand times a day. We still do.

There was a time when we want to sit at a counter to eat something, drink from a public fountain, or attend a decent school, we couldn't. We can do so now but, if you come to the deep south and walk around you will still see many signs, faded and barely visible but still there on fountains, door jams, bathrooms and pools that say, "whites only." Even now as a black person, in some remote areas, to walk down a street, vote, get a job, or use a public pool, we often have to find alternatives. This was in spite of the fact that our ancestors had come to America long before any of the whites who hated us.

Darius continued, "But I want to talk about a different threat. I want to talk about climate change and our environment. I believe these are the most important threats to our lives right now. They are even more critical than COVID-19. There is evidence that climate change impacts vulnerable populations with much more intensity. Something has to be done soon.

"We've talked about deniers who just dismiss the problem. Scientists have told us that 2020 will be the hottest year on record. In the last week of July, Sonoma County, California, recorded a high of 112 degrees. Death Valley recorded 134 degrees, reportedly the highest temperature ever recorded on earth. Greenland's ice has almost completely melted, as have large sections of Antarctica. Many do not realize that these ice sheets are our primary defense against UV radiation from the sun, a major source of skin cancer.

"Ocean temperatures are as much as 4 degrees above normal, when only 2 degrees is enough to dramatically alter the dynamics of our oceans. The powerful storms in the Caribbean and along the East and Gulf Coasts have become more dangerous and more common. Scientific estimates suggest that more than 50 million people will have to relocate inland within the next twenty to thirty years."

"Darius, you sure do keep a lot of facts in your head about the environment," Angela interjected.

"I have to. It's the only way to explain the urgency. Look, we're witnessing the same degree of manmade threat to our air, water, land, and natural resources as we are to our climate. Many realize that water's the new oil—it's expensive and increasingly scarce. Did you know that the total amount of fresh water on the planet is exactly the same as it was four billion years ago and only a small percentage of it is potable? We've almost managed to pollute it out of existence. Agriculture, meat processing, and manufacturing have polluted our rivers, streams, and lakes to the tipping point. Methane production from cows alone represents one of the biggest threats to air pollution, second only to transportation.

"It is critical that we accept our responsibility and get to work. The irony is that technology has brought down the cost of renewable energy to a point that it's currently below the cost of fossil fuels as an energy source. Renewable energy also offers an opportunity for new paying jobs for thousands of people. If we were to reduce our consumption of red meat and shift to local produce, we could substantially reduce air pollution. The reduced transportation costs from that change would alone give us significant relief and the air quality benefit we need to survive. Electric cars are a boon, but only if we move all production of electricity to renewable sources."

"Wow! I think you should run for office, Darius," said Anna. "Maybe Congress? You could work on the Green New Deal."

"Well, maybe I will. Seriously, though, there's no doubt that the modern way of life is life-threatening. Fortunately, the same creativity that helped get us into this mess can get us out of it."

It was obvious that Darius had really done his homework. His passion and commitment were even more so. This bright young man has a future as a public person and I really hope that he gets the chance to follow his dreams.

"Thank you. Darius," I said. "I'm impressed with the amount of research you must have done. If everyone knew a fraction of what you know, I think the number of deniers would be close to zero. As you say, the evidence is overwhelming. The damaging role people and industry have played can no longer be in doubt. We don't have much time. I personally feel guilty knowing that my generation has created a mess for yours to deal with. I can't tell you how gratified I am knowing that you and your generation will try to save us and not let this problem we created go unresolved. You guys really rock."

Anna laughed. "Oh, Professor, you really give us a lot of credit," she told me.

"Well, as a professor, I only give credit when it's due," I responded, giving her a wink.

Anna was the last student to speak and she had clearly prepared. "I won't introduce myself, since you've known me since I was a baby," Anna said and smiled. "I will, however, say that for my entire life, I've had to sit through debates between you and my dad on every topic under the sun. That's where I first learned about the specific topic, I would like to bring up tonight: the role of government and how policies have trended toward the right over the past fifty years. This has had a major impact on our lives, that I don't think is for the best and at the root of what our group has been talking about since we first got together.

"I learned from my reading that following WWII, the USA was the manufacturing and financial savior of the world. The Marshall Plan and our willingness to rebuild Europe and Asia after the war made America a highly respected partner. As the world struggled to meet the demands of the post-war period, America enjoyed economic growth, prosperity, and peace that led to a host of major advancements and opportunities that we willingly shared with our trading partners.

"At the same time, we were suffering from an unacceptable level of poverty and systemic racism, both of which had been partially dealt with during President Lyndon Johnson's administration when he passed the Civil Rights legislation, the Voting Rights Act, and Great Society programs. But around that time, our government gradually began to be taken over by special interests in business. Our elected officials became beholden to those special interests rather than to their constituents. We also saw an increasing concentration in some economic sectors like consumer products, energy, and pharmaceuticals. Rapidly advancing technology coupled with an increase in global economic competition mostly from China also led to more monopolies. On the political side, Citizens United, gerrymandering, together with the ideological movement from center left to far right, all contributed to the loss of trust of most American citizens have in their own government. This move to the right was also evident in several of our global trading partners."

"You are absolutely correct, Anna, this is not singularly an American issue." I interjected. "Please, go on."

"My position on this might have been influence by you and Dad, but I do feel that the American voter is our only defense in an all-out war against our democracy. Our freedoms have been increasingly restrained since the 1970s. With a few exceptions, that was the last decade that the average American worker had an increase in real disposable income, which is one of the most solid measure of the spending power of our families.

"Ever since the 2000 election that was determined by the Supreme Court, our problems have only increased. It is the opinion of many scholars that the court never should have gotten involved in that decision. That election gave us an administration that was blindsided by 9/11. Rather than capitalize on world sympathy for a good purpose, the Bush administration, led by Cheney and Rumsfeld, manipulated all of us into an inexcusable and incredibly expensive war with Iraq over the completely fictitious existence of WMDs. Like all wars in this day and age, the joint wars in Iraq and Afghanistan cost us enormous loss of life and trillions of dollars. I remember you and dad talking one night about how thirty-nine billion dollars found its way into VP Cheney's former company, Haliburton. The Bush administration did not tax the public to pay for that war; it was financed by the Chinese who bought our Federal notes. This is now *our* debt and it is left to my generation to pay it off. It's worth the time to think about how a President Gore would have responded to 9/11.

"Obama gave us eight years of indecisiveness as the Republicans controlled Congress for six of those years under Senator McConnell, who made it clear that he was disappointed with the Obama victory. McConnell made it clear to his colleagues at a luncheon the day after inauguration that President Obama would have a tough time getting anything past his desk in the Senate. Almost every Obama initiative for the next eight years was stalled. Obama tried and failed to break through the McConnell juggernaut with diplomacy and negotiation. With the exception of the contentious Affordable Care Act, his two terms ended far less successfully than they otherwise might have.

"Trump's candidacy was in the right place at the right time. Never has a person been so unprepared for the Oval Office. This man has managed in less than four years, to eviscerate laws that made up the fabric of America. He led us backward in our effort to achieve that elusive more perfect union. Historians will devote hours to figure out how a man of Trump's limited public sector skills and experience managed to win the 2016 election. Should he win reelection in 2020, many more hours will be spent trying to understand how we, as a nation, elected him twice. That of course, assumes that we will be allowed to undertake scientific, scholarly, or anti-government research during a second Trump administration. He will continue to marginalize science and minimize the role of education in America. He even brags that he likes being around uneducated people. I shudder to think of what our environmental, judicial, and congressional institutions will look like if he continues on this same path for another term. Our State Department has already been decimated with the resignations of many long-serving staff! We have yet to fill several ambassadorships, which has further reduced morale in the department. The same is happening in other agencies.

"There is nothing, including outright lies, cheating, and ballot manipulation, that Trump won't employ to win in 2020. He's already shown that by compromising the Post Office and by encouraging white supremacists to open or liberate states whose Democratic governors have closed them down to combat the virus and save lives. He encourages his followers at rallies to shout 'lock them up' about anyone who disagrees with him. Trump encourages *his* justice department to do everything it can to suppress the vote. He's even threatened to cut off funds to blue states and send more federal money to red states. What kind of a president does such things?

"Like so many civilizations before us, we are on a descending path that will only accelerate with four more years of Trump. As Richard said, ancient civilizations all had several hundred years of power and glory. Sadly, the American example has not yet lasted a hundred years. There's been one benefit from this administration. For several decades we have seen the income and wealth inequality gap grow. We have seen racism and poverty become more widespread. We have maintained our hawkish stance on war and shunned the negotiating table. The Trump administration has made all of these, shall I say "deplorable" aspects of America abundantly clear. Now we know the game. We also know the only way back to the true roots of our nation's grand experiment is to do the right thing. As professor Pryce has said, we the people, we the voters, must rise up. If we don't, we may meet the enemy and find that he is us.

"Capitalism as an economic system and democracy as a political system can succeed if they are allowed to function fairly and equitably. My dad and Professor Pryce were always quick to agree on one thing. As great as democracy and capitalism are, they are also the most vulnerable of systems.

We have seen how greed, corruption, and incompetence can weaken them. If we allow capitalism or democracy to fall under the control of powerful, self-centered, dictatorial leaders, they will both fail. Apathy is the enemy here. We have left our democracy to others for several decades. These are people who do not necessarily have our best interests in mind. The burden is on the voters— there is no other trusted, capable, or willing entity out there at this point to do what only we can do. We have seen the solution and it is also us."

She sat down, visibly shaken. The room was again quiet until they all began to clap.

"Wow, Anna! That was wonderful. You are clearly your father's daughter," I said as I, too, began to clap. "How long has all that been festering inside you?" As adulation was being heaped on Anna, I said to myself, these were just the types of students I had been longing to teach. In that moment, having listened to these incredibly bright young people, I made up my mind. I wanted to teach again, and I wanted to do it at NYU. I wanted to be around these bright, involved game-changers. I would even pay them to let me teach students like these. The room was unbelievably still. Then everyone began talking at once. They reminded me of the idealistic students around me during the '60s and '70s. This was a genuinely great evening for me, and I think for them as well.

"Professor Pryce," Clarita Alvarez interjected. "This has been a wonderful evening and I am so glad that I was able to attend. We sent you a long list of issues we talk about all the time. We only had time to cover a few tonight, and I'm asking how we can find a way to have you or someone like you available to discuss the other issues, some of which bother us a lot. We care about how many of us were raised by single moms. We care about student debt, abortion, and women's rights. I personally care about getting a job. This virus is killing the economy, and jobs are disappearing right before our eyes. How can I justify spending all this money on an education knowing that my career opportunities are fading away each day? I do not know what it was like for you when you were in school, but we are really hurting, and we don't know where to turn."

Clarita really hit a major sore spot for me. One of the findings Andrew and I noticed was that in all likelihood, this next generation of graduates will most likely, for the first time in America, not live as well as did their parents. Clarita saw this and knew it to be the case. I am sure that every student in their group was also aware of this problem, made even more acute due to the current cost of an education.

"Clarita, I cannot imagine what you and your friends are going through. I had none of these problems when I was graduating, but over time I have seen them beginning to take over our lives. That is why I chose the profession I did. I wanted to make a difference. One thing I'm going to do is approach the chairman of the economics department and offer to teach a course I have wanted to do for a long time. It is a course on the history of economic thought that will focus on how economists have worked for thousands of years to understand and deal with the very issues you have just mentioned here tonight. I am willing to teach the course for free. I promise you that even if I can't get the course approved, I will pull it all together and offer it for free online and then wherever we can find a classroom. You might think you learned something here tonight, but I assure you, I am walking out of here having learned the most.

Darius blurted out, "What do you mean thousands of years? I thought economics started in the eighteen hundreds with the publication of Adam Smith's book?"

"No, Darius, in fact, I think of Aristotle as the first economist. I also go back to the time Homo Sapiens began to first form communities, which was about 60,000 years ago. Economics played an important part in their lives, just as it does for you guys today."

"I hope you get that course; I want to take it."

"Me too, Darius, me too. I really love you guys. I love you for all that you care about and for the intelligence and effort you are going to put into your professional lives. The world is going to be a better place because each of you are in it. I feel humbled and honored to have had this opportunity. I thank you."

I thought this would be a good moment for Carlos to fill up our sangria mugs and bring us some more tapas. I walked to the bar area to find him when I noticed the men sitting near the door. I recognized them as my unwanted federal guards. I turned away from them, ordered the food and drinks, and returned to our room. Moving to a corner of the room, I pulled out my burner phone to call Ari. I let him know what was happening. Ari instructed me to give the burner to Susan who was at the bar and to leave as soon as I could. AO had just warned us that these are White House goons here to arrest me. Ari wrote, "We're right outside the restaurant and I see some Escalades parked up the block. There may be more Feds outside, be careful."

I hung up and settled down to give myself time to process the situation. I asked for any questions or comments, but there were none. We were all pretty exhausted. We sat around, finishing off the delicious tapas and talked about the various issues. We agreed that the topics as presented were those that really mattered to their generation.

I mentioned the list that they had compiled. "Some of those topics were discussed tonight, others were not, and, like you, I consider all of them important. As Clarita pointed out, you guys have put together an agenda for the next administration. I'd like you to figure out how to get it to Biden if he wins. I am going to work on this myself and put my thoughts into how you might expand on your concerns. Regardless of what happens, I will get my comments and suggestions back to Anna for distribution. If you should want to meet with me again, I am at your service."

I ended our time together by sharing my fervent wishes for all of our young people. "Get involved, stay involved, and vote for the changes you want! Please get out there as soon as this pandemic is over and meet people from other places and nations. Nothing expands your heart and mind like learning about other peoples and their cultures."

We fist or elbow bumped each other as the group began to leave. All agreed that it was a fun and enlightening evening. We began to collect our things. The students drifted through the main room toward the exit and I noticed that they were not bothered by my goons. For the first time, I noticed Susan, who was taking her apron off. Ari had somehow known that something was going to happen and stationed her there. Susan called out to Anna, "Are you ready to leave?"

I turned to Anna and, with a nod, indicated that she should leave with Susan. Understanding, Anna quickly packed up and said goodbye to her friends. Then she came over to me. As she side-hugged me goodbye, I whispered that something was wrong and that I wanted her to stay with Susan until she heard from me. I handed Susan my burner. I didn't make another move until I knew that all the students, Anna, and Susan were out the door. Then I called to Carlos and offered to help clean up. He came in with a tray. "Thanks, I could use the help, and the company, too!"

We started cleaning up and I mentioned my concerns about the two guys sitting near the door. I told him that I knew who they were and that they'd been following me around for weeks.

Carlos said, "Be careful, you never know what these people have in mind."

Actually, I knew exactly what they had in mind—they intended to arrest me. "Have you ever seen them before?"

"Never."

We finished cleaning up, and I picked up my bag and walked casually toward the exit. I noticed the men begin to shuffle and maybe stand up. Halfway there, I changed my mind. I noticed my cover was across the street, and I knew that Ari was close. I walked to the table where the Feds were nursing their beers. I pulled up a chair and sat down.

"May I join you?" I asked conversationally.

Two very startled men stared at me. Actually, there were four startled men as I caught the eye of my covers who were staring at me from across the street, wondering what the hell I was doing.

I smiled and asked, "Should you guys be drinking on the job?"

"What do you mean? What are you doing?" the heavy one asked suspiciously.

I gazed at them for a moment, leaned back in my chair, and said, "Look, I've seen you hanging around for several days now, and I thought it might be constructive if we just talked for a few minutes." I put my open hand on my back, signaling to Ari's guys that I needed five minutes.

"Why would we want to talk to you?" grumbled the other agent.

"I guess I figured that if you're going to spend all this time tailing me, we might as well get acquainted. Who do you guys work for? Is there something I can help you with? Do you want to see my notes? My phone?"

"Now, why would we want to do that?" sneered the overweight guy.

I could tell that he was going to do all the talking. Maybe the other guy had another skill.

"Because you obviously have an interest in me, and frankly, you make me extremely uncomfortable, especially when I'm with students. I wouldn't want them to get hurt or get involved in whatever it is that you think I'm doing."

"We were just instructed to keep an eye on you, nothing more. They're concerned about who you are working with and what you're doing. You seem to be angry. We think you don't like being American."

I burst out laughing. "Do you mean what transpired at this dinner? There's nothing covered or discussed here that has not been on the front page of the *New York Times* or the *Washington Post*!" I then got a bit more serious. "Look, all this might be okay with you, but we don't really allow anyone to follow citizens around without cause. Do you have cause? Do you really think it's appropriate to listen in on private conversations? Who are your superiors? Maybe I should be talking to them? May I see your ID, please?"

"That is all confidential information, sir. We are not obligated to disclose anything to you or anybody else," he said, slapping the table for emphasis.

"Well, strictly speaking, that's not true," I told him, "and if you're in any way representing an official government office, you know I'm right."

"It is not," said the heavy guy. As he sat up, his shirt fell out of his pants. He looked at his partner for confirmation.

"Okay, guys. Here's the deal. I'm a retired professor and a visiting scholar at NYU. If you think you have any reason to follow me around, I'm telling you to leave my students and anyone else at NYU out of your equation. Are we clear on that?"

"We are not obligated to be clear on anything to you. This meeting is over," he told me, abruptly pushing his chair back and standing up.

I took out my phone and pretended to make a call, activating a hidden camera that I pointed at them to take their picture.

"You'll have to give that phone to us," he said, as he held out his hand.

"Hey, guys, I am not looking for any trouble," I said as I stood up and stepped back, planting my feet firmly on the floor. "You're not getting my phone unless you take it forcibly. I strongly recommend that you not try to do that." I did, however, agree that this meeting had gone on long enough. "If I see you hanging around me again, I'll call the police, who will get to hold you long enough for me to have my lawyers get involved," I warned them. "At least then I'll find out who the hell you are and why you've been following me around." I turned toward the bar and shouted to Carlos. "Mr. Carlos, will you please dial 911?" I winked out of view of the Feds. Carlos picked up his phone and pretended to dial. "There was a time when everyone looked to you guys for our national security, and you were our most trusted and valued guardians. You think that I'm a threat? You need to rethink your priorities! The biggest threat to you and your bosses is sitting in the Oval Office right now trying to figure out what valued agency he can corrupt next, and you can be sure that yours is on his list. That man, gentlemen, is a threat to everything you and I hold dear. If you and your superiors can't tell the difference between an honest and dedicated citizen and our fake president, I fear you much more than you should fear me. I have to go. I strongly suggest that you get back to DC and start working on a clear and present danger to you, your organization, and our once beautiful nation." I turned to go.

For a split second they seemed poised to stop me. I stood my ground, spread my legs, and looked at both of them straight on. Out of the corner of my eye, I saw my cover running across the street. The Feds stepped back and let me leave. I walked out without looking back. Ari was right there with another man and the three of us walked west with no particular destination in mind.

Ari took me by the arm. He could see that I'd been shaken by the whole experience and was on the verge of collapse.

"What the fuck were you doing?" Ari's angry voice startled me into alertness.

"I just wanted those guys to know that I was onto them, and I wanted to mess with their heads. I'm sorry if I pissed you off."

"What would you have done if they'd grabbed you? What if they had taken your phone? Do you know what you risked?" I could see that he was not going to let this go.

"I'd already handed our burner phone to Susan. I wasn't worried because I knew you were there, and that Carlos would come to my aid. I wanted to let them know that I was not their problem. I don't for one-minute think I made them go away, but I do think my message sunk in."

"How do you know you can trust Carlos?"

"I just do. Do we know where Susan is now? Where is Anna?"

"You surprise me, Benson," Ari smiled at me approvingly. "I'll get it from her."

"Well, you hold more surprise cards than I do, Ari. Thanks for being there for me. Did you imagine that they would follow me to the restaurant tonight?"

"As I mentioned, I got word from AO that you were in trouble, so we mobilized. You have him to thank."

I let that sink in for a minute. "That tells me that these guys are not tied to a legit agency but have been sent by the White House."

"I agree. I honestly don't know what alarmed them tonight, but someone deployed them to tail you, and we have to get to the bottom of it."

"Okay, you do that," I told him. My body ached and I could feel the events of the evening taking their toll. "But I need to get home and take a long hot shower. Where's Anna?"

Ari said, "She is with Susan and safe. No need to worry about her. We might have to sit down and fill her in as much as we can. She's no fool and now knows that something's going on."

"You're right. Let's meet tomorrow and pull this together. Did the illustrations get posted? I want to be sure that we hit as many evangelical sites as possible. Also, I put a short piece on *Roe v Wade* on the flash drive. I want the team to condense it without losing the message and publish that as well. Abortion is their biggest reason for supporting Trump, and I want to make it the non-issue it really is."

"You really are something," Ari said with astonishment. "You're telling me that after all you've just been through, you manage to think about the posts at the same time. Wow!"

"We have a job to do, and all of us have put our hearts, not to mention time and money, into getting it done. We both need to stay focused."

Ari responded. "The illustrations are out there and getting liked and shared and most importantly, our clicks are way up. I should have some specifics tomorrow. You know that you need to stay cool and should not be aggravating the Feds."

"I do. What I just did was probably a mistake. Even though, I have to say that it felt really good to me. This is why I need to have everything ready to go. I'm not important at this point. It's the team and our mission that matters from here."

"Benson, there are a lot of people who would disagree with you on that, starting with Anna. Don't forget you're still controlling all the content we post."

"Okay, I'll be more careful in the future. Please walk me home and tell me the plan for tomorrow. Is Moshe available?"

"He's already in the apartment. I have to be in Brooklyn, so let's meet in Prospect Park at 11:00. Ninth Street and Prospect Park West, by the Lafayette sculpture. Bring Moshe and be careful. I'll have a car pick you both up at 10:00."

"Thanks. I was actually scared shitless, you know. Maybe it was the sangria, or maybe I was actually scared for those wonderful students. They are filled with such incredible energy. The only thing that made it possible for me to challenge those guys was that I knew that you had my back."

"You are a strange piece of cake, my friend." Ari smiled at me and I knew we were back on even ground.

"Ari, would you please check on Anna? I couldn't bear to have anything happen to her. I think it was actually her presentation that may have riled the Feds up. They threw some pretty heavy accusations at me. I think that was when all three of us got angry. That girl is one heavy political animal."

"She's her father's daughter, and most importantly, she is safe now. You know, Anna is free from responsibilities for now and can take some time off. Maybe it's time to let her know more about what we are doing...and about her dad, too?"

"We can make some decisions about Anna and everything else tomorrow. You may be right. I'm too tired to make that call right now." We arrived in front of my apartment building. "See you in the morning. And Ari, thank you."

CHAPTER 18

SEPTEMBER 2020

MOSHE WAS IN THE APARTMENT when I got home. I was almost 11:00 p.m., and I was drained. He could tell that I was unwell. "Are you okay? I heard it was a pretty rough night." He poured both of us a Glenfiddich 25 with an ice cube and a twist of lemon, exactly how I like it.

"Yes, thank you. I may have screwed up by confronting those two dicks. I guess I was angry that they had followed me to that meeting and had heard Anna speak so passionately about what our government is doing to itself—and to us. I was also angry that they'd involved the students, and frankly, *nobody* messes with my students. They were totally out of line. They also refused to identify themselves, and I think that's against the law."

"We all have a breaking point," he said. "Ari knows you pretty well, and you know you can depend on him. You should get some sleep—we have a long day ahead of us. We need to be ready to leave by 9:45. I'll leave earlier and go to the pickup spot. The limo will be here at 10:00, so bring a change of clothes just in case."

"You're right, I should get to bed. Do you think we are safe tonight? Ari and I agreed that these guys are not official agents; they are with the White House. Something's wrong here, and I have no idea what is going on."

"I agree, this is strange. As for tonight, I'm not sure we're ever going to be safe again. I will cover for you, and Mr. Bonaparte is on duty in the lobby. Get some sleep."

★ ★ ★

THE SUN WAS JUST PEAKING OVER the downtown skyline as I woke up. I think I slept for seven hours straight, a record for me. I was rested and knew that I had to get going. I could smell the coffee. Moshe was already dressed and watching the news. Trump had just tested positive for the virus, along with some of his staff members. A million thoughts raced through my head. *Will he die? Will they use this to stop the election? What would a President Pence be like?* I knew it was probably inevitable given POTUS's refusal to recognize the virus. I honestly hadn't given a moment's thought to him getting infected—I am sure he didn't either. Troublesome times.

I hopped into the shower and let the hot water pour over me for as long as I could stand it. I got dressed and stuffed some spare alternate-colored clothing into a shopping bag, as instructed. No croissant, so I had some cereal with fresh frozen blueberries. I'd found a box of those sweet tiny Maine blueberries on the way home. I wolfed down a cup of espresso, and we were ready to go. The security computer and all drives and papers were safely stored in the other apartment.

Moshe left before me. I suggested that I stay someplace else tonight to give him a break. He didn't disagree but told me to ask Ari. I left 15 minutes later and stopped to ask Mr. Bonaparte where I might be able to spend a few nights.

"I'll have a key for you when you return. Best you come back here, but not stay in the apartment."

"Thank you. I should be back after lunch." How does that man keep more up-to-date on my activities than I do?

"I'll still be on duty."

I glanced outside and could see my car. I ran out the door, up the stairs to the sidewalk, and directly into the car. I didn't look around, assuming my driver had already done so. We took off as soon as the light changed. We drove west on Thirteenth Street as fast as we could, then turned downtown on Seventh Avenue and pulled over next to a fire hydrant to see if we were being followed. Seeing no one, we pulled out and headed downtown toward the Brooklyn Bridge. We both kept an eye out in back as we darted in and out of the early morning traffic. The Brooklyn-bound bridge was almost empty, so we made good time. We headed into Brooklyn Heights and onto the BQE, another detour. We were still clear. At the Thirty-fourth Street exit we headed back into the depths of Brooklyn toward Prospect Park, one of my favorites.

In addition to getting more people to the polls, our mission now was to prevent Trump from winning a second term. We knew how much he wanted to win, but was our almost invisible campaign really important enough to warrant all this attention? Maybe they thought we had more going on than we did? I made a mental note to discuss this with Ari.

I could see Moshe sitting on a bench in front of the Marquis de Lafayette. That rather large relief had been a gift of an American Francophile to honor the efforts of the marquis during the Revolutionary War. The marquis was highly respected and won the favor of General Washington who had appointed him as a Major General in the Continental Army. He returned to France and convinced the French government to dramatically increase its financial and military aid to the colonial revolutionists.

I was dropped off a block away and told to meet the car on Ninth Street and Eighth Avenue when we were done. I thanked the driver who remained nameless. Walking back to Ninth Street, I saw Ari heading down the path that leads to a pond and what is now called Prospect Park Dog Beach. Moshe was 200 feet behind him. I sat on a nearby bench for a while to make sure none of us were being followed. After what seemed an eternity, I started on the same path. I felt my burner go off and wasn't sure if I should stop to check it.

The temptation was too strong. I took a left toward the Tennis House and a clutch of trees just to get out of sight. The short message from AO was coded with a red X emoji, meaning Code Red. Code green is a green check mark.

"POTUS major breakdown after testing positive, and press focused on COVID. On the attack, intel agents split and not sure who to trust. Barr at his side, Trump bouncing off the walls, watching five stations at once, and eating everything."

That was the last thing I wanted to hear, even though it wasn't unexpected. Reading between the lines for the past several weeks, it was clear that Trump was running scared and somehow acting cockier than I had ever seen him. His arrogance really scared me because to me it meant that he had more tricks up his sleeve. Everyone knows that his biggest fear was being a civilian again. He knew that he would spend the rest of his life in court or possibly jail.

Ari was sitting on a bench by the dog beach. Moshe was out of sight. I casually walked over and sat down next to him. I could tell he was upset. I waited for him to speak. "Did you see the message from AO?"

"Yes, I did," I answered. "I'm going to make up a really biting, on-point post as soon as I can. AO is turning out to be a major asset for us. What do you make of the message?"

"I think I understand why we've been targeted," he said. "POTUS is running scared. He's behind in the polls and knows that he'll be either in court or jail if he's not reelected. Barr's controlling the DOJ, but not the

NSA, CIA, or FBI, and it looks like a team of agents and some White House staff are about to go after them. No comment from the military. The word is they're on our side and really pissed over Putin's bounty on our soldiers and the fact that POTUS is putting Putin first. This is an act of treason. The president is totally ignoring them and could not care less. Soldiers don't feel safe in the field, and the brass knows that. QAnon is everywhere. Some of them are running for Congress. The Proud Boys are pushing campaign trucks off the road. I think we're heading for a civil war.

"The next thing we need to talk about is that we have definitely been tagged. The tails on you were identified to me this morning as White House–based and not part of the agencies. There's some snooping at our Iceland operation, and Andrew has decided to close it down. We're going to remove everything except the transmission and reception units."

"Is that even possible? Does this mean we're out of business?"

"Not at all. Everyone will leave Iceland after we relocate the equipment. Maybe sooner. Our communications links will still be in place. The team will set up elsewhere. The Iceland base will still receive data and transmit as before, only it will all be robotic with no one on hand. We have already temporarily switched over to a new location a few miles away, and the team is cleaning up so that if we should be found, the current place will be totally cleaned. It will be as though we were never there. It will take them several weeks to find the bunker, and when they do it will self-destruct as soon as they open the door."

"Where is the new permanent location?"

"Not sure yet. What is critical right now is to get you out of New York and get Anna out of the country. Andrew and I have decided that I'll fly to Iceland tonight, help load up the plane, and get everyone out. I want Andrew and Anna separate from the team for a while. Susan's with Anna, and I haven't decided if she's at risk. I think you should go to the old safe house in Virginia. I'm preparing a new identity for you because you might need to be secluded for a while. I should have it for you tonight."

"I still can't figure out why they're so focused on us—surely there are dozens of higher-level groups doing far more damage than we could possibly create." I was losing it and started pacing back and forth. Trying to get into the head of POTUS is like navigating a Pac-Man maze blindfolded. Ari let me rant for a few minutes. "Benson, this man is on the verge of a breakdown. We're not the only ones under the gun, and these goons who are after us are just off-budget pablum to Trump. Their job is to keep the president happy and his hands off the red button. AO has made it clear that everyone in the White House is suspicious of everyone else. You can't run an operation with that kind of internal mistrust. You and our team are, however, collateral damage and expendable. We are dealing with the White House here, and the president of the United States running around the White House in his bathrobe shouting orders at a bunch of people trying desperately to hold the nation together."

Ari offered his usual steady hand. "Look, Benson, calm down, you're certainly right about POTUS, but I have everything under control. We're going to split up now. You will get back into the car and get back to your apartment and start clearing it out."

"Do you think we're still on their hit list? My guess is that those guys from last night have been recalled to deal with bigger fish."

"You might be right, but I'm not taking any chances. I think we have a window. I want to get you and Anna out of the city. You aren't needed here since everything is in place and on schedule for posting, and you can work anywhere. I need to make a few calls. I want you to go back to the apartment and get our secure computer, notes, and flash and all hard drives and bring it all with you. Clean out the apartment and take what you will need for a few weeks. Bring your passport and remove the security devise I installed. Mr. Bonaparte will scrub the place and store what you cannot take. I'm going to put you in a temporary safe house for a few days while I scope out what's actually going on. This has moved way too fast for me, and that tells me that something else is happening."

"What about you? I will need to take my other laptop and the secure external drive with me, it has all our data for our posts on it. Will you be alright?"

"I'll be okay, Benson. I have more than enough cover. I leave it up to you to decide what to do about the external drive. Destroy it if you think it is incriminating."

I lamented. "I need to think all this through. I'm totally blown away that we have managed to be identified as a target. I'm not flattered. Do you think Anna and I can go to Iceland? Remember they know that Andrew is alive."

"That was actually my first thought. We have enough backup there and a safe house for both of you, but I think you might be safer in the States. Besides, I think it's time that Anna and her dad reconnect."

"I couldn't agree more. Can you get us another flight? I think we have enough cash to get through a month or so. Do you have enough for you and your people?"

"Yes. Thank you, Benson, if I get short, I have some of our cash in the safe deposit box in Jersey."

"Do not take any chances; I am not sure what would happen to me if anything happened to you. Maybe bring the cash with you in case you guys need it."

"I've been taking chances all my life. It's what I do."

"Ari!" I shrieked with exasperation.

"Okay, okay. I hear you. Right now, you and Anna are the priority. Walk down to the Third Street exit, and I will let the driver know to have the car meet you there. Watch your back."

"Is Moshe safe? He's a very competent man and good to have aboard."

"Moshe is my kid brother. He insisted on going to work for me. It was a real battle with our parents. They finally gave in and he won. You're right; he's going to be better at this than me in a few years. I also think they knew he would be safe with me."

"Your brother? Will I ever know how much of your life is a secret to me?"

"Never. Now, get going. The driver will take you to the apartment and get anything you need. When you get back to the lobby, the driver will come in and scan everything you have with you, including yourself."

"You really do think of everything."

"And be careful. The guys who want our data and systems and to shut us down are every bit as competent as I am. Don't forget; they also trained me."

I just stared at him for a moment. "They trained you?"

"We don't have time for that right now."

WE WERE BACK AT THE APARTMENT before I knew it. I got everything cleaned and packed up. I gathered my personal computer, notes, passport, cash, and whatever clothes I thought I would need. I suddenly realized that I'd probably be in hiding for a long time, maybe even through the election. I would have a lot of time to relax and read. So, I packed some of my favorite books and put the rest on the kitchen counter. Mr. Bonaparte would save them for me. I was out the door in less than fifteen minutes.

My driver was waiting in the lobby when I came down. Mr. Bonaparte had the secure laptop and all the drives and notes with him. The driver had a portable scanner and used it to inspect me and my bags and then did it all over again, setting the gain a bit higher. I was clean. I asked him if he would please take my things to the car. I needed a moment with Mr. Bonaparte. "Mr. Bonaparte, I need to get away for a while, and I'm not sure when, or if, I'll be back. Please stay in touch with Ari. I want you to know that Anna will be with me. I'm not sure I can say any more right now. You know how much you and your family mean to me. Please let Ramon know that I'm grateful to him and can't wait to hear how his daughters are doing. Thanks for bringing the bag from 201 down."

"You just take care of yourself and Anna. I'll have the cleaners take care of the apartment and store anything left behind."

"You know what to do. Goodbye, my dear, dear friend. I don't know when I'll see you again. There will always be a place in my heart for you."

"Thank you, Dr. Pryce. The feeling is mutual."

I noticed a sheet of paper with one of our illustrations of the president on his desk. "Where did you get that? Do you know what it is?"

"Yes, I just wanted you to know that your work is getting out there and a lot of people are talking about it. You have done a wonderful thing here, and I am so proud to know you."

"A lot of us have made this happen, including you. Stay safe and maybe put that page away."

We sped away, moving in and out of traffic and onto side streets. We drove through the Holland Tunnel toward Ari's Hoboken safe house. As we drove, I remembered that I used to keep an old car I had in Hoboken while in graduate school. Parking there cost next to nothing and the cost of Manhattan garages had been out of reach to me at that time.

I have no idea how Ari managed to set up a safe house in New Jersey, much less Hoboken. I never knew about Hoboken until a friend had recommended it to me for my car. I learned a little about the history of this tiny enclave, tucked away on the Jersey side of the Hudson River. Francis Albert Sinatra was born there in 1915. He was raised in a walkup tenement building. His domineering mother was a midwife, his father a bantamweight boxer. Hoboken had been a major port since the seventeenth century. Its busy docks eventually became an integral part of the Port of New York and New Jersey. This small town on the Hudson once claimed more bars per capita than any other town in America. It is also known as the site of the very first baseball game ever played in America. Hoboken shares long and important historical events in the formation of the colonies, pre- and post-Revolution. Despite all that, Frank Sinatra is still Hoboken's favorite son and its biggest claim to fame.

I felt like a member of the Sinatra family as we climbed the three floors to Ari's three-bedroom apartment, which was clean and tastefully appointed. To my total surprise, Anna and Susan were sitting on the couch talking as we entered. I was beyond happy to see her, knowing that she was safe. I greeted Susan and thanked her for taking care of Anna for us.

Anna scoldingly said, "Benson, what the hell is going on? Why were we hustled out of that bar, and why are we hiding out like refugees?"

"I'm so sorry, honey, but we need to be careful. I promise to tell you everything. For now, all I can say is that I have put together a team of people, all of whom are dedicated to get as many people to the polls as possible. We're working off the database your father and I built. Surely you remember it."

"I thought you gave it up when dad died?"

"I did. Last fall, I found a way to resurrect it with some tech guys Ari introduced me to. We are also doing everything we can to prevent Trump from being reelected. You need to know that we are doing nothing illegal. Well, almost nothing," I said smiling. "We're hacking into many sites and platforms to reach the voters we want to get to the polls. Right now, we think that Trump's paranoia is the problem, and that's the main thing we are running from. Can I get you anything?"

"No thanks, this place is fully stocked. The three of us could stay here for a month and never have to leave."

"That's Ari. Leaves nothing to chance."

Ari arrived at about 5:00 with three suitcases from Anna's apartment. Anna was extremely upset with us and not the least bit hesitant to let us know it.

"Benson, why are my clothes here? Why are we here? What happened last night? A beautiful evening suddenly fell apart, and I'm whisked off to Jersey with someone I've never met and plopped into a third-floor walkup. This is not like you. No one, especially you, has ever treated me this way." Anna stomped off, terribly upset.

I looked at Ari and shrugged. We had failed to talk over our strategy for Anna. Neither of us knew exactly how to handle what we needed to tell this rightfully angry young woman. I excused myself and took Ari into a bedroom to talk.

"Ari, did you get her passport?"

"I couldn't find it. I'm hoping she has it with her."

"How do we tell her that not only are we fugitives from the government, but that her father is alive and well in Iceland? This isn't going to be easy. She is going to be totally pissed at us for deceiving her. Is there any way you can get him on video or voice from here?"

"I probably can, but it would compromise our location. Let me think about it. I feel that we have to tell her now. You know her best; what are your thoughts?"

"I'm not sure. Give me a minute. What if we drove to the Meadowlands and placed a call? Could we do a video call? Don't forget that we need to let Andrew know that we're about to tell his daughter that he's not dead."

"I thought of that on the way over and gave him a heads up. He's ready to deal with Anna in any way we think is best."

"Wow, that's big! Thanks. Did you tell him that the Feds know he's alive?"

"No, I thought that should wait until I am with him."

"What do you think about going to the Meadowlands?" I asked. "I'm sure that they do not have a game going on, but there will be a lot of immigrant workers hanging around making international calls. Another idea would be to go to a shopping mall and link to their Wi-Fi. How much time would we have before having to fly out?"

Ari wasn't keen on that idea. "Let me think. I'll come up with something. Why don't you go brief Anna on the project? That will hopefully give us some cover and explain why her father had to disappear. We'll probably have the least amount of grief by telling her the truth."

"Fully agree. My problem is how to order the information for her. Should I first tell her that her father is alive? Or tell her what we've been doing, and then about her dad? Actually, I'm going to see if she has her passport. You come up with a way to get her dad on a line somehow."

"Sounds like a plan."

"You get so trite at the worst times. That sounds like 'the check's in the mail' to me."

"Get out there and calm her down," ordered Ari.

I took a deep breath to calm myself down, remembering my martial arts training—be calm, clear, and focused. "Anna," I started, "Ari and I need to talk to you, but first, do you have your passport?"

"Yes. My friends and I were going to drive to Quebec after the meeting last night. We've been tested and cleared for entry. You guys sure messed up those plans. Now tell me what the hell's going on?"

I sat down beside her. "Many years ago, your father and I became concerned that Americans were not voting and that our country was falling into the toilet," I explained. "We felt there were legitimate reasons why most Americans do not vote. When we realized that Trump was placing dangerous people in charge of vital departments and agencies, we knew the game had changed. These people had marching orders from him to do everything they could to destroy or neutralize the very agencies they were sworn to protect. Your dad and I decided that we needed to do something."

"Is this going to be one of your endless explanations?" she asked. She was angry. "If so, I'm really not in the mood for such bullshit right now. Please get to the point."

Another deep breath. "This really *is* the point. We began to reorganize our database to reach out to eligible, but nonvoting people. We wanted to distribute our information to voters throughout the country, right and left—we wanted to get to everyone. That meant we needed a sophisticated software team and a lot of equipment."

"Benson, why am I sitting on this couch in Hoboken, New Jersey?"

"Well, to get the job done right, we had to figure out how to hack into dozens of websites and other private accounts on social media. Basically, we needed to do *exactly* what the Russians and a lot of far-right radical groups did during the 2016 election."

Anna glared at me. "You and Dad are really the most naïve people I know. You don't know anything about that technology. What made you think that you could put together something like that? You could get caught and go to jail. Was getting a bunch of uninvolved, uninformed, and probably unregistered voters to the polls that important to you?"

She was frustrated, angry, scared, and still mourning. Things were not going her way. "Yes Anna, it was—and still is. And you're right, we couldn't have done it alone. We needed to find a secure location and get some very smart hackers to pull this off."

"Even if you could do that, there's no way you would get away with it. You'd be arrested."

I locked onto her eyes. "That is what is happening right now. The Feds are onto us. And that's exactly the rub. We needed to set this operation up offshore so that no one would get found or arrested."

I could see that she was beginning to put two and two together. I said nothing for a while. I just looked at her face and read her thought processes as she began to figure out what was going on.

"Have you set this up yet?"

"Yes, and we've begun to release our data. It's been saturating the internet for about a week now. We've managed to hack into some pretty sophisticated sites. Apparently, we're pissing off the right people. But I'm not sure that we've influenced the voters we want to reach. About two months ago, when I saw the direction the 2020 presidential election was taking, I made the decision to add an even more aggressive and complicated campaign to discredit this president and his administration. As we began to design the systems, we found a way to hack into the sites of those who were spreading all those lies to the public. It worked for them, and we thought we could make their systems work for us. We've connected with foreign, domestic, and underground platforms serving the political right and left, as far out on both sides of the center as possible.

We started hitting Trump's base two days ago, concentrating on the evangelicals, since they represent the biggest single block of far-right voters that support the president. We couldn't figure out why they'd want anything to do with a man like him. We published a simple chart on the post *Roe v. Wade* abortions that shows a consistent decline. We have reason to believe that his duplicity is beginning to get to them. Their loyalties are wavering, especially since Falwell Jr. made headlines with his sexual fantasies. I saw a recent poll that concluded that 23% of evangelicals are moving away from Trump, purely on moral grounds."

Anna was thinking again. "How did you do that without Dad? You don't even know how to set a new email password without him."

I paused. I inhaled and exhaled. "That's where this whole thing gets a bit messy, especially for you. We were very afraid for everyone involved, especially you. Your dad and I decided that we had to work from a remote and secure place that has the most up-to-date communications systems available. We knew that we couldn't do that from the States."

Anna stared at me for what seemed like an eternity. I said nothing. "Are you telling me that my father is alive?" She stood up and began walking back and forth. I've always counted on her analytical ability to think through anything on her own. Knowing her as I do, I tried to present everything in such a way that she'd figure it out for herself. Now, I let her question drift around in her head and just stared at her.

I was sure that my eyes and hers were full of tears when I opened my mouth. "Yes."

She sat back down. The room was noticeably quiet. "Why did you and Dad do that to me? Why didn't you tell me? Why didn't *he* tell me?"

I was prepared for anything. Was she going to stand up and start pounding away at me? Start crying? Look at me with total disgust? She was capable of all of the above. "Anna, it was a joint decision. We weren't sure how much trouble we'd get into, and the last thing we wanted was to have you picked up and interrogated. These people are not civilized. Remember Abu Ghraib? Faking your dad's death was the only way we could keep him out of the picture and, at the same time, protect you. He chose to have it happen from a sailboat because we knew that you'd doubt that he would die that way. We wanted you to have hope, and I know that it worked."

"I really do not know if I want to kill you or kiss you. When can I see him? Is he okay? Where is he?"

"You'll be with him in a few days. That's why we are here. The Feds figured us out even though they are still only guessing. Actually, they didn't find us. Ari thinks that White House goons or the Russians might have marked us. They're pissed that we hacked their hackers. No one knows who or where we are, but they know we exist. Every time they put something out, we're right behind them, posting to the same sources they are. We're going to make them wish they never hit the return key on American democracy. Then, as we get closer to the election, we plan to advertise in the popular and rural press. How much will depend on whether the press picks up the traffic on our posts. Ari's in the next room trying to figure out how we can contact your dad from here without compromising our position. Ari," I called, "will you join us now?"

"Be right there." He walked into the living room and sat down opposite us.

"Can we pull this off or do we have to wait until we're in the air?" I asked.

"I think we can do something. Andrew's sending something as we speak." He looked down at his phone. "I need to check the connections before I can answer that...." Before he could finish his sentence, Andrew's distinctive voice came over my burner.

"Anna, honey. I'm here," he said. Her eyes immediately teared up. "Please don't be mad at Benson. This was my idea more than his." She looked at me empathically. "We've done some important work, and we knew of no other way to get it done without compromising you. I couldn't bear the thought of you being interrogated. As it turned out, we were right, which is why we need to regroup. We'll be together in a few days, and we'll never be apart again. I promise. Love you from here to the moon and back 275 thousand times!"

The phone clicked off. Anna just sat there. She'd only begun to accept the fact that her dad was dead. As Ari left the room, she looked up at me, and we both burst into tears. I could feel Anna's relief almost as much as I could feel her anger. I pulled her to her feet and wrapped her in my arms. We both just stayed glued together, not moving, not saying anything. Andrew had banked on her strength to get her through all this, and he'd been right. It had been painful for all of us, but it was the right thing to do.

⚓

WE ALL SAT DOWN to a huge bowl of pasta with mushrooms, red and green peppers, and shrimp in a garlic and butter sauce. Ari and Susan had cooked us a gourmet feast. No one spoke until we'd finished it off, along with a couple bottles of wine. I, uncharacteristically, don't even remember looking at the label.

Ari broke the silence. "We'll leave the apartment tonight around 11:00 p.m. Benson, you will leave earlier and be driven to Union Station in Newark. You are staying in the States. We think it's best to keep as much separation between us as possible. Susan's decided to stay with us. She, Anna, and I will be driven to Teterboro Airport to board a corporate jet to Iceland. Andrew and the team will have packed everything up and be ready to board as soon as we land. Anna, you will be with your dad in about ten hours. We'll learn where we will be going after we leave Iceland and make a scheduled stop in Switzerland. Benson, please make a call to your banker and let him know that we will need some cash, I think about 100K will do it. We want nothing on credit cards for at least the next month or so. You will board an Amtrak for DC. I will have a car there for you. You know the car and the driver from our previous trip. You will stay at our safe house in Springfield, Virginia. Here's your new identity. Use it sparingly, but do not be afraid. If we have to extend past the election, I might have to get you a different ID."

"Do I have to pay the rent or utilities or anything on the safe house?"

"No, actually, you own it. You and Andrew bought it many years ago under a fictitious company. Everything is paid for from a secret Swiss account the both of you set up years ago when you had that consulting company in Washington. I told you that you're going to make a great snoop. Do not expect to get a government job for some time," Ari laughed.

"Since when did you develop a sense of humor? I'd totally forgotten about that place. Don't you think I should be out of the country?"

"That would be the most logical decision, which is why I think it's best that you stay behind. The Feds will think you're gone. I also want you separated from the team, and we need at least one person on the ground here. You'll join us as soon as it's safe for you to travel. Leave the secure laptop, papers, and flash drives with me. I want them out of the country and separate from you. There is too much information on it that we must protect. You can work from your other laptop, but don't go online with it if you can help it. That computer has been scanned, but your account might be compromised if you go online. Open a new account with your new identity in Virginia. Use a PO box in Springfield with your new ID. Keep the two burners you have but be ready to ditch them. I have people watching the Springfield house, but you will not see them unless something happens."

"Do I get to know where the team is going to be?"

"I won't know where we will be until I get in the air. When we're resettled, you will be told. It's easier for me to ask questions when we're traveling at 500 miles an hour. I want everything in Iceland to stay functional, even though no one will be there. We built in that capacity from the beginning. I wouldn't be surprised if it were already shut down and functional. Wherever we are, our posts will go out as though we were in Iceland. Should it be raided, the system will self-destruct and nothing, but some gutted and obsolete relay equipment will be found. You will get our reset, coded text from me when we are safe."

"Where will Moshe be?"

"I'm not sure. Maybe I will take him with us. You need to get ready to leave. Here's your ticket and your new ID and wallet. There's a place to hide your old ID and devices in the safe house. The driver will show it to you where it is and how to use it. Good luck, try to stay out of view at least until I am able to get back to you."

"Okay, Ari." Everything had started to feel overwhelming, and I did not want to be separated from the rest of them, even though I understood Ari's reasoning. I looked over at Anna and spoke quietly to her. "Anna, will you come with me for a moment, please?"

We walked into one of the bedrooms. I honestly had no idea what I was going to say to her. After everything that had happened to us, I just needed some time alone with her. "I want to say, on behalf of your dad and me, that we're terribly sorry. Maybe it was a mistake to deceive you. If it is, I have to take the blame. I pushed the goal line on your dad and the team. I'm still baffled about how we got on the White House's radar in the first place—nothing we are doing warrants this level of response by them. Maybe the illustrations I commissioned on Trump ticked him off? Maybe our campaign has been more effective than we thought it would be? I honestly do not know, especially given the person we are dealing with. I only hope that we can all be together soon. At least you and your dad will be together, maybe even early tomorrow afternoon."

"Well, this has been an awful lot to absorb. In some ways, I'm not surprised—I understand why you're committed to stopping Trump's reelection, but I have to question whether the risk will be worth it. Like, will you even be able to make a dent in his votes? This man is evil and totally void of even the slightest remnant of decency. Plus, if he catches you, you'll be toast."

"You're right, and we've discussed that very possibility. We've even been pushing the safety envelope with the virus, which was not a factor when we set this project up. We decided, after a lot of thought, that we have a comparative advantage with technology. We thought that we might be able to reach some potential voters. Only time will tell. You know that your dad and I are very thorough. We weighed all the risks and decided we had to do this. If we were found out, they would be on you in no time. So, we decided to keep you out of range until we were sure you were safe. We couldn't, however, make that decision for you, and that's why we kept you in the dark."

She was quiet for a long moment. "Thank you again for everything, I think. I do wish I'd known how much pressure you were under. I might have been able to help."

"It's been rough," I admitted, "but we were able to execute our plan. All we can do now is let everything play out. I'll go into hiding and maybe do some writing and keep adding content. That and some quiet downtime are looking exceptionally good to me right now. I'm so happy that you and your dad will be together again. I'm sure that Ari has a safe place set up for all of you. Now I'd better get out of here. Trust me when I say that deceiving our president has been a whole lot easier on me than having to deceive you. That has without doubt been about the most difficult part of this entire affair. I know that your father shares that sentiment." I decided not to let her know that I was with her dad a few weeks ago. Insult to injury is not our style. "Oh, and thanks so much for setting up that meeting with your friends. I enjoyed them so much. It's been a long time since I've felt so energized and optimistic. You guys are really going to make a difference and what your dad and I are doing is paving the way for all of you. I think I'm going to ask NYU if I can teach that course. I will donate the money to the student union or something. I miss being around smart young people who are eager to clean up the world that my generation screwed up. I hope those Feds do not bother them."

"Believe me, they can handle it and would actually be proud of what you have done if they ever knew. Maybe I'll write a book on this someday," she said.

"Please don't. We would all have to join your father in some obscure place to hide out for the rest of our lives."

"Benson, you be safe, and I'll make sure that Dad knows that I did not throw you out a window or anything," Anna said, giving my arm a punch.

"He will be most grateful; I did think that doing so was a viable option on your part. But seriously, I could not love you more. This has been so hard for me."

We hugged. I picked up my bags and said goodbye to everyone. I side-hugged Susan, too. "Thanks so much for staying with Anna," I told her.

"I'm glad to have been of help. You guys are doing something really special, and I am proud to be a part of it."

"Thank you, Susan, you are a dear, and I am glad to have met you."

Ari walked me to the car. "Anna and the team will be safe," he assured me. "I'm so sorry not to be able to take you with me, but it's best you stay apart for a while. Work on the new content and send it over on the first burner I gave you. Do not use the AO burner for anything outgoing. Forward anything he sends you, and I will hand it off to the team to publish as they see fit."

Ari is all business. It is a rare moment when his hard edge is challenged. This was one such moment. I felt his relief that we will all be dispersed safely, and that Anna is now informed and on her way to reconnect with her dad. Ari leaned in and opened the car door for me, and placed both of his hand on my shoulders, for the first time in all the years we have worked together. He was having an intense internal moment with himself, and I felt every pore of his body's reaction to the moment.

"Benson, I need to tell you that working with you these past months have been just about the most gratifying experience of my life. What you in particular, and the team have done here is nothing short of amazing. I could not be prouder, and I'm honored to have been a part of it."

"Thank you, Ari, that is a lot to say given your career and the many missions I can guess that you have worked on. None of what we have done would have happened without you. I sincerely hope that all this works out so that one day we can all sit in a café somewhere, maybe Paris, and reminisce. To say thank you, fails to recognize how important you are to me in so many ways."

"Our bond is complete and permanent. You stay safe and I will keep you as informed as I can. We will surely not meet again until well after the election. We have to be careful. We don't want AO compromised. He's been incredibly helpful. I cannot imagine how hard it is for these guys to have to be around that man every day, picking up after him, and keeping his tiny fingers off that red button. Take this phone to make any domestic calls—it's clean. I gave you a new number. It's not linked to your old phone. I need to take that one from you. I'll drop it off in Europe someplace that will be in motion. That should keep them busy for a while. I saved all your contact and data on this flash drive. I can give that to you now. Store it away with the burners and do not call anyone unless they or you are bleeding. I will get back to you as soon as I can. I also want to give you this package of COVID masks, they 're the best on the market. Take care, Benson."

"Thanks again, stay safe yourself. Is Mr. Bonaparte safe?"

"Absolutely, he knows what he's doing."

I got into the car. Ari's driver sped off toward Newark and my train. I was confident that Ari had everything under control.

★★★

CHAPTER 19

OCTOBER 2020

EVERYTHING HAPPENED TOO FAST. Our fairly tight team had been on a well-defined mission. Now we were scattered to the winds. Ari had done what was necessary to save the project and us. On my way to DC, I tried to process it all. Maybe someday I'd understand why everything happened this way. At least the pleasure of the train ride helped soothe my raw nerves.

My driver was waiting at the main entrance near Union Station as expected. We headed toward Virginia on I-395. As we drove away from the station, I looked out on the lighted monuments and the Capitol building. I reflected on our nation's glorious and sordid history. And here I was, being hustled off in the dead of night to a safe house, with government higher-ups out to get me.

For the first time in months, I felt the dark energy that had taken over my whole being gradually float out the window, disappearing into the cool night air. I had to assume that the team got picked up and was on their way to locations in the world that Ari deemed safe. Any concerns for their safety would have to be stored in an inactive file until Ari next contacted me—I hoped soon.

I had my notes and an external drive with all the data Andrew, and I had compiled. I could work offline for the voter posts and the bulk of the election-related posts. And send everything via text on the burner Ari programmed for me for that purpose. Nevertheless, I was hoping that in Springfield I'd have access to a library, hopefully with Wi-Fi. I had yet to memorize my new identity. That was a task for the morning.

Feeling the car backing up woke me from a deep sleep. My driver told me to wait a bit until he checked the place out. I knew he was going to scan inside and out to make sure that the safe house was secure. While waiting, I noticed that this dead-end street had about five other similar cottages along each side. In less than ten minutes, we were inside. The lights had been turned on. I was shown where everything was, including hiding places that had been built for small devices. I was shown where the security device was installed to let me know if the space had been violated. It was the same one Ari had put in the Thirteenth Street apartment. I suddenly remembered to tell Mr. Bonaparte that I had removed that unit. I thanked my driver, knowing that it was not my place to tip him. He handed me another burner, a 24/7 direct line to him. "My partner and I are never more than an hour away," he told me. He wrote down a place where I was to meet him if I had to abandon this site. I agreed to check in with him daily on this unit as instructed by Ari. Like Ari, he was gone before I knew it, and I was alone.

In less than a minute, I heard a knock on the door. I looked out through the curtain and saw my driver at the door and the car still in front. I double-checked to be sure no one else was lurking. I really hated this part of what we were doing. I'm not good at it and knew how dangerous it would be to screw up.

I opened the door slowly. The driver was standing back from the door with his phone in his hand. "I just got a text from Ari. They've taken off and are on their way to their first destination. Everything's going smoothly." I thanked him as he turned to leave. I felt a great sense of relief as I watched him drive off. Finally, I sensed that we were all safe.

The clean, well-appointed two-bedroom cottage was appropriately discreet. I knew I'd be comfortable there and selfishly looked forward to leaving the theater of the absurd behind me for a while. I now had three burner phones, each with its purpose. I decided that I'd better label them so I wouldn't make a mistake. I found some stickers in a drawer and stuck a different colored dot on each device and made coded marks of the same color on the reproductions on the wall to remind me which was which. I put the devices, my original identity wallet, and the flash drives in the clever hiding place. There was even a remote *destruct* button I could carry with me that would obliterate everything within five feet of the hiding place, but I had to be within thirty feet to set it off. I temporarily put the external drive in the same box. I would need that almost every day, so I knew that I had to find a more convenient hiding place for it.

I put my clothes in the bedroom closet. I took a shower, made some coffee, and went on the back deck to think. There was a dense forest thirty feet away. My cottage was the last one on a block of identical structures. The sun was starting to peek out from behind the trees when I decided to take a walk around my new neighborhood and get an idea of where everything was. I checked out my new identity. I was Brian Prensky, from Berkeley, California. According to the note attached, I was a retired researcher working on a book on Abraham Lincoln, and I would be in town to take advantage of the Lincoln collection at the Library of Congress. I also planned to spend time at the Memorial and take advantage of other academic resources available in and around DC. That is, assuming they weren't closed due to the virus.

Springfield, Virginia, is a small town. I could walk almost anywhere or catch a bus if necessary. There were lots of parks and two well-stocked libraries, each with Wi-Fi. I discovered that the Springfield Hilton had a pool and a gym that I could use for a fee. Lots of small restaurants and a supermarket were within walking distance. Andrew and I had chosen well, and Ari was wise to pay off the mortgage and put the tax bills and other expenses on automatic payments from our Swiss bankers' offices. I knew that as long as I kept to myself, I'd be able to ride it out for as long as necessary.

THE NEXT SEVERAL WEEKS FLEW BY, and the election was just around the corner. I managed to send a lot of content for the voter awareness posts, and we were building a solid inventory of relevant posts that were being read, liked, and shared. For obvious reasons, I wasn't receiving any data on how popular our sites were. We'd decided to keep all communications as short and infrequent as possible. We were blasting out proof of how much the quality of our readers' lives was being manipulated by those at the top of the economic food chain. This was even more apparent in the economic recession caused by the virus. I continued to use only data that could be easily understood and discussed: wealth, income, housing costs, healthcare costs, education costs, and the comparative prices for day-to-day items. Everything was fully documented and verified to the reader, an important step for credibility. I did notice that the popular press and some cable TV stations were picking up our posts and covering them. This was great news and exactly what we'd hoped would happen.

I found several ways to show how far we were from being a heavily taxed nation. How much we pay is not nearly as important as how our tax dollars are used—that part of the equation is rarely mentioned. The money we spend on defense, government pensions, health benefits, and the lifelong perks our elected officials enjoy, are not generally known to most constituents. We employed creative and illustrative ways to present them for impact. Most Americans have no idea how rich elected officials become while in public office. These benefits carry forward when they leave, and I made that point in every post we sent out.

We collected information on insider trading and how congressional committee members take advantage of stock purchases linked to legislation they or supporting lobbyists write and pass. This has been going on for decades and is blatantly illegal. Several members of Congress were recently caught red-handed and had to resign their committee memberships. Rarely do they actually resign their offices, even though their legislative power has been compromised. Two Republican senators from Georgia who had recently been exposed for profiting on closed-door committee meetings they held on specific COVID-related PPE equipment were up for reelection. The companies were given major government contracts to step up production. Everyone in the room knew that their stock would make a big jump as soon as that went public. Both of those senators, who were already massively rich, took advantage of insider knowledge from similar committees they sat on to capitalize on the companies' stocks.

Several of our posts focused on the inadequate infrastructure expenditures over the past five administrations. This deficiency has put our roads, highways, bridges, airports, water, and energy distribution systems into great peril. These projects could be major employment opportunities, which heightens the ignorance of not updating infrastructure. This neglect was made even more absurd when considering the extremely low interest rates, making the financial issues of these decisions irrelevant.

"We, the people" has become a slogan of the past with little relevance in the current lives of most Americans. We were gaining traction and people were talking about our messages, which deliberately lacked vitriol and anger. TV commentators particularly liked our sense of humor and carried it forward in their reports. The seriousness of what we were doing did not seem to be lost on anyone.

Our campaign was doing its part by publishing the truth, backed by data. We'd begun to see that a lot of people across the political spectrum were getting onboard. They were using their considerable influence for good and leaving the past four years on a sidetrack to rust and decay itself into oblivion. With no effort on our part, a lot of long-time Republicans had been coming out in support of the Democratic ticket.

WE HAVE TO TAKE RESPONSIBILITY for the fact that we as citizens have not fulfilled our obligation. There's no excuse for any of us not to vote. Many nations fine their citizens if they do not vote. We make it easier for those who want to take away our right to vote if we do not vote. We published several posts on the topic of voting rights and obligations. Our posts have shown the seriousness of having so many of us restricted from voting. The extent of voter suppression in 2020 is only now coming to the fore. The threats to our voting rights and the subversive activities of selected initiatives are finally on the front pages of local newspapers. Only the Republicans fight to keep as many people from voting as they and their creative thinking can keep from the polls. Democrats, on the other hand, fight even harder to get as many people to register and vote as they can. Neither party is doing enough to educate voters so that they can vote intelligently.

The libraries are open on a restricted use basis. Several times a week, I went to the local library or a local café to check us out on social media. I opened an account under my new identity, and I searched through all the basic social media to find our posts. I was delighted to see that we were everywhere. I was silently gleeful every time I saw a post, even more so when I saw all the likes, knowing that this was how the message would spread. The press continued to pick up on the traffic we are creating. I even found a few articles that reproduced Professor Mike and our cartoons of the president as part of their articles on the impact we are having. This was all we hoped for. My only concern was not knowing if we had penetrated all of those fringe and Rust Belt citizens on our list. We knew that it would be a hard statistic to measure and only time would tell.

The Feds now knew that Andrew was alive. I only hoped that they didn't know where he was. In fact, even I didn't know where he was, which made me wonder if separating us was Ari's strategy for keeping me safe. I wouldn't put this past him. It's how Ari thinks every day; the details never get by him.

I'd been receiving texts from Agent Orange and forwarding them to Ari. It had become obvious, as we moved closer to the election, that Trump was losing it. He was totally unhinged due to his ratings in the polls. The pandemic was not going away, even though he pretended it was. The economy was recovering a bit, but not even close to what it had been before the pandemic. We had yet to return to pre-pandemic levels. The president only reported growth and not the fact that we were considerably below where we had been in February. Fortunately, it took only one very simple chart to defuse that lie. He also liked to take full credit for the "best economy ever," ignoring the fact that the path from the Obama years was largely unchanged right up to February 2020. There was no Trump bump. The 2016–20 economy was inherited. We published a chart showing the economy from 2010 through 2019 with the Obama trend and without. There was no difference, proving that Trump was merely riding Obama's economic coat tails. We published another that showed the pandemic economic decline, which Trump did own. We labeled it as such.

Watching his rallies, I was captivated by how he was able to look right into a camera and at his supporters and lie. Not little lies, big ones: the pandemic was disappearing, the economy was back, and he was killing the Democrats in the polls. All facts to the contrary somehow managed to completely escape him and his loyal followers. Talk about living in a cave!

Agent Orange mentioned that those around the President were assuring him that the polls meant nothing. They cited his own polls in 2016 as proof. Trump couldn't control his attachment to Twitter, and he put out Tweets that compromised both himself and his party. He seemed to have lost touch with reality—there was a rising level of concern among some members of his party, but the fear of crossing him kept them quiet. One of Agent Orange's messages revealed how staff members hid certain memos from the president because they knew that if he saw them, he would become angry and send out Tweets. Some Republicans, who were up for re-election, found ways to distance themselves from him. There was a growing acceptance that the Senate might actually be in play. But the pundits were still not putting down hard money, given what happened in 2016.

All of a sudden, a rash of tapes were released, not necessarily by us, that showed in Trump's own voice just how little he cared about his base when off camera. Trump's sister is recorded stating that her brother has no principles, and he is not to be trusted by anyone. Apparently, what he says in private is vastly different than what he says in public and at his rallies. Another set of tapes from interviews with Melania disparaged Trump and Ivanka—most embarrassing. Shock Jock tapes of his bragging about getting draft deferments based on false medical statements were particularly hurtful to his base, even though the Access Hollywood tapes were not. His "suckers and losers" comments on fallen soldiers would ride the two-week news cycle, so we found ways to give them recurring life throughout the American hinterland. We did the same for his uncalled for and hurtful comments about Senator McCain, a universally respected hero. Again, we could not measure the impact, but we knew it was out there on a repeat basis to an audience not sympathetic to such statements, especially when made by our president. Agent Orange sent us a tape of Trump's rantings in the White House. We do not know who produced it, but it was his voice, and we got it out there along with others who got a hold of it. The major point was that Trump's duplicity was becoming known to his base, and we could only hope that it would matter to them in November. We had to be careful not to expose Agent Orange, and I could tell that we were on top of that by having others release information we were given, thereby deflecting from our source.

The press played all this up, but most didn't believe for a minute that Trump should be counted out. Trump made it abundantly clear that he was going to win. If he lost, it would be, he said, because the election was rigged against him. Once again, he was claiming that his rivals would do the same thing to him as he was doing, putting out fake news, stealing votes, almost driving the Post Office out of business, encouraging other candidates to run and take away votes from Biden. Trump filed numerous lawsuits to deny ballots to steal the election, something he all but admitted he was willing to do. Antifa, which did not exist as a real organization, the radical left fascists, an oxymoron of moronic proportions, and of course the liberal press, all of whom hated him, were targets for his complaints. The laments that he was never treated fairly were part of his daily chants of victimhood. Trump, the draft dodger-in-chief, was Swift-Boating the electorate. He denigrated the military and our generals and enlisted soldiers alike. I ask myself how he and the Republicans were able to convince a significant proportion of Americans that he *was* the party and the candidate of the people? They managed to bring whole blocks of blue-collar workers into their fold yet did nothing to make their lives better. When the extreme right wing of the Republican Party saw a way back on top in the mid-60s, they determined that they could, if they worked smart, take away the New Deal gains, and bring small government under their tent. They did just that. We've allowed a wall to be built between the two parties, and it has become impossible to rationally debate our nation's needs. Divide and conquer has ruled public discourse in America for decades. A wedge has been driven between the two parties and competing ideas, the result of which has destroyed dialogue and negotiation. Those seeking absolute power have used Citizens United money to make it impossible to pass meaningful legislation. I often wonder what the Eisenhower-era Republicans would think if they could see their party in 2020. I think they would find it difficult to recognize. Who would have thought that blue-collar workers, stalwarts of the Democratic Party, would find a home with today's Republicans? It happened because Democrats were also deflected away from their base, many of whom gradually realized that no one was listening to them.

We do not see just how far we have moved from our once prosperous baseline. All the checks and balances, law and order, democratic rights, and our trusted means of oversight have failed the American citizenry. This was why our team and many others decided that the American citizen/voter holds the most powerful weapon to turn this around. The overriding sadness in all this is that it would be almost costless in the long run to move America to a far more equitable economy where all classes shared fairly. We lack only the will to act.

⋏ ⋏ ⋏

HAVING WRITTEN AND SENT OFF ENOUGH POSTS for our voter awareness and reelection campaigns to cover us for the ensuing weeks, I decided to take advantage of some much-needed downtime. I had been looking forward to reading and exercising. I needed to set up a routine to get myself back in shape, both mentally and physically. The last several months had been so intense that I neglected good eating habits and exercise.

I started taking daily walks before breakfast. I enjoyed going into different sections of this quaint suburban town and watching people go about their day. Memories of when I stayed here more than forty years earlier began to come back to me. That company was a fun project. A few colleagues and I started an economic consulting company in the early '80s that helped states plan for what they could expect to receive from the federal government. State governments had no way of knowing the federal receipts under then President Reagan's budgeting system, Fiscal Federalism. I enjoyed the work until I eventually sold my shares to my partners and moved on to new things.

I balanced my walks with swimming and weight training at the hotel gym. It really did not take long for me to begin to feel the benefits of moving my body again. I also enjoyed just walking into town, having a cup of coffee, and going to the supermarket for food and supplies. I stopped at a bookstore or shopped for new sneakers, T-shirts, or underwear. For the first time in what seemed like a lifetime, I felt like a standard-issue American citizen, just living his life, unencumbered by all that had been absorbing me for years.

As I became more comfortable in my new life, I decided it was time to dive into the many books I had brought with me. Getting to know my surroundings and building up an exercise routine had been just what I needed to erase the tension of the last several months. Now I could turn to the pleasure of reading. As the weather cooled, my back deck became less inviting. The upside was that I had to find comfortable places to go when I wanted to read. It was really becoming a drag to deal with this damned virus. We can blame our president for making it particularly hard for Americans, especially when compared to many other nations whose leadership had been far better prepared. I returned to the libraries whenever I could and luxuriated in the comfort of reading rooms. I brought my earphones with me. When I felt like it, I could walk to the computer center, search for anything I might want to download, and check on our posts to see if we were still out there. We were becoming more visible as were a whole lot of other efforts like ours. We were all using available social media platforms to express our opinions and commentary. I was pleased that we were not the only game in town. There is safety in numbers.

It really is difficult for the average, hardworking, time-starved citizen to know how to differentiate fact from the multitude of "alternative facts" out there. A democracy, especially ours, protects free speech. It also protects its citizens from distorted commentary that, if believed, can distort the course of events. Evidence abounds attesting to the fact that significant segments of our population believed the president who, even after being diagnosed and hospitalized, still hinted that the virus was not a threat. Despite the tens of thousands of deaths and millions of cases, far too many people continued to believe that the virus was no more than a flu.

Trump no longer called it a hoax or Democratic plot to deny him re-election. It was now something that would just go away. He held many super-spreader events himself often inside with hundreds of people, as more among his staff and acquaintances became infected. His refusal to wear a mask and social distance his guests has made many of his loyal followers sick. The master of branding managed to use his own case as one that proves that this virus was nothing to worry about, he felt stronger than ever after absorbing a huge amount of our resources receiving medical attention unavailable to others. He really was able to make everything about him.

Our factual messages sailed to viewers on the power of Google, Facebook, Twitter, and others. These companies value revenue over truth. The degree of invasion into our privacy and their ability to manipulate millions of data points to increase their bottom line had become unconscionable. They represent an ever-present threat to our democracy. At some point, a regulatory effort will have to protect the public from the lies they publish. One must wonder if those at Google remember their own motto, Do no harm?

We cannot, at least at this point, rely on social media to separate fact from fiction. For the moment, we must rely on common sense. I took comfort knowing that most of us could do that objectively. Our mission was to help those who, for a host of valid reasons, cannot.

My days began and ended with a walk. The days here in Virginia were still warm and inviting. The mornings had that cool, clear feeling of fall gradually arriving. I've always taken great pleasure in seasonal changes. My walk took me back among the rustling dried leaves underfoot, a fresh pizza tucked under my arm. I felt invigorated; nature has always been my dearest companion.

These feelings may have been stimulated by my choice of reading for the day, Henry Thoreau's *Walden*. Several years ago, I randomly picked up that book and found peace within its pages. I had taken a few days off back then and driven up to Walden Pond to try to duplicate the paths Thoreau had taken while he sequestered himself in his tiny cabin. It was in the fall, so all the tourists were gone, and I was able to share the smells, sights, and sounds as he described them. This was why I had chosen to read this timeless work once more. Certain books and movies never seem to go out of style. As I walked toward my cottage retreat a thousand miles from Walden pond, I could hear his words describing the distant wail of a train and the wind drifting through the pine needles creating soft music in the form of nature's poetry.

My pizza was still hot as I entered my cottage. I took a beer from the fridge and found Vivaldi's *Four Seasons* on my iPod. My relaxation was interrupted by a knock on my back door. I had to think for a moment since this was the first time anyone had invaded my solitude. I quietly worked my way to a window that would let me peek out to see who was at my door. Why the back door? To my relief, I saw that it was Moshe and that he was alone. I opened the door and we greeted each other warmly. It was good to see him, despite the fact that my weeks-long reverie ended. Moshe's presence brought back the tensions I had allowed to slip away. Nevertheless, I was pleased to see him, and I invited him in and offered to share my pizza and beer. I could tell that he was jittery, which was unlike him. That only made me nervous.

"Moshe, what brings you here? I hope it's good news, but the look on your face tells me otherwise."

"You're right. I just got word from Ari that we're in trouble. Agent Orange has told us that the White House has learned that you are in the States, and there is an all-out search to find you."

"What the hell for? Are they that upset with our posts? At this point in the election cycle, it would seem to me that they would have a million other things on their plate."

"It's weird, but it's also happening. Ari wanted me to get this information to you."

"I'm glad that Ari's talking to you. I haven't heard a word from him or anyone else. Are they safe? Where is everyone? Where is Anna? I can tell that the posts are coming out regularly and that we are getting a lot of likes and shares."

"Ari did tell me to let you know that everything on their end is going smoothly. Everyone's safe, but I honestly don't know where they are. Ari did say that Andrew and Anna are together, but they do not stay in one place more than two or three days. I don't even know where they, Ari, or the team are."

"Well, we know how cautious he is, and I'm sure that he's doing the right thing. I've been following our progress and pleased that we are most definitely making a difference. I do, however, feel somewhat abandoned. My only defense has been to drop out of the whole project and live my life. I've sent enough information for posts right through the election. I have shut down my computer to be on the safe side, and I only sign onto the internet from the library and then only using my new ID. I have actually begun to enjoy the peace and quiet of suburban life."

"I'm afraid your dream world is about to crash. Ari thinks it's only a matter of time before they find you. He did not say why they might be looking for you, but facts are facts, and we need to figure out how to handle it. AO's message was marked urgent. There are less than three weeks till the election, and we all want to stay underground."

"What is Ari's new plan?"

"He's afraid to contact you because he feels that his locations have been compromised, although he has no idea how. Ari knew that I would be the only one who could safely deliver a message that you would believe. Basically, he wants you to go back to being Benson and make your way to DC and allow yourself to get caught. He wants to protect the existence of the safe house, and he does not think you are in physical danger. The Feds just want information, and they want to know who we are and where our team is."

"I can think of dozens of other sites and efforts out there that are much more proficient than we are. I still can't imagine why they're after us. And that unknown is what scares me the most. It just does not make sense."

"That is the one thing we all agree on, which is why Ari thinks that we can find out if we let them catch you. Only then can we get to the root of this. We have somehow gotten under the skin of POTUS, but that's not hard to do, there are dozens of others who want him to lose the election. Why us? Is he going after others as well? I honestly do not know, and neither does Ari," shrugged Moshe.

"Maybe AO has been targeted?"

"No, he's still in the clear and actually feeding a lot of intel. You're probably not seeing all of them. We are hacking deep into some sites that you would not normally see. AO stopped texting you because he saw this threat coming. Keep the burner Ari gave you to contact AO but shut it down completely when you aren't using it. AO is the one who told us that you are on their list, and it was agreed by everyone not to compromise you any further."

"Okay, I get brought somewhere to be interrogated. What do I tell them, and what do I not tell them?"

"Ari's leaving that up to you. He did suggest that you admit to pulling the data together as requested by some fictitious person. You do not have to admit culpability beyond that, which is true, for the most part, at this point."

"What if they get aggressive with me and things get messy with truth serums or a reenactment of Dustin Hoffman in *Marathon Man*. I do not do well with torture."

"Ari does not think that's what we are dealing with, but you will not be alone. Besides, you are far from an unknown person. You have a professional reputation and are visible in circles where these guys would not want to be talked about. They're not going to hurt you."

"I see it differently. If what you say is true, these goons will make sure I jump off a bridge somewhere and then find a note I ostensibly left someplace that I could not take it anymore."

"You need to do only one thing to protect yourself. Make sure that you're not hidden in some lead-lined room that shuts out any signals."

"What good will that do? I will certainly be scanned for devices. I wouldn't want to wear one because, once found, they might be able to trace it back to Ari. None of us wants that to happen."

"We'll be able to listen to every word within twenty feet of you, and they won't find any devices on you."

"How? We both know that's impossible. Ari once said that these guys are as smart as he is, and we always have to be conscious of that one fact."

"And he's right. All you have to do when you are being interrogated is wear your glasses. It does not matter if you have your reading or distance glasses on, both are operative. If they are on your nose, we are listening to you. There is no way anyone can find anything in the way of a chip or device if you have them off."

"What if they take my glasses off?"

"We have a contingency that will go into effect within five minutes of a negative signal."

"Why do the glasses have to be on me?"

"Because the device has to be connected. If that connection is broken, both devices are completely ineffective."

"That means that I have a device planted somewhere in my head?"

"Actually, you do. Remember last spring, I think it was in May, you decided to have cataract surgery because you failed the visual portion of your driver's test?"

"Yes, but how did you know that?"

"I didn't, but you did tell Ari, and if you recall, he recommended a doctor to you for the surgery."

379

"He did, and she was terrific, I hate anyone near my eyes and the entire procedure was totally painless."

"You also had a chip installed that kicks in only when your glasses are on you. Otherwise, it is totally passive and undetectable."

"Ari did that to me? How is that even possible?"

"You know Ari by now, anything is possible, in any case your head and your glasses are connected so just keep them on when you are with anyone who might pick you up. Just know that should you be threatened, a threat of any kind, the place, wherever you are, will be compromised, and you will be rescued."

"Sometimes that man really scares me. I don't understand how this will work. What a frightening world we live in!"

"You know that Ari will never do anything to hurt you. He was just planning ahead, once he understood what you were doing. He had that implant done to protect you, and now you can see why.'"

"I do trust Ari, but this is rapidly becoming something much more than any one person can manage."

"You're right. I want to tell you something about Ari that I suspect you don't know."

"The one thing about Ari that I do know is that there is a lot about him that I don't know. For example, I only just found out two weeks ago that you're his brother."

"Right. I was surprised when he told me that he had let you know that. Ari plays it as close to the vest as anyone I know. Look, one thing we want you to know is that we're on top of all this and what we need to do is distract these goons until the election. After that, we might decide to go public or just close everything down and move on.

"About my brother, you know about his training in Israel and his connections in the States. You know his ability to get the most amazing things done. What you don't know is that Ari's part of a well-funded, worldwide cadre of highly trained good guys who consider themselves the anti-intel's. This group is comprised of thousands of people all over the world who know what they're doing. They are in constant contact with each other and only each other. I personally think that Snowden is a member. Many of them worked for intelligence agencies for years and realized that things were getting too invasive and out of control. They like to think that they went from the dark to the light side and are far more comfortable having done so. Ari was recruited by them during the Reagan administration and has been heavily involved with them since. He retired from all regular agencies that used him for years and gradually removed himself from the grid so that he has a lot more mobility than most of the group. He is considered a high-value asset."

"What's the name of this group? Does anyone on the outside even know that it exists?"

"No name, and no one outside has ever heard of them."

"Then why are you telling me all this? They have no name. That is the height of secrecy and maybe even paranoia. How do they recruit? Get their money? Stay invisible?"

"They just do and have, almost since the end of WWII. They recruit by observing potential candidates and test them for years, gradually letting them into the fold. They don't need nor want a name, a logo, or visibility. You might be interested to know that both you and Andrew were on the recruitment list. You've been observed for years."

"Get out! I would be the worst person to take on that responsibility. Andrew, too. How did they even find us?"

"Through two operatives in your building on Thirteenth Street, and through Mr. Bonaparte."

"You have to be kidding. I think I know who the two operatives were. Ari mentioned them to me. I served on the board of the condo with Mike. Is that how this no-named group found Andrew and me?"

"Yes, and don't forget that you and Ari met in the '60s during the Vietnam protests. He got to know you pretty well then. He met Andrew much later."

"I guess we didn't make the grade."

"Actually, you both did, but you were considered a bit too idealistic to become a full-blown operative. You were used for some important intel gathering, but you were unaware of it."

"How did that happen? I certainly would have known about it."

"Don't underestimate us. We knew your activities, public service appointments, conferences, consulting, and other professional interests. You were trusted but considered more valuable on the outside than as an operative."

"Then how did you get whatever I was collecting without my knowing about it?"

"Through Andrew. You were valued, but on the fringe. Andrew was recruited and has been on the inside for years."

"And he never told me? I thought he was my friend. We tell each other everything."

"He is your friend and that's exactly why he did not tell you. He'd do anything to keep you safe. Besides, by not knowing how you were actually helping, you were able to function without hesitation. You only had to be yourself, and that was what made you as valuable as you were, and still are. Ari has mentioned several times that, given what you two have been through the last several months, he thinks he underestimated you. You're a lot more capable than he thought. He admires you. And that's why he's asking you to take on this challenge. We're going to get to the bottom of something important, and you will be taking the lead. The one thing we're learning from Agent Orange and Ari's DC contacts is that our official intel agents are splitting themselves up all over the place. No one trusts anyone, and that's creating a huge hole in our government that our foreign adversaries are beginning to take advantage of. Trump is at the head of that list, and we do not even know if he knows about it."

I needed a minute to process all this. Andrew has been a spy for some dark or light underground group for years? More astonishingly, I have been a spy for the same amount of time, and I did not know it? Was this even possible? Did I even have a choice? Too many people close to me were even closer to this effort than I could have imagined. Also, the very reason I got myself involved was because I shared the objectives of this no-name group. And they knew that to be true. Moshe then said something to me that I could not have expected. "Dr. Pryce, Ari told me to tell you that he and Andrew are training Anna to join the worldwide team. The decision was made that they had to begin reaching out to younger people who fit the profile to carry on what has been developed."

"Anna, a spy? Why would they even think of that after what we have just put her through?"

"That's exactly why they are. They concluded that she would bring a special skill to the effort and she has agreed to be trained."

"Wow, that's a bolt out of the sky."

"Dr. Pryce, we need to get back to the issue at hand. Time is short."

Clearly, I had no choice. I needed to see this through. My only reservation was that I was not sure that I had the skills to pull off being captured and interrogated without compromising myself, my team, and my friends. We finished the pizza, opened two more beers, and drank them in silence. Moshe knew exactly what was going on in my head. Unlike me, he was trained, and like his brother Ari, he was trained by the best. These two brothers have a connection few people ever achieve. It goes beyond respect and knowing that they have each other's backs. There's a mutual admiration that flows between them in both directions, born of family, purpose, core values, and an unqualified love for each other that, like an onion, adds new layers each day. I looked at Moshe and said to myself, *I wish I had a brother, or even a son, like him in my life. Ari is a lucky man.* "Okay, what's the plan?" I asked finally.

"You are to assume your Benson ID. On Monday morning, you check into the Dupont Circle hotel but go first to the Lincoln Memorial. You'll be pretending to do research on Lincoln taking some notes. That afternoon you will go to the Library of Congress and take some books on Lincoln to the reading patio and relax. On the way out of the library, you will be picked up in a black limo. We do not know where you will be taken, but as long as you have your glasses on, we'll be able to track you. If it looks like they're going to scan you, just take off your glasses and you'll be safe. As I have already said, you can use either you're reading or long-distance glasses, they are both fitted with the tracking unit. Ari did tell me that they won't be able to hear you if the glasses are in your pocket or around your neck, but they will be able to tell where you are. He wanted me to let you know that he will extract you if things go south."

I had no idea how Ari could pull that off, but I did know that if he said he could do it, he could.

"Will someone be with me while I'm in DC?"

"Yes, someone will be close at all times. Change identities before you leave here. Leave all things identified with Brian with me, along with all burner phones. Take only your normal phone and Benson's wallet. I'll take your computer and the external drive and devices with me now. A car will pick you up around 9:00 a.m. No need to protect your personal phone, that car is secure. Give back the phone the driver gave to you. You will be dropped off near Union Station, so they will think you just came into town. You need to remain calm. Don't even try to fool them. They are pros and will be able to tell if you are lying. Best to deny or just say you do not know whatever they are asking if you think it may be compromising. Remember they know your history; they are not going to expose themselves to something they cannot cover. We wish we could say more, but that is the best we can do for now. Ari did mention how well you handled the Feds who came to you in New York. Stay ahead of them, and we think it will go well. The main thing is to keep them off our backs until the election. We can all decide what to do once this mess is over."

Moshe and I sat outside on the deck for a while, filling the air with small talk. I knew he was trying to calm me down and make me feel secure. I also just learned how closely he had been watching out for me. Like his brother, he is a most competent and comforting person. I gave Moshe the devices and drives he asked for. He finished his beer, handed me the bottle, and walked back toward the woods carrying almost every means of communications I had. I watched him for as long as he was in sight. I sat on the deck and tried to go over everything I'd just learned. It was a lot to process. I only hoped that I was up for this challenge.

The best thing to do in such circumstances is to open a pint of Cherry Garcia and pig out, which is exactly what I did. I turned on the news and ate away, devouring the entire pint. Decadence personified. I had two days to get myself on an even keel and become as strong as possible to face my intentional capture. These guys tend to be focused, informed, and brutal when necessary. That did not give me any comfort.

CHAPTER 20

OCTOBER 2020

MONDAY MORNING CAME, and as promised, my car was at the curb at 8:45. I was ready to go. I had my original ID, my fully charged phone, my trusty leather bag, and, of course, my glasses, which had taken on a whole new level of importance. I put a phone charger, some research notes, and a writing pad in my bag. I had my credit cards and plenty of cash. I was sure to secure the alarm for the cottage before leaving. I thought of taking my iPad but couldn't remember what was on it that might be incriminating, so I decided to leave it with the driver.

We arrived at Union Station at 10:10. I walked through the main room and out another exit to hail a cab to the Lincoln Memorial. I knew I needed to spend some time there to keep the guys who were going to pick me up from being suspicious. Since I'd never really studied it closely, I began to walk around the outside first. The proposal to build this monument and the statue of Lincoln inside was approved by Congress in 1913. The thirty-six columns of the structure represented the number of states in the Union at the time of Lincoln's death.

The interior of the Memorial contains the sixty-foot statue of Lincoln cut from white Georgia marble. There are also inscriptions of the Gettysburg Address and Lincoln's second inaugural address. It is a fitting memorial for our sixteenth president whose accomplishments belied his humble nature. I wandered around inside and out for a little more than an hour, until I figured it was long enough. As I started down the steps, I noticed three seri-

387

ous-looking men in black suits waiting at the bottom of the stairs. I assumed they were waiting for me. I was right.

"Dr. Pryce, would you please come with us?"

"I am sorry, sir, who are you?" I was actually a bit nervous because this was different from what Moshe told me to expect. I removed my glasses and put them safely into my bag. I assumed that Ari had someone stationed nearby, and I was afraid if there was a tussle, my glasses might get knocked off.

"We're with the government, and we have a few questions."

"Well, I'm pretty busy, so please ask, so that I can get on with my day."

I looked around to see if I had any cover. I saw no one I knew and that bothered me. "We need you to come with us."

"Am I under arrest?"

"No, but if you refuse to come peacefully, we will have to place you under arrest."

"Might I ask why?" I was stalling. I hoped Ari's people could see what was happening.

"We'll discuss that in private."

"I would need to see your authorization to arrest me. If you don't have one, I would ask for your cards, so we can set up an appointment. I would be happy to show up with my lawyer. Surely, if you are with the government, you know that we do not snatch people off the streets in America. You realize that we are standing in front of a memorial to President Lincoln who took us to war with ourselves to avoid this kind of behavior toward our citizens."

"Dr. Pryce, we need to leave now."

"Well, then, you'll have to place me under arrest and drag me off in full public view."

I immediately began to shout as loud as I could. I got the result I wanted. It is almost impossible to do anything, especially in DC, without someone taking a video.

The last thing I recall was a mist of some sort engulfing my face. I vaguely felt myself being dragged off with a goon at either side holding me up. I hoped that whoever Ari assigned to me was close enough to witness this and learn where I was about to be taken. My next memory was waking up in a barren and windowless room. I was on a bed, and there was a desk with a plastic glass and pitcher. Rising hesitantly since I was still woozy, I tried both doors in the small room. One led to a bathroom, also windowless. The other door was locked. My bag and its contents had clearly been inspected and were laying on the desk. I immediately put on my locating glasses and checked for my wallet, phone, and other items inside the bag. Everything was intact and undamaged.

I filled the pitcher with some water, drank it, and lay back down. I was still dizzy. My watch said it was 2:30. I realized I must have been out for several hours. I closed my eyes and drifted off again. About an hour later, I heard a knock on the door, and it opened immediately. An orderly walked in with a tray of food. "Where am I?" I asked.

The orderly put down the tray, and without looking at me or answering my question, left the room, locking the door behind him. I could tell I was in some sort of government building. The tray was from a cafeteria, like those offered to civil servants who work long hours in bland, cavernous government buildings. The food looked decent. It was hot, and I was hungry.

I did not have anything to read, and my phone had no service. I only hoped that my personal location unit was working. I was sure that whoever had been watching me earlier followed my abductors to wherever I was. It was deathly quiet. I was tired and again went right to sleep. I awoke around

4:00a.m. I had lights, the bathroom worked, and not a sound could be heard. I lay on my bed trying to go back to sleep. When I couldn't, I did my normal morning exercises. Then, I walked around the room, trying to locate a hidden camera or microphone. None was evident.

At 7:30 in the morning there was another knock on the door and a different orderly walked in with breakfast and a pot of coffee. I did not bother to ask any questions. I ate leisurely since I had no place to go. I did begin to hear sounds from outside the door, but I could not make them out.

An hour later, there was another knock, and the same two men who'd dragged me away entered and stood at the door. I was informed that I would be brought to a conference room at 9:00 for questioning. I was handed an electric razor and a standard government-issued bathroom kit, which I accepted without a word.

9:00. My door was again opened, and I was guided down a long, drab hall to a conference room about a hundred feet away. We walked into an equally nondescript room with no windows, artwork, banners, or plaques. There was a narrow strip of glass at the top of one wall in the room. I could see that it was a bright, sunny day, but nothing else.

"Dr. Pryce, we have a few questions for you. Answer them, and you can go. Where have you been for the last several weeks? We know that you were working with some people in New York who took you someplace. Who were they, and where did they take you?"

I looked around the room, trying to size up my interrogators who now numbered four. One of the new men looked vaguely familiar, but I could not place him with his mask on. I shifted my position to face my inquisitor. "Before I answer any questions, I need to know who you guys are and who you work for. I also need to know where I am, and if I'm still in America."

They glanced around and then back at me. "*We* ask the questions," the lead guy barked. "You are here to answer them."

"Well, then, this will be a short meeting. In fact, it's now over. I have nothing to say to you. Will someone please take me back to my cell, or shall I go by myself?"

"You're not in a cell, and this meeting is over when we say it is. Again, this can all be over right now, or it can go on for a long time."

I said nothing and shifted my position only slightly, more to annoy them than for any other reason. I was kind of digging my heals in and I wanted them to know it. The room was silent. My original inquisitor repeated his questions. I just stared at him, saying nothing. I had my glasses on and assumed that if the windows were real, I was within earshot of Ari's technology.

"Dr. Pryce, we have many ways to make you talk, and they will not be pleasant."

"Are you actually threatening me? Young man, that will not work. I'm too old and tired to care about you or your cronies, who seem ignorant about the law. I have a right to a phone call and a lawyer," I continued. "Until you've answered my questions, I have absolutely no incentive to answer yours. If you represent an authorized government agency or department, you know that I have a right to the information I have demanded, and I have a right to make that call. For all I know, you could be foreign agents who've mistaken me for someone else. If that were so, I could later be charged with treason for cooperating with a foreign government. I will not and cannot do that." I needed to be as defiant as possible if this was going to work. I assumed that these guys were part of the White House intel group and not an authorized part of the FBI or any official government agency. That was most likely why they did not want to show me any identification.

The room was quiet for a long time. Then, they all looked at each other, stood up, and left the room. I used the time to see if there was a mirror, microphone, or camera hidden in the room. I bent down ostensibly to tie my shoe and looked under the table. I did see something that could be a device of some sort. When I sat back up, I noticed a tray with paper and pencils in the middle of the table. That tray conceivably could have a hidden mic in it.

After several minutes, the same men returned, sat down, and the original interrogator spoke up. "We are FBI agents assigned to the White House. You're still in Washington." I did suddenly recognize the familiar face as one of the men sitting at my table at the NYU reunion several months earlier. "Dr. Pryce, we have reason to believe that you are mixed up in a plot against the government. We believe you're working with foreign agents trying to infiltrate our government. We are investigating these activities to determine the extent of your involvement. We have the right, in the name of National Security, to detain you for as long as necessary and will do so until you cooperate and tell us what we need to know."

"If that is so, why did you ask me questions assuming that I was guilty? Is that how professionals conduct an interrogation? National Security is a concept that is bandied about quite freely these days. I still have no proof as to where I am or who you guys are."

"We're only trying to find out what you know and how deeply you are connected to this plot."

"I am not nor have I ever been involved in a plot to take over our government. I am a veteran and a patriot, and I deeply resent you thinking that I would be involved with such a thing. Where is your evidence? Who put you and your goons on me? Do you honestly believe you can drug a citizen and drag him off the street at will? Are you connected with those who have been following me around in New York?"

"Dr. Pryce, we ask the questions, and you answer them."

"I just did. Now, please let me go before people who know me start to wonder what's happened to me. I make no claim to be someone of political importance, but I do have friends capable of making a lot of noise if I am held for much longer."

"Is that a threat, Dr. Pryce?"

"The only threat going on here is the one to my rights as a citizen. I trust that at some point you're prepared to defend your actions against me. I must respectfully ask one more time. *Who* do you represent? I do not think a responsible FBI agent would drag a citizen off the streets. Where am I, exactly? What evidence do you have that supports these charges? I'll answer no questions nor offer any information other than my name and address until you answer me. I would offer my military serial number as required, but I have forgotten it."

With that, the two original men entered the room and escorted me back to my cell. That indicated to me that there was a listening device in the room. On the desk was hot coffee, water, and snacks. My leather bag that had been moved, but not opened, lay on the bed. Not knowing how long I'd be there, I wished I had brought my iPad so I could at least get caught up on my reading. Amazing how you don't miss things until you don't have them.

I wasn't sure how long I could continue to play this game. If subjected to torture, I knew I would cave fast. I could only hope that I'd convinced them that I wouldn't. If they were pros, they wouldn't ask any question that they didn't have the answers for. So far, nothing of any depth had come out, and I began to think that I was going to be there for some time.

About an hour later, I was taken back to the same conference room. A different set of people, older, looking a bit more "establishment," but wearing the same type of suits, was sitting across from me. I sat down and said nothing. They rustled some papers, offering an occasional glance my way. I sat motionless, surprised that I was actually comfortable.

"Professor Benson, where have you been for the last two weeks? We've been concerned about you."

I said nothing and let myself visibly drift into my own mind by looking past everyone in front of me. Did they really not know where I had been, or was this a part of the game? The question was repeated. Why "Professor Benson"? Did they not know my last name, or was this a ploy of some sort?

"Listen, I made my conditions clear to your previous squad. Without proof about who you are or where I am, I feel no obligation to answer your questions. I can play this game as long as you can. In fact, I'm raising the ante. I want a stenographer in here, and I'd like these sessions recorded. Also, I respectfully request some reading material in my cell. *The Washington Post* and *Times* would suffice. Do you guys have names? I need some paper and a pen to keep a log of what's happening to me so I can be prepared when we meet in a legitimate court."

"You're not in a cell, and you won't be getting any newspapers, nor will we be supplying a paper or pen," growled the older man.

That indicated to me, by assumption, that my sudden and public abduction had made the press, and they did not want me to know that.

I responded, "Such definitions can and do vary. I call it a cell, and since I'm the one who's being unlawfully detained, I'll call it what it is to me." I heard the door open as I stood up and began to walk toward it. As expected, the goons, who I had not seen until then, appeared and blocked my way. We just stood there looking past each other. "Are you going to drug me again, or do you only do that in public?"

"Sit down!" I was told.

I didn't move.

"Professor Pryce, we know that you've been handing off information to some subversive groups. We know it's from you, and we want to know precisely what you are involved with."

I noticed they now used my correct last name. Was this designed to confuse, or were these guys amateurs? I retained my position in the face of the goons and said nothing. They were both slightly taller than me, which gave them an advantage on this stare down. I didn't let that impact me. Minutes passed without anyone moving, and nothing further was said.

I was soon taken back to my cell. This time, nothing had been moved. I took off my shoes and shirt and lay down on the bed.

In less than ten minutes, I heard a knock on the door. I waited. Another knock. I got up and opened the unlocked door. A new person, a woman, was in front of me and asked if she could come in.

"Surely, you jest. You are the one with the key. This is your cell; I'm just a temporary occupant."

"Professor Pryce, we don't want this to go on any longer. We need to know what you're up to. We have reason to believe that you are supplying data to some people who want to subvert the government. We know that their organization has been tapping into several confidential agencies."

I tried to size up this woman. She had startlingly white hair, cut short and styled. She was medium height with tinted glasses, loosely fitting business attire, and modest makeup. She could've been anyone. She gave off an air of authority, but wore no badge or ID. I could not tell how high up the chain of command she could be. I am not sure I even cared. She wore expensive shoes.

I took a chance and asked, "Exactly what organization am I supposed to be running or supporting? Look, this is getting out of hand. You know that it's only a matter of time before my public disappearance will be plastered all over the media. That is a level of publicity that I'm sure you don't need, whoever you are. If you have some specific charges to level against me, do it. Otherwise, you have to let me go."

"We're in a bind here, Professor Pryce. We told you we work for the White House. We are with the FBI and are bound by our oath to follow up on any threats to our government. We do not have anything specific on you or your group, but we know enough to keep you here as long as we need to."

She had a tempered yet strong voice that did command authority. I noticed a definite New York accent, more from Long Island than the boroughs. I said quietly, "I'll admit that being associated with this particular White House is not, to me, a badge of honor for you or the agency you claim to represent, with or without proof of my potential guilt." I think I'd just learned that this room was not bugged, that pressure was building, and that they were running out of time. Ari most likely had news of the abduction released to the press. One more reason why a democracy needs, indeed, *demands*, a free press.

There were likely pictures of me being dragged off on CNN, MSN-BC, and maybe even on Fox. I decided not to challenge my guest with that thought. I'm an economist, and we gleefully make assumptions all the time. This time, knowing Ari as I do, I put a high probability on my assumptions regarding my public abduction were reasonably correct. "Take me out of here and put me in a hotel or someplace more civilized and then you and I can talk. I want to know exactly what's bothering you people. And I want to know where I am and who you are. I do not answer questions while captive and possibly under the auspices of a foreign government. Then and only then, will I try to help you out."

I decided to test her to see if the barrier I had deliberately built could be broken. I didn't want to risk being tortured, knowing very well what that could entail. We stared at each other for several seconds, which seemed much longer.

I asked, "What's your name and title?"

"My name is Special Agent Beverly. I'm a Director of Special Operations, and I work out of FBI Headquarters on Pennsylvania Avenue."

"What number Pennsylvania Avenue, Special Agent Beverly?"

"Nine thirty-five. I prefer to be called Bev." Her answer was quick enough to be believable, although that address is pretty well known to most people in DC. I decided to go on instinct. I did not know if Beverly was her first or last name.

"Thank you. Now, about the information I was accused of handing off... I was approached several weeks ago in New York by someone I didn't know. He told me that he worked with a group and that they needed my help. Apparently, this guy knew of our database, which I'm sure you know about, too, since it's published research. I did ask what he wanted it for. He said that he was launching an effort to increase voter participation. I was told that they work on their own and are not affiliated with any group. Their concern is that people don't vote in America, and they wanted to change that. They also did not want me to know who they were, and now I know why, don't I?"

"Who approached you? A man? A woman? Young or old? An American?"

"He was young and looked like a student, about six feet, very thin, decently dressed. I do not remember much else about him. Was he an agent under your supervision? I asked."

"Why would you do business with someone like that?"

She did not answer my question. "Like what? Pretty judgmental on your part. As I said, there's nothing in our data banks that is illegal or threatening. We have data series on economic, social, and political trends, not only for the U.S., but for other nations as well. Nothing we have is confidential, so I had no reason not to help them. This is what I do. I'm an economist. Luckily, I can afford to compile and maintain my own data. Is that the organization you are referring to? If so, it's a public, not-for-profit company called Sociometrics, a 501-C3, registered in New York for more than forty years. You'll get more information there than you will from me. My memory on details like that is fading. Besides, I like what that fellow is doing a lot more than I like what you are doing."

Bev stared at me for a while. Then she stood up, excused herself, and left. I washed my face and sat down to think.

About an hour later, there was a knock, and my two familiar goons were outside. They asked me to get dressed, pick up my personal items, and come with them. I put my glasses back on and stuffed as much as I could into my bag and left the food and toiletries behind. It was about 11:00. I was escorted out of the building and into an enormous Cadillac Escalade. The two goons sat in the front, and Bev was next to me. I noticed that she'd changed her shoes; they looked comfortable, business-like, and also expensive. I wondered if they had red soles.

She turned to me. "We'll be going to an agency facility that is both secure and inviting." She looked directly at me and said very clearly that she hoped that we could manage to have a productive exchange on our mutual concerns.

I thanked her for her forthrightness. I agreed to talk to her as long as I wasn't asked to do or say anything that I might consider subversive. At least I knew for the first time since I was abducted that I was still in America. I thought I would play the patriot card for a while and see what they were really after. I'm not sure it worked, but it felt good. For some reason, I take great pleasure goading these Feds. I knew that I was now definitely within earshot of Ari's team.

"A video of your sloppy and unprofessional abduction was released by a citizen and broadcast on almost every channel last night," Bev told me. "The director realized how vulnerable that made the agency, so he assigned me to take over from the White House unit who'd been ordered to seize you. They were ordered to pick you up by the president. They had been told to take you by any means necessary."

I most certainly do not know who that citizen whistleblower was, but I'm absolutely sure that Ari or his people were close to the action. That had been Ari's plan, and that was why Moshe had told me not to worry. We were in control of the narrative. I also began to think that his plan was bigger: leave me in the States and expose my whereabouts to the Feds was also part of it. I kept silent until I was sure as to how the new situation was unfolding. I was sensing a turn in the tide, but I wasn't sure how much in my favor it would be. I knew I was about to find out.

The caravan of vehicles drove through a gate as we worked our way around the back to a separate building that looked like a hotel. We all got out, and I saw the metal detectors on each side of the door. I removed my glasses and followed my escort. He was in a hotel uniform and took me to a penthouse apartment with windows all around. I found a change of clothes laid out on the bed. Coffee and healthy snacks were on the side table by the window. I was glad to see them.

"Professor Pryce, someone will be back in about a half hour," my escort said. "Please make yourself comfortable. Agent Beverly will be accompanied by other agents when she returns."

I stared at him and said, "She prefers Bev."

I took a long, hot shower. I changed into my new clothes that fit perfectly, though they were not my style. I was beginning to feel like I was in a James Bond movie. I poured a cup of coffee and tried to relax in the living room as I went over the events of the past few days. I didn't see a newspaper, and there was no TV. My phone was still blocked.

Then there was a knock on the door, and I opened it. Bev was there with two other agents, both of whom I knew.

"I hope you remember Dennis and Dean? They will be joining us this morning."

"Yes, I do. Nice to see you guys again. Did you ever get to that diner I suggested?"

"No, sir, we left the city right after our meeting."

I was surprised to see them, especially together. I decided to keep cool and not say anything about Agent Orange or Dennis's role in that part of our effort.

Bev broke the silence as soon as we sat down. I had my glasses on and imagined that I'd already identified who was present to Ari's team. It was an interesting exercise knowing that everything we said was being recorded without the FBI's knowledge. Hopefully, we'd never need to use whatever came out of this discussion.

I remained silent. This was Bev's meeting, and I was more interested in where she was going to take it. "Professor Pryce..."

I wanted to break the ice a bit. "Benson's fine, unless you have decided to pay my consulting fee."

"I'm beginning to think that we could never afford you, so this one will have to be pro bono."

"Fair enough."

"Dean and Dennis told me about your meeting. We recalled them back to headquarters from the White House unit when we learned what they were told to do. We've looked over your publications, consulting, and career from even before you started graduate school. We are convinced that you aren't subversive and that you're indeed a patriot, albeit not in the same category as those who often claim that mantle for themselves. Why did you not start college until you were twenty-eight years old?"

"Long story," I said, "let's just say that the opportunity was not there until then."

"But you walked out of NYU less than six years later with a PhD. Is that not a bit strange?"

"So, I've been told. Chalk it up to motivation. Can we get down to business?"

Bev responded, "We know that your long-time friend and partner, Andrew Lawson, is alive and well. We know where he is and that his daughter is with him. We also know Ari has actually taken the lead in your little enterprise. By the way, you may or may not know this, but Ari's not his real name."

That was a lot to dump on me at once. Bev had established her credentials. I was not totally surprised that Ari had kept his real name from me. I had surmised that he used a different name for each of his clients. That's how he keeps them apart. I was surprised, however, that they knew where Andrew and Anna were. Bev didn't mention the rest of our team at all. Nor did she say that she knew where Ari was. I was not sure if that was a deliberate oversight or a test. No mention of Agent Orange either. My guess was that she knew nothing more than what she let on. Yosef and Lavi, along with our art team were unknown entities.

"If you know where Andrew and Anna are, you know more than I do," I said. "I don't even know where Ari is." Saying this, I was admitting my complicity for the first time.

"We know a lot," she responded. "It's our job to know where people of interest are. You need to know that as innocuous as your posts were, the Seven Sins cartoons really got to the president. He treasures his connection with the evangelicals, and your posts did him no favors with them. He's been getting a lot of phone calls from evangelical leaders who are pressuring him and questioning their loyalty. He knows their loyalty is waning. Your chart on abortions in the US and how *Roe v. Wade* could be considered an anti-abortion platform really hit home with some of the more reasonable members and followers."

I decided to let our work hang out a bit, since they clearly knew what we were doing. I was still not sure if they knew how or where. "We thought that they would," I responded. "As crazy as some of those evangelical leaders are, their followers are, for the most part, reasonable people looking for something to hold onto. Their lives have become more vulnerable because of political forces they don't understand, and that frightens them. I have no respect for their leaders who often take advantage of their faith and bleed them of their relatively meager funds."

I still couldn't tell if Dennis's activities were known to his associates, and he was giving me no sign one way or the other. Best to play dumb on that one and let him take the lead.

Bev asked, "What were your objectives with this effort?"

"Very simple. It's an extension of a project Andrew and I started many years ago to build a system that could reach Americans who have not been participating in our election process. Many have never registered to vote—others have registered and never gotten to the polls. As this election cycle evolved into an insane agglomeration of misleading statements, we decided to reactivate our effort. I was particularly upset that the president's rallies had become increasingly absurd. It was my decision to make the cartoons. We eventually expanded the effort to actively try to prevent the reelection of the president. I apologize if this offends any of you, but for a sitting president to lie so often and on such important issues in front of people who admire him is, in my opinion, tantamount to treason. His behavior incites them to actions that are not based on the facts, which is dangerous. He seems to enjoy making people angry."

"Is that why you feel so strongly that he should not be reelected?" Dean asked.

"I'm not sure if you took notes from our meeting in New York. I know that you bugged my office, but I don't know if the conference room where we met was also bugged. I assume that there must be a record somewhere—if not I have it on my phone. Andrew and I felt strongly because I know exactly the kind of a person he is, a man out for himself with no loyalty to anyone else. That includes our nation. In fact, I do not think that he cares one fig about America. He's using his office as he uses everyone, for self-aggrandizement and profit. He's dangerous, and not only for his corruption, greed, and narcissistic behavior. He can't visualize the consequences of his actions. He learned early on in his sordid career that whatever screwups he initiates, his bevy of lawyers will tie everyone involved up in court. He's only just realizing that he can't run the country the way he ran his business."

Bev interjected, "He is the president and that still has standing in this country."

"True, but we're all accountable for our actions, particularly so for elected officials."

"Reasonable point that certainly needs more support."

"His brilliance is his ability to visualize an opportunity to enhance his brand," I continued. "That's partially why he ran for the presidency; he craves the spotlight. He is, however, unable to see the consequences of his decisions. If he had lost to Hillary, he would have gathered all the publicity from the campaign and used it to pay off his debts or forestall having to pay them off. His incompetence in managing his business built on sand has come back to haunt him. If Trump really understood the consequences to him, his companies, and his brand, not to mention the responsibilities of becoming a public servant, I think he would never have run. Our problem is that he sees everything in terms of branding and has no concern about secondary consequences. Trump was unprepared for the scrutiny of the press. He most likely never thought he would win."

Bev surprisingly said, "Most of us at the Bureau believe that to be true. By becoming a public figure, Trump made himself incredibly vulnerable. He could no longer control the narrative of a relentless media, hungry for the next scandal. His lifelong ability to hide his many shortcomings was no match for the *New York Times* and the *Washington Post* and cable TV, notably Rachel Maddow and Anderson Cooper. Much to his surprise, his lawyers couldn't protect him from the media once he became a public figure. This is what happens when people who have no actual public sector experience decide to run for office. The public sector world is a completely different universe than is the private sector. That reality is only now becoming clear to the president."

"So true," I agreed. "Trump has some strong characteristics. If he had been smarter, he might have made his presidency a lot more effective. The press gave him a hard time, but it was not as critical as it should have been, he deserved much more scrutiny than he was given. I have often felt that if the market share and profit-driven press hadn't given him so much airtime and ink, he wouldn't have been elected."

Bev interrupted. "You need to know that we did not bug your office. Are you sure it was bugged?"

Wow. Big change of subject. Why wasn't she responding to what I'd just said?

"Absolutely," I responded. "I was also followed on several different occasions, and once you involved a group of students I had agreed to meet with. No one messes with my students, and for that one act itself, I'm considering legal action against the agency."

"You are welcome to proceed," she said. "The agency had no part in that action, but I can guess who did. We will take care of that in-house if that is okay with you."

"If I have your word on that, I won't sue," I said. "The fact that you didn't know about activities going on in your own house reinforces why I felt compelled reconstitute the project. Apparently, the Bureau, along with a whole lot of other people who should know better, doesn't see what's been happening to our country. The concentration of money and power has gotten to a point that it might not be reversible. The wealth and income gaps are unacceptably huge for a representative democracy. Those gaps and their rates of increase have become ingrained to a point that they are feeding on themselves and might be unstoppable. Perhaps you don't comprehend the consequences of this concentration of wealth and power, and that alone is what bothers me more than the gap itself. The election of Trump is directly related to this trend in our economic and our political systems."

Bev responded, "We did not realize until too late what the administration was doing with our agents assigned to the White House. That's never happened before. Once we figured it out, we recalled our agents back to headquarters. The problem was that he found a way to hire others from the private sector. Dean and Dennis asked to meet with me after they met with you. That meeting made them most uncomfortable because they knew that they were not following FBI procedures."

"I could tell how uncomfortable they were. I actually felt bad for you guys," I said. "Maybe I should have been nicer."

Dean smiled for the first time. "Look, we're all sitting here about two weeks from the re-election of someone who has systematically been raping our economy, our government, and, as Joe Biden has said, the soul of America. This president is dangerous because of the office he holds, which he views as a means to achieving his personal and financial goals. He has no interest in the long-term aspirations of our nation. He is also deathly afraid of losing the election because of the many legal actions that are waiting for him when he becomes a civilian again. 'He does not even want the job. All he cares about is the power, and the protection of his brand. No one's above the law. Sitting presidents, if anything, should be setting an example for the rest of us. A president ought not to be able to break the law and hide behind his presidential shield. What could possibly be more of a travesty than a sitting president having broken the law and his oath to our Constitution without consequences?

I agreed with Dean and offered further support. "I need to point out that the president is not even our biggest problem. He's merely the result. A long time ago, some rich people decided that they didn't want to live in a representative democracy. They like the concentration of decision-making in the hands of a few and not the many. Republicans, unwittingly or not, represent these powerbrokers. Why is it that for so many years, Republicans have done everything conceivable to stop people from voting? Just look at the rising concentration of wealth and income over the last forty to fifty years. The poverty rate may be going down but look at the thousands of middle-income families drifting into poverty almost by the day. The pandemic is one reason, but inaction from the administration and the unconscionably rising health costs are a longer-term cause. The rest of the world pays a fraction of what our people have to pay for basic healthcare. Why is education perceived by many on the right as a waste of time and money? I think that the reason is that they, like our president, find it easier to manipulate the uneducated. Education lifts people out of the poverty of the mind by giving them a set of viable alternatives to generational oppression and ignorance. An education is also the most productive investment we have to help someone gain financial independence. I know that to be true because it worked for me."

Bev interjected, "So, you are a socialist"

"No," I snapped. "I'm a realist, and I know that if we do not make basic public investments in our nation and our people, we can't compete. Most people have no idea what socialism is. I always like it when I hear people on the right or politicians, some who have lived off the government for their entire lives and never cashed a private sector paycheck, talk to me about the evils of socialism, present company excluded of course.

"Shall I mention housing? Redlining is now against the law, but do you think for one moment that a successful black family has equal access to available housing? Assumed genetic inferiority, laziness, drugs, or family values on the part of many rich white people are often used to explain poverty. But it is white privilege and its attendant policies and attitudes that are largely responsible for creating these conditions in the first place. The fortunate thing for America is that those who feel this way are dwindling as a percent of our population. The next generation is prepared to take on the establishment and create a more just America. These young people are asking us to get on board addressing their concerns or stand down."

"Are we getting a lecture in economics?" asked Dean.

"You might say so. It's on the house." I continued, "I cannot imagine where this president gets his ideas. He simply does not know government well enough to come up with all the initiatives that are literally destroying decades of social and political legislative achievements."

"We have reason to believe that our president gets phone calls every morning from people hell bent on the goals of the extreme right. We have targeted several think tanks and institutes who freely give Trump these ideas. We have them on a watch list because we know they are potentially violent or purveyors of violence against the state," said Bev. "We think that they feed him ways to crush our democracy. They instruct him about where and who to attack next. Their objectives are to destroy any substantive agency, department, organization, or individual that might stand in their way of absolute control. Trump's objective is to use these institutes to show his base just how smart and powerful he is. The problem, which will come as no surprise to you, is that he uses his private phone, which we can't tap."

I responded. "These people are hell bent on destroying what they call New Deal Socialism, without even knowing what that term means. They are using Trump as their mercenary to get the job done."

Was she baiting me about the phone calls? I knew what she was saying is factual. Agent Orange had told us as much. Even though he was unsure who'd been on the other end of the phone, such calls were regularly made to the president's private line, usually in the mornings, on the phone he was not even supposed to have. Could Agent Orange be a double agent?

"Like you, I suspect that several rightwing think tanks are behind most of these initiatives," I said. "The impact of his actions on the overall economic growth and stability of our nation never enters his mind. I do not want you to think for one moment that what I'm saying is a conspiracy theory. It's not—I'm just not sure who's involved. If you doubt any of this, just look at Trump's knowledge base and compare that to what he is doing to our government."

"Your theory has merit," Bev responded. "We can confirm that the president has several people outside of government who are spurring him on. One of your cartoons with him subserviently listening to his daily instructions really ticked him off. He does not like being perceived as not in control."

"Who were the goons who drugged and arrested me?"

"FBI agents who were assigned to the president and were only doing what they were told. And we apologize." She seemed genuinely embarrassed.

"What can I say? If anything positive results from our meeting, I should thank them. Assuming, of course, that you're no longer going to subject me to torture."

Bev laughed. "That was never a real threat."

"It felt real to me at the time. I expected Dick Cheney to walk through the door any moment carrying a water board. Look, I agree with Dennis, we're sitting here right before the election with an incumbent who has told more than 20,000 outright lies. How is it that his lies alone do not render his right to reelection null and void? Politicians sometimes bend the truth for professional reasons. But this man lies to build himself up. He knows that as president, his word means something to people who want to be heard. He inflames them to gain their votes with no intention of solving their problems. They are clueless and don't realize he'll throw anyone who he no longer needs under the bus. There are hundreds of cases to prove that point, starting with his ex-wives."

Dennis spoke for the first time. "You must be hell as a professor!"

"That might be true, Dennis. After all, I've been at it for a long time. I am consistently evaluated by my students as well-informed in my field and overly passionate about anything I care about. I do tend to drone on, but that's also an extension of my passion."

Bev broke in. "Benson, we know that a lot of what you're saying is accurate. Our problem is that we are constrained by what we can do about it. It's both the benefit and the curse of a democracy. It is also the reason we let people like you off the hook and hope that you won't stray too far."

"Okay, but why do the good people follow the rules, and the bad people get away with breaking them?"

Bev answered, "That's why we have you out there on the front lines. There are a lot of groups like yours that operate just inside, and sometimes, outside of the rules. If we think your intentions are good, we look the other way. If not, we come down on you, fast and hard. It is extremely difficult to separate who is who, but we do a rather good job. We eventually decided that you were valuable to us and that is why we left you alone, and that is exactly why the president and his people could not."

"So, we are unpaid and unwitting consultants for the government?" I asked, only half-joking.

"Precisely."

"How is it that I have no idea where some of the most important people in my life are, and you do? Why am I here when you know damn well that, other than wanting to help bring down a clear and present danger to our nation, we have done nothing illegal?"

Bev smiled. "Hold on, cowboy."

"Why do people keep saying that to me?"

"Because despite all your honorable intentions, you're always on a very short fuse."

"I plead guilty, with cause."

Bev took over. "I know that you know just how sophisticated our surveillance is. We watch everyone, and we've watched you for years. We did not know exactly what you were up to, but we had a good idea. You're really good at staying under our radar."

"We have Ari to thank for that," I said.

"We let you continue because we knew that somehow you'd ferret out some element of corruption. We wanted to be there when you did. Driven by honor, passion, and patriotism, people like you are able to do things we can't. All we had to do was watch and wait until the you-know-what hit the fan. That was our clue to step in."

"So, we've been operatives for you—something like the characters in that NBC series *The Blacklist*?"

"Your hacking activities constitute a felony. And having broken into the deepest caverns of the Russian government, you may have put us in an untenable diplomatic position with our Russian adversaries."

"Whoa. Wait just a minute," I said. "We've done nothing of the sort. We did use the 2016 Russian model to get to people who don't read establishment news, but hacking into the Russians themselves? Never."

Bev paused, looked squarely at me, and said, "Maybe you aren't aware of it, but your team, whoever they are, has slipped deep into the bowels of the Russian government. You guys have been downloading a hoard of top-secret Russian information that, if made public, would be embarrassing to them, and frankly to us. The Russians actually think the FBI, CIA, or some other US governmental agency is behind it all. They're really on us for invading their government, and a whole lot of Russian oligarchs are furious that their systems and personal bank accounts have been hacked."

Bev paused and looked directly at me, gauging my reaction. If what she was saying was true, it is a wonder that we are still alive.

Bev continued. "A prominent German bank is now under investigation because of some documents that were leaked, we think by your people. The Suspicious Activity Report System article released last year really scared them and embarrassed some pretty big banks. They will have a lot to answer for after the election. Other individuals, including your former mayor, know a lot more than they've admitted to."

"What mayor?" I asked.

"Rudy. We know you worked for him and were fired for not falling in line."

I began to see that this woman had a lot more muscle than I'd thought. I could see that she was really pissed that we apparently entered doors that they themselves have been unable to penetrate. Maybe I should have been more circumspect. When will I ever learn to cool it? I was also astonished at the revelation and could not imagine that *we* were agitating the Russians. I think I just found out why we are so popular with these agencies and constantly being followed and harassed. We did something they couldn't. What I didn't know was if their problem was technical or professional. Either way, I had just gained a lot of respect for the team we put together. "Look, none of this originated with our team," I said. "You even said that we were only one group that you have on a long leash. Besides, the SARS and money laundering exposure were done way before we were even operational. This cannot possibly be our doing."

"So you say. Let's take a break for lunch. I have something I want to show you. You will be free to go before dinner. I suspect you have people out there waiting for you to be released."

How did she know that? I wasn't sure if I was annoyed or impressed at how much information these people had on us. How was it that they didn't know where I'd been the previous few weeks? Maybe they did!

My guests left. I washed my face and sat down to figure out what had happened over the last... I'm not even sure how long I was there. I really wished I could talk to Ari before meeting with them again. What did I know for sure at that point? I learned from Moshe that I'd unknowingly been an underground spy for years with my best friend as my go-to agent. I worked my ass off to protect myself from getting caught, only to find that I was an unpaid consultant for the very people I'd been trying to avoid. I just learned that we cracked the Kremlin and that my handpicked team might have been in this business long before I even knew them.

And Ari, or whatever his name was, had said that I'd make a good spy. I laughed. I can't even spy on myself!

Lunch turned out to be easy. Only Bev and I were there. It was delivered and we ate in her office. We talked about a whole range of life experiences we'd both had. I learned that, like AO, Bev came from generations of dedicated public servants. Like many women, she hit the glass ceiling in the Bureau early on, but she had a lot of people behind her and that was what mattered in this business. She clearly cracked through the double-plated bulletproof glass ceiling of the FBI.

Over coffee and dessert, I decided to put my economist's hat back on. There was something I wanted her to know. "Bev, I want to thank you for understanding what we've been trying to do. We never once had a thought of trying to subvert our government. On the contrary, we considered our effort as one that would save us from ourselves. I do want to mention one concern that did not come up in our discussion this morning. One of the biggest costs of this administration's isolationist Make America Great Again philosophy is that Trump has almost destroyed our position in the global community. The press has covered the embarrassment of leaving the Trans-Pacific Partnership and the Paris Climate Accords and his disdain for NATO and other global initiatives. The disruption he has caused with so many of our trading partners, not to mention China and his Russian buddy, is going to come back to bite us. This president has no understanding of the terms of trade or the dangers of relying on tariffs to make a political point. To this day, he still thinks that our tariffs are paid by the nations he imposes them on. He has no clue that they're actually a tax, paid by American importers and American consumers. He's been forced to spend billions of tax dollars to bail out our farmers because they've lost their best customers due to his tariffs on China. These payments have only increased our deficits. Such payments don't really help the farmers in the long term, especially since they foster dependency. The pandemic has caused a temporary stall in our trade balances problems, but if his trade war continues, it will start to rise again. China is significantly better situated to ride out this trade war than we are.

The politics is understandable and not to be minimized. If Biden wins this election, he knows that we have a long way to go to rebuild trust in America. If he does not win, we'll find ourselves on the brink of a rabbit hole that we may never be able to crawl out of. I want to talk about what we can expect to happen to the dollar. Reading between the lines in a lot of the business news, it is clear to a lot of people who think that, in a second Trump term, we can expect some serious damage to the dollar to occur. We're already witnessing a rise in our national debt and deficits; these are numbers we haven't seen since WWII. Currencies fluctuate on the global exchange markets by the moment, and its folly to even try to predict their rates.

"The Yuan and Euro are becoming stronger relative to the dollar. Should that trend continue, the dollar will become more expensive because importers have to give up more dollars than before to buy goods made elsewhere. This is a decrease in purchasing power for American consumers. On the positive side, American goods become cheaper to our trading partners because they will be able to get more dollars for each unit of their domestic currency. The fluctuations in foreign exchange markets can be traced to the activities of a nation's central bank. Overall confidence in a nation's economy and its political stability plays an important role in the value of its currency. As America continues to undergo these social and political conflicts, largely inflamed by this White House, we have to expect some blowback from the global markets.

"We need to restore stability to avoid a major depreciation in the dollar. When that happens, as it does anytime people get nervous about any commodity, our trading partners will dump dollars and buy more attractive currencies if they lose confidence in us. They will flood the market by selling US treasuries, which will further lower the value of the dollar and threaten its status as a world reserve currency. Many of our major trading partners, China and Japan in particular, hold trillions in US treasuries. They will gamble on the strength of America, but only as long as they think their holdings in US paper have value.

"More than sixty percent of all foreign reserves are in dollars. That's what makes the dollar the global reserve currency. This status gives America many advantages in world trade. If those who buy and sell currency to facilitate trade lose confidence in the dollar, they will shift to another currency that is more stable. For instance, a recent China/Russian currency swap was created, specifically to take advantage of our national stress and to diminish the value of the dollar as a reserve currency. The administration's trade war with China and other trading partners has eroded confidence in America, and therefore the dollar. We need to get on top of this problem before it becomes irreversible."

Bev used this moment to inform me. "We actually had a workshop on economics several months ago. We had our own economists, some from the administration and a few from business and academia. There was no specific agenda since we asked each to bring a paper on whatever concerned them. The biggest concern was our national debt and deficit. It was felt that the 2017 tax reductions were mostly to blame, and thought was given to how they could be reversed. The trade war was introduced, but politics dominated the discussion. Wealth and income inequality gaps were of major concern and tax alternatives were introduced as the quickest way to give those issues some relief. Of major concern was the large numbers of American falling below the poverty line, mostly due to the pandemic. The consensus was that about eight million Americans fell into poverty this year. Economists from the Urban Institute estimated that the unemployment rate went from 3.5 percent in February to nineteen percent in April. They estimated that over half of all adults over 18 lived in households that experienced a loss in income. The Congressional Budget Office's best estimate for the unemployment rate for the end of the year will be eleven percent. It was a most depressing afternoon to be sure."

"That is why economics has been labeled the dismal science," I said.

"Is that true? Who did that to you guys?"

"Thomas Carlyle in the 1820s. He was at a conference with economists that apparently was as depressing as yours."

"Look Bev, China and Japan are among the largest holders of US treasuries. If they decided to sell these holdings, we'd quickly see our interest rates climb, which would spill over into higher rates for American home buyers, capital investments, and consumer credit. China and Japan hold these notes because they don't want their exports negatively impacted by a weak dollar. As China has become an economic power, they've also greatly expanded their own middle class. This means that China will begin to depend much less on exports, because their domestic consumption of all that they produce will be more robust. They will simply no longer need to hold so many treasury notes and can start selling them on the foreign exchange market, which will result in higher domestic rates of interest for us."

"What are the chances that this will happen?"

"Always hard to say, but anything that has to do with China is possible. They have really been on a roll lately. Despite many domestic problems, they are rapidly becoming the major economic force on the global stage. They desperately want to dominate global trade and have been inching toward that goal for decades. Revised estimates have been circulating that China could surpass America as soon as 2024, twenty years sooner than earlier estimates. They thrive on the dissension in other countries, and we are currently a feeding frenzy for them. I put Russia as our biggest political problem, and China as our biggest economic problem," I hypothesized.

"I don't mean to overwhelm you with a lot of economics," I continued, "but this risk stems from our rising national debt and political instability, and the perceived value of the dollar is the measure used to deal with it. Should this campaign and the election continue to be as unruly as the president is making it, we can expect the natural forces of economics to take over and create a serious global problem for America.

"If the president wins the election, international organizations and many valued nations will move further away from America as a trusted partner. Should the president lose, the rising number of right-wing angry fanatics, whose violence he has encouraged, is almost a greater problem, primarily because they are domestic. If these fanatics hit the road armed and ready to sow their hatred and express their dissent, we can expect confidence in the dollar as the prime world currency to fall through the floor, and our economy with it.

"Let me conclude with the fact that the Trans-Pacific Partnership is about to be signed. You will recall that abandoning this agreement, of which we were an original partner, was Trump's first isolationist act. We're not part of that agreement, one of the largest trade agreements ever. My warning is that whatever happens in this election, any fallout must be quelled quickly and firmly. The new administration will have enough on its plate. A civil war, as you know, cannot be won. America will lose big especially if the threat of civil unrest continues to dominate the headlines after November 3. I have no way of knowing if these points I am making are under consideration. If not, they damned well better be put on the table, and soon."

I could tell that my comments hit home and that she understood the gravity of the situation. She acknowledged my concerns and promised to bring them up at their weekly directors' meeting.

Bev asked me to join her on a tour after lunch. She took me into a large room filled with screens and the dim roar of informational input. I felt like I was in a NASA ground-control center. She showed me with the flick of a switch that Andrew and Anna were in a safe house owned by a Swiss banker. They'd been in the Azores, then in the Algarve in Portugal, before landing in Switzerland. They had clearly felt the need to be mobile. She said, "I am sure that Ari was behind that decision." She knew that Andrew had bought a sailboat in Luz Portugal, and they that he planned to live there and not come back to the States. They weren't sure of Anna's plans.

At least I knew they were safe. In fact, I knew exactly where they were since that banker is ours. I was not sure how comfortable I was knowing they were being watched by people we've tried to avoid. Bev said, "Ari's currently on his way back to the states. He might have already landed. He manages to do that frequently without us knowing until it is too late. He has been in Israel for several weeks."

I saw a blip on the screen that she said was him, but his name had been redacted. She let me know that algorithms exist that enable them to track every American citizen 24/7. They can also track immigrants, legal and illegal, and any and all diplomats at will. My earlier perceptions, as I had walked around Washington Square Park and the streets of NY, were now confirmed, far more definitely than I could have imagined.

We got into a car for short ride. We entered a building I had not seen by going down a ramp into the basement parking lot. We took an elevator down many floors. The elevator had only one button. We got out and entered a far larger room. There must have been hundreds of people wandering about or sitting at computer stations, each with no fewer than five massive screens. I was in a secret war room that watches the activities of all nations, their corporate leaders, military, and politicians.

I wasn't sure whether to be intimidated or impressed. Why was I being shown all this? These spaces were most certainly not on the White House tour!

We went back to Bev's office and sat down. She explained that this was where they had been watching people like me. "We let you go about your business because we have concluded that more positive information would flow to us by doing so." She continued. "We agree that the president must go if we are to stem the damage his policies and behavior have caused. There are a lot of people in our government who feel the same way. But our hands are tied on how active we can be to counter him." Bev admitted that neither she nor her colleagues would violate the law, even though the president does so frequently. "The days of rogue underground departments in the intel world are long gone," she told me. "The digital world has made all that you just saw possible. It has also put us under public scrutiny as never before."

We agreed that the election could go either way. "With the cheating and manipulation, Trump's campaign may well overcome the will of the people," she said. "If he succeeds, we will have a horrendous battle on our hands for the next four years. One thing is clear to both sides of this battle. There's no limit to what he'll do to win. He knows that if he loses this battle, he will either be in court or jail for a long time." She suddenly got more serious. It was as though an entirely different person had just come forward. "There is one more point that I need to make. None of us in the intel business will interfere in the election. Those days are over. We have to live with the will of the people, even though we know that the will is often subjected to vicious underground influences. We know the actions of the alt-right, white supremacists, and of course Russia. All we can do is fight back within our constitutional constraints and the law, which are not effective in this new age. Our hands are not totally bound, but we are pretty constrained."

It was my turn to weigh in. "We're going to know in a few weeks which of two distinct worlds we'll be living in. If the Democrats can prevail, the battle will be easier. The problem is that we'll need a major clean-up from the damage that has been done over the past four years. There remains the real threat that he will be able to wreak havoc before leaving office on January 20. There is also the threat, that win or lose, Donald Trump will not go away quietly. I think Senator Romney just said something to that effect."

Bev got up and shut her door. She sat back down and said something to me that I never thought I'd hear from a Fed. "Benson, we really don't know how this election's going to turn out. I can say with absolute certainty that a whole lot of people in DC hope with all their hearts that Biden is strong enough to win this. Those people are not Republicans or Democrats, they are Americans, and they know exactly how dangerous the conditions we are facing are to the very fabric of our country. We think that you and your partners are making a difference. We know that he's furious at your posts, especially the ones directed at him. We do not, however, know how effective you've been with the electorate. That is the biggest reason that, despite the problems you have created for us with Russia, we are not going to stop you.

"The problem as I see it, and I think you do as well, is that whatever happens on November 3rd, the battle has only just begun. We are, however, prepared for either eventuality, and that is what I want to talk to you about." Bev continued, but far more earnestly than before. This woman was under a whole lot of stress. I had not seen it earlier, a testament to her resolve and professionalism.

"It's going to take a major restructuring of our economic, social, and political systems to put us on a path back into the global community. We agree that our government has not only lost the trust of our people, but we've also lost the trust of our global partners. We realize what it will take to win back that trust. Regardless who wins, we'll have to undertake an enormous effort to bring our nation back to an even keel.

"Whenever we go through game-changing situations like this, we tend to fall into the same traps we have just gotten out of. If the president wins, there will be no change to his agenda. But with a win, he'll be emboldened and more aggressive—there will be nothing to stop him. If Biden wins, I've been informed that I will be working on what he's calling a New Priorities

Agenda. The biggest asset we have with Biden at the helm is that he knows people, and he knows who he can trust and who he can't.

"Biden will place people from many disciplines on designated committees to determine exactly what our priorities should be as we move into 2021. None of us knows who else has been appointed and we won't, of course, until after the election. I don't have a clue what I can contribute, but I'm looking forward to working on this team, since we've been told explicitly not to be burdened by the past. Biden told us in his memo that we'd need to take bold steps, partially to appease the extreme left of his party, who feel left out. He must also address the fact that the past four years have resulted in several steps backward. He wants to focus on the future, but these skeletons will be in the closet. I would like to be able to call on you for help."

"Is this the only committee he's formed so far?"

"No, and it's not even the first. Biden recognizes the COVID-19 crisis as issue number one. He also knows he might have a civil war on his hands. If he wins, he'll have to deal with a bunch of angry Trump voters, many of whom are armed. And like every president-elect, Biden has about 4,000 positions to fill on day one, not to mention his cabinet and major agency and department administrators. Most of those choices will be made by the inauguration."

I jumped in. "Because of who he is, Biden can solve a lot of our global problems with just a phone call. For the cabinet, staffing, and public sector appointments, you're right, I'm sure he will be able to pull that together between the election and January 20. The pandemic is a major problem because of Trump's refusal to act. Two thirds of the deaths we have suffered would not have occurred if he'd had a plan like New Zeeland, South Korea, or Taiwan. I personally think he should be brought up before the International Court of Law or Human Rights for Crimes Against Humanity. The whole world has confronted this virus more successfully than he did. America has among the highest case and death rates in the world. Hundreds of thousands of Americans have died on this man's watch, and that is inexcusable." I could tell I had made my point and that I was beginning to wear her out. I nevertheless continued. I have always been much more effective in the classroom than at the consultant's table. I think I lack patience and always want to get onto the next topic. "The president's base has been so charged up. As you said, they are primed for civil war and that is something that cannot be tolerated. They're angry about a lot of things that are simply not true, but they believe Trump and his tweets. My recommendation would be to put together a team of streetwise people to try to open up communication with them. Find out what they're angry about and be prepared to offer solutions that would matter to them. Establish a dialogue and assure them that they have a voice, and that they will always be told the truth. That may be naïve of me, but it is worth a try. Possibly ex-police officers who have worked with these groups could make a difference. Just be prepared to have something to put on the table, so that no one's wasting their time. Build trust and go from there." I paused. "Outside of that, what can I do?"

"We need your economic and political expertise. Nothing until after the election, however, regardless of who wins, will happen. Either way, this committee will continue. We'll be up front if Biden should win, but out of view to everyone if Trump is reelected. I need a position paper and some guidelines as soon as possible. When could you get that to us?" asked Bev.

This was nothing I could possibly have expected when I was seized off the street. I took a moment to think about my options. I asked her if she could get me access to a computer and a tape recorder. "Of course," she said. "What do you have in mind?"

"A few weeks ago, I was asked to participate in an evening with some very bright graduate students. They wanted to talk about the direction the country is taking as they moved towards graduation. They don't want to enter the real world as mature, educated people only to slip into the world our generation has left them. Frankly, I've learned that this year's graduation class is totally dismayed by what they see around them. They're just not sure about how to deal with it.

"They know we've made a mess of things, which might possibly be irreversible. Our mistakes are our own, and they're not going to allow them to continue. These young people are going to make a difference, and they have the right ideas and the moral compass to see them through. They need only the guidance and opportunity to make it all happen. They've asked me to get them started. They submitted a list of their priorities and I was incredibly impressed with it. I embellished it for them and I think you will find it instructive for what you have asked me to do."

"How did they get to you?"

"That's confidential, and frankly it doesn't matter. You have to believe me when I say that win or lose this November, there's a whole new vanguard entering the work force who aren't going to fall in line. They're called the Gen Z'ers, and one of the primary demographics we focused on with our voter project. They did not come out in numbers in 2016, but I think with a little encouragement, they will do so this time around.

"These young people are going to make things difficult for whoever's in charge. Occupy Wall Street was a millennial initiative that failed because they were unsuccessful in identifying a leader. These young graduates will not make the same mistake, trust me."

Bev commented, "This is news to me. My children are older, and I don't have much contact with young people anymore."

"Give me an hour and access to a computer. I need to download a file. I have the list of topics that most concerned them in my email account. I'm willing to give you the output of that meeting. If you have recording capacity, I can give you a short verbal presentation to introduce you to the topics and make a tape for you. That should give you the help you requested."

"Given my experience with you, I doubt that it will be short. I'll get you set up right away. Is this room okay?"

"Sure. Please get me a clean flash drive as well."

I knew I had the outline of the student meeting on a file I could access. I also had more notes in my online folders that could be accessed by email. I thought of trying to communicate with Ari when Bev left the room but decided the risk was too great. Besides, I had the feeling that I would be out of there in an hour anyway.

★ ★ ★

Chapter 21

October 2020

Bev gave me the hour I asked for. She brought me a printer that was already hooked up to the laptop so I could make notes on paper for my proposed presentation. I got into my email account and downloaded my files from the meeting with the students. That only took a few minutes. I printed the document, read it over making minor changes, and saved it to their flash drive. I had some time left, so I lay down to take a twenty-minute nap before we planned to meet. I got up in time for a quick shower, got dressed, and was ready to go when I heard the knock on the door.

Bev, Dennis, and Dean entered with two other men and a woman who I recognized as part of the Biden campaign. Bev told me that they were all working for Biden. "I called them and briefed them on the relevant parts of our discussion and mentioned your offer. They're interested in what you have to say and asked to attend. Do you mind?" she inquired.

I looked at everyone in the room, including Dennis, from whom I received a slight nod of acceptance. Knowing the identities of the people in the room, I felt that I did not have to be as guarded and could freely express my thoughts and concerns to this group. I wanted the broader points and the economics of my presentation to dominate the discussion. Most of all I wanted to leave them with exactly where and from whom these ideas came from. The students deserved the bulk of the credit for putting this document together and I wanted these people to know that. There would be time for them to consider the details after the election.

"Not at all. I sincerely hope you guys will still have a job after the third," I started. "My verbal presentation will not be as detailed as the write-up. As everyone in the room will attest, I tend to ramble, and it's late in the day. I did, however, want to be here for questions and leave you with something to work from."

I handed my presentation to an aide who left to make copies. "I want you to know that the specific list of items was given to me by a group of graduate students who labeled it Building a Better America. That should be familiar to you. The title was their choice and might have been lifted from the Biden campaign. The comments under each topic are drawn from our discussion and my own thoughts following our meeting. Bev, I liked your use of the word 'priorities' and took the liberty of subtitling the report 'Prioritized Capitalism', which is, I believe, appropriate. I might also add that these are not in any order of priority since the students told me they could not agree on a ranking and view each as vital. They're angry that we've drifted from our core values and feel that we're no longer the land of opportunity. They are also angry because for the first time in America, these students know that they will not be able to live as well as their parents have. Of importance here is that none of these students are from wealthy families; they're all middle income and were at NYU because they are exceptionally bright and motivated. They're also committed to making a difference. These young people will enter their next phase with a mission to take back our planet and put equality, justice, and love up front.

"One thing they did agree to prioritize was the issue of trust. They're fed up with elected officials and business leaders lying to them. It is their opinion that anyone who lies should have to pay a price. They feel they can't function as citizens if they're lied to. They researched approval ratings of Congress and the Supreme Court and were astonished to learn how low they were. Without trust, nothing can be accomplished. They believe that there's been a tremendous amount of misinformation on social media. I agreed with them. Building trust is never an easy task, and this will without a doubt be a formidable one for the next administration." I noticed everyone looking around at each other and nodding. "Climate change was also a major concern. These young people know their lives hang in the balance if we don't solve this massive problem. Science must take the lead, elected officials can no longer be among the deniers, and business must be incentivized to participate in a positive way. They demand immediate action to save our planet. They like the Green New Deal but also recognize the political sensitivities."

"Do they realize how costly the Green New Deal would be?" asked Bev.

"I asked them the same question. Their answer was: Do you know how expensive it will be if we don't implement it? They pointed out that it wouldn't have been so expensive if we had dealt with this problem thirty years ago when the scientists first let us know about it.

"Another topic was the income and wealth gaps. Some of them come from families who experience it firsthand. The wider that gap, the more vulnerable we are to civil unrest. People are angry at the disparities, and they won't let their children starve without a fight. They mentioned that one in every five children goes to bed hungry at night in America. At the same time, one billionaire was recently reported to have made $13 billion in one day. They believe a more equitable tax system must be immediately implemented to better share our nation's wealth. No one's asking for a handout; they want only a fair distribution of our nation's prosperity. As a side bar, I read a study that just came out that those in the top economic echelons of our corporate world, Jeff Bezos and others who live in his world, have actually profited this year from the pandemic. This has happened as most of us are suffering major economic setbacks in a hundred ways from the pandemic. These are not trivial—they were reported to be in the trillions of dollars. This is not healthy and beyond the pale of decency."

Bev said, "Taxes are always sensitive, and there's no way a politician can offer higher taxes no matter how popular the issue."

"Bev," I replied, "America's one of the lowest taxed nations in the industrialized world. We have to start asking what we *get* for our tax dollars, not what we *pay*. We also have to address the loopholes that permeate our tax codes, making it possible for the rich to get richer at the direct expense of the middle class. They have a lot of empirical evidence that this is both true and unconscionable.

"They are incredibly upset with the continuation of systemic racism. Black, brown, and Native Americans, not to mention women, gays, and immigrants, have not been able to share in the opportunities our great nation has to offer. This is largely because of racism, a national disgrace in a country that's thrived on diversity. These young people are prepared to do whatever it may take to correct centuries of racial oppression. Black Lives Matter will not go away—this important movement will only grow. It does not make economic or moral sense to exclude any demographic from striving for the American dream.

"A lot of these issues go back to generational poverty. Debt and poverty get passed from one generation to the next. Their recommendation was to eliminate or at least reduce our national debt. They suggest something along the lines of those war bonds that helped finance World War II. They want financing that enfranchises working-class Americans as investors in our nation's future. They're asking for a creative financial package to reduce or eliminate national debt so we can start over with a clean slate. They want the benefits for this package be paid back to the people and not to the banks.

"These students are worried about their career opportunities after the pandemic. The world has changed, and we need to make sure that the needs of the workplace and workers are properly matched. This will involve providing training and re-training for newly created jobs. Students mentioned the need to pay attention to technological obsolescence in the job market. Miners and fossil fuel workers were cited as a case study. We can't continue to support generations of workers whose jobs are not there and not coming back.

"Our branches of government need to eliminate conflicts of interest, and self-serving power-seekers should no longer be able to take over our government. Future judicial appointments must not be political. Judges should be objectively appointed on the merits of their skills, experience, and knowledge of the law. Other nations have apolitical systems that could be a model for this change.

"We'll spend close to $16 billion on the 2020 elections. How many mouths would that have fed? How many student loans would that pay off? How many small businesses going out of business because of COVID-19 would that money have helped? We must consider some form of public financing for federal elections and get big money out of our elections. Imagine what the struggling nations out there must think of our political system? We need to eliminate any money going from a lobbyist to an elected official, whatever the reason. It is viewed as bribery. We must eliminate Citizens United; our government ought not to be for sale."

"I recall that the expenditures for the last presidential election amounted to the total GDP of the bottom thirty nations. Could that be possible?" Dennis asked.

"In a word, yes. And try to imagine the impression that leaves on those nations struggling every day to feed their people."

"Every elected official has only one boss—their constituents. We need a better system of communication between elected officials and constituents so that voters know what and who they're voting for. At the same time, we need to look into ways to make sure that all citizens are informed of the issues and prepared to vote in their own best interests. We should think of penalties for eligible voters who don't vote. Eighteen nations currently do this, and so should we.

Regulation is not a four-letter word. Regulatory oversight is needed because many businesses have proven that it's incapable of policing itself. Consumers and the environment need protection from businesses that put profit before safety and social responsibility. Until businesses can prove they are responsible, they must be regulated. The financial and pharmaceutical industries were offered as clear examples of irresponsible corporate behavior. In particular, the students are extremely concerned about the proliferation of lethal weapons. This generation has grown up with shooter drills in their classrooms, fearing that they'd be gunned down while in school, in the movies, at concerts, or in church. This is a national disgrace not suffered by any other nation on earth. They think the answer can be found in the responsible gun owners who don't like the politically motivated NRA.

"Our healthcare system is both unresponsive and expensive. We currently have five layers of profit between the patient and the cure. Healthcare is a right, not a privilege. We must stop blaming the infrequent problems of a single-payer system and focus on the bigger picture. Single-payer healthcare better serves all the people. We need to devise a system that offers affordable healthcare, professionally administered and dedicated to serve every American. It is both a moral and economic imperative. America continues to fall behind on many of the recognized indicators of a healthy work force. Our inadequate and incredibly expensive healthcare system is crippling our ability to be a productive nation. Just take a look at workdays lost in America because of health issues and you will see what we mean.

"The same is true for primary and higher education. When did education become an expense and not an investment in our future? The United States has dropped near the bottom of the list in major measures of education—we used to be number one. Student debt is currently higher than all consumer debt in America. We can and must do better. Education should be available to everyone. We should also have a free higher education system for those who can't afford college. The students recommended a community service or National Service Corps requirement in their field as a payback system for those who benefit from a publicly funded higher education.

"I want to quickly run through some other items that they introduced that are more fully described in my handout. Single parent families, drug overdoses, threats to our freedom of the press, our crumbling infrastructure, immigration and the dreamers, and most important, the problems surrounding our community police forces, are all very much on their minds.

"I want to state this next point as strongly as I can. The generations that we in this room belong to must accept responsibility for leaving these young people a world that's in disarray. Political, economic, and social unrest have not only been ignored, but they also have in many cases been made more detrimental on our watch. These young people are not going to let this *deplorable* condition continue unabated. We damn well better get on board with a more responsible agenda, or step aside. They are determined, and they will not leave behind a world that even hints at the one they inherited. Whomever is in charge after this election, you are advised to reach out to these young graduates and bring them into the decision-making process. Ignore them, and you will be reporting to them before you know it. Listen to these motivated, working-class students who have lived the pain. *They* are the ones with the best solutions.

"Do not underestimate the resolve of these graduates. We talk a lot about tipping points, and let me warn you right now, these young people are going to make a difference, with or without us. We have only one option and that is to get on board and bring our experience with us. What they have presented can best be viewed as building a new and better foundation for a sustainable superstructure, a superstructure that represents our economic, social, and political strengths, and our diversity.

They want only to build a better world to pass onto *their* next generation. It will bear little resemblance to the one we handed down to them. They are also convinced that if we all work together, across demographic, economic, and social lines, we can make this happen and do so to the benefit of all. The super-rich are going to have to pony up if this is going to happen. Any short-term sacrifices on the part of the super wealthy will quickly become the means for a stronger, safer, and more equitable nation. These concepts and goals might seem politically naïve. They are not. They represent nothing more than the right thing to do. We must shift from the tracks of unwarranted discrimination, dependency, and ignorance. This upcoming generation of citizens feel that as long as the playing field is level and opportunity is distributed fairly, all boats will indeed float with the incoming tide. Social and political outliers will soon see the benefits of community and family. There is simply too much that needs to be done, and we do not, as a planet, have the resources nor the time to continue to battle each other as we now are. As these students told me, we damned well better get on board or step aside. To paraphrase Bob Dylan: 'The times they are a-changin'.'

"Should Biden win the election," I said hoping, "this economic planning committee should have a longer life. The Employment Act of 1946 put the responsibility of maintaining full employment on the government. It also established the Council of Economic Advisors, reporting directly to the president. It is important for the council to produce economic outlook for the president. The next council, however, should take up some variant of each of the issues mentioned here. They must be incorporated into the day-to-day deliberations of the planning cycle with explicit and ongoing recommendations made to both Congress and the president.

"One way to start is to correct the historical apathy of our voting citizens, which is why we initially launched our Voter Awareness Project. Our current track record is abysmal, but I have faith in the future. From what we can see, we are going to have a much larger turnout in 2020 than we have had in many decades. We are going to learn how powerful the voter is and how that power can preserve our democracy. All the economic and political power in the world can't prevail over the common sense and moral compasses of an informed people. The voter is the ultimate negotiator in this battle. It is our job to make sure that the information given to voters is presented such that busy, hard-working people can digest it and vote intelligently, and in their own best interests. Thank you for your time."

Our guests from the campaign excused themselves and thanked me for my presentation. I had no idea if our work would ever see the light of day. That ball is in their court, and we can only hope that reason will prevail. Once we were alone again, Bev turned to me. "We do see all of this, Benson, and that's why I grabbed you from your abductors. One of the next administration's best weapons will be an expanded and robust economic development plan. You have given us a head start, though I have to admit that it's not what I expected. These issues are quite different from those typical of an economic planning committee. I agree that they must be front and center if we are to bring the fringe back into the fold. We might well have been putting the cart before the horse. I hope that you'll be available to work with us for at least a year. You see the big picture. Most of us are stuck in the trenches and barely get a moment to lift our heads. We desperately need your insight. I am asking you to work with us on whatever terms you are comfortable with after the election related smoke has settled, assuming it ever does. Can we count on you?"

"Let me understand. Your people drug and abduct me, charge me with committing a felony and treason, threaten to torture me, and then want to hire me to help straighten out the mess we have created for ourselves?"

"Something like that."

"I think that would be one for the *Guinness Book of Records*."

"I can see you sending that into them as an entry. Please don't," cried Bev.

I promised that I wouldn't. "I want to thank you for that vote of confidence, and I will certainly be available to serve my country. I would, however, like to wait until after the election. I still have a big job to do, and I will not walk away from it. One of the most nerve-wracking aspects of the last four years has been waking up every day to drama that never seems to stop. Those of us who try to see the big picture can barely grab a breath before he sends us off in an entirely different direction, causing us to forget what he did yesterday, or even what he just said in the previous sentence. My hope is that reason and justice will prevail and that with all his manipulations and cheating, the voters will see through him."

"You are as naïve as you say you are," teased Bev. "I only hope you are right. Don't people say that economists often have their head in the clouds? Your faith in human nature is admirable."

"We tend to make a lot of heroic assumptions, but do not forget that we have successfully predicted nine of the last five recessions."

"For real?"

"Another definition of an economist that has floated around for many years: 'We are often wrong, but never in doubt.'"

"Okay, I hope that's not true. Maybe I should take back my offer?"

"The truth is, Bev, economists are willing to take on tough issues, and that tends to make us the brunt of everyone. It is one thing to defend the big bang theory, gravity, or why the sky is blue. It is quite another to understand human behavior and why we do the things we do. Politicians are of course in an entirely different and far more complicated realm. Unless you accept the hypothesis that they only do what's needed to get reelected."

I did ask that she not hurt the two goons who drugged me. "They were only doing their job. Let them know that I got over it." Bev walked me to the main lobby and the exit. We parted. To my complete surprise, Ari and Moshe were right outside leaning against our car.

How in hell did they know I was going to be released? I caught Bev and Ari giving an ever-so-faint nod to each other. My question was answered. *Will this man, and now his brother as well, ever cease to amaze me?*

I received a heartfelt hello from each of them and settled into the comfortable seat, ready to go home. Ari asked, "Are you okay?"

"I'm fine, but you have a lot of explaining to do. Have we really broken into the Russians as I have just been informed, and if so, what are we doing with all that information?"

"The answer is yes but keep it to yourself. I want to hold off on any decisions regarding what we do with that information until after the election. Depending on who wins, we will have to decide how to handle it."

"How did this happen, and aren't they going to figure out who did it?"

"It was accidental. We found a gateway as we were hacking into their hackers. Don't worry about it for now, besides, the Russians think the government hacked them, not us. When we realized what we had, we were surprised at how primitive the Russian security systems are. Their ability to hack into others is far more sophisticated than are their own protection systems."

"And you think that makes us safe, especially since the Feds know who we are and what we have?"

"Neither the Russians nor the Feds are sure what information we have. In any case, we are going to keep it as a trump card, pun intended, to leverage after the election, win or lose."

"Another of your apt idioms? Were you able to record my ordeal over the last two days?"

"Yes, almost everything. I am quite surprised that they let you that far into the organization. That could prove to be most helpful."

"What do you mean?"

"Let me just say that I have a few people I want you to meet."

We stared at each other for a long moment. Then I glanced at Moshe and got a wink of approval.

I have worked with this man for more than forty years. It turns out that I do not even know his name, much less the extent of his involvement and authority. I do know that I will never learn the whole truth about him, yet I will forever trust him with my life. In fact, I already have.

"Look, Benson. We and many other groups have been working to win this election for Biden. As AO has told us, Trump is really bouncing off the White House walls, and he has only himself to blame if he loses. He has run a campaign based on hate and lies, and despite that fact that he is good at it, the chinks in his armor are beginning to show. We have to step up our efforts which we know are working. Despite the many roadblocks in place to restrict voters, not to mention COVID, nothing is stopping people from getting to the polls this time. This was our major goal as defined by you, and it is happening. It looks like the turnout is going to be big and that is a good thing.

"That is good news, Ari, there are a lot of other groups out there with us. The Feds told me that our posts, especially the cartoons on Trump, have done their job. I am feeling hopeful. Did you hear the discussion about Andrew and Anna? They know where they are and where they have been since you guys took off from Jersey."

"That was a surprise. They did not seem to know about our team, and I think they were guessing as to where I was."

"They know a lot more than we thought. Ari, the election notwithstanding, we have a lot of work before us if we want to empower the American voter and restore our democracy and economy. This challenge will not end with the election, which some people think is going to be a blow-out. I do not. In either case, we are going to have a lot of people on opposite sides of the political spectrum who simply do not trust each other. This is what happens when people in leadership positions lie to those who want desperately to believe that they matter. We are now all living in the swamp that is filled with anger and doubt. Our first task will be to build a trust in our intentions which must be focused on the creation of a just, equitable, and fair nation that embraces our differences. This nation must bring its polarized forces together. We must first throw down our swords and pick up our plowshares. Our nation is capable of providing enough for all of us, but we must work together to succeed. Building a trust in each other that we all have good intentions and desires are the first seeds we must plant and harvest.

"We have our truths, they have theirs. Closing that gap that has been wedged between us is going to take a huge effort that is much bigger than anything we have faced in this era."

"And you think we can do all that?"

"No one person or entity can, we have to do it together. A polarized nation is doomed to fail. What we have just lived through has been wrenching, and we are all wounded. The vulnerabilities of our democracy and our economy have been made as vivid to all of us as has their strengths to survive adversity. That might turn out to be the legacy of the Trump presidency. We need to rebuild so that our cherished systems are stronger than any one force."

"Let's get through this stage before we worry about the next. We must do what we can to ensure his defeat."

"Ever the pragmatist."

We pulled out of the FBI compound and headed toward New York.

"Ari, will you ever tell me your real name?"

The silence that followed left me with one more unanswered question. At least this time he did not disappear into his self-created mist.

★ ★ ★

Afterword

A Post-Election Assessment

I FINISHED THIS NOVEL ABOUT TWO WEEKS BEFORE the 2020 election. The time it takes from writing the last word of a book and getting it to print has provided an opportunity for me to reflect on the outcome of the election and the actions taken by the president. That task was seriously complicated by the speed and complexity of the post-election events, driven mostly by the disruptive behavior of a president who was living in an alternative universe and could not accept reality. Trump was resoundingly defeated, and the voice of the American voter rejected his desire to move us toward an autocracy fed by a constant stream of lies and desecration of our Constitution. Our democracy was left standing tall, in spite of an orchestrated effort to stomp it down. We can all take pride in that as we can now move towards rebuilding our nation.

I wrote this chapter as an afterword for *2020: America on the Brink,* a novel that chronologically traces a year of unparalleled tension and drama, and one we have barely managed to survive. The events of 2020 reveal much more than the obsessions of a candidate whose campaign of chaos, anger, and hate led to his downfall. The larger picture revealed an orchestrated attack on our democracy and way of life embedded within the actions of a president whose respect for our representative democracy was nonexistent. Trump's many followers were blinded in their faith that failed to see the true colors of their duplicitous hero. His base contained many decent people who wanted desperately to believe in him, so much so that they looked past the threat he posed to everything America stands for. It will take time for them to climb out of the dark pit of hypocrisy he drove them into, and we must help those who are willing to accept it with positive love.

Could another Trump-like candidate enter our political arena, one who is smarter and has a better working knowledge of our systems? Absolutely, this is the cost of democracy. Such a person could prevail and take our democracy down as Trump tried to do. It is the voter's obligation to become more informed and aware, so that such a threat never happens again. We did it in 2020; we will do it again.

None of us has been left whole from this ordeal, neither has our nation, however, valuable lessons as to our strengths and vulnerabilities are important experiences that we need to keep close to the surface as we begin the task of restoring our democracy and our economy for the good of all Americans.

THE NIGHTMARE THAT WAS TRUMP

THE PEOPLE HAVE SPOKEN. The 2020 election itself went off almost without a hitch. Biden won a clear victory to the complete and unacceptable amazement of Trump. Republicans gained or held seats the pundits said they would lose. Democrats held onto their majority in the House but lost valuable seats to Republicans. The chaos predicted by the press emanating from anticipated foreign meddling and disruptions at the polling stations apparently did not occur. One could arguably credit Trump for how smoothly everything went. Knowing that he'd use the courts and any means whatsoever to challenge any votes that he felt were illegal, put everyone involved from the secretaries of state right down to the individual counters on the defensive as never before. Pride in their jobs and faith in our most visible example of democracy resulted in an election that was magnificently managed by all states to ensure accuracy and fairness.

What have we learned over the past four years under the Trump administration?

Possibly the biggest lesson for us has been an awareness of the serious problems we have been ignoring for decades. They were brought out into the open and made obvious and immediate with the election of Trump. We have also learned that while flawed, our particular forms of democracy and capitalism have historically been the strongest and best systems available for many reasons. Based on freedoms of choice and trust, our political and economic systems are also incredibly vulnerable by virtue of their definition. Dictators rule differently; they offer no choice; government-controlled economies do the same.

We used to think that we could trust our supposedly free markets to serve us with safe, fairly priced products and services. We now see that economic concentration creates an irresistible urge to increase market share and profits at the direct expense of the working-class consumer. We thought that our constitutional, representative democracy was able to function putting the best interests of its constituents first. Over the last several decades, the concentration of wealth and power over government decision-making has dictated how our tax dollars are spent. Legislative decisions have largely ceased to represent our nation's citizens. These were the factors that contributed to Trump's victory. 2016 was a perfect storm. As the reality of a host of major social, economic, and political issues came to the fore, we found ourselves in a highly polarized environment. People and institutions were trying to survive as our nation found itself sliding down a well-defined slope of mistrust that enveloped the venerable institutions; we had thought were there to protect us. Generations of middle-class workers finally realized that they had not made the economic gains they expected, especially when compared to those in the upper income classes who were earning relatively indecent amounts, at the direct expense of the middle class. There are reports of executives earning hundreds of millions a year in stock options and bonuses while hard-working families are choosing food over prescribed medicines defies belief. These super-rich have only become more so in 2020 since COVID attacked our shores.

The American dream of working hard and respecting others that would lead us to a decent standard of living and social mobility failed to materialize. As much as we never really liked politicians, we always felt that the provisions of our constitution and the separation of the branches of government would prevail and our best interests as a voting public would be preserved.

What many saw by 2016 was that our treasured democratic and capitalistic systems were neither self-sufficient nor independently strong. They are systems of free markets that, we had thought, were constitutionally designed to protect our personal freedoms. Ensuing events revealed that they were extremely vulnerable. Over time, powerful forces were able to take control of our political and economic systems to such a degree that we the people began to realize that we no longer mattered as participants. Neither our political nor economic system was serving the American voter and consumer. Dissention, frustration, and anger replaced trust, opportunity, and hope. We lost faith in the establishment and felt as though we'd been cast out of our own homes, communities, and nation. Average Americans found themselves in survival mode, often forced to choose between household necessities as the rich and powerful accumulated ever more money and power.

The genius of Donald Trump was that he saw this and knew that it was his time to do something he had only talked about for years. He had been trained by his father to see an opening and know exactly how to jump in for his benefit. He had done this several times as a New York real estate developer, often leaving bankruptcy and chaos behind. Hillary Clinton ran her campaign based on her vast experience and the strength of the establishment. Trump ran his as a wealthy renegade, totally outside of the establishment. His excesses and complete lack of preparation for the job mattered little to the disenfranchised and angry voter. That lack of preparation and his ego made his tenure in office a virtual nightmare for the whole country.

He told us that he was going to clean up the swamp; Hillary and her companions *were* the swamp. Trump won. The establishment lost. America was about to enter four years of exhausting and debilitating chaos for everyone, Republican and Democrat alike. Every day, we were bombarded with a series of tweets that seemed to land from outer space. Everything we had learned to trust and lean on was suddenly thrown off the table as the insatiable needs and ego of our president, who was largely ignorant of his responsibilities, were all that mattered. That was our world for five years, including the months of the 2016 campaign.

ENTER THE ELECTION YEAR 2020. The world was quickly absorbed by COVID-19, which dramatically threatened every nation on the planet. America was the leader in cases and deaths. Our economy slid off its almost ten-year track of steady growth. An increasingly insecure president deliberately ignored the worst pandemic in a century, a failing economy, and a host of political, legal, and global crises, as he focused only on getting reelected. The country suffered. The year leading up to November 3rd election was like living at the center of a multi-laned bowling alley with an equal number of players speed-rolling ten-pound solid lead balls at us from every direction. We became exhausted and numb with only our hope for the future holding us up.

As we neared the election, the raging pandemic influenced voters to use the option of mail-in or drop-box votes to avoid the crowds. Most of the mailed ballots were from Democrats who chose not to take a chance with COVID-19. Trump had encouraged his loyalists to vote in person on Election Day and not worry about the virus, which they did do. This request by Trump was followed up with commands, issued by his chosen Postmaster General, to slow the delivery and sorting of our mail. This action caused a serious disruption in our time-honored mail service. It also caused a false illusion of victory for Trump on election night because the millions of mailed ballots could not, in most states, be counted until Election Day. Despite a throng of interferences, everything went incredibly well. So much so that Chris Krebs, Trump's Director of Cybersecurity, concluded that "there is no evidence that any voting system deleted or lost votes, changed votes, or was in any way compromised." Attorney General William Barr backed up that statement several days later. Both statements were not received well by the White House. Trump fired Krebs because of his statement and publicly considered firing his AG, who soon after, resigned before he was fired.

In another attempt to resort to the courts to overcome his failure at the polls, the president initiated a bevy of unwarranted post-election legal efforts. This time, his efforts were interpreted as a direct effort to subvert our democracy and rile up his base around a completely unsupportable lie. He sent more than 300 tweets to supporters with deliberate untruths about the election, implying that Biden stole it. This not only discredited our election system and the efforts of thousands of hard-working public servants and volunteers, it also cast doubt on the legitimacy of the president-elect.

Trump reluctantly let Biden commence the transitional effort, stepping aside only because of the political pressure. He has, however, yet to concede, and it is unlikely that he ever will. Throughout the post-election period, he has blamed everyone but himself for losing the election. Trump is among the few American presidents to have never sustained an approval rating above 50% at any point during his entire term of office. He never even attempted to reach beyond his 40% base to gather the needed majority for an election victory. The importance of this deficiency was never appreciated by the president. A two-candidate presidential election cannot be won with fewer than 50% of the voters. It is critical to recognize that most down-ballot Republicans did well in 2020, making any challenges to the election by the president, a direct threat to Republican winners. Trump lost because, unlike many of his Republican colleagues, he did nothing beyond bluster, lie and threaten to entice voters. Reaching across the aisle for supporters was an untenable exercise for Donald J. Trump.

Despite the pandemic, almost 67% of the eligible voting population showed up at the polls in 2020, a record not matched since 1908. Biden ended up with 306 electoral votes to Trump's 232, a perfect inverse of the 2016 electoral votes. Biden, however, received seven million more popular votes than Trump: 81.3 million, to Trump's 74.1 million. This exceeds Hillary Clinton's popular vote of three million over Trump in 2016. Trump has explicitly claimed that the "fake news" is lying about the entire process. For his entire presidency, Trump made it his mission to discredit the press. His manipulative skills in getting an unconscionable amount of free press are dwarfed by his unrelenting chastising and criticism of our Fourth Estate as failing and fake. If any story is not complimentary to the Don, it is by his definition fake news.

Trump lost, but that did not stop him from eventually launching a powerful campaign of more than 60 lawsuits to turn selected states around and into his column. He has lost every one of his baseless suits, even when those rendering the decisions were Republicans. Two separate suits were brought before the Supreme Court, because he was convinced the judges would be sympathetic to his position. They were not and firmly ruled against the increasingly frustrated president. Most disturbing was that the Republican leadership reneged on its moral and professional obligations to accept the results. What the president did accomplish by ramping up his lies was creating a perception among his followers that the election had been stolen from him and that Biden is not a legally elected president. Trump managed to convince his base, who should have known better, that the election was stolen. Trump fell back to his time-honored strategy of repeating an outright lie until it became believable. The Republican leadership and elected members should never have allowed itself to be a party to what Trump was doing.

THE 2020 ELECTION MIGHT GO DOWN as one of the most bizarre, confusing, and hate-filled in the history of US politics. Fallout threats from 2016 of foreign meddling, rigged ballots, mail fraud, and the ongoing effort to subvert and restrict select demographic groups from voting, dominated the 2020 headlines. COVID-19 surges, economic recession, and failed leadership from Washington did not deter the voter. In addition, the visible rise of white supremacy and QAnon vied with the virus and the election for front page coverage. They did so with encouragement in the form of tweets and proclamations from the president. These efforts accomplished little, but they did succeed in eroding trust in our election processes.

Trump is incapable of kindness or decency and seems to revel in that. The number of people who have died on his watch proves how unprepared his administration was as the number of virus victims exploded right up to and past the election. His comments regarding his fellow candidates during the 2016 primaries were disgusting. He still can't talk about a political adversary without tagging him or her with some kind of repulsive title. His persistent criticism of Senator McCain, a national hero is a behavior never before seen emanating from the Oval Office. The untimely death of the Senator fed into the presidents' vile words and actions. He is a man without shame. The quoted report while visiting Arlington Cemetery, of Trump calling our fallen hero's losers and suckers will surely be attached to any historical article or book about the 45ᵗʰ president. Shame must be also assumed by those of us who let this behavior continue as accepted and expected in public discourse surrounding this president.

McConnell & Co. continued their longstanding assault on American justice throughout 2020, with an unabated flow of unqualified and/or politically motivated judicial appointments, culminating with a third controversial Supreme Court appointment. With the appointment of Amy Coney Barrett to the court, a fifty-year goal of the Republican right has been achieved. The political leanings of all of these lifetime appointments Trumped reasonable regard for judicial prudence, professional and legal objectivity.

Many pundits and voters alike felt strongly that Trump has never wanted to be president, witnessed primarily in the amount of tax-supported time and money he has spent at his own properties and golf courses. His complete disinterest in the vital President's Daily Briefs (PDB) and his total lack of empathy for the victims of COVID-19 were exceeded only by his unwillingness to develop a viable plan to deal with this deadly virus. These actions alone caused the discerning voter to question why he wants this job. Trump has continued to deny the pandemic by not issuing a single word of sorrow for the rapidly rising COVID cases and deaths since the election.

Trump has not improved our global standing or our balance of trade. He will leave office with an unconscionable deficit and national debt, opposing everything fiscally sensitive Republicans stand for. His signature tax cuts, and jobs act of 2017, became an engine of public debt, provided a windfall for corporations and the one-percenters. It did precious little for the average middle-income voter or for job creation as promised.

The president was more interested in playing golf and twisting the American political system around to his self-serving interests than he was in fulfilling his constitutional and presidential obligations. His obsession with reelection was driven more by a justifiable concern over the many legal issues he would face as a civilian than by the privilege of serving for another four years.

⁂

2020 WAS HARDLY THE BLOWOUT ELECTION that some pundits had predicted, but it was definitely a clear win for Biden, both in the electoral college and the popular vote. This makes Trump's absurdly expensive and politically disruptive efforts to overturn the decisions in select states futile, not to mention extremely damaging to the democratic process. The 2020 election process was exactly the same one that elected Trump in 2016.

One big question is: What did Trump hope to achieve by claiming a rigged election even after it was obvious that there was no voter fraud? His own lawyers rarely if ever mentioned outright fraud because they were not going to jeopardize their reputations or possibly getting disbarred over frivolous lawsuits. A wise strategy, since absolutely no substantial evidence of fraud was found in any of the contested states. Trump claimed his right to challenge the count to get his petitions before the court, probably knowing that they had no chance of survival. Was he simply trying to stall the inevitable? Was he hoping the decision would be left to the Supreme Court? Did he actually believe that he had won? Was he trying to be as disruptive as possible to discredit our election process and possibly our democracy? Or was he trying to raise money by launching a campaign to fight for recounts and against voter fraud? All of the above are viable reasons. The leadership of the Republican party refused to let Trump know that his actions were not in the best interest of their party or our nation—that action on their part was unconscionable. Elected supporters of Trump, either out of fear or for possible personal gain, refused to stop Trump from potentially destroying our faith in our election processes. Shame on them.

The Election Defense Fund, a post-election PAC Trump set up to pay for the challenges was actually being used to raise money for a another run in 2024 and to pay off campaign debt. To date, more than $200 million and counting had been collected from unsuspecting supporters who thought it was a fund to fight fraud. The fine print on this request for funds from his loyal base states that legal battles to turn the election are only a tiny portion of where these funds will go. All of this gets at the importance and intensity of Trumps base and what they may mean for the country and under the Biden administration in the next four years.

            ᴸ ᴸ ᴸ

THE DEGREE OF POLARIZATION which has been evolving for more than four decades in America is the single biggest reason Trump got elected in the first place. Electing Trump in 2016 was America's version of an Arab Spring, and until we can "heal," as Biden has promised, nothing else the new administration does will matter. Trump voters are angry at a system that has ignored them for too long. If any effort to appease these folks is even slightly perceived as shallow, it will fail. It will also galvanize them well beyond any motivation to "heal."

The bulk of the people who voted for Trump in 2016 and 2020 did so because they'd given up on sharing in our nation's prosperity. Promises had been made to them for decades. *2020: America on the Brink* highlighted the working-class participation in the growth and prosperity of the post-WWII period. Wages, household incomes, home ownership, decent standards of living, health and pension benefits were all an integral part of the postwar working family's economic solvency. These were the good years when labor productivity and profits rose side by side, and, except for people of color and the poor, all other income levels did well despite generally high tax rates. Eisenhower's national highway program represented a major infrastructure investment that created many jobs. We built many schools, universities, and community colleges that, along with innovative scholarships, the GI Bill, and advance placement programs, many more students could now go to college. This period also saw the construction of hospitals, entertainment centers, movie theaters and a multitude of shopping opportunities for affordable necessities all of which contributed to a period of prosperity for all, workers and owners alike.

Beginning around 1970, we witnessed a flattening of household incomes, an observable disappearance of health benefits and pensions, a decline in the influence of unions, a significant transfer of jobs from our shores, and most of all, the steady erosion of equality and polarization caused by our nation's increasing wealth and income gaps. These are the conditions that contributed to the anger that led to the 2016 election of a political neophyte over arguably the most qualified candidate ever to run for president.

The above issues were at the foundation of the uprising that led to Trump's 2016 election. They were real and evident. They were not, however, among the rallying cries that he used to win that election. Pushing against immigration, constructing the wall, punishing the Clintons for corruption, and appeals to racism, nationalism, populism, and everything Obama-related were the major topics expounded upon at his many successful rallies.

Immigration has never been a valid reason for complaint in America. We are a nation of immigrants and with precious few exceptions, immigrants have always been a positive, social, and economic force. Who among us is not an immigrant?

Many have proclaimed that the Trump campaign motto, Make America Great Again, was actually a call to make America *white* again. Our inherent racism represents a festering sore that infects every aspect of our democracy. We can no longer accept the humiliation that accompanies the existence of racism in America. Legislation helps but cannot solve this problem. If we really want to repair our racist nation, we will need a shift in our social values and in our nation's moral compass towards an attitude and behavior that is more inclusive and just.

Trump ran as a populist and a nationalist. Make America Great Again might sound like a reasonable platform. It is not if it relies on racism and isolation from the global community. Many of the positions Trump took during his administration and even before he ran for president indicate that he is racist, and seriously unbelievable as a "man of the people." Trump has shown a disdain for people of color since the DOJ discrimination suit against him and his company in 1973 and more obviously in his abhorrence of what he recently referred to as "shithole countries." What president talks like that? Other than a small COVID-related bump, his trade wars did nothing to alleviate our trade balances. Trump does not, to this day, understand what a favorable trade balance is. A self-proclaimed master negotiator, he resorted to tirades and tantrums with our trading partners. He threatened long-standing agreements, most of which had been effective and kept us at peace. Imposing tariffs on so many of our trading partners was a failure at the negotiation table. We have hundreds of years of trading history with solid proof that, with minor exceptions, tariffs do not work. There will be inevitable retaliation, and consumers and importers end up paying higher prices. The animosity that is most often the biproduct of trade wars ends up causing major shifts in global trade that rarely benefit the initiator of tariffs.

Furthermore, Trump's trade wars nearly decimated our farmers. Ultimately, he had to pay billions from our treasury to make up for his failed trade policies, which constituted a form of double taxation for the average worker. Nationalism and populism often sound great on the campaign trail, but rarely are they translated into a more prosperous nation. Every candidate who campaigned on nationalism or populism—such as Stalin and Saddam Hussein—have been closet autocrats or dictators. Even a casual reading of *Mein Kampf,* Mussolini's *My Life,* or Mao's *Little Red Book* reveals a pattern of takeover by dictators, who were definitely not candidates for their people. Their goal was to be elected, or simply take power by any means, usually in times of trouble, and take advantage of the real suffering of the people. Once in power, their first objective was to do all they could to discredit the press. It is extremely hard for a dictator to survive with a free press. They typically then begin to eviscerate key segments of government that served the people, serving only at the pleasure of the "Dear Leader." If religion was a complication, it was neutralized. The evangelicals in America have traded their souls for the hope of the eliminating *Roe v. Wade.* Nothing else Trump did mattered to them as long as abortion was made illegal. Next, the dictator must go to work on the nation's educational system. A successful dictator can't have an educated population. Knowledge is the enemy of dictators.

All of these traits should at this point be familiar to everyone supporting Trump's administration and his futile attempts at overturning an election he clearly lost. Trump was an aspiring dictator and to support him is to deny that America is a representative democracy. Trump went a major step further as he humiliated, chastised, and vilified the leaders and nations we have long relied on as allies. He also chose to cozy up to leaders we have long viewed as enemies. The political motivations behind this behavior truly defies logic and must have other, possibly compromising, reasons. If possible, the dictator will use his power to establish a lifetime presidency. Trump hinted at such a possibility for himself when he saw that China and Russia had successfully established long terms of office for their leaders.

TIME WILL HAVE TO BE THE ULTIMATE JUDGE as to whether Trump was a great president, as most of his followers still believe. Current thinking is not favorable. Those who are not loyalists believe that he was the single biggest disaster ever to befall our nation. The temperature in the Trump kitchen is currently much too hot for either side to think or react rationally. We can, however, say that Trump loyalists have some valid reasons to have followed him. Never Trumpers know that to believe in Trump is to ignore his horrendous behavior, humiliating statements, and disdain for science, truth, and facts. Trump lacks empathy, diplomacy, decency, and competency, basic requirements for leadership. His followers desperately wanted a better deal and had grown tired of not participating in the prosperity of our nation. Their concerns are real and backed by empirical evidence. Trump loyalists do not care that he's often crude and behaves boorishly. They look past his thousands of lies, racism, and misogynistic behavior. He really could shoot someone on Fifth Avenue, grope women, make money off his presidency, and violate his oath and the Constitution, and they would not care. Why not lock up anyone who disagrees with him? It means nothing to them that he bases his entire platform on a tangle of lies. Imagine for a moment the anger and frustration it must take to willingly embrace a leader who exhibits such abhorrent behavior.

Nevertheless, many of Trump's supporters deserve to be heard. They desperately want to be recognized for who they are and for the economic and political benefits that have eluded them for decades. Trump used language and promises that appealed directly to those concerns. Truth, integrity, and character were of little value in their world. It is unfortunate that a block of supporters who are white supremacists locked onto the Trump band wagon. These angry people must be considered separate from traditional Republicans who never vote otherwise and the group of desperate suffering working class Trump believers. Even more unfortunate was the fact that these dangerous people are the very block of supporters that Trump called upon to pick up his violence-ladened mantle on January 6, 2021, to attack our Capitol and our democracy.

Despite Trump's failing battle to win the election, they honestly still believe that he will deliver what has been denied them, regardless of his actions to overturn the election, no matter who gets hurt, not even our democracy. He's incapable of accepting that he lost, even though *he* is the reason he did. It is incumbent on the next administration to acknowledge the grievances of those who continue to back him and create a viable and believable plan to address them.

A miracle of the century can be laid at the doorstep of the Georgia voter. Not only did Biden squeak out a victory, both Democratic candidates for the Senate prevailed in the January runoff. One of our nation's reddest states has become just blue enough. This also happened despite Trump's rallies and an infamous phone call to Republican office holders to "find" 11,800 votes for him. That phone call, like the one that got him impeached the first time, was a in total violation of our Constitution and Georgia state law.

The days after the Georgia election has been recorded as one of the darkest days in our nation's history. The president's lawyer, Rudy Giuliani, his son, Don Jr., the president himself, and several elected Republican officials, incited tens of thousands of extreme right loyalists to storm and invade our Capitol, while Congress was in session. Never before have we witnessed such a blatant violation of and direct threat to our democracy. History will not be kind to Trump for having deliberately incited these people to do what they did. The video and subsequent actions of those he incited will make the case against him hard to defend. The House has just passed a resolution of impeachment against Trump, the first time ever that a president has been impeached twice. The calls for his accountability on his many legal and moral acts will surely continue long after the Biden's inauguration. As I write, evidence of insider assistance, possibly by elected officials, to the invaders has been discovered. These people actually built a gallows next to our Capital and threatened to hang VP Pence. They tried to capture and detain selected members of congress. They invaded the halls of congress and rifled through personal papers and documents. People died and many were injured. These people were armed and angry. This horrendous event could very well have ended far more violently. This was a sad day for America, a day that no one could have predicted.

Donald Trump has continually shown just how violent, unpresidential, incompetent, and self-serving he can be since he first came down the escalator to announce his candidacy. We did not listen close enough and gave him a bye for four years. His call to arms on January 6, 2021, was the final straw, proving his complete lack of respect for our nation and its democracy. Those who have tolerated his excesses, those who have actively supported him, and everyone who has blindly served this horrendous person, must take partial blame for what happened on that sad day. People died, our elected officials,

Republicans and Democrats, were threatened with their lives, as was our Vice President. This was a horrific day in the history of our nation. If FDR were alive today, his speech following the attack on Pearl Harbor would bear repeating. Each of us must do everything we can to make sure that a man like Donald J. Trump never again has a chance to run for any office, much less that of the president of our United States, which he has vowed to do in 2024. We must bring him to justice, not out of revenge, but to set precedent that such a person never again gets to hold public office in America.

A BIDEN ADMINISTRATION

AS MENTIONED, IF BIDEN IS GOING TO WIN over supporters and bring them to the table, he's going to have to convince the Trump loyalists that he has a better deal for them. Fail on this one issue, and he will reign over a deeply polarized and angry nation. Despite a host of unbelievable roadblocks put in his way by Trump, The Biden team did not waste any time once his election was secured. Biden will honor the platform upon which he was elected to the best of his ability.

Biden must choose carefully with every appointment he makes. Biden and his team must return government to the people and at the same time deal with a list of critical issues the likes of which few incoming administrations have ever had to face. Biden will not have to be reminded that Obama did everything in his power to respectfully bring Republicans into the fold to achieve the goals he was elected to meet. Obama failed and Biden knows that the post-Trump senate is now possibly more dug in than it was for Obama.

Party is important to every elected official. However, our country must come before party, and if any leader does not see that, he or she must be bypassed by all means possible. A more aggressive, LBJ-style approach of tough love backed by threats of recriminations will come much closer to winning over recalcitrant Republicans. Biden's team must identify those who are up for election in 2022 and make it politically undesirable for them to follow McConnell. Even with the miracle in Georgia, we cannot expect McConnell and his Republican colleagues to get in line with the Biden administration. McConnell must pay the political consequences of his actions, especially for those of the past four years. Mitch McConnell has refused to bring valid legislation passed by the House to the floor of the Senate. More than four hundred of these bills lay untested on his desk. McConnell has done this either out of fear that the bills might actually pass, or to protect other spineless Republican senators from going on record in support of or against these vitally needed laws and expenditures. No leader should have that kind of power over our democratic process. The Biden team must read and adopt the LBJ handbook on how to bring errant elected officials on board.

President Biden will know what needs to be done. Joe Biden has the experience, temperament, transparency, and ability, to be the absolute perfect person to take over the post-Trump White House. Biden is a decent man who will be our trusted, respected, and treasured elder statesman. He will set a tone that will bring government respect and trust back. He will appoint the best people to carry out his goals and do it without scandals, indictments, or dictatorial demands for loyalty.

Joe Biden will make calls to each of the world's leaders who have rightfully concluded that America is not a trustworthy partner. They will give President Biden the slack time needed to regain trust. Biden will put together an experienced and diversified team that will recognize the devastation of COVID-19 and reduce the pain we've suffered to acceptable levels witnessed by most other nations. Biden won't solve the inherent racism in the United States, but he will move us in a positive direction toward respect and acceptance of minorities as contributing Americans who only want what white people want for themselves and their families. Minorities ask only for justice and equality in education, healthcare, the job market, and the purchase of a home. They want nothing more than a chance to thrive, just like anyone else and to no longer live in fear for their lives.

President Biden will bring our economy back and make it even stronger than he and President Obama did in 2009. President Biden will not tolerate deniers of climate change. He will attack this existential threat to life on our planet with the creation of new jobs and technology that will prove to be the biggest single contributor to our economic recovery. Renewable energy is currently one of our largest areas of growth. Our environment and the dangers of climate change will have a new, strong, and committed champion who will work with the Paris Accords and all nations, because these issues, like COVID-19, know nothing about borders.

President Biden will, to the surprise of our nation's police forces, also become the champion they did not have with Trump. Biden will not defund the police; he will enrich them with resources that meet the mental health and physical safety needs of our communities. He will redirect our police to be the guardians of our safety. Police precincts ought not be perceived as a militarized threat to the members of the communities they serve.

President Biden knows the importance of maintaining the coequal role of our three branches of government. Congress makes the laws, the executive carries them out and leads, the judiciary is charged with protecting and interpreting our Constitution without prejudice to party. Justice is balanced, blind, and must be administered equally to all. Powerful interests ought not to have sway over those who lack power. The devastation Trump and McConnell have wrought on our judicial system by making appointments around political objectives has only dramatically reduced the trust we as a nation can place in our judicial system. This is particularly evident in the Supreme Court, where appointments have recently been made that do not reflect the professionalism, experience, or objectivity required of that court.

How we choose judges and how we run our elections, noting the obvious limitations of the electoral college, must be reviewed by objective committees that are free of political bias and dedicated to the preservation of our democracy. It has been estimated that within two decades, unless major changes to our electoral college are made, 30% of our senators will be representing 70% of our population. We've also had five presidents lose the popular vote but still win office with electoral votes. The system is not working as intended, and it is desperately in need of review. In addition, we need to implement a system that holds our elected officials fully accountable to their constituents for their actions. They must be equally transparent regarding where and from whom they receive funding of any kind. Citizens United has put our democracy into an auction-driven market, and that is unconscionable. Our democracy ought not be sold to the highest bidder. Furthermore, information concerning every vote and decision on behalf of all constituents must be effectively reported and distributed such that voters know exactly what their elected representatives are doing.

Voters must be made accountable as well. America is among the lowest in voter participation for elections in the world and that must change. Systems to ensure that voters know exactly and honestly who and what they are voting for must be devised and implemented. Penalties for not voting might be considered and implemented. Eighteen nations currently impose penalties on their eligible citizens who do not vote.

President Biden has without doubt inherited an angry and seriously polarized nation. He will address those issues just mentioned because he said he would. Many of them have plagued us for decades and might not get resolved within his term of office, but he will get that ball rolling in the right direction, which will constitute a major victory for America. Biden will be forced to spend considerable energy mending fences and rebuilding trust in our government, a trust that has been decimated in many key areas where trust is fundamental to cooperation. He will be fighting an incalcitrant Republican half of Senate that has already made it clear that they will be exceedingly difficult to work with and have little interest in the Democratic platform. Biden has vowed to find the key to healing our nation, which means that he's aware of the political gap exacerbated by his predecessor. It will be difficult to convince 48% of the voters that Trump's lies, and malignant behavior were not the truth they desperately wanted to believe in. Convincing these Americans that there is really only one set of facts might prove to be the new president's most formidable task. A significant portion of Trump supporters are so far dug in and angry that there may be no way to bring them around as a part of the solution. Violence can no longer represent a constant threat to any American. Those who seem to know of no other way to be heard, will also represent a formidable task to Biden and frankly to all of us.

⌁ ⌁ ⌁

THE PEOPLE HAVE SPOKEN. Those who feared another four years under Trump know that a bullet has been dodged with this election. The destruction to our nation would have been devastating with a second Trump term. We would have, at the end, been unrecognizable as a democracy. To those who did support him, the fear of not having him for four years was equally incalculable since they trusted him as their champion. Trump managed to persuade his loyal following that he and only he had their best interests at heart. They were comforted and emboldened by his post-election actions, despite the danger he is posing for the future of his party and the nation. Donald J. Trump has promised that he is not going away. He has vowed to make another run in 2024 and has already deceptively been collecting the funds to do so. We simply cannot allow that to happen.

The majority of Americans must live with the hope that Biden will find a way to slice through the solid walls and roadblocks of political obstruction he will inevitably confront. Biden has the needed experience and will appoint only the best and most qualified administrators to get the job done. We leveled out the political downturn with the election of Biden. He will need the support of every American if we are ever to regain all that we have lost over the past four years. Fortunately, thanks to Georgia, we won a Biden-favorable senate. This will make the job of rebuilding significantly less difficult to achieve.

An Author's Dilemma

I **HAVE THOUGHT LONG AND HARD** about my lack of political fairness in these pages. Every time I sat down to look for a balance, seeking good and constructive thinking or actions from those defending the president and striving to get him reelected, I was met with nothing short of the Theater of the Absurd. The impeachable events of January 6th cemented any doubts I had that Trump had good intentions and respect for our democracy. I constantly asked myself, *what have Republicans done before and after this election to display themselves as a responsible rational political party?* The ranting and ravings of Trump, incapable of accepting the obvious, pushed our post-election political system into a frenzy of demonstrative lies of voter fraud, devoid of even a shred of validation, that almost brought our democracy to its knees. The Republican leadership sat this out in silence. About one month after the election, the *Washington Post* published a survey of every elected Republican in Congress asking if they recognize the Biden victory. Only 25 out of 249 Republican members of Congress acknowledged that Biden won the election. Two members stated in the survey that Trump actually won the election. 222 congressional Senate and House republicans refused to even say who won. This despite the fact that at that moment, Biden had seven million more popular votes than did Trump and more than enough electoral votes to win as well. When did the vote count cease to matter? This followed four years of fear-driven servitude to an aspiring dictator who managed to abduct the GOP and transform it into a herd of personal servants whose quest for votes and re-election suffocated their oath of office and their pride. How can a major political party find any justification for such behavior as that which so many Republicans displayed on this issue alone? America is a two-party nation, and we need both parties to be responsible to and respectful of our constitution.

Instead of striving to hand off the best possible economy and a stable, functioning political structure as every transitional administration has done in the past, Trump has deliberately sabotaged everything he could get his hands on. He engaged in delays, antagonism, and obstruction, preventing the Biden team from doing its constitutionally established transitional functions. During the transitional period, Trump fired administrators, replacing them with unqualified loyalists whose mission through January 20, 2021, was unknown. This was most disastrous for the Department of Defense. Secretary Esper was fired which left this critical department to be run by novice loyalists to Trump. This action represented an inexcusable and direct threat to our national security. Trump's total negligence on COVID-19, despite horrendous numbers of cases and deaths, would put any executive on notice for legal action. This list could go on, but the point has been made. The search for redeeming positive actions on the part of his administration with the passive support of his party have been nothing short of irresponsible and dangerous. We have lost respect as a world leader, and for the mature representative and constitutional democracy we have always thought we were. The events of January 6th did nothing to redeem the fallacies of the Republicans who have supported Trump despite a mountain of undemocratic positions and self-serving behavior that has put us on a dangerous path. Shame on them for not standing up to a clear and present danger to our nation.

The incredible actions taken by Trump to overturn the election in states that did not vote for him was an abuse of our system never before witnessed. Contacting state level officials, more than sixty failed court appearances, two Supreme Court rejections, blatantly illegal calls to state officials demanding they overturn the election, attempts to control the electoral college process, and inciting insurrection to defy the congressional authorization of the electoral votes were an amazingly futile effort on the part of a desperate president. Each of these actions on the part of the president were impeachable and done with the passive acceptance of many Republicans.

How could the leaders of the Republican party abandon their own values and oaths of office? The press has reported, and we have observed first-hand, violent incidents from disenchanted Trump supporters. People have died, hallowed halls have been defiled. We must give pause to just how angry and disenfranchised these people must feel to even think of the actions some have taken and are still proposing to take against our democracy. The hate being spewed by Trump, Giuliani, and some of his most fervent supporters is also nothing short of frightening and treasonous. Some of them talk of civil war, and it is well known that no one wins a civil war. We can only hope that their real numbers are small and manageable.

My sincere attempt to find justification for those who were willing to follow Trump to inevitable defeat, failed miserably. If there were champions of justice in the party that I have not been able to identify, I offer my apologies. Those people, especially those in power who claim to be patriots and leaders, knew what they were doing and if justice has any validity, they all should, and hopefully will, be held accountable. I single out Ted Cruz and Josh Hawley who immediately following the January 6th attack on our democracy, persisted in promoting a lost cause purely for political posturing. All those Republicans from both houses, who voted for the electoral college challenge leading up to that attack must walk themselves back to a woodshed and learn exactly what it means to enter public service. We need a strong two-party system in America and one of them is currently in total disarray. It is my fervent hope that those Republicans who respect the privilege of their elected positions will be able to redirect their party away from the self-serving, fear-based decision makers of the past and find their moral compass as a contributing force for good for our future.

Many of us feared the worst because the president was actively inciting violent actors. His encouragement to those prone to violence against the state is shocking. His multitude of untruths publicly made to faithful supporters and his tendency to call in the military to combat lawful protests are actions never before seen from the Oval Office. Military intervention into the election was threatened. If such a thing had been even suggested by a military officer, that officer would be facing a military court martial and serious punishment. That these statements were attributed to our commander in chief leaves us with much to be pondered.

It is shocking how irresponsible and self-serving the majority of Republicans are to what Trump was doing. Led by Mitch McConnell, Republicans have abdicated positions they have long stood for as systemic to their party. Every day that passed in which they refused to recognize a lawful, acknowledged, and remarkably fair election was a day of political irresponsibility.

We can only hope for a smooth, violence-free transition where congress will begin to work together as it did in the past. One of my biggest concerns is that forces might come into play, as with Nixon, that will give a free ride to Trump from the legal and moral indiscretions of his actions. I sincerely hope that that does not happen. I say this not because I want revenge. It is critical and just that Trump does not walk away with all the damage he has caused. Pardoning him or not holding him fully accountable for all the harm he has done would set an unwise precedent for our justice system. Each action against our Constitution should be objectively reviewed and adjudicated to ensure that America remains a representative democracy and a nation of laws. This retribution should also be administered to all those in his administration who willfully failed to responsibly do their jobs and respect the constitution they took an oath to serve.

We are not a nation that vilifies its past leaders. However, we do not want future presidents or anyone else to think that such behavior is permissible. As of January 20, 2021, we must take definitive actions to ensure that we will never allow someone like Donald J. Trump to occupy elected office, especially the Oval Office, again.

The silver lining to all this corruption of our democracy is that the American voter came through. Despite all the roadblocks put up by this administration to prevent us from voting, and despite COVID, we turned out in record numbers to vote. Congratulations to all of us, we have shown the power of the vote and the will of the people prevailed.

As voters, we have an important task to undertake; we must ask ourselves how was it that one man was able to totally take over the narrative of the most powerful representative democracy on the planet. We must recognize that for what it was. We must also recognize that what we have just been through could happen again. The next aspiring dictator, however, might not be as flawed and ego driven and might manage to succeed where Trump failed. We the people must engage in a serious examination of our electoral system to make sure that such an unqualified and mean-spirited person will never again enter the halls of our political system. That same examination must also consider a review of those aspects of our electoral system that are no longer working for us. One person one vote is our motto, and we must restore it without qualification. We must also ensure that all voters are informed and ready to vote their best interests.

We have one other pressing issue that has revealed itself as an existential threat. Seventy-four million people voted for Trump for a wide range of reasons. There were those who always have and always will vote republican, there were those who remain disenfranchised and believed in Trump, not recognizing his true colors, additionally, there were also a band of race-based voters whose anger may never find peace, and surely there were others among them. For those who invaded our Capital, white supremacists and race-driven, we now recognize them as a growing presence in America. We must find a way to find a hopefully peaceful way to deal with them as a clear and present threat. We should not be forced to live each day in fear of a Civil War, any more than should we live knowing that there are many American citizens out there who are so misguided and angry that any one of us could die at any time. For all other Trump supporters, it is up to the new administration and all other Americans to find a way to enfranchise them and make them part of the solution we all seek for America.

We have endured and survived possibly the greatest internal threat to our system of government we have ever faced. President Biden has one of the most challenging sets of problems that must be solved. COVID is killing us, The Russian Solarwinds hacking, our economy is suffering a terrible setback, millions of people cannot find jobs, and we are facing a potential civil war that is being fostered by a growing threat that might have reached into the halls of our congress. None of these clear and dangerous threats to our nation are republican or democratic, they are real threats to every American. I would love to see all the embattlements set up between the aisles of political discourse thrown down in the name of country, where wisdom, justice, and a mission of effective policy and programs emerge that will indeed make us that more perfect union we all like to talk about and embrace. We are a nation that has taken adversity and turned it into opportunity. We can do it again. Actually, we have no other choice. Now is the time to come together and build stronger and better America for all.

Who we are as a nation is based on who we are as a people. The new administration and the respect of every nation is on the line. Our representative democracy is on the line, and the actions we take in the ensuing months to restore our standing in world politics are crucial and urgent. The importance of reestablishing domestic and international trust for America cannot be understated. The world is watching.

APPENDIX

Gen Z: Building a Better America through Prioritized Capitalism

Baby Boomers through Gen X: Get on Board or Step Aside

WHILE NOT EXHAUSTIVE, the following list of national issues are of paramount importance to the graduating class of 2021 and their peers. They are not listed in order of priority, in that no definitive agreement could be reached. Each is considered important, some more urgent than others. All are deemed vital to the health and viability of the just and equitable nation in which we wish to live and pass on to our next generation.

1. **Trust:** We've lost trust in the institutions and bodies that were established to protect us.
   A. **Congress and the Supreme Court** are not trusted by the public.
      I. Decisions appear to be political and not in the interest of citizens
   B. **We do not trust** business and corporations to do the "right thing."
      I. Overwhelming evidence that many put growth and profit before social responsibility, pharma, cigarettes, chemicals, financial services.
   C. **Local** police, fire, educators, courts, etc. must faithfully serve the public as their first priority.
      I. These services exist to serve the public, protect their safety
      II. Services provide to all persons equally and fairly
   D. **Our legal system** benefits the rich and is not fairly or equitably administered nor is it equally available to all citizens.
   E. Public oversight:

I.   If you lie, cheat, steal, or abuse your office you will be punished,

II. No shifting the burden of penalties to shareholders or others. Violators of the public trust and safety that break the law should individually pay the price with Jail, fines, or their positions.

III. Accountability goes with the job. Executives, elected officials, religious leaders, public service administrators, have a responsibility to respect best practices and behave in a professional and ethical manner.

2. **Climate change:** National recognition of crisis and life on our planet.
   A. **Rejoin global community**, Paris Accords, UN, and others.
   B. **Incentivize** energy, agriculture, and transportation companies to reduce pollution.
   > I. Tax policies as incentives, not punishments
   C. **Public awareness** on urgency of this problem.
   D. **Assert** science as the lead.

3. **Income and Wealth Inequality:** There can be no democracy compatible with the grossly unfair and economically inefficient wealth and income gap.
   A. **Rewrite and simplify** tax code to distribute national income and wealth more fairly.
   > I. Nonpunitive and geared towards economic efficiency and fairness.
   B. **Reduce** public sector financial burden of generational dependency
   C. **Create** meaningful incentives and opportunities for all through education, health care policies, and jobs.

D. **Poverty** is a persistent drain on a nation's potential that must be addressed.

4. **Racism:** America can no longer tolerate systemic racism, either economically or morally.

   A. **Protect** the civil and human rights of all citizens and immigrants

   B. **Ensure** proper education and health care as a fundamental right to everyone.

   C. **Establish** Independent Minority Economic and Opportunity Zones.

      I. Modeled after pre-riot Tulsa Black Wall Street model.

   D. **Confront** extreme rightwing and leftwing groups, especially those that promote violence.

      I. Meet with and find out what white supremacists and racist groups want. Enfranchise them, inform then that they must live within the law.

      II. Violence will not be tolerated

   E. **Law enforcement:** Our policemen and women are our guardians and not militants armed to kill.

      I. Establish national commission to define limits and responsibilities of all community-based police forces.

      II. Ensure full funding for all required services performed.

      III. Establish access to mental health professionals within all precincts to aid in domestic calls.

      IV. Ensure system of accountability on excess violence and actions against the public.

      V. Define the duties (and non-duties) of the police.

5. **Accountability in government:** Government is there to serve the long-term interests of the people and act as a facilitator of efficient utilization of private and public sector resources for the safety and prosperity of its citizens.

   A. **Debt Reduction:** Consider innovative financial incentives to pay off public debt created by COVID-19 and unfairly initiated tax policies.

      I. Create a viable plan to write off our public debt through the issue of modern-day version of WWII war bonds

         1. Re-structure our current national debt to start over with fair return to purchase of a public sector refinancing instrument, priced to be available to all citizens. Earned interest distributed to the public, not to the banks.

      II. Reduce or eliminate the interest on student loans with reasonable payback schedules.

   B. Redefine government operations to re-establish co-equal branches of government

      I. Oversight and checks and balances to prevent concentration of power and conflicts of interest.

      II. Define responsible subpoena power and rights of congressional oversight on executive and judicial.

      III. Evaluate and resolve areas of potential for abuse and conflicts impacting elected officials and public sector administrators.

      IV. Hold all elected officials and public sector administrators and decision makers to legal, moral, and ethical standards. No one, especially public servants are above the law.

   C. Remove politics from judicial appointments

  I. Set up permanent committee of standards and qualifications with potential candidates from which all judges are considered for appointment.

    1. No Obama, Bush, Trump or Biden judges, only fully qualified judges.

 D. **Rewrite tax code** to make it morally progressive and fair

  I. Government expenditures are to serve only the public, not special interests

  II. Create public awareness and accountability on all public sector expenditures revenues.

    1. Create a periodic report on all elected officials votes and actions to their constituents that is easily readable and distributed to all registered voters.

  III. Eliminate transfer of any and funds form lobbyist to government officials. Our government is no longer for sale.

 E. Gun Control

  I. Maintain and reinforce second amendment to meet rights and safety needs of the 21st-century public.

  II. Create commission of responsible industry professionals and gun owners to make all citizens safe from guns.

    1. Take the lead to establish an alternative association to the NRA made up of responsible gun owners and manufacturers.

    2. Link marketing and sales to public safety and responsible gun ownership.

  III. Remove all liability limitations on gun owners and manufacturers.

1. Make them legally responsible for their product like all other industries. This will ensure built in safety measures on each gun.

IV. Eliminate sales of assault weapons from public consumption. and provide buyback program for those already in hands of citizens.

F. Create a Voter Awareness Strategy

    I. An educated and informed voter is critical to functioning democracy

        1. Create a system of information flow from elected officials to all constituents to keep them fully informed of all financial contributions and policy initiatives and laws passed

        2. Make these reports legible to the average voter.

        3. Distribute to each and every constituent.

    II. Re-establish National Voter Rights Act.

G. Elected Officials are Accountable to Constituents

    I. Ensure constant flow of information from all elected officials.

        1. Format and distribution structured to serve all constituents.

    II. Create a hacker- proof, universal system of voting

        1. Monitor and fund a foreign and domestic voter meddling commission to stop voter meddling and prosecute anyone found guilty.

        2. Construct registration and voting systems that encourage every eligible voter access to the polls and the right to cast the ballots.

    III. All candidates must make taxes and any financial assets and activities public.

        1. Eliminate any possibility for bribery and conflict-of-interest

    2. Financial reports and tax reports to be made public prior to running.

    3. If this cannot be done, the candidate cannot serve the public.

  IV. Public servants, elected or civil, are responsible first and foremost to the public they serve

H. Publicly Financed Elections

  I. Evaluate and restructure Electoral College: one person one vote.

    1. Incentivize smaller states to insure voter participation.

  II. Repeal Citizens United

  III. Any and all contributions or donations to a candidate or elective official above $2,000 must be reported and made publicly available to all constituents.

  IV. Review and regulate all PAC's to make sure they are serving the public and not the candidate.

  V. Return to mandated free candidate promotional public service time for all broadcast news and commentary stations.

  VI. Set time limits on how long campaigns can run, four months is suggested.

  VII. Consider revising and tightening current campaign finance and operations laws.

6. Jobs and Careers: Everyone deserves the right to a decent living wage

  A. Raise national minimum wage, permanently eliminate subsistence wage policies on labor and working-class people.

  B. Recognize post COVID-19 alternative job market

    I. Redefine concept of a job, no longer 9-to-5, office-based employment.

II. Work from home, consider environmental and climate change opportunities

C. Consider placing economic value on domestic output of homemaker.

D. Retraining and education to meet next generations of jobs.

    I. Retrain workers displaced by technology or environmental changes. sea and river rise, pollution, drought induced crop failures

7. **Public Healthcare for all,** with Private Sector Option: Healthcare is a right and a vital investment of our future.

    A. Establish accountable public Sector Health Agency appointments and management separate from politics.

    B. Offer a choice between public and private sector option at set periods

    C. Establish scope of public sector options in terms of preventative and basic health care services to be part of the public sector option.

    D. Public Sector Option

        I. Tax based and financially available to all citizens.

        II. Create premium political free administrative and management system

            1. All public sector health officials paid fair market wage with normal benefits and incentives to want to work for this entity.

            2. Establish budget process for funding of all functions accountable to congressional oversight.

        III. Private Sector Option as a Choice for Elective and non-Basic Health Needs

8. **Affordable Education**: Education is a right and a not a line-item expense

    A. Reconsider public funding to create equality across income and wealth classes.

    B. Promote and define higher education as an Investment in Our Future

        I. STEM, Science, technology, engineering, mathematics,

        II. Establish fair exposure to the arts-they are not a luxury and foster creative thinking.

    C. Universal and equal educational primary and secondary opportunities available for every child

        I. Establish national public/private pre-kindergarten programs for working parents.

    D. Publicly funded post-secondary option

        I. Required community service in the field as payback for all graduates.

9. **Government Regulations**: Needed to create level playing field for all.

    A. Establish responsible regulations on all private sector entities to ensure public safety and financial responsibility for all goods and services provided.

        I. Protect the public from predatory excesses such as those of the cigarette and Pharmaceutical, chemical, and financial industries.

        II. Establish fines, arrest, jail, and loss of employment and benefits for individual offenders.

    B. Protect public and consumers from Unethical and Libelous Corporate Behavior.

    C. Profit and Not for Profit Enterprises are subject to Best Practices and equal under the Law.

D. Redirect all net fines and penalties back to those aggrieved. Loser pays all court and legal fees, outside of any settlement.

10. **National Service Corps.** Public service option to replace student debt.
    A. Public Service Option for Non-College Bound to Learn a Trade
    B. Collaborate with Military and local public services
    C. Coordinated with public sector Community Service Commission for higher education

11. **Single Parenthood.** Local based services for children and families in need.
    A. Too many children growing up in single-headed households.
    B. Consider programs to aid and assist these families to prevent generational dependency.

12. **Pharmaceutical**s: Enforce best practices management and accountability on products.
    A. More Americans die each year from opioids than died in the Vietnam War.
    B. Eliminate all advertisements for prescription drugs
        I. Leave such choices up to the doctors and medical practitioners.
        II. This will dramatically reduce the costs of prescription medicines; estimates range from 18-25% for marketing costs of a product the consumer cannot buy without a prescription.
    C. Corporate leaders, not shareholders, are to be personally and financially responsible for illegal and unethical business practices that injure the public,

13. **Make mental health a national problem**, Policies and practices.

A. We must reduce suicide rate especially among teenagers.

B. A national problem that costs us more to ignore than it will to address

C. Incentive mental health providers to aid community service providers

14. **Student debt:** Find a solution to pay off student debt and change the way tuition is paid for higher education.

   A. Education is an investment in our nation's citizenry, not an expense item

   B. Public service option to pay back loans

   C. Re-establish the separation of Church and State.

   D. A politically active clergy is its own greatest threat

15. **High tech and Communications industry regulation:** Consider separating, community, family, commercial platforms from opinion and commentary, and news.

   A. All news and commentary posts must be fully identified as to source and made legally and morally accountable for content by source and or distributor

   B. Strict oversight provided for the use of any and all private data collected and stored.

   C. Maybe nationalize them as natural monopolies.

   D. Force financial and legal accountability by source or distributor for lies and misinformation.

16. **Abortion:** A most horrendous decision and not within the purview of anyone but those directly involved.

   A. We cannot threaten access to abortion, family planning, and contraception.

 B. Establish a national right to family planning and contraception and the problem will be solved.

 C. It is a woman's right to choose the size of her family

  I. It is her right to consult with those she chooses to assist in that decision.

17. The Fourth Estate

 A. Separate professional journalism from media-based commentary and opinion

 B. Incentivize major newspapers to create financially independent local and regional editions and offices with local advertising and reporters.

  III. They print locally and get selected sections from parent newspaper electronically and for free

18. Infrastructure

 A. America must address its infrastructure

  II. Low interest rates, and job creation benefits demand positive action

  III. The rate of crumbling highways, bridges, waterways, etc. is a national problem

19. Immigration

 A. Immigrants are not a net negative; they contribute and have proven time and again that they are good citizens.

ABOUT THE AUTHOR

Photograph by Sybil Holland

DR. WILLIAM J. LAWRENCE was a professor of economics and business ethics whose research and professional interests were mainly focused on the economics of the City of New York. He enjoyed a productive and rewarding career as a professor, advisor to city government, consultant, and an entrepreneur. He retired early from Pace University, after which he taught at several universities in the States and abroad. He has published several papers and books on regional economics, art fraud and theft, entrepreneurship, and cloud computing and has sat on several academic and not-for-profit boards. He currently resides in Brooklyn. He holds master's and PhD degrees from NYU and a bachelor's from LIU.

Made in the USA
Middletown, DE
07 July 2021